JAKE
BUCHAN
DOUBLE
VISION

A challenging case of brutal murder, drugs, gambling and false identity

Mereo Books

2nd Floor, 6-8 Dyer Street, Cirencester, Gloucestershire, GL7 2PF
An imprint of Memoirs Books. www.mereobooks.com
and www.memoirsbooks.co.uk

DOUBLE VISION
ISBN: 978-1-86151-981-8

First published in Great Britain in 2021
by Mereo Books, an imprint of Memoirs Books.

Copyright ©2021

The address for Memoirs Books can be
found at www.mereobooks.com

Mereo Books Ltd. Reg. No. 12157152

Typeset in 11/15pt Century Schoolbook
by Wiltshire Associates.
Printed and bound in Great Britain

Acknowledgements

Whoever said that writing a third novel would be any easier clearly has never done so!

Without the help and advice of others I could not have written *Double Vision*. I would especially like to thank retired Detective Sergeant Terry Parkhouse, Charlotte Jones, Drs Gordon and Maureen Crosby, Captain Joe Walford, Nick Randall-Smith, Neil Rees, Nick Passmore and Donald McIntyre (whose van really does have Vancouver, Brisbane, Sydney and Singapore written on the side).

I am again grateful to Chris Newton, Editor in Chief, Mereo Books for pointing out the errors of my ways and giving the manuscript its final polish.

I would never have reached the end without the love and support of my wife Trish.

Dedication

To the memory of Quentin Cramb, my former
English teacher. A man of vision, to whom I owe so much.

About the author

John ('Jake') Buchan was born in Aberdeen, Scotland, and moved in 1981 to Mid Wales, where he worked as a family and hospital doctor for over thirty years. This is his third novel featuring DI John Steadman, the blind detective. The first two books, *Blind Pursuit* and *Second Sight*, are also available from Mereo Books.

For more information see https://www.jakebuchan.com

CHAPTER 1

It was a typical mid-January morning: damp, dreary and depressing. Two men and a large black dog were walking briskly along the boardwalk towards Helmsmouth's eastern beach, trying to keep warm and dispel the winter's blues.

The larger of the two men turned towards his companion. 'You know John, I hate January,' he said in a broad Scots accent. 'Christmas has gone, Hogmanay's over – all that's left is the credit card bill. Maybe we should hibernate until March. God knows, I've eaten enough in the last three weeks to last me for a couple o' months.'

His companion smiled wistfully behind his dark glasses as he tried to replace his memory of Detective Sergeant Alan Munro with a chubbier version.

'A few games of rugby and you'll be as fit as ever, I suspect,' he replied.

Alan Munro looked at his colleague, who, despite the recent festivities, remained woefully thin. His green fedora was covered in tiny droplets of moisture, as were his dark glasses, not that the latter mattered. His bony left hand loosely held his dog's harness.

Munro shook his head.

'You could do with a bit of fattening up yourself, John Steadman. Either that or someone to look after you.'

'And just who do you think would want to take on a blind, widowed ex-detective inspector, not to mention his guide dog?'

Robbie, the dog, turned his head. It was almost as though he knew he was being spoken about.

DS Munro didn't answer. Although some time had passed since the shooting that had left DI Steadman blind and Holly, his wife dead, Munro still felt uncomfortable talking about it. He turned red and was about to mumble an apology when Steadman spoke again.

'No, I don't fancy hibernating. My son Ben has the right idea. He's gone south for the winter with his alternative circus. He is in Brisbane just now enjoying the Australian sunshine. His only gripe is that it's too hot to sleep at night.'

'My heart bleeds for him,' replied Munro flatly. 'How is he, anyway?'

'Ben? Much the same as usual, I guess. Laid back to the point of being horizontal. I wouldn't say he was carefree. He worries about the bigger issues – the environment, politics – but never about himself. You'll see him fairly soon. He hopes to come back later in the month.'

'I wouldn't if I were him. I mean to say, just look at it! The sky's grey, the sea's grey, even the ruddy beach is grey on a day like this.' He paused, then added, 'I suppose your world is always grey – sorry.'

'No need to apologise,' Steadman replied. 'My world is more of a nothingness now. It's very hard to explain – you know when you go to bed and you switch off the light, the room suddenly seems very dark until you close your eyes. It's a bit like that – you only notice the darkness with your eyes open.'

The dog started tugging at his harness.

'Steady, Robbie, steady,' commanded Steadman.

'Am I walking too fast?' asked Munro.

'No. Robbie knows we're almost at the beach and he gets a bit excited, that's all. Now, if my calculations are correct the tide should be far out. How's the beach looking?'

Munro was puzzled for a moment, but he knew his former boss liked others to paint a picture for him.

'Soft sand and dunes to your left leading to the high-water mark with the usual detritus of seaweed, bits of fishing nets and plastic bottles. Then a large flat expanse of hard, wet sand.'

'Any rocks, stones or pools?'

'No, flat as a pancake.'

'Anybody else about?'

'There's somebody in the distance, crouched on the sand – could be an angler digging for lugworms. He's too far off to be certain. Whoever he is, he's got his own personal flock of seagulls.'

'Good,' replied Steadman. 'Let's get below the tideline.'

The two men walked over the sand to where the tide had receded. A huge smile spread across Steadman's face.

'This is why I asked you to bring me here, Alan – freedom! It's flat and empty. I don't really need Robbie, a cane or even your arm. I don't have to scuff my shoes, worry about bumping into people or tripping over things. If I had thought, I could even have put on a pair of trainers and gone for a run. Just give me a nudge if Robbie and I get too near the water.'

Just then, as if to add to the occasion, a thin watery sun appeared through the clouds.

The two men walked for some minutes without talking, enjoying the silence between friends. All that could be heard was the gentle lapping of the sea and the occasional mewing of a gull overhead.

Quite suddenly Robbie stopped and started barking in the direction of the man squatted on the sand.

'That's odd,' said Munro.

'What's odd?' Steadman asked.

'The man I mentioned – he's got up and he's running as fast as he can towards the dunes.'

'Maybe he's frightened of dogs,' Steadman suggested.

'He's left a bundle of some kind lying on the beach,' Munro continued.

Robbie stood stock-still, his hackles raised, barking incessantly.

'Quiet, Robbie. What is it?' Steadman tried to calm him with a gentle stroke.

'Something is seriously upsetting him, sir.'

Afterwards, Steadman was to recall that moment vividly. It was as though a switch had been thrown and two friends out for a stroll had, in an instant, become police officers: DS Alan Munro and DI John Steadman, the blind detective.

Munro fought down the urge to run towards the shape lying on the sand.

'What do you think the man has left, sir?' asked Munro as the three of them made their way over the beach.

Steadman had been pondering exactly the same question. Robbie was highly trained and had never behaved like this before.

'It must be something important and I can only think of one thing...'

'You're not going to believe this, sir,' Munro interjected, 'I think it's a body.'

Steadman nodded. 'The thought had occurred to me.'

Munro could resist no longer and ran the last twenty yards, leaving Steadman and Robbie to follow.

'Dear God alive!' exclaimed Munro.

'What is it?' asked Steadman.

Munro had moved a few paces from the body and was retching. Steadman reassured his dog and gave him a small biscuit while he waited patiently for Munro's return.

'Sorry about that, sir – it's pretty grotesque. Bugger off you,' he continued, swinging a half-hearted kick at a couple of gulls intent on trying to resume their grisly feast.

'Describe please, Alan,' said Steadman.

'White, middle-aged male. I doubt if he's been in the water for long. The most striking thing is that his head has been split vertically, twice – it looks like the Ace of Clubs. The damned birds have eaten most of his brains. Go on, shoo, the lot of you!'

'Is that what killed him, do you think?'

Munro peered at the body again. 'Well, if he wasn't dead before he certainly would have been after.' As he spoke, he pulled on a pair of vinyl gloves. Carefully he lifted the man's tie. 'Nah, two bullet wounds to the chest. I'm no expert, but they look as though they've been fired at close range.'

Steadman pressed the button on the side of his watch. A metallic voice informed him that it was eleven thirty-five.

'Better phone the Eyesore, Alan. The tide will be on the turn in a little over twenty-five minutes.'

The Eyesore was the nickname for Helmsmouth

Police Headquarters, a ghastly example of the worst of 60s architecture.

'Good point,' Munro replied, retrieving his mobile from his pocket. The phone looked ridiculously small in his enormous hands.

Sergeant Grimble answered.

'Do they never give you a day off?' asked Munro.

'And what would I do with a day off?' replied Grimble, a portly, balding man who lived for his job of desk sergeant. His age, like his shambolic filing system, was a closely guarded secret. 'Now, I presume you're not calling to ask after my well-being, young man. What have you found?'

Briefly, Munro outlined where they were and what was lying at his feet. He turned to his companion. 'They are on their way, sir,' he said as he pocketed his phone.

'In that case, you have less than ten minutes, Alan, to improve on your brief description.'

Alan Munro paused for a moment then began, 'I doubt if he was killed on the beach. I think the body has been washed ashore. I'm sure Dr Rufus, the Home Office pathologist, will confirm. My guess would be that he has been in the sea for less than twenty-four hours. With the damage to his head, I can't say what he looked like other than he had dark wavy hair and was clean-shaven. He must have been reasonably tall. No jewellery and no obvious tattoos. Black socks. His shoes look new. The trousers are dark with a thin stripe.'

Steadman grunted; suit trousers, he thought.

'White shirt with natty cuff links in the shape of tiny roulette wheels. Other than that, he's only wearing a tie, and that looks a bit unusual.'

'Unusual?' In what way?' Steadman asked.

The sound of approaching sirens prevented Munro from answering. In truth, he wasn't exactly sure why the tie struck him as peculiar.

Two uniformed officers appeared over the dunes. In their wake strode an elegant lady with blonde hair pinned back off her face.

'They've sent DS Fairfax,' said Munro.

Steadman had worked with DS Fiona Fairfax on several cases. She was methodical and diligent. Some officers thought she was aloof. Not Steadman: he had a lot of respect for her.

'Morning, gents,' she said. After a quick look at the body she continued, 'Well, that would certainly spoil anyone's Sunday morning stroll. Did you find the body, Alan?'

'No – when we arrived on the beach there was somebody crouching on the sand. It wasn't clear what was going on. Initially I thought it was just some bloke digging for bait. Robbie started barking. At which point, whoever it was legged it over the dunes leaving that lying there,' said Munro. He pointed at the body with the toe of his shoe. 'We only realised what it was when we were much closer.'

Robbie nuzzled into Steadman's thigh and was rewarded with another pat on the head.

'You didn't get a look at the person?' Fairfax continued.

Munro shook his head, 'He was wearing trousers and an anorak. Judging by the way he ran off, I would think he was little more than a youth.'

DS Fairfax instructed the two uniformed officers to see if they could find any trace of him.

'Forensics should be here any minute,' she said.

'I don't think he was killed here,' suggested Munro.

'No,' Fairfax agreed, 'probably dumped at sea. Any ideas about the head?'

Munro felt another wave of nausea well up in his stomach. Steadman struggled to visualise the scene. He had an inkling of what might have caused the injury. He was about to make a suggestion, but instead he asked, 'Is Dr Rufus coming?'

'I'm afraid not, sir. He's giving evidence in the Old Bailey tomorrow morning and he's already up in London. Dr Bathgate's on his way – he's a GP who doubles as police surgeon.'

A car door slammed. More heads appeared over the dunes.

'Forensic team, sir,' Munro explained to Steadman.

Other than take photographs, there was not a lot they could do. The sun had gone in and the rain had started again.

Kim Ho, who led the forensics team, looked intently at

the body from several angles. 'He's wearing an American tie,' she said at last.

'Why do you say it's American?' asked Munro.

'Let me guess,' ventured Steadman. 'It has diagonal stripes and the stripes run from the wearer's right shoulder to his left hip. Diagonals on a British tie traditionally run the other way. Am I right?'

Kim Ho gave a nervous laugh. 'Exactly right, sir.'

'What amazes me is where you learn all that stuff. Now you're going to bamboozle us as to why the stripes run in a different direction,' said Munro.

'Oh, there's been all sorts of speculation, such as not wishing to offend old Etonians and ex-army officers, although I suspect the Americans simply wanted to be different. Fiona, I'm getting concerned about the tide coming in.'

'The mortuary van is here – we're just waiting for Dr Bathgate.'

The roar of a very powerful and expensive engine announced his arrival. It was a young man who slouched over the dunes. He didn't take his hands out of his pockets as he looked around him with unsettlingly disinterested eyes.

'Which one of you is DS Fairfax?' he asked.

'That would be me,' Fiona responded.

'Well, DS Fairfax, exactly what part of the body do you think is still alive?'

Steadman was having none of it. 'Come now, Dr

Bathgate, you know the rules, ridiculous as they are. Only certain people can pronounce death before we're allowed to move a body and we need to move it soon.'

Dr Bathgate gave a faint snort, looked at his watch and grudgingly said, 'Fine, he's dead – you can move the body.'

'Before you go, doctor, any thoughts on how his head ended up like that?' asked Munro.

'I'm not a pathologist. Possibly the Grim Reaper having a couple of practice swipes with his scythe, though I wouldn't put any money on it.' And with that he turned on his heels and left.

'What a tragedy!' exclaimed Munro. 'To be so young and yet so cynical. I hope his car gets stuck in the sand.'

It didn't, and Dr Bathgate roared away.

The two men from the mortuary van arrived. With Munro's help, they put the corpse in a body bag but not before Kim Ho and DS Fairfax had done a preliminary examination. The dead man's pockets were empty apart from a handkerchief and some small change. The entry bullet holes at the front of the chest were matched with exit holes at the back.

'We're just in time,' remarked Fairfax as the first wavelets of the incoming tide rolled up to where they were standing.

'Here,' said Munro, 'I'll give you lads a hand over the dunes. You take a front handle each and I'll take the back.' He lifted the stretcher as though it were nothing more than a half-empty bag of shopping.

Robbie was wet and shivering, having sat patiently on the damp sand at Steadman's side throughout. Slowly, Steadman, DS Fairfax and Kim Ho followed the stretcher like some bizarre funeral procession. The two uniformed officers had found no trace of the youth who had fled the scene. The other members of the forensic team were already sheltering back in their car.

'One thing strikes me as very peculiar,' Steadman announced.

'Only one! You mean apart from a body washed up on a beach with two bullet holes in his chest and a head that looks like it has been used as a chopping block,' Munro replied.

'You're right, Alan. Of course, those need explaining. But I'm wondering why he wasn't wearing a jacket. From your description, I presume those were suit trousers he had on. You didn't find a wallet. I guess it could have been stolen, although I think it's more likely to have been in his jacket pocket. So why did he take it off?'

'Couldn't it just have come off in the water?' asked Munro.

'Possibly, but the sea has been dead calm for days.'

'What if his killers had simply pulled down the jacket at the back to pinion his arms before shooting him?' Fairfax suggested.

'Pulling down a jacket like that only works if you're standing directly behind the person. Not the ideal spot to be if someone is shooting a powerful weapon at point-blank range. Remember, the bullets exited the body. No, I think he removed his jacket before he was killed.'

'What are you thinking, sir?' asked Fairfax.

'I think he was murdered indoors and somewhere he felt familiar enough to slip off his jacket without causing offence. Somewhere nice and warm and dry. Which is where we would like to be right now, isn't that so Robbie?'

CHAPTER 2

Munro's car soon warmed up. 'Are you going back to your flat for lunch, sir?' he asked.

'I've been invited to my sister's house. If it's not too much trouble, would you drop me there?' Steadman replied.

'No problem, sir. I hope Linda doesn't mind the smell of damp dog. I don't know whether it's something in the sea air, but your dog isn't half pungent!'

Robbie, who was curled up at Steadman's feet, opened an eye and gave Munro a mournful look.

'I'll swear that dog knows he's being talked about,' said Munro, glancing down at Robbie. 'Mind, I'm not sure I fancy any lunch after what I've seen today. At least you were...' His voice trailed off in embarrassment.

'At least you were spared that, is what I think you were going to say.' Steadman waved away his apologies.

'True. However, I have a very vivid imagination. It may well be that the pictures in my mind's eye are even more gruesome than the reality.'

'I think it was the herring gulls that really did it for me – ugly brutes at the best of times. Ah well, no lunch for me anyway. I'll have to go to the Eyesore and write up my report.'

Steadman felt a pang of jealousy. He could imagine the buzz of excitement, the speculation, and the deduction as all the bits of evidence were being gathered and brought together. He longed to be part of it. He knew he would only be brought in if there were exceptional circumstances. Were there exceptional circumstances, he asked himself? He didn't know the answer, and there was also a new Divisional Superintendent he had not yet met.

The rain was persistent now. Steadman could hear heavy drops falling on the roof, the rhythmic slap of the wipers and the hiss of the tyres on the wet road surface. January rain had a different quality, he thought, dirtier, wetter, colder. It was the type of rain that seeped through shoes and clothing as if it were determined to penetrate right to the bone. He gave an involuntary shudder.

'Shall I turn the heating up a wee bit, sir?'

'No, I'm fine really. I agree with what you said earlier – I hate January too.'

As the car pulled up outside Linda's house the door was flung open and Linda scurried towards the car underneath a large umbrella.

'I was keeping an eye out for you,' she explained unnecessarily, as she gave her brother a hug. 'You're absolutely soaking wet!' she cried. 'And poor Robbie looks as though he's been half-drowned. Where have you been?'

'We went for a walk along the eastern beach,' Steadman explained. 'We ran into complications.'

'What sort of complications? Alan, I thought you had more sense.'

Munro blushed. 'I think I'll let the boss explain. I have to dash. Give me a ring if you want a lift home, sir.' He put his foot down and the Audi shot off at a pace to match Dr Bathgate's.

Of course, Linda had old towels waiting behind the door. Her husband, Dominic, was instructed to attend to Robbie while she peeled off her brother's sodden overcoat.

'I'll hang this by the boiler. Pass me your hat.' Steadman obliged. 'John, your trousers, socks and shoes are wet through. You can borrow some of Dominic's.'

Steadman knew there was no point in arguing with his sister. It was much easier simply to go with the flow.

Fifteen minutes later he was sitting in front of a cosy fire with a hot mug of tea.

'Would you like a dash of whisky in that?' Dominic asked. 'Don't worry, it's not a precious malt, only what you might call cooking whisky.'

Steadman doubted that, for Dominic, although

useless in the kitchen, prided himself in keeping an expansive cellar. He declined the offer, uncertain as to the combination of whisky and tea.

'How's the world of antiques, Dominic?' Steadman asked.

'Absolutely dead. I only deal in fine art now. There is always room at the very top of the market if you can get your hands on the stuff. I've also opened a small gallery for new artists. It's great fun. I go round the students' final exhibitions up and down the country seeing if I can spot up and coming talent. When I think somebody has potential, I will buy a piece or two, then offer to exhibit a few more. So far it's working out quite well. It keeps the wolf from the door, and I like to think I may have helped to launch three or four youngsters on to good careers. Are you beginning to warm up?'

'Yes, thank you,' Steadman replied.

Before Dominic could ask any more questions, Linda came in and announced that lunch was ready. Gently, she steered her brother through to the small dining room.

Steadman hated eating with others, even if it was only his sister and brother-in-law. Cutting up food was a trial, vegetables had a habit of falling off the plate, likewise soup and sauces were a nightmare. Added to that, he had to touch his food to know where it was on the plate and, in so doing, he was quite liable to knock over his glass.

Linda knew all this and had, with her usual foresight, planned accordingly. Even so, Steadman didn't eat a lot.

He was unusually quiet, and Linda thought he looked preoccupied.

When at last they were settled back in front of the fire with a coffee and a decent malt whisky, Dominic asked, 'Well, John, what are you thinking about?'

'The whisky? Highland Park – Orkney's finest, and very pleasant,' he replied.

'You're right about the whisky, but that was not what I meant, as you know full well.'

Linda had joined the men. 'Come on, you can tell your sister what happened on the beach this morning.'

Steadman rubbed the back of his neck. Doubtless the story would be splashed all over the papers tomorrow and perhaps it would be better coming from him; at least the story would be free from journalistic embellishment.

'We found the body of a man.'

'Dead?' asked Dominic.

'As dead as your antiques business,' Steadman replied.

'How shocking!' exclaimed Linda. 'Had he drowned?'

'Oh no,' Steadman replied, 'that would have been too easy. Almost certainly murdered, and not on the beach either.' Steadman gave a very brief account, skipping lightly over the injuries to the man's head. 'Strictly speaking,' he continued, 'we didn't find him. A youth was by the body, but he ran off when Robbie started barking.'

'Do you think he was the killer?'

'Highly unlikely, although I'm not sure what he was doing.' He paused. 'I have just had a thought...'

'Don't you think he was merely emptying the man's pockets? You said he didn't have a wallet on him.'

'I think he was taking something all right, except not in the same sense,' Steadman said enigmatically. He drained his whisky. 'Are my clothes dry, Linda? I think I would like to go home now, if you haven't had too much to drink.'

'Clothes are all laundered, and I've been on soda water all day.'

Steadman smiled. 'You are very kind to me.'

'That's what sisters are for, as I keep telling you. When's Ben coming home?'

'Later this month. However, you know Ben – he'll turn up when the mood takes him.'

Steadman stood up and held out his hand to Dominic. 'I enjoyed our chat. I like the sound of your new venture. Bear me in mind if you spot a rising sculptor. Where has Linda gone?'

'I'm here. I've just taken Robbie out to water the hellebores, so to speak!'

It was still raining and now getting dark. Steadman lived in an apartment above Lloyds' Café, not far from the Eyesore. The Lloyd family looked after him, and his former colleagues were always popping in for a bite to eat. It was an arrangement that suited him well.

Linda concentrated on the road; she was not the most confident of drivers. Periodically she glanced at her brother, who seemed lost in thought. When they eventually arrived, she turned to him and asked, 'Do you think you'll be asked to help in the investigation?'

Steadman shrugged. 'We are too alike, Linda. I was thinking exactly the same thing.'

★ ★ ★

Steadman slept fitfully. He woke at one point with a pounding headache, prickly eyes, and a sore throat. Cautiously, he groped his way to the bathroom, opened the small cabinet above the wash-hand basin and located a packet of paracetamol. His fingers lightly touched the Braille on the packet: it was meaningless to him. He had made an attempt to learn not long after he had lost his sight, but had found it nigh on impossible. It didn't matter; he only kept paracetamol and a bottle of indigestion medicine in the house.

He ran a thumbnail round the foil and, cupping his other hand, popped out two tablets, placed them in his mouth and put the packet back in the cabinet. The tablets tasted bitter and wouldn't go down easily despite a glass of water. He swallowed again and decided to take the glass back to his bedroom.

What sleep he had was punctuated by disturbing dreams. He found himself back on the beach trying to gather up a pack of cards that were being blown over the sand. The only card he could not reach was the Ace of Clubs, which was being jealously guarded by a vicious flock of seagulls. Every time he tried to get near, their sharp beaks would peck at his hands and arms. No matter how hard he thrashed out at them, he was no nearer his goal.

He woke with the sound of a loud crash. For a second or two he lay motionless, not sure of where he was. Yet something had certainly crashed. He dangled an arm out of the bed and touched the floor. *Damn*, he said to himself, feeling the puddle by his bed. He had knocked the glass onto the floor.

He was fully awake now and rolled on to his side. The most important thing was to find the glass, or the remains of it, before either he or Robbie, who was scratching at the door, stood on them. The glass was under the bedside table. Carefully he traced a finger round the rim and the base; good, it appeared undamaged. Tackling the spill was more problematic. There was a towelling dressing gown behind the bedroom door and using this, he did his best to mop up the water.

The doorbell rang, and an excited Robbie pushed open the bedroom door.

'Calm down,' said Steadman in a hoarse voice. 'It will only be young Tim Warrender coming to take you for a walk.' Tim was a schoolboy who had been helping him ever since Robbie arrived.

Steadman's throat was still sore, and his headache was returning. The bell rang again, and in his haste, Steadman stubbed his toe on the half-open door. He swore under his breath and reached for his dressing gown before remembering he had used it to mop up the spill.

He trailed a guiding hand down the corridor wall, reached the front door and opened it.

'Sorry about the state of my dress, Tim – bit of an accident.'

'It's not Tim, Mr Steadman. It's me, Sally. Tim twisted his ankle yesterday.'

Sally was Tim's younger sister. Although Steadman had met her on numerous occasions, he felt acutely embarrassed standing there wearing only pyjamas which he knew had wet patches on them. He mumbled an apology and an explanation. In truth, Sally barely noticed, being far too taken up with a very excited Robbie.

Steadman took another two paracetamols. He wondered if he had a fever.

The phone rang irritably.

'All right, all right, I'm coming,' he said out aloud. He massaged his forehead and picked up the phone.

Before he could speak, a familiar voice bellowed, 'Have you seen the morning paper?'

It was Dr Rufus, and he was well aware that it was some time since his friend had actually seen a paper. If there was anything of interest, Marco Lloyd would read it out to him when he brought him his morning coffee.

'I'll take your silence as a no,' Dr Rufus continued. 'Listen to this headline in the *Echo*. "Mad Axeman Loose in Helmsmouth" – utter scaremongering balderdash! I've tried phoning the editor, but the sluggard is still in his bed. I've left a blistering message on his answerphone. Do you want me to read the rest of the piece?'

Steadman frowned. 'I thought you were giving evidence in the Old Bailey this morning?'

Rufus guffawed loudly. 'Oh that! No, when the defence read the damning details I was about to produce they changed their tune sharpish. They'll be spending the morning plea bargaining, no doubt. I came back last night and I've been in the mortuary since the small hours.'

'I presume you're talking about the body found on the beach?' Steadman queried.

'Do you know of any other corpses in the neighbourhood who have had their heads chopped open?'

'Fair point. How did you find out about it? No, let me guess – Sergeant Grimble.'

'Of course, who else! Have you had breakfast yet? Because I haven't, and I could do justice to a Lloyds' full English.'

'Come and join me, just don't come too close. I think I caught a chill on the beach yesterday and my throat's a bit sore.'

'That's the second bit of rubbish I've encountered today. You know perfectly well that there is no such thing as "catching a chill" – far more likely you've been coughed at or sneezed upon. I'll bring you some lozenges to suck.'

'Will they help?' Steadman asked.

'No earthly idea, but they may stop you spouting

nonsense for a few minutes.' And with that, Dr Rufus hung up.

Steadman pressed the side of his watch and a tinny voice told him the time. If he was quick, he could have a shower and get dressed before Sally came back.

He was pulling on his jumper when the doorbell rang.

'I'll give him a rub down with a towel,' Sally said. 'He's a bit wet and his paws are muddy.'

'Will you be back this evening?' Steadman asked.

'Probably.' She laughed. 'Poor Tim, he hates school almost as much as not taking Robbie for a walk. Mum says if he's fit enough to walk the dog then he's fit enough to go to school.'

Dr Rufus arrived shortly after Sally had left. He was a much shorter man than Steadman, but heavily built. With his larger-than-life personality and air of authority he always seemed to occupy more space than he actually did. Despite his blindness, Steadman swore he could always tell when Dr Rufus was in a room even before he spoke.

As Dr Rufus bolted down an enormous breakfast, Steadman recounted how he and Munro had discovered the body.

'I note you have the newspaper with you,' he said. 'Will you read me the rest of the article?'

Dr Rufus didn't bother asking how he knew he had the paper. He cleared his throat and read, "'The *Echo* has received exclusive photos of the mystery body washed up on Helmsmouth's eastern beach yesterday. The pictures are too horrific to publish. However, they clearly show a man with his head brutally chopped into three pieces." Not true,' Dr Rufus interjected. 'The head was quite neatly sliced.'

'I had a suspicion that was what the young man might be doing before he ran off,' said Steadman. 'He was taking pictures with his mobile phone. DS Fairfax will no doubt be wanting to have a quiet word with him.'

Dr Rufus shook the paper, 'The article goes into some detail, then concludes, "The only reasonable explanation is that this man was hacked to death in a frenzied attack." You get a mention as well – "Was it just coincidence that Detective Sergeant Alan Munro and former Detective Inspector John Steadman, the blind detective, were walking along the beach? The *Echo* thinks not. So far, Helmsmouth Police have declined to give an official statement."' Dr Rufus folded up his newspaper and gave a contemptuous sniff adding, 'Appalling tripe! Surely you've worked out the cause of the head injury, John?'

'Tell me about the rest of the post-mortem. I have some ideas, although I don't think I'm right,' Steadman replied.

'Post-mortem was straightforward – white, male, in his forties, in good health, had recently drunk some champagne...'

'Champagne? That's interesting. Sorry, I interrupted you – do go on.'

'The cause of death was two shots to the chest from a large calibre gun fired from no more than a couple of feet. One of the bullets tore through the left ventricle. Death would have occurred within seconds. Unfortunately, neither bullet was found in the body.'

'Any idea what sort of gun?' Steadman asked.

'Can't be certain, of course,' Dr Rufus replied. 'My money would be on something that fires 9mm rounds. The bullet wounds were less than an inch apart – the first to take the man down, the second to make sure he was dead.'

'So possibly a professional hit man,' mused Steadman.

'If you are going to get fanciful, John, tell me how you think he got his head injuries?'

'I did wonder if he had been hit by a jet ski, then I remembered a jet ski only has a large nozzle underneath. Next option was somebody on water skis.'

'Close, but no cigar!' said Dr Rufus.

'I can't see how a boat could cause two parallel cuts unless it had some sort of fancy keel or rudder.'

'I'll give you a clue,' said Dr Rufus. 'Both cuts were slightly curved.'

Steadman shook his head, 'Go on Frank, put me out of my misery.'

'Simple really – his head was run over by a moderately large propeller from either a big outboard or an onboard motor. Chop, chop – neat as you please! It's a classical injury if you know what you are looking for, and I do.

There used to be a black and white photo in my forensic pathology textbook of exactly such an injury. I've seen a number of propeller injuries, but nothing quite as... extreme.' He was going to say "good", but stopped himself just in time. 'It's a bit like playing billiards – all about chance and angles.'

Steadman thought for a moment, trying to reconstruct the accident in his imagination. It was not a pretty picture. 'Is there any possibility of reconstructing the face?' he enquired.

'Only if you wanted to design a Hallowe'en mask,' Dr Rufus replied. 'Both eyeballs and half the nose are missing, and the facial bones are in smithereens. What is a smithereen, anyway?'

Steadman put his fingers together. 'I believe the origin is from the old Irish word *'smidirin'* meaning 'little bits'. I'm not sure you can have a single smithereen.'

'Trust you to fill your head with such trivia. I can't do a face, but I have done fingerprints and arranged for DNA testing. Kim Ho and the forensic team may come up with something. I gather his tie was American.'

Before either man had time to ponder the tie's possible significance, the phone rang again.

'Will I get that?' Dr Rufus offered.

Steadman nodded, and Dr Rufus picked up the phone.

'The very person I'm after,' said Sergeant Grimble at the other end. 'I thought you might be with Inspector Steadman. Is your mobile not working?'

'I'm sure it is,' replied Dr Rufus. 'I just don't know where it is.'

'Are you free this afternoon? DCI Long wants to hold a case conference. We have a name for the mad axeman's victim.' Sergeant Grimble struggled to keep a straight face.

'Don't you blooming well start as well. I've already tried to get hold of the blasted editor.' Dr Rufus paused. 'Damn it, you knew that already, didn't you?'

'It had been brought to my attention. Would you ask if DI Steadman is free as well? DCI Long has specifically requested his presence.'

Steadman, who clearly had overheard all of this, asked, 'Why?'

Dr Rufus passed him the phone.

'Apparently the victim was well known to you some time ago,' Sergeant Grimble replied.

'Name?' asked Steadman.

'Strictly under wraps until 2 pm this afternoon.'

CHAPTER 3

Dr Rufus's old red Volvo pulled up in front of the Eyesore at one forty-five. Steadman opened the passenger door, glad to get some fresh air. Robbie too seemed anxious to get out and tugged on his harness.

'Wait your turn, Robbie. Remember who's the boss,' said Steadman as he eased himself out of the car.

At one point in the journey, he had asked Dr Rufus, 'Do you never clean the inside of your car? It stinks in here.'

'Can't say I've noticed,' replied Dr Rufus whose nose had been rendered impervious to most smells from years of working with decomposing bodies. 'I did spill an Indian take-away in here a couple of weeks ago, maybe it's that. I suspect you're a bit over-sensitive.'

Sergeant Grimble was on desk duty. He was shuffling papers, moving them around from one apparently random pile to another. He stopped as Steadman and Dr Rufus entered.

'Well, my favourite dog has come to see his Uncle Bertie!' he exclaimed.

'I think our desk sergeant is beyond hope,' Dr Rufus remarked.

Unabashed Sergeant Grimble continued, 'There's quite a crowd in the conference room. I'm sure Robbie would prefer to stay with me, and we can have a nice little walk later on – can't we Robbie?' There was a faint rustling from behind the desk.

'On the condition you don't give him too many of those doggie treats,' Steadman replied.

'I wouldn't dream of it,' Grimble responded, surreptitiously slipping a bone-shaped biscuit into Robbie's mouth. 'Our new Divisional Superintendent may want to meet you afterwards – the fearsome Olivia Campbell.'

'Why do you say fearsome?' asked Dr Rufus.

'How else do you think a woman would have made it through the ranks?' Grimble replied.

Steadman's brow furrowed. He thought the name sounded familiar, yet he could not recall why. 'Apart from me, is anyone else being brought in?' he asked.

Sergeant Grimble grinned and winked at Dr Rufus. 'Had you anybody particular in mind, sir?' Steadman's cheeks flushed. Grimble could not resist adding, 'Someone like an attractive Welsh forensic psychologist?'

'Possibly,' Steadman replied drily.

Sergeant Grimble feared he had gone too far. 'Sorry sir, I don't believe Dr Griffiths has been asked as yet. If she is, I'll make sure you are the first to know.'

Steadman was about to express his indifference, but he couldn't. He and Sam Griffiths had worked closely on Helmsmouth's last murder. Too closely or not close enough, he had asked himself, and concluded it was probably the latter. Her voice had haunted his dreams even though he knew he was still grieving the loss of his wife. Would that ever stop? And besides, what could he, a blind ex-detective, offer her?

Realising the other men's silence, he hastily thanked Sergeant Grimble and handed Robbie over to his care.

Dr Rufus took Steadman's arm and led him through the double doors and along the corridor lined with photographs of retired officers. He wondered if his photo would ever appear there.

As if sensing his thoughts, Dr Rufus remarked, 'Your picture isn't on the wall yet. You must still be of some use to Helmsmouth Police Force.'

They continued up the stairs to the large conference room. Judging by the noise, it must be almost full, Steadman thought.

'Anybody here I don't know?' he asked turning towards his companion.

Dr Rufus surveyed the room. 'The usual team are here. They've just opened a new box of uniformed recruits by the looks of things. They're the ones making the racket at the back. There are a couple of new plain clothes officers that I don't recognise.'

'I've saved you a couple of seats over here,' said a Scottish voice. Only DS Alan Munro had the capacity to hide two empty chairs under his outstretched muscular arms. Dr Rufus guided Steadman to the nearer of the two.

'Any thoughts on who our mystery victim could be?' Munro asked.

'No, not really,' Steadman replied. 'Someone from my past apparently, though I don't know if it's recent or distant past. Doubtless it will all be revealed soon enough. What time is it?'

'Almost two. Here comes the chief now.'

DCI Long was one of the few officers who could match DS Munro in height. He was, however of a much slighter build. The years of responsibility hung heavy on his shoulders, and he now had a slight stoop.

He walked slowly to the front of the room, placed a file on the table and turned to face the assembled gathering. From under bushy eyebrows, he peered around the room and frowned. Someone was missing. The minute hand on the wall clock indicated that it was precisely two o'clock. DCI Long confirmed its accuracy on his own watch and, with a small grunt of satisfaction, began.

'Thank you all for coming, or almost all. The purpose of this meeting is to bring everyone up to speed on what we know about the body on the beach, decide what further investigations are needed, what lines of enquiry need to be pursued and divide out the responsibilities. The body appears to have been discovered by a person unknown who decided to capitalise on his discovery by taking photos. Whether he took anything else, we don't know. He is a person of interest, and we need to speak to him. DC Lofthouse, that's your job and take DC Osborne with you. He sold the pictures to the *Helmsmouth Echo*. I suggest you start there.'

DC Cleo Osborne had newly joined the plain clothes division. She looked towards Will Lofthouse who, as usual, appeared to be in the middle of a daydream. He turned towards DCI Long with a start.

'Very good, sir – I'm on it.' And with that he rose to leave.

'I hate to stifle your enthusiasm, but it can wait until after the meeting,' DCI Long replied.

Someone at the back of the room sniggered as DC Lofthouse sat down again.

'I think we can be certain that the victim was not murdered on the beach,' DCI Long continued, 'so let us start with the post-mortem findings. Over to you Dr Rufus. I gather you disagree with the newspaper's conclusion,' he added with just the merest trace of a smile.

'Fantasy and claptrap!' Dr Rufus exclaimed. 'I have told them exactly what caused the injuries to his head, although I doubt if they'll print a retraction. And for those of you who have not worked out the glaringly obvious, the victim's head was not hacked by a mad axeman but run over by a propeller. Not that he would have cared as he was already dead from two shots to the chest fired at close range and less than an inch apart before being chucked in the sea.'

'He was definitely dead before being jettisoned?' asked DCI Long.

'Beyond any doubt. Death from the gunshots would be instantaneous and, besides, there was no saltwater in his lungs. Otherwise he was fit and well and had been enjoying a glass of champagne very shortly beforehand. Not bad for your last drink on earth. Personally, I would prefer Château Margaux if given the choice. Oh, and he was unquestionably in the water for less than twelve hours.'

'Thank you, Dr Rufus,' said DCI Long, and turning to Kim Ho, he continued, 'What have we learnt from forensics?'

Kim Ho was by nature somewhat nervous and had to be prompted to speak up.

'All his clothes, even his underwear, were made in America, quite new and of good quality. Only his shoes were old – they could easily have been mistaken for new as they had been re-soled and heeled very recently.' She gave DS Munro an anxious glance.

Nothing seems right, thought Steadman. *If he was from*

America, why did he end up here? And he certainly wasn't pushed off an ocean liner. Dr Rufus was adamant he had only been in the sea a matter of hours.

'Somewhere along the way he had lost his jacket,' Kim continued. 'He had no form of ID on him, no wallet, not even a watch, although the marks on his wrist indicated he regularly wore one. He was wearing novelty cuff links in the shape of roulette wheels. I haven't been able to trace where they were made.'

'Thank you, Kim,' DCI Long replied. 'There you have it – it seems highly probable the victim has been recently living in America. In view of that, and the fact we now know who he was, I will be leading the investigation. His fingerprints confirm that he is, or was, a gentleman by the name of Seth Shuster.'

This announcement was greeted with a puzzled silence. DCI Long turned and wrote his name in a beautiful cursive script on the whiteboard.

'Do you know who he is?' Dr Rufus whispered to Steadman.

'I only know of one Seth Shuster, and that was well over ten years ago. If it's the same person, and I'm sure it must be, he was a lot of trouble.'

'Inspector Steadman, I'm certain you recall the name,' Long continued. 'Apart from myself, the only other person who is old enough to have had dealings with Seth Shuster is Inspector Crouchley, and he doesn't appear to be here.'

Inspector Eric Crouchley, renowned for his foul language, was a difficult man. He had scant regard for rules and little respect for authority. Young recruits idolised him in the mistaken belief he was one of them but, in truth, Crouchley did not care for them either. He was tolerated only because he got results. The means were often questionable.

DCI Long looked at the young PCs sitting at the back of the room. 'I don't suppose any of you know where he is?'

A pink-faced officer replied with a grin, 'He said he had something better to do and that he might be here later if he could be bothered.'

The hush that fell on the room was absolute. Some turned their heads to stare at the young constable in disbelief whereas others, Steadman included, merely raised an eyebrow and sighed.

DCI Long glared at the man with incredulity.

'Shall I box his ears for you, sir?' offered Dr Rufus.

'I don't think that will be necessary. Perhaps one of his colleagues could remind him of the correct way to address a senior officer.'

The young PC was now scarlet and looking desperately at his colleagues for help. Someone whispered something in his ear. After a moment's hesitation he added an apologetic, 'Sir.'

'Thank you,' replied DCI Long. 'What is your name?'

'PC Myers,' and after another pause, 'sir.'

'Better. In future when speaking about your superiors please give their rank and name. The *he* that you refer to is Inspector Crouchley. Do I make myself clear?'

'Yes, sir.'

Still looking at the uniformed officers, DCI Long continued, 'Who is the most senior among you?' A beefy sergeant raised his hand. 'Please take notes. We have on file photos of a much younger Seth Shuster. Our photographers have created a likeness to indicate how he probably looked before he died. Because of the injuries to his head, it is only an approximation. Copies will be distributed. I need to know where he stayed, which means trawling all the hotels and guest houses. It may help to know where his shoes were repaired. They are, I gather, quite distinctive. You will be provided with the shoes and approach every cobbler and shoe repairer in Helmsmouth. I would like to find his jacket. Samples of material from the trousers will be supplied and I want every charity shop checked as well as every rough sleeper and hostels for the homeless. Got all that, sergeant?'

'All written down, sir.'

'Excellent. Perhaps now would be a good time for DI Steadman to enlighten us as to Seth Shuster's past. I am sure all of you, even you PC Myers, know of DI Steadman. He has been brought in at my request to help with the investigation.'

'Shall I come to the front, sir?' Steadman asked.

'I think it would be better,' replied DCI Long.

Alan Munro leapt to his feet and steered Steadman to the front of the room. 'There's a table right behind you, sir,' he whispered. Steadman turned, leant on the table, stroked his chin, and appeared to be gazing at the ceiling. He pursed his lips and shook his head slightly as he gathered his thoughts.

Dr Rufus broke the silence by bellowing, 'In your own time, John – no rush!'

Even Steadman smiled. 'What would I do without you Dr Rufus – my nemesis and saviour rolled into one. I was wondering whether to start from Seth Shuster's beginnings or when I first had dealings with him. I think the second option would make more sense and I can fill in the gaps as I go along. Although it is a long time ago, twenty-six years to be precise, I can remember my first encounter with Seth Shuster as if it were yesterday.'

As he started to speak the door opened quietly and a lean woman with coffee-coloured skin and soft features pulled into a frown sidled in. She had short dark hair flecked with grey and wore half-moon glasses. This was Divisional Superintendent Olivia Campbell. DCI Long nodded a greeting to her, and she raised a finger to her lips.

CHAPTER 4

'I can recall the events of twenty-six years ago with unerring clarity, because it was my first day on the beat,' said Steadman. 'I had barely completed my probationary period and was probably no older than PC Myers, and if it's any consolation to the young man, I made a gaffe that was considerably more significant than failing to address a senior officer in the correct manner.'

'Not your last either,' Dr Rufus butted in.

'Indeed not, Frank,' Steadman replied, 'To get back to the story, it was a two-man beat and my colleague was a tall skinny fellow by the name of McAllister. I believe he is now a social worker in Islington. Even then his heart was not in the job and, for reasons best known to himself, he decided to pretend the kerb edge was a tightrope. With outstretched arms he walked heel to toe for about ten feet before slipping off and badly spraining his ankle, although at the time the swelling was so bad, I thought it was broken. An ambulance was called. He was whisked away, and I was left alone, and in truth, quite scared. Within five minutes of the ambulance leaving, a call came through on the radio. The signal was poor, but the gist of the call was that a couple had had property forcibly removed from their flat. It all seemed rather odd. However, as the flat was quite close, I was instructed to go and see what it was all about.

'From the outside the block of flats looked poor and squalid. Sadly, the inside was no better. Everything was worn and grubby. It was difficult to conceive what there possibly could have been in the flat that was of any value. The couple were called Raymond and Shirley Walker. Raymond was small with long hair and a drooping moustache. He was thin – not athletically lean – more the sort of thinness associated with not having enough to eat. Shirley, on the other hand, was...' Steadman screwed up his eyes in concentration. 'I think podgy would best describe her, pale and podgy – too much fast food and not enough fresh air, I guessed. It was Raymond who did all the talking; Shirley stood behind him chewing her nails and occasionally nodding.

'Raymond informed me that someone had forced his way in and removed a brand-new kettle and toaster. "Could he describe the man?" I asked. "Oh yes," he replied, with Shirley nodding in the background. He was tall, dark-haired, well-built, and so forth. I duly wrote it all down along with a description of the kettle and toaster. I told them I would write up their statements and they could either come to the Eyesore or I could bring them back for signing. To my surprise, Raymond asked, "Don't you want to know his name?" I said something stupid like, "That would be helpful." Of course, the name was Seth Shuster.' Steadman paused and cleared his throat.

'Would you like a glass of water?' DCI Long inquired.

Steadman took the glass and continued. 'I was by now completely out of my depth. So, I did what I should have done from the outset, sit down and listen. Seth, it transpired, lived with his grandmother, who was a money lender, or more accurately, a loan shark. The Walkers had borrowed money from her on more than one occasion. In this instance they had fallen behind on their payments and Seth had called around to redress the balance. I got the impression he rather liked doing this bit of his grandmother's business. Raymond knew where they lived. "He has no right to take away our stuff," he pleaded, adding, "I'm not so stupid as to go around there myself – he'll smash my face in." I radioed in to ask for advice and was told that I was a big boy now and to go and sort it out myself.

'It wasn't far. With some trepidation I knocked on the door and was met by Seth Shuster's grandmother. She was a terrifying woman who could not have been further removed from the fairy-tale image of a benign, cherubic white-haired smiling old lady baking cakes all day. Her name was Adelina Monke, spelt with an "e", and I suspect that throughout her childhood other children must have added a "y" at every available opportunity. This could in part, I suppose, have accounted for her unpleasant demeanour.

'She was a large lady with cold, staring eyes and a tight, unsmiling mouth. I recall she had huge strong hands, like a man, and she was constantly opening and clenching her fists. She was, to say the least, reluctant to let me in. Her house was like an Aladdin's cave with an ill-assorted mix of quality antiques and, what could only be described as fairground trash. There was also a collection of power tools, white goods, and television sets. Doubtless the Walkers were not the only ones to have fallen behind with their payments.

'Seth Shuster was in the kitchen having a coffee, and I took an instant dislike to him. He was tall and dark and would have been quite good-looking if it hadn't been for his perpetual scornful, sardonic smile and general air of arrogance. He made no attempt to deny that he had been to the Walkers' and removed their new kettle and toaster, stating that these were rightfully his grandmother's as they had borrowed money and not paid it back. I pointed out that what he had done was illegal. He laughed and challenged me to arrest him there and then. Being young, impetuous, and rather angry at his attitude, I handcuffed and arrested him. This amused the grandmother enormously. She cackled and told me I was making a big mistake. I looked at her and I remember thinking that despite the laughter her eyes remained icy.

'She was right. I had made a mistake – a mistake which I'm sure PC Myers is dying to hear about. Seth Shuster was only fifteen at the time. He was, on that occasion, handled with kid gloves, given a caution, and made to return the Walkers' property. About three weeks later, the Walkers' flat was torched. Nobody was hurt, but they lost everything. We never did find out who set the flat ablaze, but I have no doubt in my mind it was Seth Shuster.'

The room had fallen completely silent. Everybody's eyes were fixed on John Steadman; all were hanging on to his every word. Not knowing how to interpret the silence, Steadman turned towards DCI Long.

'Shall I continue, sir?' he asked.

'Please do. Like you, I believe the more you know about the victim, the more likely you are to catch his or her killer.'

Steadman nodded. 'In due course, I met Seth Shuster's mother. Her name was Claudine Turner, and she was one of the most pathetic creatures I've ever met. She must have been pretty at one time, but years of drug abuse and prostitution had taken their toll on her appearance. She had become pregnant as a teenager and had never married. Seth Shuster took his name from the alleged father, an American airman with whom she had had a one-night stand. Seth used to brag about his father – to the best of my knowledge they never met. Seth was a good actor and could do a passable American accent which he used to impress the girls.

'Because of Claudine's drug habit, he was threatened with being taken into care on several occasions. Always, the grandmother stepped in. When a pimp and dealer realised he could make a lot of money out of Claudine if he took her to London, Seth moved in with Adelina Monke on a permanent basis. Claudine died shortly afterwards of a drug overdose.

'She had an elder brother and sister and I did wonder why Seth was never put into their care – that is until I met them. The brother was called Joshua Reynolds, so maybe Adelina thought he would become a famous artist. He preferred to be called Josh as it was easier to spell. He did wield a brush, but only as a painter and decorator. His other occupation was as a small-time crook. He reminded me of a robin – cocky, cheeky, self-confident, and ferociously vicious in defending his own territory. He would make copies of the keys wherever he was working, then go back and ransack the properties at his leisure. He also handled stolen goods – probably from Seth Shuster.

'The sister, Clara Drinsdale, was another thing altogether. She combined petty criminality with inordinate foolishness. Let me give you an example – she was a prolific shoplifter, and on one occasion she took an expensive bracelet back to the shop as the clasp had broken. When asked for a receipt, she replied, "Don't be bleeding stupid. I haven't got a receipt, I nicked it!"'

Once the laughter had settled down, Steadman continued, 'It was little wonder that out of the possibilities, Seth was left with his grandmother. The sharp-eared among you will note that the three siblings all have different surnames. Hard though it was for the young PC Steadman to believe, grandmother Monke had been a thing of beauty in her day and one of Helmsmouth's leading ladies of the night. She too had named her respective children after their putative fathers.'

Steadman paused to draw breath, and in the brief interlude Dr Rufus piped up, 'I hope you're paying attention at the back – there will be a short quiz following the inspector's presentation.'

Steadman smiled and shook his head. 'Let's return to Seth Shuster. He developed a taste for what he perceived as the good things in life. He was no fool despite only sporadic school attendances. Given his background, it was little wonder that he started dealing in drugs as well as money lending. And, following his mother's death, he callously added procurement to his portfolio. He had several brushes with the law and a string of convictions. Somehow, he was always able to hire expensive solicitors and barristers who milked his upbringing for all it was worth.

'But Seth Shuster was bad news. He was responsible for a series of grievous assaults, either personally or by paying hired heavies to do his dirty work. He ruled his little empire by fear and intimidation. The few that were willing to press charges soon backed off.'

Steadman took another sip of water. 'I've interviewed him several times over the years. He had good looks and charm. Undeniably, there was, lurking just beneath the surface, a ruthless and malevolent greed. He changed tactics shortly before disappearing from Helmsmouth. He decided an easier living could be made from gambling. It was illicit at first – dog fights, bare-knuckle boxing and so on. Eventually he had his own casino where, if you knew who or how to ask, you could be provided with cocaine, heroin, and the like, as well as companions of your choosing.

'It wasn't just the law he was in trouble with. These activities were already ruled by a criminal elite, and Seth Shuster stepped on one toe too many. He left Helmsmouth in a hurry and headed for London some years ago. I doubt if he lasted long there. He thought he was a big man, but he soon found that organised crime in London was in a different league altogether.'

Steadman turned towards DCI Long. 'Unless you have more information on what has happened in the intervening years, that's about all I can tell you regarding Seth Shuster.'

DCI Long cleared his throat. 'Thank you, I think you have painted a very vivid picture. One of our priorities will be to find out where he has been during the last ten years and, of course, what he has been up to. The only thing I can add is that we are fairly certain he has not been in this country for the most part, although when he arrived back on these shores is still unknown. Are there any questions for DI Steadman or myself?'

There was a general murmur in the room as though someone had disturbed a beehive. In the chatter a tight-lipped Divisional Superintendent slipped out of the room without casting a glance at DCI Long or John Steadman.

Alan Munro put his hand up. 'Do we know if the grandmother, brother or sister are still alive?'

'I can answer that one,' replied DCI Long. 'The grandmother is in a care home. Josh Reynolds is still working part-time. The sister, Clara, has never really held down a job. Occasionally she picks up the odd dish-washing shift in one of the large hotels. Neither of them has married and, I gather, they moved in together about five years ago. They need to be interviewed.'

DS Fairfax spoke next. 'I have a question for Inspector Steadman. From what you know of him, do you think Seth Shuster was capable of murder?'

There was no hesitation in Steadman's reply, 'Most definitely. Seth Shuster was morally bankrupt from an early age. I have no doubt that he was capable of killing anyone that got in his way, probably without giving it a second thought.'

'What about Josh Reynolds and Clara Drinsdale? They would be Seth's uncle and aunt,' added DS Fairfax.

'I don't think so. Clara was too stupid. Josh was a

bully and had a temper, but somehow I can't see him as a murderer.'

The door burst open with a loud crash and everybody's head turned. For a second or two, Inspector Crouchley scowled around the room. His eyes eventually alighted on the whiteboard and Seth Shuster's name.

'Don't tell me that piece of excrement is the body washed up on the effing beach!' he exclaimed. 'If I had known you were holding a celebratory party, DCI Long, I might have come earlier and brought some cake.'

Again, there was some sniggering from the back of the room. Probably PC Myers, thought Steadman.

'Hardly a party, Inspector Crouchley,' DCI Long replied. 'For all his failings, Seth Shuster was murdered on our patch. I don't like unsolved murders, which is why I have specifically requested your help. Only three of us here remember Seth Shuster...'

'And you want me to reminisce,' Crouchley interjected. 'Steadman's no doubt painted you a rosy picture of a poor down-trodden boy from a sad and broken background. Don't be taken in! All you need to know is that Shuster was born bad, grew up worse and went downhill from there. A complete nutcase in my opinion. If we catch his killer, I will personally shake his hand and put his name forward for a national honour.'

DCI Long sighed, 'I'm sure that there are some who would agree with you...'

'But I am not one of them,' Steadman finished the

sentence. 'Seth Shuster may well have been all the things you said. Your argument, however, applies equally to whoever killed him. And I will do whatever I can to help bring those responsible to justice. Justice, Inspector Crouchley, not mob rule.'

Before Inspector Crouchley could reply, the door opened again and Sergeant Grimble, preceded by Robbie, entered.

'Sorry to barge in, sir, only Robbie's getting fretful,' he said.

The dog nuzzled up to Steadman. Without being asked, Munro passed him the dog's harness. Somehow the sight of Steadman harnessing his dog appeared to irritate Crouchley even more. He snorted and strode to the back of the room to join the other uniformed officers.

'Oh – and our new Divisional Superintendent would like to meet you in her office as soon as you have finished, Inspector Steadman,' Grimble added.

Steadman's brow furrowed. Olivia Campbell? He was sure he had come across the name before, but for the life of him, he couldn't place it.

CHAPTER 5

It had been several years since DI Steadman had visited the fifth floor of the Eyesore. The rooms here were larger and grander, as befitted the more senior officers of Helmsmouth Police Force, including Divisional Superintendent Olivia Campbell.

Steadman, Grimble and Robbie squeezed into the tiny lift which clunked its way laboriously up to floor five. Sergeant Grimble noticed the Braille numbering next to the lift buttons. He recalled Steadman telling him how difficult they were to decipher. Feeling a bit like a naughty schoolboy, Grimble closed his eyes and traced a finger over the raised dots, hoping his colleague would not notice. They were virtually impossible to interpret.

'Having fun trying to read the Braille numbers?' Steadman asked with a smile.

'I'd swear sometimes you aren't as blind as you make yourself out to be, sir,' replied a shamefaced Grimble.

'Sadly, I am – and I don't recollect ever being in a lift since I lost my eyesight when somebody hasn't surreptitiously tried their hand at reading Braille.'

Grimble opened his eyes and swiftly changed the subject. 'Why do you think so many people of Jamaican origin have Scottish names, sir? I'm surprised Munro isn't foaming at the mouth.'

'I presume you are referring to our new Divisional Superintendent. I gather there are more Campbells per head of population in Jamaica than in Scotland,' Steadman replied.

Sergeant Grimble was taken aback. 'You surprise me, sir. Any idea why?'

'Apparently it started with Oliver Cromwell shipping out a load of Scottish prisoners of war in the mid-seventeenth century to work on the sugar plantations. If memory serves me rightly the boat was called something like *The Two Sisters*.'

Sergeant Grimble raised an eyebrow. If Steadman thought it was "something like" *The Two Sisters*, he would bet his police pension that he was correct.

'But most of the Campbells,' DI Steadman continued, 'are reckoned to have descended from one man, Colonel John Campbell. He had a large family, sugar plantations and, of course, slaves who were often given their owner's name. Rather than foaming at the mouth, I suspect it's a part of Scottish history that Munro would prefer to forget.'

The lift stopped with a shudder and the doors opened.

'I still can't imagine our new Divisional Superintendent in a kilt doing the Highland Fling, somehow,' Grimble remarked. 'Anyway, she was most insistent that I drag you to her lair.'

Steadman was subconsciously counting the steps as they walked along the corridor. 'I doubt if it's a social call,' he replied cautiously. 'I wonder if she perceives me as some sort of threat. I can't think why – my involvement is only as a consultant.'

'She's a difficult lady to read,' Sergeant Grimble whispered. 'Doesn't like to get too close to people. Likes a place for everything and everything in its place, if you know what I mean. A stickler for protocol and not much sense of humour either. I can't imagine she and Dr Rufus becoming bosom buddies.'

'I'm certain we haven't met before, yet the name is definitely familiar.' Steadman drummed the fingers of his free hand on his thigh. 'No, I can't remember – maybe I'm wrong, and it wasn't her at all.'

'You're seldom wrong, sir. You'll remember in time, you always do. Here we are. She's got a big enough sign on her door – no mistaking whose office it is.'

Grimble knocked lightly on the door. Steadman had tallied the number of steps and committed them to memory.

A voice called out, 'Enter.' Even in that one word

Steadman could detect the slight musical lilt of a Caribbean accent.

'DI John Steadman, ma'am, and his dog...' Grimble was not allowed to continue.

'I am quite sure Inspector Steadman can tell me his own name, Sergeant, and if needed, that of his dog. For the record, Sergeant, I did not choose the size of the sign on my door.'

Grimble didn't bat an eyelid. 'Of course not, ma'am. Probably selected for the benefit of my advancing years and failing vision.'

Certainly not for mine, Steadman thought.

Grimble bent down and gave Robbie a small biscuit from his bulging trouser pocket. 'I was only going to tell the lady your name,' he mumbled. And in an even quieter voice Steadman thought he whispered, 'Bossy cow!' in the dog's ear before leaving.

The room was vast, and as sterile as a surgical theatre. There were no pictures on the wall, no shelves bursting with files, no family photos; almost nothing to indicate that anybody worked there. The desk was laid out as neatly as a dining table at the Ritz. Two pens lay at exactly right angles to the length of the desk, parallel to the in-tray whose position was precisely mirrored by the out-tray at the other end of the desk. Even the telephone and desk clock were lined up with military precision.

'Is he senile?' asked Superintendent Campbell.

'Sergeant Grimble? Far from it, ma'am. He knows

everything that's going on in the Eyesore. If you want to speak to someone and can't find that person, ask Sergeant Grimble. He will not only know where they are, but give you their mobile number, home phone number and probably even their date of birth.'

'You do surprise me, Inspector.' She looked at her own immaculate desk and recalled the shambles that was Sergeant Grimble's. 'Won't you take a seat?'

'You will have to help me, ma'am, with some directions.'

'You really are totally blind?' she said incredulously.

'Not totally, ma'am. I can sometimes make out a bright light in the darkness, but only if I cover one eye. Unfortunately, my eyes no longer work together in any meaningful way. I don't have any useful vision as such.'

Olivia Campbell was about to say, 'I see', but bit her lip just in time. 'The chair is about two feet in front of you and to your right.'

Steadman stretched out his right hand and stepped forward. He found the back of the chair. 'May I take off my coat, ma'am?' The room was quite warm.

'Of course. I would open a window, but not only are they filthy, they all appeared jammed.'

'A design fault in the construction I fear, ma'am, and no money in the budget to make good either,' said Steadman as he hung his coat over the chair and placed his hat on the floor.

The Divisional Superintendent made no reply. For a moment or two she simply stared at him.

'I was impressed by your performance in the conference room,' she said at last.

'I was unaware of your presence, ma'am. In some ways I am very lucky. Most people who have been shot in the head either die or are left with significant brain damage. All I lost was my sight – and, of course, my wife.'

'So I gather.' She nibbled her thumbnail, not sure how to carry on. 'Obviously, the background information you gave is helpful... and the press seem to like you,' she continued hesitantly. 'Having said all that, I feel asking a blind person, albeit a former detective, to assist with a serious criminal investigation reflects badly on Helmsmouth Police Force.' She paused and moved one of her pens a fraction of an inch. 'I wonder why, exactly, you have been brought in?'

Steadman was unsure if the question was rhetorical or directed at him.

'Well, what do you think?' she said breaking the silence.

'I have a mantra,' Steadman replied, 'the more you know about the victim, the more likely you are to find the culprit. Seth Shuster's murder was no accident. As I see it, or more correctly, visualise it, only DCI Long, Inspector Crouchley and myself knew Seth Shuster and his family. It was DCI Long who requested my assistance, perhaps you should speak with him.'

Again, there was a pause. Steadman reflected that

Superintendent Campbell liked to choose her words with care.

'I would have thought Inspector Crouchley knew them as well as you.'

'I believe I had more direct dealings with Seth Shuster and his family,' Steadman replied diplomatically. 'It really is not my place to say why I have been brought in, ma'am, although I am more than willing to offer what help I can.'

The ticking of the clock suddenly got louder. Maybe she had moved it, Steadman thought, or corrected the time. Robbie stirred, and Steadman snapped his fingers. Immediately the dog spread-eagled himself on the floor at his feet.

'I wish I could train my officers like that,' Campbell remarked.

A smile spread across Steadman's face as he conjured up a picture of Alan Munro flattening himself on the floor.

'Is there something amusing you, Inspector?'

'Yes, ma'am. I just had an image of you snapping your fingers and DS Munro falling at your feet, that's all.'

'Quite so,' she replied as she adjusted the position of a file in her out-tray.

'In reply to your earlier question,' Steadman continued, 'I wonder if I would get more from Seth Shuster's family, given that I know them, and they know me. They may find me less intimidating.'

'Now it's my turn to imagine something. I'm trying

hard to imagine conducting a police interview with my eyes shut – and it doesn't work. How, for example, can you tell if someone is lying? You wouldn't know if someone was not looking at you, or indeed about to hit you, would you? And I'm not sure that a formal interview shouldn't be intimidating. Perhaps you could work with Inspector Crouchley?'

'He would never agree to it,' Steadman replied. 'He finds my presence an embarrassment, as I suspect you do too, ma'am.'

Olivia Campbell started to say something, but Steadman held up his hand. 'I'm not offended – I understand your position.' The room suddenly seemed very hot, and Steadman was glad he had removed his coat. 'I usually work with DS Munro or DS Fairfax. Alan Munro's very presence is intimidating, and I've seen hardened criminals lose their nerve under Fiona Fairfax's steely gaze. Both are extremely good officers.'

Superintendent Campbell pushed her chair back and stood up. Steadman could hear her pacing up and down between her desk and the windows. She wiped one of the panes with a tissue. It made no difference.

'Is there no way these damned windows can be cleaned?'

'May I suggest, ma'am, you ask Sergeant Grimble,' Steadman replied. 'If there is a way, he'll know.'

She dismissed the suggestion with a wave of her hand. 'You are very fond of Sergeant Grimble, but not so keen on Inspector Crouchley? Crouchley gets results.'

'He does indeed, ma'am.'

'You don't like his methods, do you?'

A melody sprang into Steadman's head, a little minuet by Bach. Without being aware, he started to tap out the rhythm on his thigh. Should he be honest with the new Divisional Superintendent? The music stopped.

'No, ma'am, I do not. Inspector Crouchley regards rules and regulations merely as recommendations – another person's opinion, if you like. Even the law is open to his personal interpretation.'

'And his attitude?'

'I would rather you formed your own opinion, ma'am.'

Steadman disliked where the conversation was going. He hated disloyalty but hated hypocrisy even more.

Thankfully, the phone rang. Steadman could only make out snippets of the conversation: 'Yes he's here… No, I'm not finished… Then you will have to wait.'

Campbell put the phone down. 'That was DCI Long. You appear to be in demand, Inspector Steadman.'

Steadman half-rose from his chair. Robbie stood up and gave himself a shake.

'We are not done yet, Inspector.'

Reluctantly Steadman sat down again. He gave Robbie a reassuring pat and the dog nestled back at his feet.

'I want to know what your first impressions are,' said the Superintendent.

'I dislike making assumptions, ma'am. However…' Steadman hesitated. 'I can elaborate a little on what I said in the conference room. Some of what I am about to say is fact, some is conjecture. I doubt very much that Seth Shuster's return was welcomed by his family. He was hardly the prodigal son. And there are others, no doubt, who would also not welcome him back. He knew how to make enemies and left a trail of corruption and chaos in his wake. Furthermore, he cared not one whit for the lives he ruined or destroyed.'

The Superintendent had returned to her seat. She was now listening very closely to Steadman. Leaning over the desk, she asked, 'Lives destroyed? Do you mean deliberately?'

Steadman pushed his dark glasses onto his forehead and rubbed the bridge of his nose between long, bony fingers. 'I have no proof – also, I have no doubt. In some ways I am surprised he has survived this length of time. He was an angry boy who turned into an even angrier young man, always trying to prove himself, always trying punch above his weight. He had delusions of grandeur, fuelled by low self-esteem. And he had many flaws. One of these was his inability to make friends. He was a loner and never surrounded himself with other people. He thought he could run organised crime without an organisation, other than paying for the occasional thug. Inevitably, he was forever outnumbered. I believe that's why he left Helmsmouth all those years ago and, I suspect, it's why he left London, presumably to go to America...'

Steadman faltered, his faced screwed up in concentration.

'What are you thinking?' asked an intrigued Superintendent. Her icy coldness towards the man sitting opposite her was starting to thaw.

'If he was following a life of crime in America, ma'am, and why wouldn't he, that's all he ever knew – why were we never contacted or informed? All I can assume, and I hate assumptions, is that he was living there under a different name, possibly even with a completely new identity.'

CHAPTER 6

Summer in the southern states can be unbearable. Even when you can't see the sun, the air is thick and uncomfortably warm. Leon Fitzroy squinted at the fan in the ceiling. Its paddles turned lazily, stirring the air in a derisory attempt to provide a draught.

He squinted because he could only open one eye. The other was swollen and badly bruised. He had met with an accident, at least that's what was recorded in the book. Could not getting out of the way of a guard's fist be construed as an accident? He laughed to himself, which brought on a paroxysm of coughing.

Eventually it subsided. He reached into the patch pocket of his orange shirt, not easy with both hands shackled, and produced a grubby handkerchief. He spat and was not surprised to see blood. Over the last few weeks there had always been blood.

The guard, a thickset bulldozer of a man called Frobisher, took not the slightest notice. Drips formed on the end of his nose, and he wiped them away carelessly with his sleeve. Great damp patches appeared under his arms. Leon Fitzroy looked at him and shook his head. Thirteen years of prison life had taught him, among other things, not to sweat.

A fly buzzed around the guard. He tried swatting it with his big fat hand, the same hand that had caused Leon's little accident. Unlike Leon, the fly was too quick. It soared up to the ceiling. Leon followed it with his one good eye as it made its escape through a barred vent. 'Lucky bastard,' he mumbled under his breath.

Maybe it was because of all the weight he had lost that the heat no longer bothered him. Glancing down at his scrawny wrists he wondered, just for a moment, if he could slip out of his handcuffs. Doubtless Frobisher would find that reason enough to give him another pounding.

The two men were sitting in a brightly lit windowless corridor. The walls were half-tiled and painted a dirty off-white. They were devoid of decoration. A sign stencilled on the door to Leon's right read, 'Montgomery Franks, Warden'. The lettering was starting to peel, a sure sign that Warden Franks was close to retiring. He had been in charge of the prison for more years than he cared to recall. He clearly remembered Leon Fitzroy's arrival; a disaffected young man then, a victim of an impoverished upbringing who turned to crime not out of necessity but from ignorance. Despite having two previous convictions he had agreed to deliver a package for his uncle. The package was "hot". The police had been tipped off and before he knew it, under the three strikes law, Leon now faced a life sentence. It was a harsh judgement swayed by the assertion by one of the arresting officers that Leon had brandished a knife, lunged at him, and gashed his uniform. Leon swore he had never seen the knife before. However, the officer was white, and Leon was not.

Montgomery Franks never knew who to believe. Over the years he had given up trying and simply accepted whatever came his way. Still, he had a soft spot for Leon Fitzroy. The angry young man had turned into a docile model prisoner who caused him no trouble. Leon's request for a quiet word was unusual, and Warden Franks was intrigued; intrigued enough to grant him an audience, although he had a sinking feeling that he knew what it might be about.

The door opened, and Warden Franks nodded to Leon and the guard. Frobisher hoisted Leon roughly to his feet. Leon was about to take a step when a fat hand grabbed his shoulder and a voice hissed in his ear, 'Not one word about your accident, or you may find yourself involved in another – understand?' Leon did not reply.

'Prisoner Fitzroy, sir,' Frobisher announced unnecessarily.

'I can see that for myself, thank you,' answered Franks.

'Sit down Leon. For goodness sake take off the man's cuffs.'

'Regulations, sir.'

Franks stared in disbelief. 'I am Warden of this prison and your view on regulations isn't worth a plugged nickel, Frobisher. Your rank is Correctional Officer and if I say remove his cuffs, you take them off without question. If you ever get to sit in my chair, and that's not likely, you can chain prisoners up to your heart's content. Until then...'

Frobisher was fuming. Reluctantly he removed the handcuffs and gave Leon a menacing look.

'Now leave us,' added the Warden.

'I'll be by the door if there's any trouble, sir.'

'Trouble?' Franks looked at the emaciated figure sitting before him. 'What do you think he'll do? Steal a paper clip? No, you will not be by the door, you will go and freshen up and get a change of uniform. And that's an order.'

'I think you've upset him,' Leon said as Frobisher slammed the door behind him.

'Lord preserve us! My days of worrying about people like Frobisher's feelings are long since over,' sighed Franks. He put his fingers together and gazed at the man on the other side of his desk through half-closed eyes. This man doesn't have long for this world, Franks was thinking.

At last he spoke. 'I know why you're here.' The prisoner shot him a quizzical look. 'But you know the law as well as I do. Your sentence is life without parole – even in your circumstances, I'm afraid.' He spread out his hands and gave Leon an apologetic look.

To his surprise, Leon started to laugh, stopping only when the coughing began again. He pulled out his blood-streaked hanky. The Warden grimaced, rummaged in his drawer, and passed Leon a box of tissues. He looked the other way as Leon hacked and spat.

'Hell no, sir, I'm not here to ask for parole. Where would I go? My last visitor was over three years ago, and she only came to ask if she could borrow money. Nobody writes, mostly cause they're lazy, but some out of lack of learning. This prison is my home. I've lived here longer than any other place in my life. I've got lung cancer and I'm dying. I'd rather stay here surrounded by people that know me – even if some of them don't like me too much.' He fingered his swollen eye. 'Besides, I wouldn't be welcome outside.' He paused and for a moment he simply stared at his feet, lost in his own thoughts. 'I can just imagine them, sir, arguing over whose bed I was soiling and who is going to pay for the funeral.' A solitary tear ran down his cheek. The Warden remained silent.

'I know I'm no angel and was a bit wild in my younger days,' Leon continued. He raised his head and said firmly, 'I did not try to knife that officer. He was an evil-hearted son of a bitch, just like the bastard who blackened my eye. You know, sometimes I wish I had knifed him – knifed him good and proper. I would have been out of all of this years ago. A nice quick death. I would have preferred a fatal injection to a slow lingering death.' He looked steadily at the Warden. 'Can you promise me one thing? When my time comes, and I know it's coming fairly soon, they won't let me suffer?'

The Warden nodded. 'I'll do what I can, I promise. About your injury, I was led to believe you had an accident.'

'Accident, my ass – if you pardon the expression. The only accident I had was not being able to dodge Frobisher's fat fist quick enough. The record book is just a collection of fairy stories. I sometimes think that each entry must begin with "Once upon a time..." and end with "...and they all lived happily ever after."'

Warden Franks knew this perfectly well. He was also wise enough not to say anything.

'Do you want to hear something funny, sir?'

'I could always do with cheering up,' the Warden conceded.

'The doctor tries to break it to me gently that I've got the big "C". He's dancing round the subject like a wasp round a jam jar. No, it's too far gone for an operation, and no, drugs won't help much either. So, I ask him straight up, "How long have I got, doc?" He shrugs and looks the other way, evading the question. "Could be weeks, months maybe. Nobody can tell," he says. And then, honest to God, without a blush he says, "I would recommend you give up smoking."' Leon's face broke into an enormous grin. 'Have you ever heard such a piece of bullshit in your life? Give up smoking, with weeks to live! Talking of which, you couldn't spare me a cigarette?'

Warden Franks opened another drawer and pulled out a packet of Dunhill International. Leon let out a soft whistle. 'They must be paying you more than I thought.'

Franks placed both his hands on the desk. 'If you're going to have a bad habit, might as well make it a good one.'

Leon inhaled deeply, leant back in his chair and gently blew a smoke ring up to the ceiling. 'You haven't asked me why I'm here.'

'Oh, I had one guess and was wrong. I figured you'd tell me in your own time.'

Leon let some smoke trickle out of his nostrils. 'You've always been fair with me, Mr Franks, and I thank you for that. Thank-yous are nice but worthless. You've recently had a mishap that I guess caused you no end of embarrassment.'

Montgomery Franks pulled a face. It was not a subject he particularly wanted to talk about.

'I'm going to give you some information on the one condition – you do nothing 'til I'm dead,' said Leon.

The Warden started to say something, his tone soothing, almost patronising, but Leon talked over him. 'I want no bullshit from you either,' he said giving him a wry smile. 'I've got two, maybe three weeks at the most and I want to talk while my brain is still clear.'

'OK, you have my word,' Franks agreed. 'Go on.'

'You recall the prisoner who gave you such a red face. He was in the cage next to me for a time.'

The Warden remembered only too well. An odd fellow who was pulled over by a patrol car for no other reason than his car had New York plates and he seemed lost. As the highway patrolman approached the car to see if he could help, the driver wound down his window, pulled out a gun and shot the officer dead. Before fleeing the scene, he put a hail of bullets in the patrol car, injuring the driver. It wasn't long before he was picked up. His papers were false, his ID was false, even the number plates on the car were false. He had said very little, offered no plea and was almost certainly facing the death penalty, even allowing for the court's nagging doubts about his sanity. He never got that far.

'He didn't talk a lot,' Leon continued. 'One night he says to me, "Leon, is that guard as crooked as I think he is?" – meaning Frobisher. I don't know how he could tell. "More bent and twisted than most of us," I reply.'

'Hold on a minute, Leon. This is not some petty revenge for getting socked in the eye, is it?'

'I'm way past revenge, sir. Only if he knew what I was going to tell you, he'd beat me to a pulp. Do you want me to carry on?'

The Warden nodded.

'He wants to know what his weakness is, so I tell him – it's gambling. Everyone knows about Frobisher's addiction. Well, he just smiles to himself as though he'd already worked it out. Now, I don't know how he got them – I guess he had the occasional visitor – but he got some hot tips. One time, I see him pass a bit of paper to Frobisher. Two days later the fat fool is wandering around smiling like Santa Claus. A week later, in the dead of night I hear them talking about horses and a boxing match. Within a month, he's got Frobisher in the palm of his hand. What does he want in return? A mobile phone and his watch back. So, the tips go on and he gets his phone. I guess he got his watch as well, but I never saw him wear it.'

The Warden frowned, scribbled something down on the pad in front of him and underlined it twice.

'And all this time Frobisher is smirking like a cat that's got the cream. I swear I even heard Frobisher call him sir! Who do you think arranged for that meal – double salmon steaks on the bone – the day he was due back in court for sentencing?'

It had always puzzled Montgomery Franks where that last meal had come from. Sure, he turned a blind eye to the odd pack of cigarettes, cake or chocolate being brought in. Drugs were a strict no-go area, yet somehow, they always slipped through the net. True, the prisoner had given him no problems, no signs of violence – nothing. If, as seemed very likely, he was to be handed a death sentence later that day, then he wouldn't be coming back under Warden Franks care. So what if he was being given a special meal before he left?

Nobody would have said anything had he not started to choke. Montgomery Franks had been called. The prisoner was gagging, frothing at the mouth and gesticulating like crazy at his throat. At one point, Franks was convinced he had turned navy blue.

The helicopter landed twenty minutes later. Franks had made sure the prison was in lockdown, every other prisoner back in his cell, all doors secured. Three men got out the helicopter: a paramedic, an anaesthetist and an ear, nose and throat surgeon. The pilot remained on board with the motors running.

What happened next was still a blur. Shortly after take-off all radio contact was lost, and not long after that the helicopter disappeared from the radar. Everyone presumed there had been a crash.

A day later the barely conscious bodies of two people were discovered in the trunk of a car parked behind the helicopter station: the real pilot and the paramedic. They could remember only snatches of their ordeal: two men dressed as cleaning staff who turned out to be heavily armed, ominous threats, blows to the head, then nothing until they were roused by the trunk lid opening. Their ankles and wrists had been securely bound and their mouths gagged.

Of the two doctors on board the helicopter, the body of the anaesthetist was discovered in the desert three weeks later. Death had resulted from a fall from a great height. The remains of the ENT surgeon were never found. Presumably they were out there somewhere, if they hadn't been eaten by the wildlife. Despite an exhaustive search, no traces of the helicopter or its other occupants were ever found.

Leon was coughing his lungs out again. The Warden got him a glass of water and helped him take a sip. His hand brushed against his cheek. *Christ,* he thought, *he's burning up.*

'Leon,' he said, 'let's get you to the hospital wing for a few days. You're sick and I don't care for the way Frobisher was looking at you.'

'That would be appreciated, sir. You know, I reckon Frobisher is missing him. He seems down on his luck.' A twinkle appeared in his eye. 'I couldn't resist but offer him a tip myself. The sucker fell for it – I told him to shove his fat head up his ass and do us all a favour. He didn't see the funny side of it.'

'Is that why he bopped you in the eye?'

'That, and as a warning to keep quiet.' Leon looked longingly at the pack of cigarettes.

'Have another,' Franks offered, and seeing as it was half-empty added, 'Keep the packet.' He phoned the hospital wing. 'Somebody will be over for you shortly.'

'Want to know some more about the one that got away? His name wasn't Adam Monke. I guess you knew that.'

'Any idea what his real name was?'

Leon shook his head. 'I can tell you something else though – he wasn't American.'

'Oh? How do you know?'

'Easy, he talked in his sleep. He was a Limey – as English as roast beef and Yorkshire pudding.'

CHAPTER 7

DI Steadman was still feeling very warm. Despite that he put on his hat and coat before leaving the Superintendent's office; it was easier and safer than carrying them.

'I have no doubt we'll meet again,' said Olivia Campbell. She held out her hand to Steadman and then felt very stupid, for the gesture, of course, went unseen. 'Are you sure you'll manage to find your own way to DCI Long's office?'

'Quite sure, thank you, ma'am. Robbie has yet to let me down. I will try not to ruffle too many feathers,' he replied, forcing a smile. Although feathers will be ruffled if needs be, he mused.

The door closed softly behind him. Robbie turned to look at him as if making sure he was ready. Either he had miscounted his steps or had been taking shorter strides when accompanied by Sergeant Grimble, for Robbie stopped suddenly. Steadman put out a hand and felt the lift door.

'Damn it, Robbie, I can't remember which side the call button is on.'

The dog jerked his head and Steadman traced a hand gently over the dog's muzzle. Robbie's head was tilted upwards and Steadman followed its direction, reaching forward until his fingers found the button.

'Robbie,' he said, 'you never cease to amaze me.'

The lift stopped with a clang and they got in. This time Steadman remembered where the control panel was. Could he read the numbers in Braille? The sign indicating numbers was fairly easy – a backward L made up of four dots. DCI Long's office was on the first floor. Could he make out the single dot to the top right-hand side of the L? Perhaps. He pressed the button and with a lurch, the lift descended.

As soon as the doors opened his ears were assailed by the familiar sounds of typing and chatter. From somewhere down the corridor, the unmistakable booming laugh of Dr Rufus assured him he was on the correct level. He stopped to think for a minute, trying to recall the layout of the offices.

'May I help you, DI Steadman?' It was a woman's voice and not very old, thought Steadman.

'That would be appreciated, but first tell me who you are?'

'Sorry sir, of course. I'm DC Cleo Osborne – very new to the unit.'

'I'm very pleased to meet you, DC Osborne,' Steadman replied and held out his hand. The hand that shook his felt as though it belonged to a child.

'Please call me Cleo – I don't feel old enough to be called DC Osborne yet.' The voice was young too. She's probably not even as old as my son Ben, thought Steadman.

'Oh, don't worry, you'll soon get used to it,' he replied reassuringly. 'Shouldn't you be out with DC Lofthouse, hounding the editor of the *Helmsmouth Echo*?'

'I should, but he forgot and left without me. Is he always in a bit of a daydream?'

'Usually, although he can be quite brilliant at times.' Steadman did wonder about mentioning that DC Will Lofthouse was also a serial heartbreaker, believing himself to be the most handsome and irresistible man in Helmsmouth's police force. Maybe he would ask Alan Munro to have a cautionary word with her.

'Are they keeping you gainfully occupied, Cleo?'

'I'm busy phoning round the car rental dealers to see if anyone with an American accent has hired a car in the last two or three weeks. I would guess that Seth Shuster may have picked up an accent if he's lived in America for the last ten years. It might give us a clue as to where he's been staying.'

Steadman had not thought of this possibility. 'Very

interesting,' he replied. 'Did DCI Long ask you to do this?'

'No sir. I thought about it myself. I haven't told him yet. Do you think he'll be cross?'

'I very much doubt it. In fact, he'll be delighted you're showing some initiative. Will you lead me to DCI Long's office?' He proffered his arm and they set off down the corridor. 'I'm surprised you're not at the meeting,' Steadman continued.

'Far too lowly a rank,' she replied with a girlish laugh. 'Here we are.'

In response to his knock, a voice inside bellowed, 'Come in if you're good-looking.'

Steadman opened the door.

'Oh, it's you – come in anyway!' said Dr Rufus.

'Nice to hear you're still giving the old jokes their annual airing, Frank,' Steadman replied.

Dr Rufus was unabashed. 'You're looking pale, John. Was the headmistress not nice to you? Did she spank you?'

'I do worry what goes on in your life, Frank.'

'Not a lot, that's the problem. I could just imagine Superintendent Campbell in…'

DCI Long interrupted him. 'I think we should not dwell on your wild imaginings, Dr Rufus. Come in, John. Alan, will you find a seat for Inspector Steadman?'

DS Munro lifted a chair from the other side of the table with one hand and gently steered his colleague into it.

'Who else is here?' Steadman asked.

'DS Fairfax is sitting to your left,' DCI Long replied. 'How did you get on with our new Divisional Superintendent?'

'I think she has her doubts about me. I suspect she is a lady who likes everything in its proper place, and I stick out like the proverbial sore thumb. She did suggest I team up with Inspector Crouchley.'

'Like that's going to happen,' Munro chipped in.

'Quite so, Alan. I may have used different words, but the sentiment was the same. I allayed her doubts as best I could and promised to keep a low profile. At least we parted on more friendly terms than when we met.' There was a murmur of approval. 'Before I forget,' Steadman continued, 'I've just had an interesting conversation with DC Cleo Osborne.'

'Shouldn't she be off with Will Lofthouse?' DS Fairfax asked.

'I gather that should have been the plan, but somehow DC Lofthouse left without her,' Steadman replied. 'However, she is phoning all the local car rental agencies to ask if anyone with an American accent has hired a vehicle recently.'

'That never occurred to me,' said DCI Long. 'I'll make a note. Thank you, John.'

Steadman nodded. 'Now, what would you like me to do, sir?'

'The first thing I would like you to be involved with is interviewing the various family members.'

Steadman's heart skipped a beat at the prospect of doing real detective work again. 'If Seth Shuster had been back in Helmsmouth for any length of time, sir, my guess is that he would have visited Adelina Monke, his grandmother. They were genuinely devoted to one another.'

'Birds of a blooming feather,' Dr Rufus remarked.

DCI Long ignored the interruption. 'I agree. I think you should go with DS Fairfax. Fiona has been doing some digging around.' Turning to DS Fairfax, he continued, 'Perhaps you would take up the story?'

Fairfax spoke in clear ringing tones. 'Adelina Monke moved into The Oaks Care Home a little under a year ago. She had become forgetful and prone to suddenly losing her temper for no apparent reason. She was found walking in the streets in her nightclothes abusing passers-by on several occasions. According to the matron of the home, Barbara Hodge, she has settled in reasonably well, although her memory and mood can be variable. As she so delicately put it, her behaviour can be challenging.'

Adelina Monke has been like that all her life, Steadman mused.

'I thought it might be too late to go today, but the matron informed me that Adelina has slept until lunch and now would be a good time to speak with her, as long as we leave before it gets dark. She is always worse as the sun goes down.'

'Sounds like a good plan,' said Steadman. 'What about Seth's uncle, Josh, and his aunt, Clara?'

'They can wait until tomorrow,' DCI Long replied. 'However, I have been looking at Josh Reynolds' record. He has a string of convictions involving violence, the last one quite recently. He does not appear to have mellowed with age. Without sounding patronising or insulting, I would prefer it if you went with DS Munro. Is that all right, Fiona?'

DS Fairfax nodded and gave a slight shrug. 'I'm sure I could manage him if things got out of hand, sir.'

'I have no doubt you could, Fiona. I would just prefer it if, in the circumstances, things never reached that point,' he replied, giving Steadman a meaningful look. Heaven knows it was hard enough justifying a blind detective's presence to the new Superintendent, he thought, let alone having to explain how he came to be assaulted.

Steadman pressed the button on the side of his watch. The metallic voice informed him that it was almost four o'clock.

'Shall we go, Fiona?'

Robbie was first to his feet. Dr Rufus helped Steadman on with his coat.

'Thank you, Frank. You've been very quiet.'

'I was wondering if Adelina Monke will remember you,' he said handing Steadman his hat.

★ ★ ★

They took one of the small patrol cars. It was a tight fit, but Robbie managed to curl himself into a remarkably small ball and nestled himself at Steadman's feet.

'Does Alan Munro never let anyone else use the Audi?' he asked.

'Oh, I borrow it sometimes just to annoy him, especially if he has been bragging about winning at rugby again. I believe it does him good. Besides, when I'm not driving this, I ride a Norton Commando motorbike. It's old but it will still blow the pants off his precious Audi!'

'Is it the 750cc or the later 850cc model?' Steadman asked.

DS Fairfax was impressed at his knowledge. 'It is the 850cc model, sir, made in 1977, and I believe one of the last to roll out of the factory.'

The Oaks Care Home was a little way inland on the other side of town. It was still raining, a fine drizzly rain that smeared the windscreen and made driving treacherous. They pulled up at a set of traffic lights.

'Don't you think it's odd, sir, how sometimes your mind plays tricks with you?'

'In what way, Fiona?' Steadman answered cautiously. DS Fairfax was not given to flights of fancy.

'We've all been poring over the photos of Seth Shuster as a youth and the photofit pictures of how he may have looked before he was murdered. Well, as we got into the car, I noticed a young man standing in the car park, albeit a bit in the shadows. For a moment, I thought he was young Seth Shuster's double. When I turned the car, he had gone.'

Steadman frowned. He couldn't think of an obvious explanation. 'You're probably right – a trick of the light and your brain working overtime, something like that.' A tiny alarm bell rang in his head. 'Only do tell someone if it happens again.'

★ ★ ★

The Oaks Care Home was a former country house that must have been fairly grand in its heyday. The winding drive leading to the house would have been impressive were it not for the potholes. Several of the lamp posts were not working and DS Fairfax noticed that the glass in some of them had been smashed. Broad steps led up to the main door. The sandstone portico was crumbling. There was an impressive brass bell push on the door. Clearly this no longer worked as a cheap plastic button had been screwed just above it. To DS Fairfax's annoyance, it was askew. A Dymo label read "PRESS ONCE AND WAIT".

The door was eventually opened by a stocky, middle-aged woman with short hair and heavy framed glasses. She was wearing a housecoat that sported a handmade name badge.

'DS Fairfax and DI Steadman,' said Fiona holding up her ID.

'I'm Barbara Hodge, Matron. Do come in.' She pulled the door fully open. Only then did she notice the dog. 'Oh!' she exclaimed, then added, 'Of course, DI Steadman – I've read about you in the papers. I should have remembered. And what a beautiful animal. Our residents would love to meet him. We used to have a dog, but he died last month. Actually, we had to have him put down. He was ancient and had become quite cantankerous. It bit Mr Peebles, although I can't blame the dog. There are days when even I feel like giving him a nip! I don't really mean that, obviously. Follow me, I'll take you to Adelina's room.'

The house was a maze of wandering corridors and stairs. Steadman doubted that he would be able to find his way out again unaided. Perhaps the various smells would help, he thought. There were the all-pervasive odours of cooking and humanity. Behind these there must be an army of air fresheners, diffusers and the like he concluded, for at every turn his nostrils were met with a new perfume: lavender, orange blossom, vanilla and others that he could not name.

Barbara Hodge knocked gently on a door and entered without waiting for a reply. Steadman would have probably recognised Adelina Monke instantly. She had already been an old woman, or so he thought, when they had first met. Her hair was now perhaps a shade whiter and sparser, her hands a bit more arthritic. Her face was more pinched but unlined, and her eyes remained bright and mistrustful. Her gaze flitted rapidly between her visitors as if trying to place them. Her voice, when she spoke, was unmistakable.

'Who are you? What are you doing here?'

In gentle tones, Barbara Hodge explained, 'Don't you remember, Adelina? These are the two police officers I told you about. They've come for a little chat.'

Adelina's arthritic hands clenched in a pathetic attempt to make two fists. 'I hate the police. They are all filthy scum.' She spat the words out defiantly. 'What did you say their names were?'

'This is Detective Sergeant Fairfax, and this is Detective Inspector Steadman.'

'Why has he got a dog?'

'I'm blind, Miss Monke,' Steadman replied.

Adelina froze in her chair. She stared with bird-like suspicion at Steadman. 'Take off your glasses so I can see your face.'

Steadman obliged. In the ensuing silence the ticking of Adelina Monke's brain could almost be heard.

'You arrested my son when he was only fifteen, didn't you? You got yourself into all sorts of trouble.' She laughed. It was a harsh, mocking laugh. 'And that wasn't the only time you hounded my poor Seth. But they got you in the end, didn't they? Shot you in the head. Pity they didn't finish you off good and proper.' She sat back in her chair looking very pleased with herself.

'Adelina! How could you say such a thing!' said Barbara Hodge.

Steadman waved her remarks away. 'We want to talk with you about Seth, Miss Monke.'

'Ah – my Seth, my little darling. The only one who has ever shown me any affection or gratitude. I raised him from a pup into a full-grown handsome man, despite you lot haranguing him and interfering. You leave him alone.'

'When did Seth last visit you?' Steadman asked.

'I said, let him be!' Adelina's voice rose in anger.

'We can't do that, Miss Monke,' Steadman replied as calmly and steadily as he could. 'You see, we have found Seth's body. He's been murdered.'

Adelina Monke let out a piercing wail like a wounded animal. Barbara Hodge went to put an arm around her but was pushed away. 'You're a liar, all police are liars. My Seth's not dead.'

'I'm afraid he is, Miss Monke,' added DS Fairfax. 'His body was washed up on Helmsmouth's eastern beach. He had been shot through the heart. Death would have been instantaneous. We have to catch his killer.'

Adelina Monke had folded her arms over her chest and was rocking in her chair. She started to wail again, yet there were no tears. 'My Seth dead – it's not true, it's not true! And all they can send is a woman and a blind detective,' she mumbled incoherently.

Steadman got the impression that their time with Adelina Monke was running out. He didn't want to appear cruel but pushed on. 'We need your help. If you won't talk to us, we could send Inspector Crouchley.'

The old lady visibly started. 'Crouchley! He's a bigger bastard than the rest of you put together.'

'Has Seth visited you recently, Miss Monke?' DS Fairfax said.

'Leave me alone. I don't know, I don't know anything.'

'Does she have many visitors?' Steadman asked the matron.

'Hardly any. Visitors are meant to sign the book by the main door. Nobody ever bothers. I can ask the other members of staff.'

DS Fairfax handed her a copy of the photofit picture. 'That's what we think Seth would have looked like.'

Steadman raised his head. 'Can I smell flowers?'

DS Fairfax looked around the room. There was a small table behind the two officers by the window. In the fading light, she could make out a large bouquet in a chipped glass vase. 'Those flowers are very pretty, Miss Monke. Who brought you them?'

Adelina Monke made no reply. Her eyes were closed, and she was muttering to herself.

'Did Seth bring you the flowers? Has he been to see you?' Steadman persisted.

She started to howl again. 'You've murdered my boy and now you want to rape me. RAPE! RAPE! HELP!' She shouted the last three words.

This time Barbara Hodge succeeded in putting an

arm around her. 'Nobody is going to hurt you, Adelina. I'll make us both a nice cup of tea.'

DS Fairfax had gone to examine the flowers. 'I can't find any card, sir.'

Adelina Monke was now silent and pretending to be asleep.

'I don't think you'll get any more out of her today,' said the matron. 'It's getting dark. Let me put on the light and draw the curtains. Maybe someone will remember who gave her the flowers. I'll ask.'

As she drew the curtains something fluttered onto the floor. DS Fairfax glimpsed it from the corner of her eye and jumped up.

'I'll get it,' she said pulling on a pair of vinyl gloves.

'What is it?' Steadman asked.

'A florist's card, sir. There's no shop name unfortunately.'

'Is there a message, Fiona?'

'It's very odd, sir. It's in block capitals and all it says is TGMLYS.'

CHAPTER 8

Steadman arrived back at Lloyds' café later than expected. Roberto Lloyd, Marco's brother, saw the car arriving and rushed to open the door.

'You have visitors, Inspector Steadman.'

'Oh, who?' Steadman asked.

'It's only us,' replied a boy whose voice was clearly breaking.

'Tim! Is your ankle better? From what Sally told me, I thought it must be broken in at least three places.'

Tim Warrender turned bright red at Steadman's teasing.

'I hope Roberto has been feeding you. Is Sally with you?'

'We're both here,' Sally replied. 'Tim insisted he would be OK. Mum says if he manages, he'll have to go to school tomorrow. I came with him in case he falls again.'

'Robbie, you're spoilt. Two people wanting to take you for a walk tonight.' He slipped off the dog's harness and clipped on his lead. 'What have you two been eating? It smells really good,' Steadman added, realising that he too was hungry.

'Pizza and chips,' croaked Tim as he helped Steadman into a chair.

'Sounds good. I think I'll have the same while you take Robbie out. Come up to the flat when you return.'

Sally and Tim jumped to their feet, squabbling as brothers and sisters do, over who was going to take the dog's lead.

'Tim on the way out, Sally on the way back,' Steadman said firmly.

'They're good kids,' Roberto remarked. 'You know, they always try to pay for their food.'

'I hope you don't accept. When I'm late, the deal is I pay for their food. Now, what about some pizza?'

Roberto shouted the order through to the kitchen.

'Join me in a little glass of white wine, Inspector – on the house.'

Steadman knew not to refuse. Roberto poured out two small tumblers of straw-coloured wine and placed one in the Inspector's outstretched hand. He chinked his glass on Steadman's.

'*Saluté.*'

'Cheers!' Steadman replied.

The pizza and chips were delicious. The café

was otherwise empty, and Steadman ate without embarrassment. After the meal Roberto led him through the kitchen to the stairs leading up to his flat.

'I'll manage from here,' said Steadman.

Subconsciously he counted the steps and in no time was at his front door. He ran a finger down the serrated edge of the key, making sure it was the right one and, at the second attempt, he found the lock and let himself in. Without thinking, he switched on the lights. The flat was chilly. Steadman fiddled with the thermostat until a click told him that the heating was back running. All he needed now was to find his favourite old blue jumper from the back of the drawer and he could settle down for the evening.

Tim and Sally returned, flushed and out of breath. Steadman thought they smelt of fresh air, unlike Robbie, who was exuding a decided aroma of damp dog. They dried him and fed him.

'Did your ankle hold up, Tim?'

'Yes – worse luck. I'll have to go to school tomorrow.' Tim's voice wavered between a squeak and a growl.

Once they had left, and Robbie had made himself comfortable, Steadman sat down at his piano. He needed to think, or at least let his mind drift over the problems. It had to be Bach. Tonight, it was the Goldberg variations, just the first movement played slowly over and over again.

The message: six letters that must mean something. The flowers – surely, they were from Seth. If they were, he was willing to bet, Seth had sneaked in and out of The Oaks Care Home unnoticed. Was Adelina Monke as muddled as she made herself out to be? Her distant recall was much better than her memory for recent events. Maybe she really couldn't remember Seth's visit, yet she was a wily old bird to be sure. And the matron; caring, overworked – how much of Adelina's past did she know about? DS Fairfax on a motorbike – now there was a thought, and tormenting Alan Munro to boot. Did she really see Seth's double in the car park? He was still troubled by Divisional Superintendent Olivia Campbell; not so much by their meeting, but by something in the past that he couldn't put his finger on. And lastly, Seth Shuster – troubled, difficult, dangerous, and doomed from the start. Why had he come back to Helmsmouth?

He stopped playing and checked his talking watch. 'An early night, Robbie. Doubtless Alan Munro will be here at first light.'

Reluctantly Robbie got to his feet and gave a shake that started at his head and finished with his tail. Then he led Steadman down the stairs and out to the small garden at the rear of the café.

Steadman yawned as he climbed back up to the flat. The door on the first floor was slightly open and old Mrs Lloyd, mother of Roberto and Marco, peeped through the crack.

'It was lovely to hear you playing this evening, Inspector. You must be working again, but I won't ask,' she said, trying very hard to keep the curiosity out of her voice.

'I don't think it is a secret, Mrs Lloyd. The body found on the beach was a man I have known for many years. It is all a bit of a mystery and I've been brought in to see if I can shed any light. Not very successfully so far – it's early days.'

'I'm sure you'll solve it, Inspector Steadman. You always do. Goodnight.'

It was with some relief that Steadman eventually put his head on the pillow. Within seconds he had drifted off into a deep sleep. And in an instant, he was back in the Eyesore; a young, dashing detective constable, brim-full of confidence and looking forward to a glittering career. A not-quite-so-bald and not-quite-so-fat Sergeant Grimble looked up from his desk.

'You appear pleased with yourself, young man. What have you been up to?'

'I've just had that ne'er-do-well Shuster's statement typed up. He denies everything, of course, but I think there is enough evidence to charge him this time. All I need is to get him to sign it without making a fuss,' Steadman replied.

'I wish you luck. Be careful – he's a real slippery customer,' cautioned Grimble.

Steadman waved the warning away with a laugh. 'His solicitor will advise him to sign. For some reason, he believes Seth Shuster's story.'

Back in the interview room an arrogant, sneering young man sat slouching in his chair. His solicitor, taciturn and uneasy, was trying to engross himself in some papers he had pulled from his briefcase.

'Here we are,' said Steadman. 'If you would read through your statement and sign on the bottom.'

Shuster yawned and stretched. He made no pretence of reading the document. With a flourish, he signed his name. Steadman noticed that each S had a distinctive squiggle on its tail, making them look like two small snakes. And as he stared at the signature the two snakes grew larger and larger. Seth Shuster and his solicitor were obscured from view. The two letters S slithered off the page, their forked tongues flicking in and out tasting the air. They moved slowly towards Steadman's hand which, to his horror, lay frozen to the desk. No matter how hard he tried he could not move it. The snakes' tongues curled round his fingers. The sensation was surprisingly warm and wet. Now they were prodding his hand with their heads, gently and persistently.

He woke with a start. Robbie continued to nudge Steadman's hand with his muzzle and lick the outstretched fingers.

'Do you need to go out?' he asked the dog.

He found his dressing gown, freshly laundered and back in its usual place. The two of them made their way to the Lloyds' little garden. There were already noises coming from the kitchen and an enticing aroma of freshly ground coffee. I could do with some of that, he thought.

On the way back up to the flat, he noticed his pyjama cuff was damp. A spark, a memory flashed through his mind. Somebody or something other than Robbie had been licking his hand. Snakes in a dream! Where had they come from? He paused on the landing and suddenly he recalled the signature and Seth Shuster's fancy letter S. Why should that be important? His brain was racing now. Robbie nudged his hand again, confused as to why they had stopped.

'Wait a second, Robbie, I've almost got it,' he said out loud.

Old Mrs Lloyd opened her door. 'Are you all right, Inspector Steadman? Do you want me to give Marco or Roberto a message?'

Message! That was it – six meaningless letters, TGMLYS, on a florist's card. If the S matched Seth's signature, it would be the first proof that he had been back in Helmsmouth alive.

'Mrs Lloyd, you're a genius,' he replied, much to her astonishment, and almost ran up the last flight of steps. He fed the dog, showered and dressed. All the time his mind was fixed on the other letters in the message. He barely noticed Tim Warrender coming to take Robbie for his morning stroll. Surely the L must stand for 'love', he thought, and if that's the case then the only logical explanation for the Y must be 'your' That left only the TGM to decipher. How did Seth address his grandmother, he tried to recall? Of course, he said to himself with a sigh of relief, Grandma Monke – GM. The T could simply be 'to' or possibly 'thanks'.

Steadman pressed the side of his watch. It was only ten past eight. Time enough for a coffee and a croissant before phoning the Eyesore, he concluded.

'How was Robbie on his walk, Tim?' Steadman asked.

'He was great. I think he knew my ankle was still sore and went a bit slower than usual.'

The coffee and croissant arrived.

'Have you got time for a glass of squash and a KitKat, Tim?'

Tim almost always had time and space for an extra snack.

'Must go,' he said through a mouthful of biscuit. 'Don't want to be late on my first day back.'

Steadman finished his croissant, sat down, and took out his mobile. Slowly and carefully, he keyed in the number for the Eyesore.

'Good morning Sergeant Grimble.'

'And a cheery good morning to you too, Inspector Steadman. Who would you like to speak to?'

'Could you put me through to DS Fairfax if she's in?'

Fiona Fairfax answered on the second ring. Steadman explained briefly about Seth's signature and the ornate S. He didn't mention his dream for fear of appearing foolish.

'I can tell you without checking that the S on the florist's card has swirly loops on it, sir. Shuster's records are in DCI Long's office. I'll check if the S matches with his old signature. There are only partial prints on the card – not enough to get a match, I'm afraid. I'm planning on doing a bit of legwork later this morning, visiting the florists, starting with the ones closest to the care home. Any ideas on what the letters mean, sir?'

Steadman gave his interpretation of the message. Somehow it seemed a lot less plausible in the cold light of day. DS Fairfax was more convinced.

'That would make sense, sir. Has Alan Munro arrived yet? He said he was going to pick you up first thing.'

In answer to her query, there was a very loud knock on Steadman's door.

'That's him now,' he replied. It could only be DS Munro. For some reason he always pounded on the door rather than ring the bell.

'Is that coffee I can smell? I wouldn't mind a cup if we have time – just to perk me up, you know.'

'I doubt if Josh and Clara are early risers. Go on – call down to Marco and get a coffee sent up.' The Lloyds had insisted on an intercom being fitted in Steadman's flat. 'And I would recommend the croissants as well. They're still warm.'

An enormous smile broke out on Munro's face. 'A croissant filled with crispy bacon – heaven on a plate! Don't tell Maureen.'

Munro's wife was perpetually trying to trim Alan's waistline, with only limited success.

'How is Maureen?'

'Great. She says you must come over for supper soon. She's found a new recipe that she's dying to try.'

'That would be nice. Why don't we wait until my son Ben is home? He'll want to see you and the girls.'

Munro had two daughters, Melanie and Annie. They were very fond of Steadman and had unofficially adopted him as their 'Uncle John'. Ben fascinated them with his beard, ponytail and earring and, of course, his magic tricks, which always left them bewildered, as handfuls of sweets seemed to appear from nowhere.

It didn't take long for Munro to demolish his croissant. All that was left was a small piece of bacon, which he slipped to Robbie.

'You're as bad as Sergeant Grimble,' Steadman remarked.

'I didn't think you would notice, sir.'

Steadman raised his eyebrows. 'Let's go.'

The Audi was warm and comfortable. Munro had switched on the heated seats, for it was still damp and chilly outside.

'I gather you're doing a bit of car-sharing with DS Fairfax,' Steadman said trying hard to keep a straight face.

'Oh, I let Fiona borrow the Audi occasionally. I think it cheers her up,' Munro replied.

How amazing that two people could view the same scenario so differently, Steadman mused.

'What do you think of the case so far, sir?'

Steadman paused. 'I think we're just scraping the surface,' he said at last.

Munro pulled a face. 'What about Josh and Clara? Do you reckon they'll be of any help?'

'Who knows?' answered Steadman. He disliked speculation. 'For what it's worth, I doubt it. I don't think they liked Seth. My guess is they will say very little. I was just trying to work out how old Josh and Clara would be now.' He paused, counting the years in his head from the time of Seth's birth to his murder. 'By my reckoning, Clara would be sixty-five and Josh was about two years older, so, he would be sixty-seven.'

'Almost spot on, sir. Josh has just turned sixty-eight.'

It wasn't far to their house. Munro had to knock several times before he got an answer. Josh Reynolds was a short man with thinning, silvery hair that was slicked back. He had watery eyes and a perpetual pugnacious scowl. His shirt sleeves were rolled up, revealing faded, smudged tattoos. The most striking feature, Munro thought, were his trousers, which were grey, baggy, and too long. They hid his feet and were so rumpled at the knee that it looked for all the world as though Josh was wearing the back legs of a pantomime elephant.

Munro flashed his ID and introduced DI Steadman.

Josh looked Munro up and down. 'It would have been

an affront to nature if you were anything other than a policeman,' he grunted. 'Come in, I've been expecting you.'

'Expecting us? Why's that?' asked Steadman.

'It's all over the front page of this morning's *Echo* – they've named the body on the beach. I see you've brought your dog with you, Inspector Steadman. That'll set Tuppence off.'

'Don't worry. Robbie's well trained. He'll ignore your cat,' Steadman replied.

'Cat? Who said anything about cats? It's what I call my sister, Clara.'

'Why Tuppence?' Munro queried.

'You've never met her, have you, Sergeant. You'll see. Clara is most certainly not the full shilling.'

Clara was in the sitting room dusting and rearranging the ornaments. Like her brother, she was short but with masses of frizzy hair. She looked terrified, even more so when she spied Robbie.

'May we sit down? We need to ask you both some questions.'

Josh nodded. Munro steered Steadman to an armchair. To Clara's relief, Robbie spread-eagled himself at his feet. She chose not to sit, preferring instead to stand behind her brother clutching a ridiculous feather duster.

'When did you last see your nephew, Seth?' Steadman asked.

Josh's answer was too quick. 'Over ten years ago.'

'You haven't seen or heard from him in the last two weeks?'

'Why should we have?' Josh retorted.

'Because we believe he's been back in Helmsmouth for at least that length of time,' Munro replied.

'What about you, Clara? Have you seen or heard from Seth recently?' Steadman asked.

Clara jumped and clutched her duster even more tightly.

'For God's sake, sit down woman,' bellowed Josh. 'Or if not, go and make us all a cup of tea.'

Clara scampered off to the kitchen.

'What's the matter with your sister?' Munro asked.

'It's her nerves. She's not right in the head, hasn't been for years, and it's getting worse. Doctors say there's nothing that can be done. Some days she hardly talks. She'll end up in a home like Adelina.'

'Do you ever visit your mother?' asked Steadman.

'What's the point? She never liked me and she doesn't talk sense anymore.'

'Somebody brought her a large bouquet fairly recently. Who do you think that was?'

'Not a clue,' Josh replied tersely.

Clara came back in rattling a tray. 'Whatever Josh says is true,' she said unexpectedly.

'Is it?' queried Steadman. 'I've known Josh Reynolds for years and interviewed him on numerous occasions.

He is a frequent stranger to the truth. I may be blind but even I can see he's not telling us everything he knows.'

Josh looked more truculent than ever. 'I've nothing more to tell you.'

'You haven't told us anything. You haven't given us a straight answer to any of our questions. And neither of you appear the slightest bit upset that your nephew has been murdered.'

'You don't need me to tell you any home truths about Seth, Inspector Steadman. You knew him as well as I did, better probably. If he was back in Helmsmouth it wasn't to get a job in the local library or to volunteer in a charity shop, that's for sure.'

Steadman reflected for a moment. What Josh Reynolds had just said was undeniably true, so why had Seth returned to Helmsmouth?

'And it wasn't to see his family either,' added Clara. 'Unless he wanted to see his...'

'Grandmother,' Josh interrupted giving his sister a filthy look. 'They were very close. Though why he bothered is beyond me. Like I said, she's in a home – nutty as a fruit cake.'

'For pity's sake, she's your mother!' exclaimed Munro.

'So what? I had no choice in the matter.'

'Could the flowers have come from Seth?' Steadman asked.

Josh shrugged. 'Certainly not from me. It takes me all my time to feed the two of us.'

Clara poured the tea, nodding enthusiastically at Josh's every remark.

'Maybe she has a secret admirer. She certainly had plenty in her younger day. Perhaps she's started working again,' added Josh.

'You're sick,' said Munro.

'And you're not welcome. The two of you can bugger off now. I've said all I'm going to say.'

'Whoever killed Seth may come looking for you,' Munro replied.

'You can't scare me.' Josh scoffed. He stood up and opened the door. 'Out – and don't bother coming back.'

★ ★ ★

The two men slowly made their way back to the car.

'He hasn't changed at all,' said Steadman.

'Is he telling the truth?' asked Munro.

'Josh Reynolds wouldn't know what the truth was if you gift-wrapped it and sent it to him as a present. What I would like to know is what he stopped Clara from saying. Who else might Seth have wanted to see?'

Munro gave his colleague a quizzical look. He barely noticed the youth that brushed past him, but for an instant their eyes met. Munro took a further three paces, then stopped.

'What is it, Alan?'

'A young man just bumped into me. Odd – he could

have passed for Seth Shuster's double.'

'Go after him, Alan,' Steadman said with some urgency.

Munro set off at a pace, only to glimpse the man boarding a bus.

'Damn! He's got away, sir.'

'Interesting nonetheless,' Steadman replied.

'Why interesting, sir?'

'DS Fairfax had a similar experience in the car park behind the Eyesore. She reckoned there was a youth there that looked like a younger version of Seth Shuster. Dr Rufus would claim, of course, it is all the work of heightened imaginations – mass hysteria, if you like. He has a point. You only have to put a picture of Lord Lucan in the evening news and there'll be fresh sightings from John O'Groats to Land's End. Yet I can't think of two people less hysterical than yourself and Fiona Fairfax.'

The two men continued in silence until they reached the Audi.

'Can you manage the seat belt?' asked Munro.

'Yes, I'm sure I can do it by myself.'

'Where to now, sir?'

Before Steadman could reply, Munro's phone rang.

'Yes… Where?… We're on our way.'

He put the phone back in his pocket and turned to his colleague.

'Another body has been washed up on the eastern beach.'

CHAPTER 9

It took Steadman several attempts to buckle his seat belt. Munro watched impatiently.

'Let's go,' he said at last, switching on the siren and the blue flashing lights. The tyres screeched and they were off.

Steadman gripped the sides of the seat tightly as Munro weaved in and out of the traffic.

'For goodness sake, are you asleep!' Munro shouted as yet another car seemed oblivious to the Audi's wail and warning lights. He drummed his fingers on the steering wheel. 'About time too,' he ranted as the car in front eventually pulled over. He put his foot on the accelerator and the Audi shot past.

Despite his apparent annoyance and frustration, it was clear to Steadman that Munro was thoroughly enjoying himself. He, on the other hand, was, starting to feel nauseous. Unaware of the shops and houses flying by, he had lost all sense of direction and now had no idea of where they were. He would have liked to ask Munro to slow down. However, he didn't like to interrupt his colleague, who was keeping up a diatribe littered with profanities in a Scottish accent that was getting stronger by the second to the point where, fortunately, it was barely intelligible.

The road seemed clearer now and Steadman surmised that they must have passed through the city centre.

'Nearly there, sir,' said Munro with a beaming smile. 'Not too fast for you, I hope.'

'No, I'm fine,' Steadman lied. His breakfast croissant was lying heavily on his stomach.

With a squeal of the brakes, Munro pulled up.

'I've parked directly behind the dunes, sir. It'll be quicker than going along the boardwalk.'

It soon became clear that he had made a wrong choice. Even with Robbie's help, Steadman struggled to anticipate where the dips in the sand lay or where there were spiky tufts of marram grass. He stumbled at almost every step.

'Sorry, sir – bad move. Here, let me take your arm.'

Not for the first time, Steadman questioned what he was doing getting involved. Maybe Divisional Superintendent Campbell was right – how could a blind detective possibly assist in a serious criminal investigation?

The final insult was getting his foot trapped in a piece

of driftwood. Munro had to bend down to extricate him.

'Put your hand on my back, sir, and lift your leg. Just as well I play in the front row of the scrum.'

Steadman couldn't help but be aware of Munro's massively strong shoulders.

'You're free now, sir,' said Munro tossing the piece of wood along the beach. Robbie's head jerked up in anticipation. 'Sorry Robbie, you're still on duty.'

Within another few paces the two men were below the tideline and on firm wet sand.

'That's better,' Steadman remarked.

They could hear voices not far off. Steadman felt a tug on the dog's harness as Robbie's muscles tensed. Could he smell blood, Steadman wondered, or might it be the memory of having to sit on cold, wet sand for what must have seemed an eternity?

They were met by a burly sergeant, the same one who was present at DCI Long's case conference.

'Sergeant Beattie, I don't think you have been formally introduced to DI Steadman,' said Munro.

The two men shook hands clumsily.

'There was no point in putting up a police cordon,' he explained. 'There's no one here and clearly the man has been washed ashore.'

'Who found the body?' Steadman asked.

'A terrified old lady who was out walking her pooch. One of my officers has taken her home.'

Dr Rufus was already standing over the corpse waiting

patiently for the photographic team to finish their job. Steadman knew that they would be taking pictures from every conceivable angle. He heard a click and for the briefest of moments sensed a lessening of his dark world as the flash went off. It seemed so trivial, yet he derived enormous comfort and reassurance from that tiny glimmer of light.

'You'll be wanting a running commentary, John,' said Dr Rufus. Steadman nodded. 'OK, here goes – white male, late fifties to early sixties, I would say, lying on his left side, facing towards the sea. His right arm is covering his face. He's fully clothed in a natty suit. From where we are standing. The most obvious thing is that he has been shot three times in the back.'

'Close range?' Steadman queried.

'Not point-blank,' Dr Rufus replied, 'but no more than several yards.'

The victim had been running away, Steadman thought.

'Any idea of the calibre of the gun?'

'Biggish, I would guess. I won't be able to say for certain until I have properly examined the wounds.'

Some gulls were circling overhead. Munro gave them a menacing look.

'Let's turn the body over and get a better look at him,' Dr Rufus continued. 'Alan, slip on some gloves and give me a hand.'

Reluctantly, DS Munro pulled on a pair of gloves and

helped Dr Rufus roll the body over. As they did so, the man's arm flopped backwards, revealing his face.

'Well, would you look at that!' exclaimed Dr Rufus. 'It's just as well the press aren't here.'

'Why, Frank?' Steadman asked.

'Half his face is missing. What would the papers say? "Mad murderer attacks man with cheese grater!" Of course, all that has happened is the body has been trapped in the rocks, the barnacles and the tides do the rest.'

Munro, who had turned a ghastly shade of white, managed a few steps then vomited profusely.

'Yet to look at our detective sergeant, you would think he was made of granite,' Dr Rufus remarked. 'What do you make of it, Kim?'

Kim Ho led the forensic team and, unlike Munro, she appeared totally unperturbed by the gruesome spectacle.

'His left shoe is very badly scuffed, and the laces rubbed through. Also, the trouser leg below the left knee is torn. He was probably trapped by his ankle.'

Steadman could visualise it all too clearly. Kim Ho was now on her hands and knees inspecting the remains.

'Expensive suit,' she said, 'and hand-made shoes.' Delicately she slipped a hand inside the man's jacket and retrieved a fountain pen and a wallet which was surprisingly dry. 'Nice pen – limited edition Mont Blanc,' she went on. 'He wasn't robbed. There must be five or six hundred pounds in here as well as bank cards and… I think these must be his own business cards. We may have a name – "Rupert H. Sidley". He is, or was a lawyer, and we have his office address.'

'What sort of parents would call a baby Rupert, for goodness sake?' asked Munro, who had rejoined them but was decidedly avoiding looking at the man's face.

'Anyone who reads the *Daily Express*,' suggested Steadman. 'The cartoon character Rupert the Bear has been a regular feature since 1920, I believe.'

Dr Rufus and DS Munro exchanged meaningful looks.

'Sad how such a good brain should have become silted up with such useless information,' Dr Rufus commented.

Steadman didn't hear the remark. He was too busy trying to place the name Rupert H. Sidley.

Kim Ho was still examining the body. 'I can't see any obvious exit wounds on his clothes.'

'In that case, I may have a bullet or two for you by the end of the day,' Dr Rufus replied.

Sergeant Beattie strolled back to the group.

'Not a pretty sight,' he said looking at the body. 'My officers have found nothing on a sweep of the beach.'

Kim Ho handed Sergeant Beattie one of the cards.

'I'll do background checks and inform the family.'

'He's not wearing a wedding ring,' Kim Ho observed. 'At least you might be spared one ordeal.'

'How long do you think he's been in the water, Frank?' asked Steadman.

'A bit longer than Seth Shuster, I would say. Odd coincidence to have two bodies washed up on the same beach only days apart.'

Steadman shook his head. He hated coincidences. 'I would be willing to bet they were shot and dumped at sea at the same time.'

In his mind's eye he saw Seth Shuster being shot first. A brief stare of disbelief at his assailant and then warm blood pulsing through his shirt, then darkness as he fell to the ground. Had Rupert Sidley already started to run? Probably.

'I'll know better after I've done the post-mortem this afternoon,' Dr Rufus continued. 'Why don't you join me, John? Don't bring Munro – I'm not having him throwing up in my nice clean mortuary.'

'Only if I won't be in the way,' Steadman replied.

'John, you are always in the way – I'll cope somehow. You can bring Robbie. I might even find him a nice bone!' he said with a loud guffaw.

'You're an appalling man, Frank. I'm not sure there's much more we can do here, Alan, perhaps we should visit the offices of the late Rupert H. Sidley. Hopefully, I can negotiate the dunes without falling flat on my face.'

'You'll be fine, sir,' said Munro. 'Robbie and I will see to that.'

Possibly because they were going uphill, the walk back to the car was considerably easier.

'Just in time, sir,' Munro remarked as it started to rain again.

'Where are Rupert Sidley's offices?' Steadman asked.

'They're close to the High Street,' Munro replied. 'There's a Tesco next door where we can park. I'll nip in, freshen up and buy some mints. Is there anything I can get you?'

Steadman made a vague gesture. He was lost in his own thoughts, wondering where on earth Seth Shuster could have been and why he needed to take a lawyer with him. More importantly, what had occurred to cause both men to be murdered.

'You're very quiet, sir. What's on your mind?'

Steadman took a little while to answer. It was as though he had to make a real effort to find his way back to the here and now.

'On my mind?' He gave his head a little shake. 'There are so many gaps, Alan, so many missing pieces. Seth Shuster has been in America – almost definitely. How did he get there? What was he doing? I would love to know. And why did he come back to Helmsmouth?' he concluded with a shrug.

'It's his home,' Munro suggested.

'I think there's something more. His grandmother maybe?' He screwed up his face. 'Something's niggling me.' Robbie stirred in the footwell. 'Are you needing to stretch your legs?' Steadman asked as he stroked the dog's head.

'We're here now, sir. I'll give him a quick walk around the car park before we visit Sidley's den.'

* * *

The 'den' of Rupert H. Sidley was situated in an incongruous Georgian house at the far end of the supermarket's car park, incongruous in as much as it stood quite alone and out of place. At one time it had been part of an elegant street, but it had been lost to the bombing of the Second World War and the ineptitude of modern-day town planners. It was hard to know which had caused the greater destruction.

The two men picked their way between parked cars and abandoned trolleys.

'He had odd bedfellows,' said Munro as he read the names on the door. 'Our Mr Sidley shared the building with a chiropodist and a funeral director.' He pushed open the large half-glazed door. The men were greeted with a pungent floral aroma.

'Hyacinths,' said Steadman. 'I don't know why, but I always associate that particular smell with funeral parlours.'

'Sidley's offices are on the first floor, sir. Let me give you a hand.'

'If you get me to the foot of the stairs, Robbie will do the rest.'

Munro knew that his former boss was fiercely

independent and said nothing. He did, however, stay close behind him on the stairs, just in case.

The first door they reached was slightly ajar. Steadman could hear the distinctive pattering of someone typing on a keyboard. A small brass plate on the door confirmed that this was indeed the offices of Rupert H. Sidley LL.B. (Cantab).

'What does "Cantab" mean?' asked Munro.

'It comes from the Latin word for Cambridge. It's where he got his degree,' Steadman replied.

'Why do you think he needed to put the name of the university after his degree?' queried Munro having read the sign out to his colleague.

Steadman shrugged. 'Convention, loyalty to the alma mater – possibly simply showing off. I really have no idea.' And we certainly won't be asking Mr Sidley, he mused to himself.

Munro knocked on the door and a voice replied, 'Come in. It's open.'

The hairs on Steadman's neck prickled. It was odd to think that only a few days ago whoever had just invited them in may have been exchanging pleasantries with Rupert Sidley. Possibly he had been standing on this very spot. Now that person was no more than a bloated corpse on its way to the mortuary.

Alan Munro flashed his ID. 'DS Munro, and this is DI Steadman.'

The young lady stopped typing. 'I know who DI

Steadman is, and I may even have seen your photo in the papers as well, DS Munro.'

'Well, possibly,' Munro replied blushing deeply.

'How may I help you, gentlemen?'

'Who are you?' Munro asked awkwardly.

In reply, the young lady tapped a sign on her desk that read, "Ms Devine".

'I'm Mr Sidley's secretary.'

It was impossible to say how tall she was as she was sitting down. She was thin with straight brown hair and a sharp fringe that framed her face. Her eyes were a dark chestnut colour, her complexion freckled, and her chin pointed. Despite being slim she had broad shoulders. A tight jumper, also in brown, emphasised her slender waist. She reminded Munro of a Toblerone chocolate bar.

'Tell me something, Inspector Steadman, could you arrest me?'

The two detectives were taken aback by the bluntness of her question.

'Should I? What have you done?' Steadman replied.

'Nothing.'

'Then nobody will arrest you. I presume you are puzzled as to my role considering I'm blind. I have been brought in as a consultant to help investigate the murder of Seth Shuster. I'm sure you have read about it in the papers. I knew Seth Shuster very well.'

If the name was familiar to Mr Sidley's secretary, her face betrayed not a flicker.

'What sort of cases do you deal with, Miss Devine?' asked Munro.

'Ms, not Miss,' she replied waspishly.

Munro frowned and tried again, '*Mzz* Devine?'

'Better. In answer to your question, Mr Sidley specialises in complex business law. You may recall the prestigious water company, Helmsmouth Upper Reaches, successfully suing a business rival for using a similar purple bottle to theirs. That was one of Mr Sidley's more notable cases.'

Steadman nodded. That was where he had heard his name before.

'Were all his clients high end?' he asked.

'What's this all about? What do you mean by *were* all his clients? Has something happened to him?'

'Sadly, Ms Devine, I regret to inform you that the body of your employer has been washed up on Helmsmouth eastern beach. He had been shot several times,' Steadman explained.

Ms Devine looked startled, but only for a moment. Her gaze shifted from one man to the other. She remained silent.

'You don't seem unduly surprised,' said Munro.

'No – not really,' she replied after a pause.

'May I ask why?' enquired Steadman.

She twirled a lock of hair round her finger and stared at the desk. 'It's hard to explain. Every evening, before he left the office, he would say, "If I'm not back in the morning, I'll have been murdered."'

'Was he joking?'

'I was never quite sure. He was a difficult man to get to know. I've worked with him for six years and I can tell you very little. He had one sister, but they weren't close. I've never heard him mention any other family. His work was his life.'

'What drove him?' asked Munro.

'What do you think? Money, of course.'

'Did he make a lot?'

'I'll say! It was part of my job to send out the bills.'

Munro scratched his forehead. The office was not lavish, in fact it was quite drab. Kim Ho had said the dead man had been wearing an expensive suit and hand-made shoes, not that Munro noticed, and that his pen was a limited-edition Mont Blanc, even so...

'What did he do with his money?'

Ms Devine sniffed loudly. 'He collected stamps. He would spend his lunch hour poring over catalogues and making phone calls. Harmless enough, I suppose... Who killed him?'

'It is early days, Ms Devine,' Steadman replied. 'His death may well be linked to that of Seth Shuster.'

'I would be interested in having a look at his diary and his files,' added Munro.

Ms Devine laid a protective hand over the ledger on her desk. 'Don't you need a search warrant?'

Munro turned on the charm. He gave her a half-smile and looked deeply into her eyes. 'Mzz Devine, I'm sure a legal secretary of your experience appreciates that the first few hours of any murder investigation are critical. Of course, we will get an official warrant. But while we're waiting for all of that…'

He slipped the book from under her hand. The entries went back over three years. Munro flicked through the pages with a scowl.

'They're all in code,' he exclaimed.

'Not really,' Ms Devine explained. 'He insisted that all his clients had nicknames, and then he sometimes used only their initials. I have no idea why he did that, and I never asked.'

'Would you describe any of his clients as suspicious?'

She shrugged her shoulders and for a moment appeared flustered. 'The same people would come to the office using different names. From time to time, he would give me a list of people that I had to fob off and others that had to be put through straight away. Sometimes I had to make myself scarce. I thought it was just a confidentiality thing. I know he kept a gun in his desk.'

'What type of gun? Automatic or revolver?'

'Automatic, I think. It's in the top left-hand drawer.'

Steadman gave Munro a barely perceptible nod.

'I'll check, sir.'

'Did he do all his work here?' Steadman asked.

'Oh no – very often he would take files home with him. He often worked evenings and weekends. Occasionally he would go away for days unexpectedly, which is why I never thought anything about him not being in this week.'

'Do you know if he had any dealings with Seth Shuster?'

'The name doesn't ring a bell.'

'It would have been very recent – last week, or even over the weekend.'

Ms Devine retrieved her ledger and flicked through the last few pages.

'According to this, he was planning to meet a Mr H. Himmler on Friday evening. Of course, that wouldn't be his real name.'

No, thought Steadman, a smile spreading over his face, he was certainly not meeting a Mr H. Himmler.

'No sign of a gun, sir,' said Munro as he returned to the room, adding, 'You're looking decidedly pleased with yourself.'

'Mr Sidley had a rendezvous with a Mr H. Himmler last Friday. I presume the H stands for Heinrich,' said Steadman.

'Wasn't he one of Hitler's henchmen?'

'Correct, Alan. Himmler was the architect and leader of the notorious SS.'

'SS? Seth Shuster's initials.'

'Precisely. Way too much of a coincidence for my liking,' Steadman replied.

Ms Devine turned ashen as the gravity of the situation sunk in. Not only was her employer dead but she was out of a job and might have all sorts of problems. She stood up and walked over to her coat to fetch a tissue. Robbie followed her movements, and as she turned the dog's sad eyes met hers. She stooped and patted the dog, trying to keep her emotions in check.

'I always thought some of his work was dubious. Am I in a lot of trouble, Inspector Steadman?'

'I wouldn't have thought so,' he replied. 'But your full co-operation would, undoubtedly be appreciated.'

'Did he have many clients?' asked Munro.

'No more than a few dozen regulars. I have them written down somewhere.' She unlocked a drawer and produced a small blue notebook. 'I think the names here are all genuine, at least, these are the people I was instructed to invoice.'

Munro took the book and slowly turned each page.

'A few familiar names, sir.' He folded down a corner, then another.

Steadman waited patiently. A song started playing in his head, a beautiful duet from *The Marriage of Figaro*, and very gently his right hand started tapping his thigh in time to the music. It was as if, at last, some of this was starting to make sense.

'We'll have to keep this, *Mzz* Devine,' said Munro. She made no protest. 'And we are going to have to ask you to vacate the offices. We'll need to seal them and get the full forensic team in. Someone will probably need to speak with you again.'

'I understand,' she said in barely a whisper. She scribbled her phone number on a piece of paper and handed it to Munro.

'In the meantime, sir, I have got some interesting names for DCI Long,' he said. 'People with business activities and violent tendencies similar to those of Seth Shuster.'

CHAPTER 10

The cloying smell of the hyacinths clung to the two men as they left the building and picked their way back to the car. Steadman sensed the rising tension in his colleague. It was barely perceptible; the muscles in the arm that Munro proffered were just that bit tighter, his stride marginally longer and more purposeful. *He has a hundred and one things to do and I'm holding him back,* Steadman thought.

'Why don't we go to the Eyesore, Alan?' I rather fancy having a sandwich in the canteen and I'm sure you have a lot to sort out.'

Munro's relief was enormous.

'Would you mind, sir? I must touch base with DCI Long. He'll want Rupert Sidley's offices and home searched, no doubt. He may even want to question Mzz Devine himself. And of course, I'll have to write up my reports. I doubt if I'll be giving my girls a bedtime story tonight.'

It should have been a short drive back to the Eyesore, but the traffic was heavy, and roadworks slowed them down considerably. Munro started drumming the steering wheel again in frustration. He resisted the temptation to put on the lights and siren. In truth, it would have made little difference, for there was nowhere for the traffic to go.

Steadman leant back in his chair and, unlike his colleague, found some of the anxiety, and even the self-doubt, he had felt earlier easing. The melody started up in his head once more, two voices in perfect harmony. He tried to conjure an image of Rupert H. Sidley. He had always found it easier to concentrate with his eyes closed. Now of course, it made no difference, and without thinking, he found himself screwing his eyes tightly shut. Clearly Sidley was a loner. Single-handed solicitors were uncommon. He had no close family. His only pleasure appeared to be collecting stamps, another solitary occupation. Even his speciality, company law, was a field more concerned with bits of paper than with people. Why would a business like Helmsmouth Upper Reaches have used him, a company that could afford the smartest of legal firms? And he had been successful. Yet a fair proportion of his clientele, including Seth Shuster, could only be described as criminals. Was he merely a crook himself? Or did he simply see each client as another

Penny Black to add to his collection? More importantly, why did Seth Shuster need the services of a solicitor like Rupert H. Sidley? Steadman couldn't answer any of these questions. He sighed and the music stopped playing.

Munro found a parking place directly outside the Eyesore. There was a small set of steps leading up to the main entrance. Robbie's head twitched and Steadman knew they were at the bottom of the flight.

Counting the steps was unnecessary. He had run up and down these steps so many times in his career. Even without Robbie's guidance he could have found his way to Sergeant Grimble's desk without stumbling.

'Well now, how is my favourite dog in the whole wide world?' Sergeant Grimble enthused. 'And you've brought back DS Munro just when I was about to phone him. You are a clever dog!'

There was a faint rustling from behind the desk. Robbie's tail thrashed furiously, and there was a sharp crunch as another bone-shaped biscuit disappeared.

'DCI Long wants to see you urgently.'

Munro turned bright red.

'He's not cross, Alan. He only wants to know about Rupert Sidley, the dodgy lawyer.'

'You know about that already?' Munro replied.

Grimble gave him a disparaging look. 'Oh please! Are you new around here? Off you go, and I'll send up some food from the canteen.'

Munro disappeared through the double doors, his footsteps receding as he thundered up the stairs.

'What about you, sir?' asked Grimble.

'I was planning to have a bite to eat in the canteen,' Steadman replied.

'I could join you if you like. I was about to go for lunch myself.'

'I was rather hoping that would be the case.'

The canteen was noisy and crowded. Grimble found a table for them in the corner. As they steered their way through Steadman could plainly hear several people speaking about him and Robbie.

'Who's that?'

'You know – DI John Steadman, the blind detective. You must have heard of him.'

'Is he allowed to take his dog into the canteen?'

Sadly, no one spoke directly to him. It was as though his blindness had rendered him deaf as well. It was distressing but not uncommon.

'What do you fancy eating, sir? Today's special is chicken curry.'

Steadman was only too aware that curry was on the menu, for the smell was all pervasive.

'Not curry, thanks – a sandwich, preferably something that won't fall apart. And a mug of standard issue police canteen tea – milk, no sugar, please.'

Grimble waddled off and returned a few minutes later. It was clear he was having the curry. He put the tea directly in front of Steadman with a thump. Very gently

Steadman slid his open hands over the table until he found the mug.

'I've ordered you a cheese, ham and mustard sandwich. They'll bring it over.'

What he didn't say was that he had ordered it specially with sliced cheese rather than grated.

The tea was exactly as Steadman remembered it; strong, almost stewed and with a slight metallic aftertaste. By the time his sandwich arrived, Grimble had finished his curry.

'I expect you'll be wanting a full update, sir?'

'Spare me no details,' Steadman replied.

'Where would you like me to start?'

Steadman tried to recall the list DCI Long had made at the case conference.

'Let's start with the jacket. I'd be surprised if they have had any luck.'

'Absolutely right, sir. A team of officers have combed the charity shops, homeless shelters and spoken to as many of the rough sleepers as they could find without success.'

'That doesn't surprise me. What would you do with a jacket if you wanted to get rid of it quickly?'

'Go through the pockets, empty the wallet of cash, stamp on the mobile phone then put the whole lot in a plastic bag and chuck it in a bin that I knew would be emptied the following day.'

'Exactly what I would have done. Nobody is going to

rake through tons of rubbish on a landfill site in the hope of finding a jacket. Did they get anywhere with the shoes?'

'Indeed they did.' Grimble wiped his plate with a fat finger and licked it. 'That was a mean curry! Would you like a pudding? I think it may be spotted dick and custard.'

'I'll pass on dessert, but I wouldn't mind a biscuit or something sweet.'

Steadman finished his sandwich while Grimble went back to the counter.

'Here, I've brought you a chocolate biscuit. There's usually an appalling joke on the wrapper. I think Dr Rufus writes them in his spare time.'

Unfortunately, the joke was, 'What do you call a blind dinosaur?' Grimble muttered something under his breath and hastily moved back to the subject of Seth Shuster's shoes.

'The shoes were much easier. There are only a handful of shoe repairers left in Helmsmouth and most of these are now in the bigger supermarkets.'

Steadman nodded recalling the kiosks situated by the checkouts that offered the unlikely combination of shoe repairs, key cutting, mobile phone screen replacements and, for some unfathomable reason, walking sticks for sale.

'A cobbler working out of Sainsbury's not far from The Oaks Care Home recognised the shoes.'

'Did he recall who brought them in?'

'No, apparently he is very short-sighted and had to peer at the shoes very closely before confirming that they were the ones he had repaired. The photos meant nothing to him. However, he did say that the man had a funny accent and, unusually, was wearing the shoes when he arrived. He was most insistent that they were mended while he waited. He paid in cash.'

'How odd,' Steadman mused. 'It does suggest he had only one pair of shoes. Why didn't he just buy a new pair?'

'Oh, I don't know,' Grimble replied. 'I have an old pair of slippers that have seen better days, but I wouldn't part with them. You can't beat comfortable, worn-in shoes – they're like old friends.'

Steadman had a sudden idea. Could Seth Shuster have spent time in some place where he wasn't allowed his own clothes?

Grimble continued, interrupting his train of thought. 'DC Lofthouse went to the newspaper's offices. The editor is being coy about revealing who gave him the photos from the beach. Maybe he wasn't being as careful as usual. It was a young man who brought the pictures in on a memory stick and demanded cash up front. We think he's a student at the Arts College.'

'Don't they have security cameras?' asked Steadman.

'They do sir, but our young man had had his hood up and was wearing a baseball cap. So clearly he didn't want to be seen.'

Steadman finished the last of his tea. It had gone cold.

'Do you want another cuppa, sir?'

Steadman shook his head. 'I don't suppose we have any inkling where Shuster had been staying?'

'Not so far. Certainly not in any of the hotels. The team are working their way through the smaller guest houses as we speak.'

'I doubt if they'll find anything. Seth Shuster's picture has been splashed all over the media – someone would have come forward by now. Do you know if DS Fairfax had any luck tracking down the florist?'

'You can ask her yourself, sir. I think she's heading in our direction.'

'May I join you, gentlemen?'

Steadman started to get out of his chair. DS Fairfax put a hand gently on his arm.

'You don't have to get up – there's plenty of room, sir. Don't worry.'

Grimble looked at her plate in disgust. 'What's that?' he said pointing a podgy finger in the direction of DS Fairfax's lunch.

'The vegetarian option.'

'It looks too damned healthy for my liking.'

'Any news about the flowers?' Steadman asked.

'I think I've trudged round every florist in Helmsmouth. I'm soaked through, I'll probably catch a dreadful cold.'

'Don't let Dr Rufus hear you say that. He'll only scoff,' said Steadman in mock earnestness.

'At least I've been successful,' Fairfax continued. 'A

small shop in Humboldt Street remembers making up the bouquet and recognised Seth Shuster's photo.'

Humboldt Street was not too far from Adelina Monke's care home. A picture was building up in Steadman's mind. The home, the florist and the shoe repairer were all within easy walking distance of one another.

'I don't suppose DC Osborne tracked down a hire car?'

'Another blank, I'm afraid,' Grimble confirmed.

Steadman was a bit sorry. He had taken a liking to DC Osborne, and finding a hired car would have given her confidence a much-needed boost.

'I do have something else,' said DS Fairfax. 'It may be nothing, but as I was showing the florist the photofit picture of Seth Shuster I dropped the bundle of pictures. She helped me pick them up and noticed the very early photo of Shuster. You'll remember it, sir – he must have been about twenty at the time. Well, the florist remarked, without prompting, "I recognise him as well. I'm sure he lives around here. His hair's different, but it is definitely him."'

'Now that really is interesting, Fiona,' said Steadman.

Grimble looked at his watch. 'I have to go to back in five minutes. What can you tell me about Rupert Sidley?'

Steadman gave him a concise account of the morning's activities, concluding with the possibility that the body might still contain bullets.

'Dr Rufus will be like a dog with two tails,' Sergeant Grimble said with a grin.

'I'm meant to be joining him this afternoon for the post-mortem. Maybe you would let him know I'm here when you get back to your desk.'

'Of course,' Grimble replied before taking his leave.

'Damn,' said Steadman. 'I forgot to give him money for my sandwich.'

'I wouldn't worry, sir,' Fairfax replied. 'The amount of overtime that man does he probably earns more than the Chief Constable.'

The canteen suddenly fell silent.

'Divisional Superintendent Campbell and DCI Long,' whispered DS Fairfax. 'They're coming this way. I think I'll leave.'

'There's no need to go, DS Fairfax,' said DCI Long.

She took one look at the new Divisional Superintendent and was less than reassured. 'That's all right. I've finished lunch and there's always paperwork to do, sir. Excuse me, ma'am.'

'May we join you, DI Steadman?' asked Superintendent Campbell.

'Please do,' Steadman replied, waving a hand in what he hoped was the direction of the vacant chairs.

Someone came and took their orders.

'I gather you've had lunch with Sergeant Grimble, so you're probably better informed than either of us,' said DCI Long with a wry smile. 'I have yet to convince Superintendent Campbell of his worth.'

Steadman had a thought. Surely, if anyone could think of a way to get the windows in Campbell's office clean, it would be Sergeant Grimble. He would have a word with him. Although seemingly trivial, it might just change her opinion.

'We now have two murders,' she said coldly. 'In your opinion, are we any nearer reaching a conclusion?'

Steadman reflected before answering.

'Yes, I think we are. I am certain that Rupert H. Sidley will be an important lead. I cannot be absolutely sure, but it is my belief that Seth Shuster was his client and that they went together to meet someone. I believe it was someone that Shuster knew.'

'Why do you say that?' Campbell asked.

'Simple – he took off his jacket. Remember, it was a suit jacket. You would only do that in familiar surroundings. He was drinking champagne. You would not be drinking champagne with someone you didn't know. I can't speak for Rupert Sidley. My guess is the meeting took a seriously wrong turn. Shuster was shot. Sidley made a run for it and was shot in the back.'

Without being aware of what he was doing, Steadman started tapping loudly on the table. Robbie stirred.

'What's bothering you, John?' asked DCI Long.

'Lots of things. I still want to know where Shuster's been living and what he's been doing during the last ten years. We are missing a major part of the story. I'm not sure if it will help us find his killer but still...' Steadman made a vague gesture with his hands before continuing. 'There are also two things nearer home that are niggling me. One is obvious – the bodies were taken out to sea in a boat. That boat must be somewhere. I know there are lots of marinas scattered up and down the coast with even more small coves and rocky inlets where a vessel could be moored. Some of these are private or are virtually inaccessible. However, at this time of year a lot of the smaller yachts are beached up for the winter. I guess the marina in the old part of Helmsmouth remains open. If my memory serves me correctly, there should still be quite a lot of the larger pleasure craft in the water. It would be as good a place to start as any. We could check with the harbour master. Dr Rufus knows him. Frank used to have a boat, maybe he still does. I can ask him this afternoon.'

'I know the harbour master as well,' said DCI Long. 'A pig-headed individual more often drunk than sober. I think he is one for DS Fairfax. She has a way of unsettling awkward men. I have wondered about the boat. I did take some advice on tides and currents. Sadly, the area of sea that the bodies could have been dumped in is quite large. As you say, there are many possibilities. I'll arrange for a number of uniformed officers to do a sweep of the coast. You said there two things bothering you. What was the second?'

Steadman took his time in replying. The last thing

he wanted to do was to make two of his fellow officers appear stupid.

'After the case conference, DS Fairfax and I went to see Adelina Monke. In the car park Fiona saw someone who apparently looked like a younger version of Seth Shuster.'

Divisional Superintendent Campbell gave a derisory sniff and was about to say something. Steadman held up his hand.

'That's not all,' he continued. 'When DS Munro and I visited Seth Shuster's aunt and uncle, Clara and Josh, on our way back to the car someone bumped into DS Munro. According to Munro that person bore an uncanny resemblance to a youthful Seth Shuster. Munro gave chase. Whoever it was jumped on a bus and we lost him.'

'I've experienced this before,' said Olivia Campbell dismissively. 'Officers in the heat of the moment, over-eager to make arrests.'

'I think you're wrong, ma'am,' Steadman replied. 'Neither DS Fairfax nor DS Munro are prone to flights of fancy. And there's one final thing.'

'What's that, John?' asked DCI Long.

'As you know, DS Fairfax has tracked down the flower shop that sold the bouquet that was in Adelina Monke's room. Inadvertently the florist saw the photo from the police file of Seth Shuster when he was a young man. The florist is adamant that she has seen the man in the photo several times and that he lives in the area.'

'Why have they never mentioned any of this?' asked Campbell.

'Fear of ridicule,' Steadman replied, rather pointedly.

'Do we know if Seth Shuster has any other relatives?'

'That's a good question, ma'am.' A small smile played over Steadman's face. 'I would ask Sergeant Grimble. If anyone knows or has heard a rumour, it will be him.'

CHAPTER 11

A slight commotion had broken out at the entrance to the canteen. Steadman's ears pricked up. That would be Frank Rufus.

'Ah, there you are!' boomed the familiar voice of the Home Office pathologist as he waded through the remaining diners. 'Grimble said you would be skulking in the corner.'

Steadman was about to protest his innocence. Dr Rufus continued with a laugh, 'Good God, John, you haven't voluntarily been eating the food here. The last person who did that ended up as an unexpected guest in my mortuary!'

The man and woman behind the counter gave him filthy looks. Dr Rufus ignored them. Robbie stirred as he pulled up a chair. 'And don't you look at me with those sad eyes. If you want another treat, you'll have to nobble

Sergeant Grimble on the way out. How are you, Hubert?' he continued turning to DCI Long.

'I'm very well, thank you,' Long replied. 'I don't think you've been formally introduced to Olivia Campbell, our new Divisional Superintendent.'

Campbell held out a hand which Dr Rufus, in his exuberance, almost squeezed the life out of.

'I've heard a lot about you,' she said.

'Have you? Well, ninety-five percent of it will be true and the other five percent will be a gross understatement.'

Olivia Campbell gave him a frosty stare. Unabashed, Rufus turned to DCI Long. 'All quiet on the gardening front, I suppose.' He looked at the Divisional Superintendent. 'Did you know DCI Long is also our resident expert on all things horticultural?' Without waiting for a reply, he continued, 'What do you do in January, Hubert? Look in seed catalogues?'

'Among other things. There's always something to do in a garden.'

'I have a large garden,' Dr Rufus declared, turning again to the Divisional Superintendent. 'It's a bit overgrown. I keep offering it to Hubert, but he's not interested. I have thought about renting it out to that TV programme – you know the one where they put celebrities and politicians in the jungle. Only I'd want to leave the whole bloody lot in there with a couple of starving tigers and a few venomous snakes.'

Olivia Campbell appeared severely unimpressed. 'I don't suppose I can interest you in my garden?' asked Dr Rufus. She shook her head. 'Pity. You're very quiet, John. I hope you aren't falling asleep. We have a bullet-riddled corpse to sort out. Unless DCI Long has a better offer, which is highly unlikely, you agreed to accompany me this afternoon.'

'No, that's fine,' DCI Long responded. 'I know where I can get hold of him if need be.'

DI Steadman and Dr Rufus stood up, as did Robbie, who gave himself a good shake which, as per usual, started at his head and finished with his tail.

'It was a pleasure to meet you, Dr Rufus' said Olivia Campbell.

'I doubt that very much. At least you can now put a face to the gossip and idle speculation,' the Home Office pathologist replied with a smile. The smile was not returned.

After they had left, Olivia Campbell asked DCI Long, 'Is he always so rude?'

DCI Long had grown accustomed to Dr Rufus. 'I think it's his job,' he answered after some consideration. 'He is quite brilliant. Personally, I can't think of anything worse than cutting up decomposing bodies. Outside of his work, I think he regards life as largely meaningless and something of a joke. I would say he was brutally honest and lacking in social niceties rather than rude. His only friend, and probably the only person he cares for, is DI Steadman. Dr Rufus sat by his bed day and night after he was shot. I'm not even sure if Steadman is aware of that, and I'd prefer if he didn't know.'

'Is there a Mrs Rufus?' Campbell asked.

'There was, but only briefly. She died on their honeymoon in a boating accident. They have that loss in common as well.'

Divisional Superintendent Campbell merely nodded.

★ ★ ★

DI Steadman and Dr Rufus paused at Sergeant Grimble's desk on the way out.

'I suppose you've heard about the sightings of a possible double for a younger Seth Shuster?' Steadman asked.

'It has been brought to my attention,' Grimble replied enigmatically.

'Do you know if he ever fathered a child?'

'There were some rumours. I don't know for certain.' Grimble pulled a face. 'I don't think anyone would be surprised if Shuster didn't sample some of his own merchandise, so to speak. However, hearsay had it that he wasn't fussy whether it was a young man or a young lady. I think Seth Shuster swung both ways long before it became spoken about or acceptable.'

'I don't find it acceptable,' Dr Rufus grunted.

'That's because you're an old curmudgeonly reactionary who doesn't get out enough,' Grimble retorted.

Dr Rufus puffed himself out and let out a loud guffaw. 'Guilty as charged!' he replied, 'and probably too set in my ways to change.'

'I have just remembered another thing for you to bend your mind to, Sergeant Grimble,' said Steadman.

'What would that be?'

'The windows in our new Superintendent's office are filthy, apparently, and causing her no end of upset. Can you think of any way they can be cleaned?'

'Tricky – I'll see what I can do.'

'It would mean an awful lot of Brownie points.'

'Well, I could always do with a few more of those. Talking of remembering things, you haven't forgotten what I told you, Dr Rufus?'

'Certainly not. I will choose my moment. Timing in life is everything,' Rufus replied.

Steadman was puzzled, but let it pass.

★ ★ ★

Dr Rufus took Steadman's arm and led him around to the back of the Eyesore, where he had parked his old Volvo. The weather remained cold and damp and a light sea mist had rolled in. Steadman could taste its salty tang on his lips. He was half-hoping they might encounter Seth

Shuster's alleged double but nothing out of the ordinary happened.

'Here we are,' said Dr Rufus as he opened the passenger door.

Steadman was hit by an overpowering scent of pine. It was so strong his eyes started watering. Even Robbie hesitated.

'Good grief, Frank! What have you been doing? Holding a lumberjacks' convention in your car?'

'What's the matter? I can't smell anything. It's you who's always complaining that my car stinks. I thought I was doing you a favour by hanging up a few of those air fresheners.' Dr Rufus seemed genuinely crestfallen.

'How many did you buy?' asked Steadman.

Dr Rufus flicked through the bunch of cardboard pine trees dangling from the rear-view mirror. 'There are six here and about the same in the back.'

'I think you're meant to use one at a time.'

'Nobody told me that. The man in the garage seemed only too happy to sell me them.'

'He probably thought you were running an illegal carwash, Frank. Do you have an evidence bag with you? If so, may I suggest you put all bar one in there for the meantime.'

Dr Rufus found an evidence bag and grudgingly retrieved most of the little pine trees and sealed the bag. Even so they had to drive to the mortuary with the windows open.

'You weren't very polite to our new Divisional Superintendent, you know,' Steadman remarked.

'Me? I was my usual self. The epitome of tact and discretion.' After a pause he added, 'Of course, you're right. I never get on with people who don't have a sense of humour. You know about her ex-husband – the disgraced MP?'

Steadman shook his head. 'Should I?'

'I can't remember his name. It wasn't Campbell – that's her maiden name,' said Dr Rufus with relish. 'He had a serious, rather old-fashioned drug addiction, opium I believe, and possibly some other unsavoury habits. He may even have been caught with his trousers down in a public toilet – something like that. She took some gardening leave, kicked him out of the house and filed for divorce. It was touch and go whether or not he would bring her down with him. Obviously, that hasn't happened.'

It was coming back to Steadman now. There was more to the story. He couldn't recall it; something unusual. Dr Rufus broke into his train of thought.

'He served time and is now out. Strings must have been pulled, because it was a very light sentence. Apparently he has a house near here, but he spends most of his time on his boat. He keeps himself pretty much to himself, I gather.'

'Do you still have a boat, Frank?'

'In a manner of speaking. It sank three years ago

about five miles out to sea. Lads from the local rugby team thought it would be a laugh to go out for a midnight sail after celebrating an unexpected victory. You know me, I've never been one for security. They were too drunk to do anything more than start the engine, get out of the marina, and point the boat in the direction of the horizon. It was far rougher than they expected, and the boat started taking on water.' Dr Rufus laughed, 'I bet the two lads never sobered up so quickly in all their lives. They found the lifejackets and made it back to the shore. They probably did me a favour as the old tub was worth more in insurance than anything else.'

Steadman thought, and not for the first time, what an odd character his friend was. Sometimes he could be so intolerant and at other times he showed remarkable indulgence.

'Do you know the harbour master?'

'You mean Captain Gherkin?'

'That can't be his real name. Why do you call him Gherkin?'

'Simple – he's always pickled. Also, it rhymes with his real name – Perkin. And I'm not sure that he was ever a captain of anything more than a boy's football team.'

'DCI Long is going to ask Fiona Fairfax to interview him. It's a long shot, but the boat that deposited the two bodies out at sea must be berthed somewhere.'

'If you see Fiona, wish her luck from me. I'd suggest the best time would be just after nine in the morning as his head might have cleared by then. But tell her to catch him before eleven. That's when he starts drinking again.'

They pulled into the grounds of the police mortuary. It was a singularly nondescript building with frosted windows set in its own plot surrounded by trees, denuded and sad at this time of year. A small sign by the entrance read 'PRIVATE PROPERTY/ STRICTLY NO UNAUTHORISED ADMISSION.' Otherwise, there was no indication of its grim contents or purpose. In stark contrast, Dr Rufus seemed to be in his element.

'I think Robbie needs a little walk before we go in. He's a bit restless, 'said Steadman.

Robbie was let out of his harness and went snuffling off into the undergrowth while the two men walked the length of the car park. Dr Rufus watched mesmerised as Robbie cocked a leg.

'The capacity of that dog's bladder is astounding. I think I may come back in the next life as a guide dog, only I don't think I could cope with Sergeant Grimble and his Uncle Bertie routine. I have to get up once a night for each passing decade. By the time I'm ninety it won't be worth going to bed at all.'

Steadman put Robbie back in his harness. Dr Rufus punched the code into the keypad and held the door open for his friend.

'I would leave your hat and coat on. It's not very warm in here.'

The smell of the mortuary was quite distinctive. It was

neither pleasant nor unpleasant, a mixture of antiseptic, floral air freshener and stale flesh.

Dr Rufus gently steered his colleague to a chair behind a large desk. Steadman sensed that Robbie was very edgy. He gave the dog a reassuring stroke. His delicate nose could probably smell death and all its horrors, Steadman thought with a shiver. Dr Rufus offered him a hot drink, which he declined.

'I don't think you have met my new assistant, or anatomical pathology technologist, to give him his full title. Nigel, this is DI John Steadman.'

A very odd-looking man materialised at Dr Rufus's side. He was tall, woefully thin and completely hairless, with bulging eyes and a fixed smile. He waved at Inspector Steadman.

'You'll have to do better than that, Nigel. DI Steadman is blind. The dark glasses and the dog are not just for show.'

Nigel moved silently towards Steadman and gave his shoulder a friendly squeeze. It was so unexpected that it startled him. Robbie clambered to his feet.

'I should have warned you; Nigel doesn't speak. He hears perfectly well.'

Steadman regained his composure and held out his hand. 'Pleased to meet you, Nigel.'

The hand that clasped Steadman's was large, soft, and disconcertingly moist.

'I've never known a man move so quietly,' Dr Rufus

continued. 'Most unnerving in a place like this. I have threatened to tie bells to your shoes, haven't I, Nigel? Have you got the X-rays?'

Nigel grinned broadly and pointed to the computer screen on Steadman's desk.

Dr Rufus whispered in Steadman's ear, 'He scares the life out of me, but he's the finest mortuary assistant I've ever worked with…

'Now, what have we here? I thought I would miss the old X-ray films, and in a way I do. However, these images are so much better. Nigel, how do I adjust the contrast?'

Nigel came over and pressed the appropriate button. Steadman could only hazard a guess as to what Dr Rufus was looking at.

'One bullet is firmly wedged in the spinal column, in the fifth thoracic vertebra to be precise. That's between the shoulder blades,' he explained. 'And the other two are lodged in behind the sternum – breastbone to you, John.'

Steadman nodded. He was getting cold and regretted not accepting the offer of the hot drink.

'The bullet in the spine would be the easiest. I think we should start there. Perhaps we could have the corpse lying on its left side?'

Dr Rufus turned around. The body was already lying in the correct position. Nigel smiled and waved a hand as though he were a magician who had just performed a clever illusion. He cast a glance in Steadman's direction before disappearing.

'Are you all right, John? You've gone as silent as Nigel,' Dr Rufus asked.

'Just a bit cold, that's all. Do carry on.'

A rattle of china announced the mortuary assistant's return. He placed a steaming cup in front of Steadman.

'Your prayers are answered, John. Nigel has made us all tea.'

Delicately, Steadman slid his hand in front of him until his fingers found the saucer. 'Thank you, Nigel – much appreciated,' he said.

'Too late,' Frank replied, 'he's vanished again.'

This time when Nigel reappeared, he was carrying a plate with three cupcakes on it, all daintily iced in pink.

'You know this breaks all the regulations,' said Dr Rufus through a mouthful of cake. Nigel put a finger to his lips. 'Did you bake these yourself?' Nigel nodded vigorously. 'Excellent – let's get to work.'

Steadman sipped his tea while Dr Rufus changed his clothes and scrubbed his hands.

'For your benefit, John, I'm inserting a probe into one of the bullet wounds on the back.' There was a barely perceptible click. 'That's definitely metal on metal. It shouldn't be too hard to extract. I'll need to be careful not to scratch it.'

For some reason Dr Rufus started singing, more to himself than for anyone else's benefit. The song was *What Shall We Do With The Drunken Sailor?* It was oddly out of keeping with the surroundings, thought Steadman, yet somehow not in the least disrespectful.

'Put him in the long boat 'til he's sober,' sang Dr Rufus before adding, 'or in this case, chuck the poor fellow's body overboard hoping nobody will ever find it.'

The singing stopped. Steadman was aware of a scraping noise. He tried to conjure up an image of what Dr Rufus was doing.

'Can I have more light, please? There – got it,' he said at last holding up the bullet.

'Any ideas?' Steadman asked.

'It's a nine-millimetre for sure. It will have to be sent to the Ballistics Service. I'm no expert, but it looks slightly unusual.'

'In what way, Frank?'

'I can't be certain. Although it is a nine-millimetre it appears to be a slightly larger calibre. Not all nine-millimetre bullets are the same.'

'And that suggests?' said Steadman.

'Possibly fired from a Makarov pistol.'

Steadman was aware of the Makarov, a semi-automatic that had been around since the fifties, widely used in Russia, China, and Eastern Europe. Not surprisingly some had made their way into criminal hands.

'Let's turn him over and do the rest, Nigel.' Dr Rufus's voice was hushed and gentle as if he were speaking to a baby. Steadman recalled him once saying, 'The human body is the most exquisite machine ever designed; even in death it should be treated with great respect'. And so it was now; no jokes, no banter, no silliness – only a man at the peak of his profession doing his work to the highest possible standard.

Very carefully they rolled the corpse over.

'Let's see what we have here,' said Dr Rufus as he made a long incision the length of the cadaver. Slowly and methodically, he opened the body to reveal its contents whilst all the time keeping up a running commentary for his friend's benefit.

Steadman was only half-listening. He had started to feel hot and had removed his hat and scarf. The smell had suddenly become quite unpleasant. It reminded him of the docks at low tide: salt, decay, and raw sewage. Without being asked, Nigel turned up the extractor fans. Organs were removed, examined, and weighed. Steadman was only vaguely aware of what was going on.

'Has the cat got your tongue, John?' Dr Rufus asked without looking up.

Nigel stared at Steadman and noticed he had gone very pale and was starting to sweat. He touched Dr Rufus's shoulder, pointed at Steadman, and made the sign of a teacup while giving him a questioning look.

'Nigel wants to know if you would like another cup of tea?'

It was the last thing on Steadman's mind. With an effort he shook his head.

'Suit yourself. I'm just entering the thoracic cavity.

The other two bullets shouldn't be too hard to find.'

There was a soft crunching sound. Steadman gripped the edge of the table with a clammy hand.

'Here we go,' said a triumphant Dr Rufus as he dropped the bullets into a metal bowl. We'll get these off to the experts within the hour. At least our Mr Sidley did not suffer – his heart has been blown to bits. He would have been dead before he hit the floor. Right, I'm going to put this all back neatly and sew him up. Then, for the sake of completeness, I'll remove the top of his skull and have a look at his brain. Nigel, is the saw ready?'

Nigel held up the instrument and flicked the switch. It buzzed into life. This was the last straw for Steadman.

'I think I need some fresh air,' he said in a pathetic voice.

'Oh?' replied Dr Rufus who seemed a bit disappointed. 'I suppose it's not that interesting if you can't see what's going on.' He tied the final knot and only then noticed his friend was looking decidedly peaky. 'Nigel, will you give DI Steadman a hand. I suppose it must be a bit whiffy in here, although if he is feeling poorly, I suspect it is more likely the result of risking a police canteen lunch.'

Nigel led him to the door and into the car park. The fresh damp air smelt surprisingly good.

'I'll be fine from here, thanks. I'll just walk about a bit. Can you give me fifteen minutes, say?'

Nigel patted his shoulder in response and returned to help Dr Rufus finish his grisly task.

Robbie led Steadman up and down the car park. Subconsciously he counted the steps; fifty up and fifty back. Slowly his head cleared and that awful squeamish feeling he had felt earlier left him. He stopped and inhaled deeply.

A twig snapped. Another noise – a stifled cough, maybe? Steadman listened intently. It could be a bird, a jackdaw perhaps, he thought. Or maybe not...

Robbie tugged ever so slightly on his harness. Now Steadman was sure he was not alone. He could sense the other person's presence and hesitation. Oddly, he didn't feel threatened. Should he say something? Should he walk towards the person?

Another cough. It was definitely a man. Steadman reckoned he was no more than fifteen yards from him and watching him. For several minutes, the two men stood motionless facing one another, neither daring to break the silence. Steadman decided he would give it another minute, then say something. He felt the seconds tick by.

He was on the point of opening his mouth when the mortuary door opened with a bang. Instinctively, he spun towards the sound and in that instant the other person turned on their heels and strode off into the gloom.

'Damn,' said Steadman under his breath as Nigel led him back into the mortuary.

He was shivering and gratefully accepted the offer of a second cup of tea.

'You're looking very distracted, John,' Dr Rufus remarked.

'There was a man loitering in the car park. I think he wanted to speak to me.'

Dr Rufus dismissed him. 'We get the occasional weirdo hanging around here. Fortunately, not too many – one look at Nigel and they usually scarper! Would you like some good news to cheer you up?'

'Go on,' Steadman replied uncertainly. He was never quite sure of Dr Rufus's "good news".

'Sergeant Grimble has told me your favourite forensic psychologist has been asked to join the investigation. Samantha Griffiths.'

Steadman felt his cheeks burning. 'When is she arriving?' He tried to sound nonchalant but failed miserably.

'Grimble wasn't sure – either this evening or tomorrow morning. I expect you 'll be wanting to go home and change the sheets. You never know, you might get lucky.'

Steadman squirmed in his seat. 'I can't believe you just said that,' he stammered.

Dr Rufus burst out laughing at his friend's embarrassment.

'You're not going to deny the thought has never crossed your mind.'

In truth, Steadman could not deny it.

CHAPTER 12

The two men barely spoke as they drove back to Lloyds' café. Dr Rufus was completely drained. Each post-mortem took an ever-increasing toll. It was as though some of his natural exuberance had been sucked out of him. He even appeared to have physically shrunk. If Steadman could have seen him, he would have sworn his friend had aged ten years in the afternoon.

As for Steadman, his mind was in turmoil. No matter how hard he tried to concentrate on Rupert H. Sidley he kept returning, firstly, to the person in the car park. If only Nigel had left him a few minutes longer... And then, with a lurch, his thoughts turned to Dr Samantha Griffiths. He and Sam had met during a previous murder investigation. There was a spark between them that was more than just friendship. Perhaps it would have been even more had Steadman not been grieving the loss of his wife. Of all the memories he had of Holly, the one that haunted him day and night was the final vision of a gun being put to her head. The guilt he felt at not having been able to save her was beyond words. And he had survived; blinded, but very much alive. 'Survivor's guilt' somebody had called it. Did giving it a name help? Steadman was never sure. It had almost become an entity in its own right – something solid and tangible, a piece of heavy baggage he would have to carry with him for ever, a leaden albatross around his neck.

Sam understood. She encouraged him to talk, share the load. They spoke regularly on the phone, often for hours. Steadman bit his lip. Were these just therapy sessions or was there, as he sometimes imagined, something more, something deeper? If only he knew, Sam Griffiths was equally confused.

He heaved a sigh. Robbie sat up and laid his big black head on Steadman's lap as if he sensed his master's unease.

'Are you all right, John? We're almost there?' Dr Rufus asked.

'Yes – I'm just thinking, that's all.'

'It does bring it all home to you, doesn't it?' Dr Rufus continued. 'The transient nature of life, the pointlessness of it all.' He pursed his lips and gave his beard a perfunctory stroke. 'I sometimes wonder how we've ended up doing such sordid work.'

It was not like Dr Rufus to be dejected, and it concerned his friend.

'Someone has got to tidy up the place, Frank. Only a thin veneer of social graces holds us all together. It takes very little for it all to break down – a rumour, a perceived threat. Laws are there to strengthen the veneer and, as you know full well, change constantly to reflect what society believes to be acceptable. However, the taking of a life, for the most part, remains the most serious of crimes. Even if that life is as corrupt as Seth Shuster's. I am very wary of the vigilante and mob rule.'

'That's very profound, even for you, John,' Dr Rufus replied. 'You've cheered me up enormously,' he continued, but there was a twinkle back in his eye. 'We're here. Now, are you sure you don't want me to come up and check the sheets for you before Sam Griffiths arrives?'

It was a feeble attempt at humour. Steadman pulled a face. 'You can never be serious for long can you, Frank?'

'No, thank God – it's what keeps me sane.'

* * *

The apartment smelt fresh. The Lloyds had insisted that one of their staff give the flat a weekly spruce up. Thank goodness it was today, thought Steadman. Would Sam turn up? He didn't dare hope. At least the place was clean and tidy.

Robbie stirred as the doorbell rang. One long ring,

one short ring and a further two long rings – Morse code for TW, Tim Warrender's initials.

'Reporting for dog walking duties,' growled Warrender.

'I'm sure Robbie will be delighted. He's been stuck in a chilly mortuary all afternoon,' Steadman replied.

'Yuk! I wouldn't fancy that. I've got some exciting news,' Tim continued without pausing for breath. 'I've got a new physics teacher – Dr Yorke. Can you believe it – a Doctor of Physics. How cool is that? I can't wait to tell DS Munro. Is he a Doctor of Physics?'

DS Munro had joined the force as a graduate entrant and had given Tim some extra tuition.

'No, I don't think so, but I believe he does have a first-class degree in it.'

Tim seemed a bit disappointed. Alan Munro was something of a hero in his eyes.

'You mustn't confuse knowledge with wisdom, Tim,' said Steadman reassuringly.

'I don't know what you mean?'

'Well, for example, knowledge is knowing a tomato is a fruit not a vegetable, wisdom is knowing not to chop it up and put it in a fruit salad.'

Tim grinned. 'I like that one. Come on Robbie, let's go.'

Steadman decided to take advantage of the peace and quiet to have a shower. What to wear? Smart casual seemed the order of the day. He felt along the rack of clothes in his wardrobe. He had recently bought some well-cut jeans.

The denim felt stiff against his fingers. These will do, he said to himself. In the drawer by his bed, he had a hand-held colour scanner. He selected a pale blue shirt and a navy cashmere jumper. Quite suddenly he was overcome with uncertainty and felt utterly ridiculous. 'Who are you kidding, John Steadman?' he said out aloud.

The return of Tim and Robbie caught him just in time, otherwise he would have fallen into the foulest of moods.

'I'll feed Robbie, then I must dash. I've got football practice tonight.' Poor Tim, his voice started as if he were gargling gravel and finished in a less than flattering squeak.

As he left a delicious smell wafted up from the Lloyds' kitchen, and Steadman realised that he was ravenous. Using the intercom in his flat, Steadman called down to the café.

'Something smells wonderful. What's cooking?'

It was Marco who answered. 'Beef in Barolo wine – one of Mama's winter specialities, served with olive oil, mashed potatoes and roasted fennel.'

Steadman's mouth watered. 'That sounds like a dish made in heaven.'

'Would you like me to bring some up? There's an interesting article in the *Helmsmouth Evening News* that I want to read to you.'

Intrigued, Steadman made his way back to his sitting room and laid himself a place at the small table. He could almost follow the progress of the food up from the kitchen by the aroma. He opened the door before Marco had a chance to ring the bell.

Steadman had arranged the table so he would have his back to Marco. He hated eating in public. He need not have worried; the Lloyd family were very conscious of his feelings.

'Mama says the meat is so tender you should eat it with a spoon. And I insist you need a glass of Barolo to go with it.'

He put a large bowl in front of Steadman, removed the fork and knife and placed the spoon by his right hand. The garnet-coloured wine was in a thick-bottomed tumbler. This he placed by Steadman's left hand. Without any coyness, he kept up a lively one-sided conversation, finishing by presenting Steadman with a large, crisp white napkin.

'Have you got a glass of wine, Marco?'

'Of course – it is a sin to drink alone. *Saluté!*'

They clinked glasses. Marco moved discreetly behind Steadman and made a fuss of unfolding and rustling the newspaper while Steadman delicately touched his food to orientate himself around the bowl. The stew was superb, perfect for a cold January day.

'Shall I begin?' asked Marco.

'Please do,' Steadman replied through a mouthful of mashed potato.

Marco cleared his throat and took a sip of wine. 'It's only a small article on page four. The headline reads,

"Mystery of Body in Freezer in Abandoned Warehouse".'
He paused and glanced up to see if there was any reaction.
The spoon had stopped midway to Steadman's mouth.
Unsure of what this meant, Marco hesitated. 'Maybe I
should wait until you have finished eating.'

'No, no – carry on. I'm listening.'

'If you're certain, here goes. "Police in Southampton
were called to a dockside warehouse after builders
made the gruesome discovery of a corpse in a chest
freezer. The warehouse had not been in use for several
years and was due for demolition as part of the port
modernisation scheme. A police spokesperson confirmed
that the remains were of a man, possibly in his thirties
and completely naked. It is believed that the freezer was
still functioning and that the body might have been there
for some time. At present, the identity of the man is not
known. The police are treating the death as suspicious".'

'Well, they could hardly do otherwise,' said Steadman
with a sigh. 'Finding a naked corpse in a freezer doesn't
exactly suggest death from natural causes, does it? I
wonder how long it's been since the warehouse was in
use. Knowing that would help.'

'Why?' asked Marco.

'Almost certainly the body was dumped after it had
fallen into disuse. Whoever put him in there was taking
a chance, though. The building could have been brought
back into service at any time.' Steadman ran the spoon

round the bowl again and was disappointed to find he had eaten it all.

'Did you enjoy the food?'

'Please tell Mrs Lloyd it was absolutely delicious.' He wiped his mouth carefully with the napkin.

'Would you like some dessert? A small gelato, perhaps?'

'No, I am replete. I couldn't even manage an espresso. Remember to put it on my account… and the wine.'

'Of course, of course,' Marco replied, not really listening.

'Thanks for reading the article.'

A shadow flitted across Steadman's mind. Something about a missing man… He screwed up his face, pushed his dark glasses on to his forehead and rubbed the bridge of his nose. He was so lost in thought that he barely noticed Marco leaving. No, the memory escaped him.

Perhaps playing the piano would help. Not Bach tonight. Something less constraining, some jazz maybe? Nothing too complicated. Art Tatum's trills and arpeggios wouldn't suit, nor would the complexities of Oscar Petersen. The beef in Barolo had warmed him up.

He slipped off the cashmere jumper. His fingers ran up and down the keyboard and without any good reason, other than it felt right, he found himself playing something by Bill Evans – slower, more subtle, more thought-provoking.

Missing people fascinated him. So many just seemed to disappear, to walk out of their lives and vanish. Where did they go? How could they drop off their families' and friends' radar? And they did, that was for sure. He recalled there was barely a newspaper or even a magazine that didn't have a distressing column tucked in the back pages. "Jamie – missing since 1998. Your family and friends are always here for you." Presumably these people were still alive, Steadman thought, but surely not all of them.

And then, of course, there was the other side of the coin. The melody changed, still soft and sad. The disasters where there was massive loss of life. There were invariably bodies left over, he mused, people with no names and nobody to claim them. Were some of them the same people as the missing?

He recalled Marco's words: 'the body might have been there for some time.' How could someone not report their son or brother missing? Maybe they had been in care and had no family, or in prison and disowned? Surely someone must have noticed.

'I bet he wasn't from Southampton,' Steadman muttered under his breath. All sorts of waifs and strays are attracted to large ports, he mused. Sailors and seamen looking for work, others simply trying to escape, anxious to move on, desperate to leave. Could Seth Shuster have travelled to America on a boat, he wondered? It was a thought. Certainly, it would be easier than flying into a country where security was so tight.

He couldn't accept Inspector Crouchley's opinion:

'Shuster was born bad, grew up worse and went downhill from there.' His fingers found another tune. Yet Shuster was undoubtedly evil. Was evil the right word? Could a child who had been brought up knowing no other way of behaving truly be described as evil? Perhaps Sam Griffiths would know. He had no answer.

Somehow society had to be protected from people like Shuster. Crouchley would argue that whoever had killed him was doing us all a favour, and there were plenty who would agree with him. Steadman was not one of them. Somewhere in Helmsmouth there was a person who had killed two people in cold blood, a person to whom life didn't matter, possibly a professional killer... and there was someone else out there, apart from the police, who cared or at least seemed interested. Someone who had almost spoken to him outside the mortuary. He felt sure that whoever it was would try to contact him again.

He continued playing without really noticing. The music suited his mood, melodies and phrases gently twisting and turning like a toddler settling to sleep.

What an odd story about Superintendent Campbell's husband. Would it all have been hushed up? Maybe his old friend Miss Bartholomew, the newspaper archivist, would be able to provide him with more information.

The tune changed again, and his thoughts turned towards Dr Sam Griffiths. Was he ready to move on? Was it remotely possible that she could be interested? Like two large black crows, self-doubt and guilt landed on his shoulders and pecked his conscience unmercifully. He realised, with a jolt, he was playing Bill Evan's version of 'Like Someone in Love' and missed his fingering.

Robbie sat up and gave a disapproving bark.

'Ever the critic, Robbie.'

But the dog was already making his way down the corridor before the doorbell rang.

Steadman's heart was racing. He stood up sharply not bothering to close the piano lid. 'Calm yourself,' he muttered under his breath. He pulled his jumper over his head and raked his long fingers through his hair. Despite his own entreaties, he found himself walking briskly down the corridor, his guiding hand barely touching the wall.

CHAPTER 13

The door was barely open a crack when a voice said, 'Hi dad, it's only me. How are things going?'

Steadman opened the door fully. A tall, thin suntanned man with long hair tied back in a ponytail stood before him.

'Ben! I wasn't expecting you.' It was impossible to keep the tinge of disappointment out of his voice.

'Sorry – I should have called. Sadly, my phone and I parted company. It went on its own adventure down a very primitive toilet in a campsite outside Byron Bay and I was disinclined to follow it. You're looking very smart. If you weren't expecting me, who were you expecting?'

Steadman looked sheepish. 'No one, no one in particular. For goodness sake, don't just stand there – come in, come in. I presume you have a bag with you, chuck it in the spare room.'

Robbie led the way. Ben put a hand on his father's shoulder.

'Oh dad, you never could tell a lie, even when I was a little boy. I remember asking you repeatedly if the tooth fairy was real. You never gave a straight answer.'

'I did wonder, Ben, if your persistence was just to torment me.'

'Of course it was. One of my favourite childhood games.'

The two men sat down and Robbie, curious as ever, sniffed and snuffled around Ben.

'Now tell me, who is this hot date?'

'Hot date? I should be so blooming lucky.'

'Dad, you're evading the question again.'

'All right, all right. I was half-expecting Sam Griffiths to turn up.'

'The forensic psychologist?'

'That's the one. We sort of keep in touch since we worked together. She's been asked to assist with the latest investigation.' Steadman felt his face flushing.

'You're working again?' Ben stretched out his long legs and gave Robbie a stroke, and a tickle under the chin. The dog closed his eyes in delight.

'You might have known if you hadn't thrown your phone down an Australian toilet.'

'I didn't throw it. It merely slipped out of my back pocket and was swallowed by the bowels of the earth. Or in this case, not so much the bowels, as their contents. Anyway, it's just as well I arrived first.'

'Why?'

'Your best cashmere jumper is on inside out.'

Steadman's hand whipped to the back of his neck and, sure enough, there was the label.

'She would have probably found that highly amusing,' said Steadman after straightening himself out.

'You like her, don't you, dad?'

'Let's change the subject. How are you? How was Brisbane, and how long do I have the pleasure of your company?'

'I'm good. Brisbane is great – very hot. I nearly froze to death when I landed back in Britain. The people are relaxed and friendly. The food is pretty decent too. How long am I here for? I can only stay for a few days, two weeks at the most. The circus is moving south to Sydney, then to Melbourne.'

'I'm surprised you can afford the flights. You must be making some money.' Steadman knew what Ben's answer would be before he opened his mouth.

'Money? I get by, but I was relying on the generosity of...'

'...a loving father. I thought that might be the case. And doubtless you will be visiting a loving Aunt Linda and a doting Dr Rufus, your kind-hearted godfather.'

'Good idea. I hadn't thought about them.'

'You lie about as well as your father,' Steadman replied.

'Tell me about the case you're working on, dad.'

Before Steadman could start, the doorbell rang again.

'Will I get it?'

'Certainly not, Ben. I have no idea how long your hair is or how shaggy your beard is. The last thing I want to do is scare her away.'

He opened the door. The fragrance was unmistakable; floral and expensive.

'I was hoping it might be you, Sam.'

'And why would I not come and visit my favourite blind detective?' She stood on tiptoe and kissed him on the cheek. 'How are you, John?'

What could he say? Confused? Excited? Hopeful? In the end all he could manage was, 'I'm well, and how about you?'

'I think I would be better if I weren't standing in the doorway.' There was laughter in her voice. 'Maybe Mr Robbie will lead the way?'

As though he understood every word, the dog turned, wagged his tail, and led them towards the sitting room.

'I have another guest,' Steadman said hastily.

'Another woman, John? I'm shocked!'

Steadman stammered before realising he was being teased.

'My son, Ben – Dr Samantha Griffiths.'

Ben stood up with the grace of a gazelle.

'Please call me Sam. I'm only called Samantha when I'm in trouble.' They shook hands. 'John, you never told me your son was so good-looking.'

'That's because I take after my mother,' Ben replied,

but Sam could see something of Steadman in the young man's finely-honed features. 'Look, I expect you two will want to talk business so, if nobody minds, I'm going to nip down to the café and grab a bite to eat.'

'Put it on my slate, Ben.'

'I'll have to, I'm skint,' Ben replied, giving Sam a wink.

'He's very nice, you must be proud of him,' Sam said after Ben had left.

'I am. Naturally, I worry about him. Just how long can you keep on the road running an alternative circus? I suppose Phineas T. Barnum, the great American showman, didn't start his circus until he was sixty and was still going strong into his seventies... I'm sorry, I should have asked – have you eaten?'

'I had something on the train. The heating wasn't working properly, and I got very cold.'

'In that case, what you need is a carefully selected malt whisky to warm you up.' Steadman, with Robbie at his side, made his way to the drink's cabinet.

As his hand glided along the back of Sam's chair, he inadvertently ran his fingers through her hair.

'Sorry, I didn't mean...'

'Don't apologise. If I didn't know you better, I would have said that was deliberate, John Steadman!'

Not knowing how to respond, Steadman, his cheeks flaming, pretended not to hear. He opened the drinks cabinet, which was full of bottles of various shapes and sizes.

'That's an impressive collection,' Sam remarked.

'Forty-two bottles at the last count. All single malts.'

Each bottle was different. Steadman's fingers danced lightly over them.

'Here we are. Dalwhinnie – the perfect whisky for a cold winter's night.'

He poured two generous measures and held out a glass to Sam. She noticed that the measures were exactly the same in each glass.

'Years of practice,' Steadman explained. 'That and the golden rule.'

'Which is?'

'Never drink whisky alone. Cheers.'

They sipped their drinks and in the silence Sam scrutinised Steadman's face.

'Excellent whisky, remarkably sweet and warming,' she said.

'Thanks. I thought...'

'John, is my being here making you uncomfortable?'

Steadman could no more lie to Sam than he could to Ben about the existence of the tooth fairy.

'Yes,' he said, 'though not in any way that is at all unpleasant.'

The ice was broken, and he smiled. 'Shall I tell you about the case?' It was a deliberate move onto neutral territory, not lost on Sam. 'Let me know when your glass needs topping up.'

Steadman's thoughts were well-marshalled. He told the story succinctly. Sam was a good listener, only interrupting to clarify a name or a relationship. At the end of the narrative, she looked at Steadman, whose fingers were gently tapping the edge of his empty whisky glass.

'A life doomed from the start,' Sam concluded. 'What a tragedy he brought so many people down with him. Do you think someone could have followed him from America?'

'The thought had occurred to me.' He shook his head. 'I think it's unlikely. The mysterious look-alike clearly knows his way around Helmsmouth, and the florist reckons he lives in the area. The disposal of the bodies was too well-arranged for the killings to be the work of a random hitman. No, I'm beginning to think this has all the hallmarks of a local score-settling. In which case, it may never be solved.'

'That won't stop you trying, will it?'

'No, if anything it makes me more determined,' Steadman replied with a wry smile. 'Talking of unsolved mysteries, Marco read me a curious tale that appeared in this evening's newspaper.'

Again, Sam listened attentively. She liked the way he spoke.

'I'm surprised that nobody reported him missing,' she said.

Steadman paused. 'Maybe they did,' he replied with a frown.

'What's bothering you?'

'A half-forgotten memory that I'm struggling to recall.'

'And what happened to his clothes?' Sam continued.

'Now that is a very good question.'

The door banged, signalling Ben's return.

'Not interrupting anything, am I? Amazing pizza – I don't think I'll eat for a week.'

'Come in, Ben. We were just about to have a second whisky. Care to join us?'

'Whisky?' Ben pulled a face. 'Is there a beer in the fridge?' He didn't wait for an answer; he knew there would be.

'Perhaps you can help solve a mystery,' Steadman said when Ben had settled in a chair. 'If you killed a man, why would you take all his clothes?'

'Well,' said Ben as he took another sip of beer, 'if I was that way inclined, I might have stripped him beforehand.'

'True,' his father replied.

'As to what I'd do with them, that's easy. If he was about my size, I'd pinch them. I'm always short of decent kit.'

Steadman looked delighted. It was as though he had found the long-lost combination to a locked safe.

'You should follow in your father's footsteps, Ben,' said Sam.

'My feet aren't big enough to fill his shoes,' he replied.

Sam drained her glass. 'It's getting late. I ought to be going.'

'Where are you staying?'

'At the Equinox Hotel.'

'Do you want me to call a taxi?'

'No, I would like to walk.'

'Mind if I join you?' asked Ben. 'My clock is all out of synch and I could do with the exercise. I'm stiff from sitting in a plane for the best part of a day. Do you want me to take Robbie?'

'No, it's his bedtime,' Steadman replied. 'I'll let him out in the Lloyds' garden then turn in myself. Take a key – there's a spare behind the door.'

Sam made as if to shake Steadman's hand, then on second thoughts, gave him a fleeting hug and a peck on the cheek.

'Thanks for the whisky and the heads-up.' Her voice was soft and warm with its lilting Welsh accent.

Steadman lost his eloquence and mumbled something about it being his pleasure.

★ ★ ★

His sleep was restless and troubled. Maybe it was the events of the day, or maybe it was the Barolo wine. His dreams were mere fragments; transient and nonsensical, like snatches of conversation overheard in a crowd. A politician with his trousers down smoking opium in a public toilet; Inspector Crouchley giving a medal to a disreputable thug; and, most disturbing, Sam and Ben laughing at him behind his back.

He woke with the sound of the front door closing. His talking watch informed him it was a little after three.

'Is that you, Ben?'

'Sorry, did I disturb you? I'm going to make myself a snack. Do you want anything?'

Steadman was awake now. He pulled on his dressing gown and traced his way to the kitchen.

'She's really nice, dad. And she likes you.'

Steadman felt uncomfortable. 'Do you think so?'

'Sure – I asked her.'

'Ben!'

'And mum would approve.'

'You know, Ben, that's the hardest thing,' he replied with a sigh. 'Thinking of them in the same breath, so to speak. It doesn't feel right.'

'One life – live it, I say. You survived, mum didn't. I don't mean to sound harsh, dad – the question is, are you going to spend the rest of your life living in her shadow? Mum wouldn't have wanted that.'

Steadman's brow furrowed. 'I know you're right, however...' he waved his hands, lost for words. 'Not that it matters,' he continued, 'but I have no idea what she looks like.'

Ben shrugged. 'No worries on that front. She looks exactly like she sounds – lively, intelligent, funny.'

It was odd, thought Steadman, that Ben chose to describe her in those terms.

'You're the one with the problems on the appearance front, dad – a dent in the back of your head and wobbly eyes that don't work! But don't let those hold you back – make a move,' Ben said mischievously.

Steadman smiled and shook his head. 'Goodnight, Ben.'

★ ★ ★

This time he fell straight into a deep sleep and in an instant, he was back in uniform as a young PC. He was standing in a poky sitting room. In front of him a middle-aged couple were arguing. It was the wife who had put the call through to the Eyesore.

'I'm telling you, officer, our son is missing,' she repeated.

'And I'm telling you, he's not,' the man retorted.

'Not what?' the young Steadman asked.

'Not missing for one thing and, as far as I'm concerned, no longer my son either,' the husband continued.

The wife howled and fled into the kitchen.

Steadman sighed, his notepad in his hand and his pen poised. 'Do you want to report a missing person or not?'

'No, and if he does turn up, I don't want to know. Now clear off.'

'What about your wife, sir?'

'Leave her to me. I'll make her see sense.'

Steadman looked at the man's hands. They were clenched and menacing. 'Go easy, sir. Whatever is going on, she's quite distressed.'

The man snorted in disgust and turned his back on the young officer.

Back at the Eyesore, Sergeant Grimble was at his most conciliatory. 'When I was on the beat, I always hated domestics. You could never win. My advice is to forget about, let it go, let them sort it out. No wonder their son left – do you blame him? Here, I've made you mug of tea.'

A voice repeated, 'I've made you a mug of tea.'

Steadman woke with a start. He knew where he was, he knew that Ben was standing by his bed with tea in hand. What he needed was a moment's silence to recapture the dream. He held up a silencing hand and Ben waited. The couple, the argument – that had really happened. He was sure of it.

CHAPTER 14

Long before she gave Seth Shuster a roof over his head, Adelina Monke had taken in the cat. It arrived one day scratching at her door, a scrawny, meowing, half-starved creature. Adelina looked at the cat. The cat, with its head cocked to one side, looked back at her. And in that brief exchange, Adelina knew she had met a kindred spirit: mean, bitter, streetwise, and devoid of anything much in the way of sentiment unless it involved personal gain.

'You'd better come in,' Adelina had said. 'The place is overrun with mice. I'll give you two weeks, then we'll see.'

The cat paused for a second as though considering the offer. Its tail twitched and it crossed the threshold.

The cat never had a name; something that had always puzzled the young Seth Shuster.

'I never told it my name, and it never told me his,'

Adelina said by way of explanation, and that was the end of the matter.

Seth was fascinated by the cat. He would stare at it for hours. This tickled his grandmother. 'Watch and learn, watch and learn,' she crowed. 'That animal is as shrewd as they come, and a born survivor.'

Seth often thought their situations were similar. Both had been abandoned, and now both had been accepted, albeit grudgingly, by Adelina Monke. Neither Seth nor the cat showed much affection, and Adelina even less. Occasionally the cat would rub itself against the old lady's legs, but only to remind her that it hadn't been fed. Its rations were meagre.

'A fat cat doesn't catch mice,' she would say, and the cat did catch mice. It would sit with infinite patience, the only movement being the slightest flicker of its eyes. The pounce, always successful, then the kill, sometimes swift and with an efficiency bordering on the elegant. At other times, as if out of boredom, the cat would let the mouse go, but only for a fraction of a second. A clawed paw would pin the mouse's tail, leaving its four tiny feet scrabbling on the floor and a look of absolute terror on its quivering face. Release – catch – release – catch, and finally, dispatch.

Seth watched and learnt – patience, cunning and cruelty.

★ ★ ★

London had become too hot for Seth and he knew it. He had made too many enemies. One in particular was exceedingly angry, having lost his father's Patek Philippe watch to Seth in an all-night game of poker. It was a thing of beauty and Seth knew his chances of getting away with the watch, or even his life, were remote. Leaving all his chips on the table he had excused himself to go to the bathroom, slipped out of the window and into the night. It was a bold move. He smirked when he recalled his escape. But sometimes he thought he could feel a cold breath on his neck, and he shivered. It was time for a change of scenery, but where to go? He had always been led to believe that his father was American. To add flesh to the myth, he had perfected the accent. He didn't know anyone in America, and no one knew him. It would be a new beginning. There was a problem: with his criminal record he would never be allowed entry. What he needed was to re-invent himself – a new identity and someone else's passport.

Flights would be too risky. What about a liner? He could work his passage. How hard could it be to sail as a steward or a barman, he asked himself, and what other opportunities might present themselves? He had some money stashed away. A plan slowly started to take shape in his mind. A passport and a new identity? He thought of Adelina's cat. He would have to be patient. He would have to kill a mouse.

★ ★ ★

Within hours of arriving at the hotel he knew he had made a bad choice. The place was too upmarket. It was like some vast sprawling private club. This was where the officers gathered. These were people who knew each other, who all had contacts and commissions, people who would be missed. Seth made himself unobtrusive. He listened, eavesdropped, tipped the porter, and asked him a question or two. He hung around the cafés, visited the bars, and mooched around the docks.

He soon found what he was looking for. It was a grubby, worn-out building lurking between warehouses, so close to the water's edge that the smell of the sea and effluent permeated every room. It was more of a bunkhouse than a hotel, a place where seamen would crash after a long voyage, uncertain of their future. Others, fresh-faced and eager with the promise of a job, stayed waiting for the green light to embark. The saddest group was what Seth called the 'desperados', individuals willing to do anything to get back to sea, older men who had spent most of their adult lives away from land. They passed their days haunting the agents and shipping offices hoping against hope for the last-minute chance of employment. Occasionally they would get lucky, somebody would take ill or just fail to turn up. Their nights were spent trying to preserve what was left of their lives in cheap alcohol.

Seth knew who he was looking for. Someone about

the same age and build as himself. Someone who was bound for America on a big liner with a large crew where he could pass unnoticed.

It was not an easy place to befriend a stranger. These people were suspicious. They had been let-down, conned or abused so many times in the past. There was also something sinister about Seth Shuster that caused alarm bells to ring. He was too good-looking, too flashy, and altogether appeared too happy to be stuck in a dump like this.

Seth should have been an actor. He stopped shaving, tousled his hair haphazardly, bought some cast-offs in a charity shop, hunched his shoulders, and stared at the floor. He had become as invisible as the ever-changing Eastern Europeans who manned the reception desk day in and day out. He was just another drifter on a downward spiral.

Even with his eyes cast down, Seth missed nothing. He remained as vigilant as Adelina's cat. Sitting in the lobby, picking at the worn sofas, and sipping a cold coffee, he clocked every newcomer – too old, too tall, a possibility... He could not believe his luck when after three weeks who should walk in but Gregory Henshaw.

They had been at school together, the same class even, but never friends. Gregory had always been a bit odd, the only child of older parents who had cut him no slack, cossetted him yet kept him on a tight leash. Seth raised an eyebrow and stared at him. How things had changed. Gregory now had spiky blonde hair and a single gold earring, and he had clearly been pumping iron. Was the tan real or fake? It was difficult to tell in the gloomy lobby. His trousers were cut to the point where they left little to the imagination. Gone was the shy, stammering boy of their school days. Seth wondered when Gregory had come out. I bet that didn't go down too well at home, he said to himself.

Seth waited and listened while Gregory checked in. Only two nights, he heard him say. He was clearly over-excited. It must be his first trip, Seth mused. He was now chattering volubly to the young man writing down his details. Seth didn't catch the name of the ship, but he definitely heard him say 'America'. Then he saw him put his hand on the young male receptionist's arm as he was chatting. 'Good grief,' said Seth under his breath, 'he's on the pull!'

Time to make a move.

'Gregory Henshaw! Fancy meeting you of all people in this godforsaken dump.'

For a moment Gregory stared at the scruffy individual, trying to place him, then a flicker of recognition.

'Seth Shuster?' Gregory looked him up and down and wrinkled his nose.

'Excuse the mess – been travelling for days,' said Seth. 'I've only just got here.' Lying came so naturally to him. 'I'm going to freshen up and get a change of clothes. Why don't we meet here in half an hour? I spied a cosy Turkish restaurant only a couple of streets away. We could have a meal and a catch up?' Seth laid a hand on Gregory's shoulder and gave him a smile. Their eyes met. Gregory's pupils widened.

'Oh!' he said somewhat surprised. 'All right – see you in half an hour.'

Seth showered, shaved, and slicked back his hair. The ratty charity shop clothes were binned. He carefully selected a clean silk shirt and casual chinos. Standing in front of the mirror, he admired himself.

'Almost, but not quite,' he said to his reflection. A gold chain, an earring not dissimilar to Gregory's, and a splash of costly cologne. Finally, he slipped on the Patek Philippe watch. 'There – you shall go to the ball.' He smiled at the transformation; it was devastating.

He checked the time and noted he was five minutes late. Excellent, he thought, Gregory would be in the foyer biting his nails. The room keys were dropped into a shoulder bag and he made his way downstairs.

His entrance was perfect. Gregory's head turned just as he appeared on the last flight. Seth paused, looked around him, pretending to search for his date. Gregory could contain himself no longer and called out. Seth waved and grinned. He really was good-looking.

Gregory wanted to say something to compliment Seth. All he could do was gape.

'Should I leave my keys?' he asked toying with the clumsy fob.

'I wouldn't,' Seth replied. 'Here, drop them in my bag.'

It was quite a large bag and other than Seth's keys, entirely empty. Gregory dropped his keys in and gave Seth a questioning look.

'I need to do a bit of shopping on the way back,' Seth explained.

★ ★ ★

The restaurant was noisy and crowded. A waiter shook Seth's hand warmly and steered him to an empty table.

'They seem to know you here,' Gregory observed.

Seth waved away the comment. 'It's an act – they're hoping for a bigger tip, that's all.'

The food was authentic, inexpensive and plentiful. Seth guided Gregory through the unfamiliar menu and ordered for them both. They picked their way through some hummus, stuffed vine leaves and Turkish flat breads followed by kebabs and salad. The wine was earthy and fragrant. Seth made sure his companion's glass was always topped up.

Little by little, he teased out his story. Gregory had left home to study drama, much to his father's disgust. When he eventually came out as gay, his father disowned him. His time at drama school didn't last and Gregory drifted to Brighton, where he worked in a variety of clubs and bars. He had kept up a clandestine correspondence with his mother for several years. That ended abruptly after his father discovered the letters. He had had a long-term partner, but that too had ended. It was a sad story. Seth was unmoved.

He discovered the name of the ship and when it was sailing. Gregory was going to work as a barman. He was not sure where exactly but hoped it would be in the casino. With any luck he might be allowed to try his hand as a croupier or a dealer on one of the tables. Seth could not believe his ears.

'I like your hair. Where did you have it styled?' he asked.

Gregory responded at great length. The wine had gone to his head.

A waiter passed and Seth caught hold of his arm.

'Can you take a photo of me and my friend?'

'Sure.'

Seth handed him his phone. They smiled and Gregory put an arm around his shoulder.

'I'll be back in a second,' Seth whispered.

He returned carrying two brandy glasses, gently swirling the one in his left hand making sure the powder had dissolved before handing it to Gregory.

Seth paid. He put a steadying arm on Gregory's waist and the two men stepped out into the darkness.

'I've found a little place where we could have some fun,' Seth said slyly.

Gregory giggled.

The warehouse wasn't far from the hotel. It was empty and up for rent. Seth had found the door at the back easy to force and, much to his surprise, the electricity had not been disconnected. The door led into what must have been the canteen, no more than a large kitchen. It didn't take long for the room to warm up. Seth slipped off his jacket and hung it on the back of a chair.

'How did you find this place?' Gregory asked, his words slurred.

'Oh, you know me. The hotel was full when I first arrived, and I just nosed around to see where I could doss down for a night.'

'You always were a wicked boy!' Gregory replied.

'I won't deny it,' Seth said with a laugh. 'How about us both being a bit naughty? I've got some cocaine.'

Seth prepared the line of white crystals and rolled up a ten-pound note. Gregory inserted it into his nostril and bent over the table. He felt Seth's hands gently massage his shoulders.

Whatever he was expecting next. it wasn't for the hands to suddenly tighten around his neck. He struggled, clawing at Seth's wrists, but he was weakened by alcohol and drugged, and the struggle was short. Gregory Henshaw was despatched swiftly and efficiently. Seth had learnt a lot from Adelina Monke's cat.

He removed the clothes from Gregory's body with

complete detachment. He might as well have been undressing a mannequin in a shop window, except that it proved more tricky than he had envisaged. Gregory was heavier than he had anticipated, literally a dead weight. Limbs flopped awkwardly.

Seth folded each item of clothing neatly and placed it in his shoulder bag. What about the earring? Why not, he thought?. As he unclipped it Gregory's head lolled to one side and the earlobe tore. It barely bled. Seth shrugged dismissively and slipped the earring into his pocket.

He knew the chest freezer was empty, as he had checked it on a previous visit. He sweated as he strained to lift the body. Eventually he got it on to the lip of the open freezer and with a small push it dropped in with a thump. The lid fell down on Seth's head. He pushed it up with a curse, took one last look at Gregory, closed the freezer, then sat down to catch his breath.

It seemed a shame to waste the cocaine. He snorted the line, unrolled the ten-pound note and put it back in his wallet.

By the time he had fastened his bag and retrieved his jacket, the drug was beginning to kick in. He felt very pleased with himself. There was a towel hanging by the cooker. He wiped the outside of the freezer, the table, the switches, and the door handles, both inside and out.

Outside it was a very starry night, or so it seemed to Seth. He was buzzing. What a night! And what a success!

He was not sure who would be more proud of him, his grandmother or her cat.

★ ★ ★

The following day Seth moved all his belongings into Gregory's room, where he found his passport and papers all neatly stacked by his bed. He smiled again at his good fortune; it was an old-style passport. The photo was slightly faded and although it was clearly Gregory, Seth felt sure he could still use it. He scanned the papers. Time was a little tight, as Gregory was meant to report for embarkation early the next morning.

Seth checked out of his own room, but not before asking where he could find a decent hairdresser.

It was a half-hour walk. The salon was just opening when he arrived. Seth showed the photo of Gregory.

'Can you do my hair exactly like that?'

'No problem, but it will cost.'

Seth flashed his wallet and was told to take a seat.

At the end of two hours, he stared in amazement at the image in the mirror. He and Gregory could have been twins.

The clothes were still in his shoulder bag. He found a McDonald's on the way back, ordered a breakfast and changed in the toilets. As a final touch, he put in Gregory's earring.

'Tomorrow will be plain sailing,' he said to himself and laughed at his own joke.

CHAPTER 15

'Are you all right, dad?' asked Ben.

Steadman inhaled deeply, then slowly let out his breath between pursed lips. 'I'm trying to recapture a dream. I doubt if it's important, but...' His voice trailed away. With a shrug, he added, 'Did you say you've brought me some tea?'

Ben placed the mug in his father's outstretched hands. Steadman blew on the mug and took a sip.

'I shouldn't have had that second whisky last night,' he said. 'What about you, Ben, did you get any sleep?'

'About an hour, that's all. It'll sort itself out in a couple of days. Sam Griffiths phoned. She left her gloves here last night. I've put them on the kitchen table. She's going to call by about nine to pick them up.'

Steadman nodded and took another sip of tea.

'What time is it now?' he asked.

'About quarter to,' Ben replied.

'Nine? Why didn't you wake me? I didn't hear the phone. Where's Robbie? Has Tim been? Here – take my tea. Have you any idea how long it takes me to get ready in the morning?'

'Chill, dad, for goodness sake. You were sound asleep – I didn't like to wake you. I picked up the phone at the first ring. Tim's been and taken Robbie for a walk. Everything's under control.'

Steadman, still cross, stumbled out of bed.

'I need to shave and get a shower.'

'Sorry, dad. Is there anything I can do to help?'

'Yes – lay out clean socks and pants. Look out my grey suit. I'll wear the shirt I had on last night, but I'll need a tie – and don't even think of putting out the silly one with the cartoon policeman on it. Oh, and can you check if my shoes are clean.'

Ben smiled to himself. He could not remember ever seeing his father so flustered.

'Leave the bathroom door open. If she arrives early, I'll send her in to soap your back in the shower,' he called as his father brushed past him.

'Not funny, Ben.'

'Maybe not, dad, but I bet it would put a smile on your face.'

Steadman could not disagree.

★ ★ ★

187

Robbie had already made his way to the front door before Sam had pressed the bell.

'You're looking very dapper today, John,' she remarked.

Steadman raised an eyebrow. 'I'm never sure if dapper is a compliment or an insult. Come on in.'

Sam squeezed his arm. 'You look fine. A bit formal, that's all. If I were a criminal and you were about to interview me, I would be quaking in my boots.'

Ben handed Sam her gloves. 'Dad maintains you left them deliberately and it was just a miserable excuse to call back this morning,' he said, giving Sam an impish look.

'I said nothing of the kind, Ben, and well you know it.'

'Take no notice of him, John, he's only pulling your leg.'

Ben yawned. 'Sorry folks, I'm going to have to go to bed. Jet lag is the pits.'

'And a good thing too,' Steadman replied, 'I was about to send you to your room!'

'That would be a first, dad,' Ben replied giving his father's shoulder an affectionate pat.

'Were you like that when you were his age?' Sam asked.

'No. I was always too serious. Ben is very much his mother's son.'

Sam was not so sure, but said nothing.

'Have you had breakfast? What are your plans?' Steadman continued.

'I ate at the hotel. However, I would love another coffee. I'm going to the Eyesore later this morning.'

'I'll walk in with you if I may. I want to ask Sergeant Grimble a question. Let's go down to the café and get a coffee. I could do with a bite to eat. Would you do me a favour first?'

Sam nodded before hastily adding, 'Of course.'

Steadman handed her his phone. 'Can you find the number of Irene Bartholomew? She is the newspaper archivist and, before you say anything, she is old enough to be my mother. She has amazing recall, to the point where she was nicknamed the human computer. Sadly, she has had a small stroke and is not quite so sharp. Miss Bartholomew has been of enormous help in the past and I need to get some information.'

Sam scrolled through the stored numbers on Steadman's phone. Miss Bartholomew was only too happy to meet Steadman later that morning.

'You're being very mysterious, John. A question for Sergeant Grimble and a secret tryst with the newspaper archivist. What's on your mind?'

Steadman paused. He always felt foolish discussing his dreams. His friend Dr Rufus had once commented that the most boring thing in the world was listening to people recounting their nocturnal ramblings. He was possibly correct.

'I had an odd dream last night about an event that happened years ago,' he said at last. 'A young man had gone missing. His mother wanted to report it, but his father wouldn't let her. I can't remember the details. Sergeant Grimble was involved. I'm hoping he can help.'

'Do you think it is relevant?'

Steadman spread his bony hands. 'Probably not. It's niggling me, though.'

'And Miss Bartholomew?'

This time Steadman went completely silent and still. Sam wondered if he had heard her.

'It's better, for the moment at least, that you don't know. Again, it may have nothing to do with the investigation. However, if it does, it's going to mean a whole lot of trouble.'

Steadman slipped on Robbie's harness. The dog stiffened, ready for a day's work. They could hear Ben snoring loudly as they left the flat.

'He'll sleep the clock round, then be back to his old self,' Steadman remarked.

The café was quiet. Steadman ordered the coffee and an almond croissant for himself.

'I shouldn't really,' he said between mouthfuls, 'but it is absolutely delicious.'

'You've got crumbs everywhere,' said Sam. 'Here, let me help you.' She leant over and brushed the crumbs from his jacket and tie.

Roberto and Marco were standing behind the bar watching them. They exchanged meaningful looks and smiled.

'I'm not sure if I should have interfered…' Sam's voice faltered.

'Oh, please do. The last thing I want to do is look like a disreputable tramp. One can't be dapper with remains of an almond croissant scattered about one's person,' he added, stifling a grin.

It was cold and damp outside. Steadman was grateful for his heavy coat and turned up the collar. Without thinking, Sam linked her arm in his. They chatted aimlessly as they made their way to the Eyesore.

'I expect you know exactly where we are, John.'

'Unless you've been leading me astray, there should be a Greek delicatessen on our right. I need to buy Miss Bartholomew some baclava. She has a very sweet tooth.'

Poor Robbie looked around the shop miserably. Like all retrievers, he was perpetually hungry.

Steadman slipped the package into one of the enormous pockets of his overcoat.

Someone was staring at them through the shop window – a young man. Sam frowned. As they left the man turned his head preventing Sam from getting a good look at him. Within a minute, it was obvious they were being followed.

'There's somebody tailing us,' Sam whispered.

Steadman appeared unfazed. 'I thought so. We picked him up about quarter a mile back.'

'Do you think he's dangerous?'

For no obvious reason, other than a gut instinct, Steadman didn't believe he was.

'I think he wants to speak with me, Sam. What I would like you to do, if you can, is get a good look at him. When we pass a shop window, perhaps we could stop, and you could pretend to be interested in something on display.'

'I have a better idea,' said Sam, and with that she opened her bag and dropped her purse. Coins scattered in every direction. The man stopped and Sam looked at him imploringly.

'Can you give me a hand?' she asked. 'My friend's blind.'

The man never spoke as he helped Sam pick up the loose change.

'Thank you so much.' She peered at him closely and added, perhaps unwisely, 'Don't I know you?'

The man turned on his heels and fled.

'Damn,' she muttered under her breath.

'It was worth a try,' Steadman said reassuringly. 'Would you recognise him again?'

'Definitely,' Sam replied without hesitation.

★ ★ ★

It was that quiet time of the morning in the Eyesore. The waiting area was deserted. The cleaners had just finished. Everywhere was clean, damp and smelling strongly of bleach. Sergeant Grimble was nursing a mug of tea.

He was about to dunk his third custard cream of the day into the steaming brew when the main door opened.

'Well, if it's not my favourite dog in the whole wide world come to visit his Uncle Bertie. And who have you brought to see me today?' Sergeant Grimble dropped his biscuit and waddled out from behind his desk. He pumped Sam's hand. 'How nice to have you back working with us, Dr Griffiths.' He pulled a crumpled plastic bag out of his pocket and produced a doggie treat.

'For a moment I thought you were going to offer me one,' said Sam.

Grimble sniffed the treat. 'It does smell rather tasty. I think I'll stick with my custard creams. I have a whole packet of them, if you'd like to join me.' Grimble retrieved the biscuits from his desk, and with an air of guilt added, 'Well, not quite a whole packet.'

'No thanks. I should be working.'

'All the files are laid out in DCI Long's office. He says that you can use his room, if you like,' he said surreptitiously slipping Robbie the treat.

'Will I see you later?' Steadman asked.

Her heart sank. It was only a figure of speech. She glanced at his face and the dark glasses and realised pity was the last thing Steadman wanted.

'You need to spend some time with your son. But you never know, I may have inadvertently left my gloves in your flat again.'

She turned and walked through the double doors leaving only a trace of fragrance.

'Don't say a thing, Sergeant Grimble. I know the way your mind works.'

Grimble suppressed a chuckle and shuffled the papers on his desk.

'I have a question for you,' Steadman continued. 'Do you remember, a good number of years ago, I went out to see a couple whose son had allegedly gone missing. The wife was very upset, but the husband wasn't having any of it and virtually denied the existence of his son. It all got very messy.'

Sergeant Grimble screwed up his podgy face and scratched his bald patch with stubby fingers.

'You advised me at the time not to get involved in domestic cases. Does that ring any bells?'

Grimble opened his eyes. 'Yes, it's coming back to me. You were worried the husband was going to hit his wife if I remember rightly. The names have gone for the moment. There was something else though. The mother came back by herself about a month later. A frail, timid lady, I recall. I was on desk duty. You were away – I think you may have been on a course or on holiday perhaps. She didn't want us to actively pursue the search for her son – she was too scared. What she did ask – and I recall it quite clearly now – was to let her know, via a neighbour, of any unidentified young men's bodies we came across. She even brought one of his old combs and a toothbrush as she'd seen a programme about DNA on the TV. We never did find her son. I do remember the lad had form. Oh, nothing serious – possession of cannabis or drunk and disorderly on a Saturday night. But as to his name… It will probably come to me at three in the morning. Why do you ask?'

Steadman didn't want to mention his dream.

'Marco Lloyd read me a snippet from the evening paper about a body found in a freezer in Southampton. It got me thinking about missing people, that's all.'

'Funny you should mention the body in the freezer. They've asked Dr Rufus to do the post-mortem. He left last night and he's probably up to his arms in body parts as we speak. I believe the local pathologist is basking in the Caribbean, lucky sod.' Grimble gazed out of the window. It had started raining again.

Steadman pressed the button on the side of his watch. The metallic voice informed him it was after eleven.

'Would you call me a taxi?' he asked. 'I need to go the old offices of the *Helmsmouth Echo and Evening News*. I have an appointment with Miss Bartholomew.'

'Tell her I'm asking for her. I gather she has had a small stroke. There's no need for a taxi. I'm sure I can arrange for someone to drive you over.'

'It's not strictly police business – not so far at any rate,' Steadman replied uneasily.

'The vast bulk of what we do is not strictly police business, or at least leads nowhere, as well you know,' said Grimble scratching his head again.

The door swung open and a slightly wet DS Fairfax entered.

'I think I've found a potential taxi driver,' Grimble announced with glee. 'Good morning, Fiona. How are you on this miserable day? Would you like a nice hot mug of tea?'

She gave the desk sergeant a withering look. 'Good morning, Inspector Steadman. Now, what are you after, Grimble?'

'A very small favour. I was wondering if you would drive Inspector Steadman to the old newspaper offices?'

'Only if it's not too much trouble,' Steadman added.

'No problem, sir. You can hear all about my encounter with the ghastly Captain Perkin.'

CHAPTER 16

Dr Rufus had advised that the best time to speak with Captain Perkin would be just after nine. DS Fairfax checked her watch, pulled on her coat, and made her way to the car park at the back of the Eyesore. Although it had stopped raining, the sky remained dark and menacing.

The small police car was cold and misted up. The steering wheel and seat both felt damp. Only after the third attempt did the engine cough into life. Turning on the headlights, DS Fairfax crawled out on to the main road.

The address she had been given was not far from the Eyesore. She switched on the radio and almost immediately turned it off. Nobody, she thought, should be that cheerful, especially on such a bleak January morning.

The house was still in darkness. Faded curtains were tightly drawn over all the windows. Did one of them twitch? DS Fairfax couldn't be sure. The garden was strewn with garbage: a rusting fridge, a discarded sofa, bits of a bike and several burst black bags spilling their contents.

Reluctantly she rang the bell. Almost at once the door was opened by a wild-haired woman with staring eyes and a rictus grin. She was wearing a dirty flannelette nightie; a torn bathrobe was pulled tightly around her shoulders and on her feet were fluffy slippers that might once have been pink.

The stench from the house was appalling. DS Fairfax wrinkled her nose. Cats, she thought, or at least she hoped it was cats. Beyond the old woman, piles of rubbish were stacked from floor to ceiling. Something small and furry squeaked and darted across the floor.

'Can I help you, dearie? You're not someone from the council, are you?'

DS Fairfax produced her ID. 'No, I'm a police officer. I wanted to have a word with Captain Perkin.'

'My nephew? He's a very bad boy and won't live with his auntie anymore. He sleeps in the harbourmaster's office down by the marina, or that's what he would have me believe.' Her eyes danced at whatever salacious thoughts were rattling around in her head and the toothless leer spread even wider.

'Thank you,' said DS Fairfax. 'I'll try there.'

'You tell him to be a good boy and come home for supper. I'm cooking fish.'

DS Fairfax nodded as politely as she could and turned towards the car but not before pulling out a hankie which she held over her mouth. She drove to the marina with the windows open.

The little rows of houses by the shore were gaily painted, each in a different colour. At the height of the summer they would have been bustling with noise and laughter. Most had been abandoned for the winter. In the winter drizzle they looked sad and lost. A sharp wind had sprung up and in the weak morning light it was as though the houses, in their summer frocks, were huddling together to keep warm. The twiggy remains of a discarded Christmas tree, blown by a gust, brushed past the car as DS Fairfax weaved down the narrow streets.

The harbourmaster's office was situated right at the entrance to the marina in a modern two-storey building that also housed Helmsmouth's Yacht Club. The original office had been destroyed by fire some years ago. Now renovated, it was a twee seafood restaurant serving mouth-watering dishes at eye-watering prices.

DS Fairfax picked her way between the boats hauled out of the marina for winter. There were still several craft in the water, mainly larger vessels but also some smaller boats belonging to hardened all-year-round sailors.

The noise was quite eerie. Wind whistling through the halliards caused countless taut lines to ping repeatedly against their aluminium masts. DS Fairfax buttoned up her coat and made her way to what she hoped was the correct door and knocked loudly.

A window above her opened and the head of man rapidly approaching the end of middle age poked out. He had the same dishevelled appearance as the old woman; his eyes, however, were bloodshot and bleary.

'What do you want?' He had to shout to make himself heard.

Fairfax flashed her ID again. 'Police,' she said. 'May I come in?'

The window slammed shut. She was about to knock again when the door opened. At least he's fully dressed, she thought. The man stank of stale alcohol and was clearly nursing a hangover. He eyed up DS Fairfax and a lewd smirk spread over his stubbly face.

'My lucky day, it would appear. Come to make an old sailor happy, have you?'

'Don't push your luck, sunshine. I'm only hear to ask you some questions,' Fairfax replied.

A little dog appeared at the captain's side and let out a small yap. It was one of the cutest things DS Fairfax had ever seen, a small terrier wearing a bright orange life vest, its head cocked on one side. She bent down and the dog licked her hand.

'He's adorable. What's his name?'

'Jack Russell,' answered the captain.

'No – I can see he's a Jack Russell, what do you call him?'

'I told you, Jack Russell, but only on a Sunday. Most of the time it's just Jack!' He chuckled at his own joke. 'Now, if you want to ask me something it will have to be over breakfast. I don't answer questions on an empty stomach.' He pulled on an oilskin, lit a cigarette, whistled to Jack, and slammed the door behind him.

'May I ask where we're going?'

'Not far,' he grunted after a bout of coughing.

The three of them set off. Captain Perkin led the way, with Jack at his side closest to the water's edge and DS Fairfax at the rear trying to avoid the cigarette smoke. They tramped past the swanky restaurant to a small unprepossessing hotel. Captain Perkin tossed his cigarette stub over the harbour wall and pushed open the door of the public bar. Jack Russell and DS Fairfax followed.

They were the only customers. The room was decorated with a haphazard scattering of nautical memorabilia, most of it cheap and imitation. The whole place was painted in unfriendly shades of grey and blue. Maybe on a Saturday night with lots of people and some music it might be welcoming, thought Fairfax. This morning it had all the charm of a down at heel dentist's waiting room.

'The usual?' asked the man behind the bar. He started pulling a pint without waiting for a response.

Captain Perkin nodded. 'And I'll have two pickled eggs and a packet of pork scratchings,' he added.

As his pint settled, he tore open the packet of pork

scratchings and tossed it on to the floor, much to the delight of Jack Russell.

'Spoilt, you are,' he said looking at the dog. With one swallow, half of his pint disappeared.

'What can I get you, miss?' asked the barman.

Definitely not a pint and a pickled egg, she mused, and settled for a coffee instead.

Captain Perkin devoured one of the eggs and belched loudly.

'That's better. So, what do you want to ask me?'

'You must have heard about the two bodies washed up on Helmsmouth's eastern beach. The police are trying to find the boat that dumped them out at sea. It was probably Saturday night or the early hours of Sunday morning. Do you know if any of the boats left the marina during that time?'

Captain Perkin had started on his second egg. He gently tapped the rim of his empty beer glass and briefly glanced at the barman. It was like an unspoken language.

DS Fairfax took a sip of her coffee and regretted not ordering tea. She needed to get some answers soon. Captain Perkin was wading into his second pint.

'The answer to your question is, no,' he replied at last. 'The *Brig o' Doon* went out on Friday for a fishing trip. She was back within the hour because of the swell. Since then, nothing has either left or docked at the marina. Now, if you'll excuse me.' Captain Perkin got off his barstool and made his way to the gents.

'I assume you're with the police, miss,' said the barman. 'You've probably not met Captain Perkin before.'

DS Fairfax shook her head.

'Don't be taken in by his drinking. If nothing else, he knows his job. If he says no boats left, then no boats left – you can be certain of it.'

She wasn't so sure.

Captain Perkin returned from the toilets. He gave the tiniest of nods in the direction of the optics and, without a word being said, was handed a whisky, which he knocked back in one.

'To work,' he declared. 'Put it all on my slate.'

DS Fairfax insisted on paying for her own coffee.

Captain Perkin's gait was a little unsteady. Jack Russell kept close to the harbourside and snapped at his ankles if he veered too near the water's edge.

'How are you so sure a boat didn't leave the marina for a couple of hours during Saturday night?'

The Captain gave her a withering look. 'Firstly, I would have heard. You couldn't have left under sail on Saturday or Sunday morning, so they would have had to use their engine. Secondly, it is impossible to moor a vessel exactly the same way twice. You wouldn't understand. It's lots of little things – the position, the ropes, the knots... I notice these things,' he said, tapping his forehead. 'I'll swear no boats left on Saturday night.'

Jack Russell snapped at his ankles again as he started to stagger precariously close to the edge.

'I suppose you know most of the people with boats around here?' Fairfax continued.

'I suppose I do, and you're going to ask me if I can think of anyone who would be willing, if the money was right, to dump two bodies out at sea.'

'And can you think of anyone?'

They had reached the harbourmaster's office. Perkin fumbled with his key and eventually opened the door then turning to DS Fairfax said, 'Maybe I can, maybe I can't – but that would be telling, wouldn't it?'

With that, he whistled to the dog, turned his back on DS Fairfax and slammed the door.

★ ★ ★

DI Steadman had said nothing throughout their journey. His face had remained entirely blank. DS Fairfax glanced at him and wondered if he had actually been listening. She need not have worried. Steadman had not only heard every word but had been with her every step of the way. He had felt the damp seat of the police car, heard the cough of the engine, walked down the old lady's garden path and, in his mind's eye, seen the litter and filth that lay there. He had been by Fairfax's side when the mad woman opened the door. The acrid stench from the house filled his nostrils, and he too felt nauseous at the thought of being made to eat one of her fish dinners.

He recalled vividly the garish little houses and how

incongruous and shabby they looked in winter. The ping, ping, ping of the halliards on the metal masts rang in his ears.

He was familiar with the harbourmaster's office and the Yacht Club. He and Holly had once spent a miserable night there as guests at the Admiral's Gala. When it became evident that neither he nor Holly knew anything about sailing and had no intention of taking up the sport, they were largely ignored and had sneaked home early.

He had more trouble visualising Captain Perkin. Dr Rufus had called him 'Gherkin' and no matter how hard he tried, the man in his imagination persisted in having prickly green skin.

He didn't know the pub they had visited, yet he felt sure he would recognise it if he ever went there. He could taste the horrid coffee; cheap instant or, even worse, yesterday's brew reheated.

More than anything he would have liked to have seen Jack Russell in his bright orange life vest. He smiled wistfully, and turning to DS Fairfax he said, 'Thank you.'

She blinked as though she had missed something and was about ask, 'For what?' when Steadman continued.

'That was fascinating. May I ask you a couple of questions?'

'Of course.'

'Do you think Captain Perkin is a reliable witness?'

'Very hard to say, sir. The barman seems to think so and he probably knows him better than anyone else.'

'True. My worry is that years of alcohol abuse ultimately undoes any wisdom gained from experience. Was he just saying those things about ropes and knots to impress you?'

'He could have been. I certainly wouldn't know any better. Motorbikes yes, boats – no.'

'Precisely. What about him hinting that he could name some unscrupulous sailors? Any truth in that, do you suppose?'

'He would only have to look in the mirror to see one,' Fairfax replied. 'And I have no doubt he knows others, but it would be purely hearsay.'

DS Fairfax bumped the police car on to the pavement and switched on the hazard warning lights. An illegally parked police car was unlikely to get a parking ticket, she mused, a small perk of the job.

'We're here, sir.'

CHAPTER 17

Steadman was aware they had mounted the pavement and was grateful for the opportunity of making a dignified exit. Too often his feet got trapped in the gutter, causing him to trip on the kerb or, worse still, stand in something unpleasant.

DS Fairfax was about to get out and assist her former boss when a young, fresh-faced girl rushed forward and opened the passenger door.

'Inspector Steadman? I'm Tracey. Miss Bartholomew sent me to help you, as the main door has swollen in the rain and doesn't open properly. You have got to squeeze in sideways. It's a real pain.' Tracey said this in a rush and all in one breath.

'I'm sure I will be in capable hands, then,' Steadman replied trying hard to not to smile at Tracey's enthusiasm.

'Shall I call back for you, sir?'

'No need – I'll get a taxi,' Steadman replied as he got out of the car closely followed by Robbie.

Tracey grabbed Steadman's arm and led him to the door. She kept up an incessant and unnecessary commentary. 'Right a bit – no, left. Sorry. Almost there…'

Even Robbie looked bemused.

The jammed door did prove difficult to negotiate and there was a moment of confusion in deciding who should go first – Tracey, Robbie or DI Steadman.

At last they made it into the main lobby. Steadman inhaled deeply. The building still held the comforting smells of dry paper and old printing ink. In its heyday the place would have been a hive of activity resounding with raised voices trying to make themselves heard over the clanking of the printing presses. Now it was as calm and hushed as the backroom of a library. Steadman loved it.

He heard Miss Bartholomew's footsteps tapping along the parquet flooring. She still limped, though not as badly as when Steadman had last visited. Click clack, click clack – a quaver followed by a dotted crotchet, thought Steadman as he imagined playing the rhythm. The steps got louder and eventually stopped. He held out his hand. The hand that shook his was small, but the grasp was firm.

'Thank you for agreeing to see me at such short notice.'

'I'm always happy to help, Inspector Steadman, you know that.' Her voice was warm and kindly. 'I'll lead the way,' she said, knowing that Robbie would follow.

As they passed the various reading rooms Steadman could hear the gentle murmur of voices and the rustle of paper as visitors trawled through the archives. Miss Bartholomew's office was compact, tidy and crammed with books. On her desk was a new computer.

'Let me take your hat and coat. It is very warm in here, I know. I never used to feel the cold until I had my stroke,' she sighed.

Steadman fished in his pocket and produced the small box of baclava. 'Baked fresh this morning, I'm assured,' he said.

'My, but you know how to win an old lady's heart.' She gazed at Steadman. The trace of a soft smile spread over her face. And a few younger ladies' hearts as well, she thought.

Steadman slipped off his coat and hat, and Miss Bartholomew guided him to a chair. He snapped his fingers and Robbie lay spread-eagled at his feet.

'Before I forget, Sergeant Grimble asked to be remembered to you.'

'Bless him,' Miss Bartholomew replied. 'A good brain, if somewhat disorganised. I suppose he's fatter than ever?'

'I guess so. He certainly hasn't mentioned dieting.'

Miss Bartholomew felt a bit embarrassed. It was a foolish question. How could Steadman know? Swiftly she changed the subject.

'The kettle has just boiled. I'll make some tea then you can tell me how I can assist you. You were very coy on the phone. I presume you had someone with you?'

It was Steadman's turn to feel uncomfortable. 'You are wasted as an archivist, Miss Bartholomew. You should have been a detective.'

'I don't think I would have passed the height test,' she replied, for indeed, she was quite diminutive. 'I've loved working here and, as you know, I'm well past retirement age and have no intention of stopping. Even my little stroke has not held me back.'

'I'm very pleased to hear it.'

Steadman wrapped his hands around the steaming mug the archivist had placed in front of him and took a sip. There was an awkward silence.

'You know, I feel a bit grubby being here,' he continued. Miss Bartholomew waited patiently. 'My request will no doubt sound to you as if I'm just wanting to dig up some dirt...' He drummed his fingers on the desk as he struggled to find the right words.

'Is it relevant to the case you're working on?' Miss Bartholomew prompted him.

'I sincerely hope it's not, and at this stage have absolutely no indication that it is, and yet... something is bothering me.'

The archivist remained silent. Steadman took a deep breath.

'I've known you a long time and I know I can count on your discretion.'

'Of course.'

'I'm sure you aware that we have a new Divisional Superintendent.'

'Yes, the indomitable Olivia Campbell. I have heard.'

Steadman's ears pricked up. 'Why do you say indomitable?'

'Her personal life is no secret. Few thought she would survive, let alone rise through the ranks.'

'That's just it. Dr Rufus hinted at all sorts of scandal. For the life of me, I have no recollection. I don't want gossip or speculation. I need to know the facts, if only to stop me putting my foot in it. We didn't get off to an auspicious start. Our new superintendent is very wary of the involvement of a blind detective.'

'Well I'm not surprised you can't remember. It all happened around the time of your shooting.' The computer on her desk whirred into life. 'I can recall most of the facts quite clearly without this thing, but it has its uses.' She typed in her password. 'To understand it fully, you have to go back several years.'

Steadman sat back in his chair. Robbie stirred and was given a reassuring pat. 'Please continue,' he said with some relief, 'I'm listening.'

'As you know, Olivia Campbell did not change her name when she got married,' said Miss Bartholomew. 'From the outset, she was determined to reach the top. Her husband was called Henry Bridges-Treston, with a hyphen. Even that's a sham. It started with his grandfather, Mr Bridges, a solid Yorkshireman who made pies – extraordinarily good pies, as it happens. He built up a very successful business which he passed to his son, Henry's father. He in turn expanded the business and made a colossal fortune. But he was not content. What he really wanted was to be accepted in society. It didn't matter that he could buy and sell most of the aristocracy, he was still a baker from Yorkshire. He was damned if his son was going to share the same fate. They called him Henry and double-barrelled his surname with that of his mother, hence Bridges-Treston. He was educated at a private school, and frankly, spoiled. He was brought up believing he was better than his parents, who indulged his every whim. He started going off the rails at university – the usual things, wild parties and drugs. His parents bought him out of trouble on numerous occasions.'

Steadman nodded appreciatively as he formed a mental picture of the man.

'He made friends at school and university – influential people from privileged backgrounds. He joined the right clubs. When his father died, he inherited the business, then sold it. Being a baker was beneath him. Politics beckoned. He became a major party donor and was rewarded with a safe seat. For a time, he was the darling of the glossy magazines. I can't imagine you ever reading glossy magazines?'

'No,' Steadman replied, 'not even at the dentist.'

'Wise man, but back to our story. Henry met Olivia Campbell by chance when he crashed his car. She was on duty.'

Steadman was surprised. 'Not at some extravagant social event?'

'Nothing so glamorous, alas. Olivia Campbell was a beauty and he fell head over heels in love. They were quite the couple for a time, but she was never fully accepted in that circle either.'

'Because of her colour?' Steadman asked.

'No, it was because she was a police officer, and not prepared to give up her career. Henry married her, I suspect, in an attempt to make her change her mind, but she didn't.'

Steadman felt a new-found respect for the Divisional Superintendent.

'Then the cracks started appearing,' Miss Bartholomew continued. 'Rumours about Henry's sexuality were rife. And he had found a new companion – opium.'

The phone on the archivist's desk rang.

'Shall I leave?' Steadman asked.

'No – if you go every time we're interrupted, we'll never finish. Hello... David, how nice to hear from you, how can I help?'

Steadman could just make out a distant voice.

'How old was Sean Connery when the first James Bond film was released? Let me think...'

What an odd question, thought Steadman, as he guessed an answer in his head.

'Well, I'm sure I can work this out,' Miss Bartholomew said. 'Sean Connery was born on the twenty-fifth of

August, nineteen thirty-two. I had a poster of him in my bedroom when I was at school...'

Steadman couldn't imagine the archivist as a little girl.

'The first film was Dr No... Yes, everyone knows that... And it was released late in nineteen sixty-two, after his birthday, so he would have been thirty-two.'

Blast, thought Steadman, two years out.

'Yes, I can understand why you were uncertain with the Americans writing the month before the day... Happy to help.'

The distant voice crackled its agreement and thanks on the other end of the line and hung up.

'That was Mr Francis, a charming man who sets pub quizzes for charity. He usually calls me once or twice a week to check up on some fact or other.'

'Why doesn't he use the internet?' Steadman asked.

'Oh, he does. However, he lives in the middle of nowhere with a poor connection and, quite wisely, doesn't trust all the information.'

Once again Steadman was amazed at the old lady's powers of recall. 'Getting back to Olivia Campbell's husband, opium seems an odd choice for a young man.'

'He was not so young by then and I think it played into his image.'

'Ersatz Victorian aristocracy?' queried Steadman.

'Something like that,' Miss Bartholomew replied. 'Their marriage was soon on the rocks. Two people leading two separate lives under one roof. She continued her career and he did too, for a time. Apparently, he became fonder and fonder of young men. To cut a long story short, he was caught performing an indecent act in a public place and in possession of a sizeable amount of a banned substance. The press had a field day.'

'I'm not surprised,' said Steadman, 'nothing like a star fallen from grace to boost circulation.'

'His defence barrister insinuated that Campbell had set the whole thing up.'

'And had she?' Steadman asked.

'No, it was never proven, and one got the distinct impression during the trial that she still had significant feelings for him. It was rumoured that it was because of her influence he got such a light sentence.'

Steadman nodded.

'His downfall was rapid – dismissed as an MP, expelled from his clubs and shunned by society,' Miss Bartholomew continued.

'I gather he has a house around here,' said Steadman.

'He does, but I believe he virtually lives on his boat. There's a picture of it on file.' Miss Bartholomew turned to her computer and flicked through several screens. 'Here it is – a rather large oceangoing vessel by the looks of it.' She zoomed in on the photo. 'His boat is called *The Poppy*. I bet that costs an arm and a leg to keep afloat. I'm surprised he can afford it.'

What Shall We Do With The Drunken Sailor started playing in Steadman's head, and he thought, I know how

I would make money if I had a boat like that. Rent boys and opium don't come cheaply either.

Miss Bartholomew was about to offer him a penny for his thoughts when there was a knock at the door. A breathless Tracey explained there was a DS Munro on the phone wanting to speak to Inspector Steadman.

'Well, put him through, child,' said Miss Bartholomew shaking her head in disbelief.

'I didn't like to interrupt,' Tracey explained fleeing from the room as quickly as she had entered.

The archivist picked up the receiver and placed it in Steadman's outstretched hand.

'Are you finished?' asked Munro.

'Yes,' Steadman replied. 'Miss Bartholomew has, as always, been most helpful.'

The old lady beamed.

'Good – I'm parked at the door. DCI Long has spoken with Mzz Devine. He wants us to interview three of the persons mentioned in her invoice book. They are all old chums of yours.'

'I'm on my way,' Steadman replied.

CHAPTER 18

Steadman found Alan Munro chatting amiably with Tracey. She was hanging on to the big man's every word. It appeared that Munro had unjammed the door.

'It just needed a wee bit of persuasion,' he explained.

Steadman knew Munro's capabilities. He could probably have ripped the door off its hinges with one arm.

A traffic warden was hovering around the unmarked Audi with his ticket book open and his pen poised.

'I wouldn't bother with that,' said Munro showing him his police ID.

'I don't care who you say you are, you're parked illegally,' then noticing Steadman and Robbie added, 'and if you are transporting a disabled passenger you should be displaying a Blue Badge when your vehicle is stationary and the engine switched off.'

'Give me strength,' muttered Munro as he ushered Steadman into the passenger seat.

'I'll let you off this time, but let it be a warning…'

The traffic warden's words were lost as Munro sped away. To prove a point, he switched on the siren and the blue flashing lights.

'How did you get on with the archivist, sir? I assume it was to do with the case. Did you find out anything useful?'

Steadman held up his hands and frowned. 'Lots of interesting things. I really have no idea if it will be useful or even if it has anything to do with the case, Alan. In some ways I hope it's not relevant.'

Munro cast a glance at his former boss. His face was as blank as an uncharted map, although lots of ideas were swirling in his head. Too few leads, Steadman mused, and none going anywhere in particular.

He turned towards Munro. 'Who are we going to see?'

'DCI Long spent some time with Rupert Sidley's secretary going through the books. He has identified three people who have had recent dealings with the dead solicitor. All would have been known to Seth Shuster. You said yourself, sir, that he was probably looking to get a foothold back into criminal activity in Helmsmouth. It's possible that Shuster and Sidley approached one or more of them. DCI Long specifically wanted you to be involved, as you have interviewed or arrested them all in the past.'

Munro wanted Steadman to try and guess, but judging by the hardened look on his face he was not in the mood to play games.

'Do they know we're coming?' Steadman asked.

'Where's the fun in that?' Munro replied. 'Seriously, sir, without the element of surprise these three would either disappear or have established cast iron alibis.'

'Come on then, Alan, put me out of my misery. I know you're dying to tell me.'

'Miles Pelham, Madam Ying Chu and Gary Draper.'

Steadman nodded. He understood DCI Long's choices. Each had a very dubious past. Were they all still active?

Pelham, he knew, imported contraband and fake luxury items. He was possibly involved in people trafficking and was known to have a financial interest in, if not actually owning, several disreputable massage parlours.

Madam Chu ran a restaurant and a decidedly dodgy casino. She operated a small chain of take-aways and was suspected of running other establishments as well. She was also a police informant, and Steadman suspected this had afforded her a degree of protection over the years.

Gary Draper was vicious. He was into the protection racket. He supplied bouncers whether you needed them or not, and at a price. He also supplied drugs.

'DCI Long said you've had a long association with all three,' Munro continued. 'I've had a quick look but could only find records for the two men.'

A glimmer of a smile flitted over Steadman's face as he turned towards the window. Munro saw him out of the corner of his eye.

'What is it, sir?'

Should he tell him? Not yet, he thought.

'Do you know any of them, Alan?' he asked changing the subject.

'Only Gary Draper. I tried pulling him in when I first joined. I got beaten up for my efforts. He set three of his heavies on me. It turned out they were his sons. I couldn't prove anything. I would love to settle that score.'

Munro clenched his teeth and gripped the steering wheel as tightly as if he had his hands around Draper's neck.

'Don't stoop to their level, Alan,' Steadman cautioned him, although he too had an old score to settle.

Robbie stirred in the footwell and nuzzled his big black head on Steadman's thigh. Steadman gave him a stroke and started humming a tune.

Munro recognised the signs. The boss was thinking, and he knew not to disturb him.

'What intrigues me, Alan,' he said after a few minutes, 'is that all these people are now getting on in life. Do criminals retire? Somehow, I doubt it. I have never met a policeman, a farmer, or a doctor, come to think of it, who has ever truly turned his back on what he's been doing for the best part of his life. I would imagine these career criminals would cling on to their dwindling empires to the bitter end. I can see why Seth Shuster may have approached them – a chance to buy himself a piece of the action.'

'I thought criminals only sold their businesses in detective novels,' said Munro.

'True,' Steadman replied, 'they are mostly kept in families. However, Pelham is not a family man, and Madame Chu has never been married, not that that matters these days. I don't think she has ever had children. Draper has three sons, but I doubt if between them they have enough brains to organise a tombola, let alone a protection racket.'

'And two of them are serving life sentences,' added Munro. 'The third was only released a month ago having served five years of a ten-year stretch.'

'Which one was released, Alan?'

'Wally Draper.'

Oh dear, thought Steadman.

★ ★ ★

Rose Villa was perched on top of a cliff. It was painted a lurid shade of pink. The Audi crunched along an immaculate gravel drive that curved through manicured lawns peppered with artfully placed topiary. It was all too pretty for Munro. His garden was lived-in and scruffy with patches of bare grass under a child's swing, a trampoline blown over in a winter's gale and a scattering of toys, some broken, that his daughters insisted they still played with and could not possibly be thrown out.

'Who would live in a place like this?' he asked.

'Hopefully, you'll soon find out,' Steadman replied.

Munro hammered on the door. Steadman never quite understood Munro's aversion to doorbells.

'I don't trust them, sir,' he explained enigmatically.

A far away voice called, 'Just coming. Keep your pants on, at least to begin with.'

The door was flung open by a man of indeterminate age dressed in what Munro could only describe as a rather tight matador costume. His hair was dyed, his face stretched by a nip and a tuck and any wrinkles smoothed with Botox. Munro knew that the man standing before him was the same age as his father. The contrast could not have been more stark. He felt decidedly uncomfortable.

'Miles Pelham?' he asked holding up his ID. 'Police. We would like a little chat.'

'Well, aren't you the hunk Detective Sergeant Alan Munro, Helmsmouth CID,' replied Pelham as he read the ID.

Munro blushed. 'And this is...'

Miles Pelham shot a hand to his mouth and gasped. 'It can't be... John Steadman! After all these years. You poor dear!' Genuine tears rolled down his face. He made to hug Steadman, then thought better of it. 'Your wife killed, and you left blind – no, I can't bear to think of it.'

His emotions appeared heartfelt and took Munro

completely by surprise. Steadman had arrested Miles Pelham on more than one occasion and had subjected him to hours of relentless interrogation.

Pelham turned and saw Robbie. 'Oh, you have a dog. I love dogs. I know, I know, you're not meant to fuss a guide dog, but I can't resist. Who was it who said, "The only way to get rid of temptation is to yield to it" – I can't remember?'

'Oscar Wilde,' said Steadman. 'Though I suspect you knew that.'

Pelham winked at Munro. 'Such a clever man,' he said in a stage whisper. Munro was not sure if he meant the Inspector or Oscar Wilde.

Steadman pretended not to hear. 'May we come in?'

'My manners – so rude! Come in, come in. We'll use the boudoir. I have a fire lit and we'll be very cosy.'

Without asking he took Steadman's arm and led him into a charming room with wonderful sea views, despite the weather. Pelham gazed out of the window and shook his head. 'Such a shame,' he said patting Steadman's arm and guiding him to a chair.

The furniture was all chintzy and dainty. The last time Munro had felt so out of place was when he had accidentally stumbled into a ladies' toilet on a drunken student night out.

'What a miserable hour to call,' Pelham continued. 'Too late for coffee, too early for lunch – perhaps a small sherry?'

Both officers declined.

'I feel wretched now. What can I do to make amends?'

'Would you mind answering a few questions, sir?' asked Munro.

'Oh, I do like a forceful man,' Pelham replied.

Steadman could sense the tension rising in his colleague and decided to intervene.

'You are no doubt aware that the murdered body of Seth Shuster was washed up on Helmsmouth's eastern beach.'

'I never listen to the news – too depressing, but I had heard. Pompous little squirt! Good riddance, I say.'

'Not just Seth Shuster,' Steadman continued, 'also his solicitor, Rupert Sidley, who coincidentally happens to be your solicitor.'

Munro scanned Pelham's face for any flicker of a reaction. Nothing. Too much Botox, he concluded.

'Both men shot, and their bodies dumped at sea.' Steadman paused deliberately, allowing the information to sink in.

'Well, well – the grubby stamp collector has got his comeuppance. Why does that not surprise me? It was only a matter of time.'

This was not the answer Steadman had been expecting. In the silence he heard Munro flick open the pages of his notebook.

'Why do you say that?'

'Oh come on, Inspector Steadman. Surely you know that Sidley was a bigger crook than the rest of us.'

Steadman shook his head. 'Not on our radar, I'm afraid.'

'The crafty sod! I always thought it was an excellent wheeze.'

'Are you going to enlighten us?' asked Munro.

'The stamps, silly boy. He was no more a collector than you are a ballet dancer, DS Munro. He was a dealer, a smuggler and above all, a money launderer. Some of those tacky little bits of paper were worth a fortune. The real collectors are obscenely rich, utterly ruthless and ask no questions. You want to check Sidley's trips abroad. You'll find some very odd destinations. I did hear he once smuggled a most valuable stamp out of a country by sticking it in his passport. They searched every last bit of him, but nobody thought to check his passport.'

Munro was scribbling away furiously.

'Interesting,' Steadman replied, 'but let us not get side-tracked. They were both murdered. It's our job to track down their killer. I may not know who was responsible yet, but I believe I know why they were killed.'

Pelham stifled a yawn. 'Do go on. Give me a nudge if I fall asleep.'

'We think Shuster may have been trying to buy or muscle his way into a business venture back in Helmsmouth. Something shady that would suit his credentials. We reckon Shuster and his solicitor visited several people who might be in the market to sell. We think he approached you.'

'Me?' Pelham's voice was too high. 'Whatever for? I'm retired now – a man of leisure, and pleasure – if I can find it.'

'According to our records you still own two massage parlours,' Munro added.

'That's my pension fund,' snapped Pelham. 'I am merely the landlord. All strictly above board and legit. Although I could arrange for one of my boys to give you a complimentary rub down after your next game of rugby. I presume you are a rugby player, sergeant.'

Munro's cheeks burned. He was appalled.

'Suit yourself,' Pelham continued. 'You never know, you might enjoy it.'

Steadman rapped the side of his chair. Robbie stirred.

'Mr Pelham, we are investigating a double murder. We need information, not complimentary massages. This is serious.'

'Nothing to do with me, duckie,' he said with a wave of his hand.

'No? Sidley looked after your business interests. His diary shows that you saw him recently. You knew Seth Shuster. You have a criminal record and despite the impressive performance, you are as hard as nails. How do I know you didn't kill both of them? You wouldn't want your pension fund compromised, would you?'

Pelham glared at Steadman.

'Sadly, a bullet in the head has not improved your manners. I don't deny I had dealings with Sidley, but killing has never been my style, besides, I haven't seen Shuster for – I don't know – years.'

There was just the slightest hesitation in his answer. Steadman pursed his lips.

'You're lying. I've interviewed you on numerous occasions – I can tell. You never could lie.'

Miles Pelham looked at Steadman. He felt that behind the dark glasses Steadman's blind eyes were staring right through him. He shuffled awkwardly in his seat.

'I need a drink.' He made his way to a dresser on the far wall and poured himself something out of a fancy decanter. 'All right, Shuster and Sidley did come to see me last week.'

Steadman breathed a sigh of relief. The gamble had paid off.

'When exactly?' he asked.

'I can't remember.' With that, Pelham opened the door and shouted, 'Stefan, come here a moment.'

A tall, thin young man with jet black hair entered.

'This is Stefan. He helps me around the house.'

And no doubt in other ways, thought Munro.

'Does Stefan have a surname?' asked Steadman.

'Radu, if you must know. Stefan, these gentlemen are from the police.' The young man froze. 'No, nothing to do with you,' Pelham reassured him. 'Can you recall when Seth Shuster and his solicitor visited us?'

'You mean the good-looking one that kept smiling at me?' Stefan answered. He had a strong accent that

Steadman couldn't place.

'If you say so,' said Pelham cattily.

'Sure, I can remember. It was Wednesday evening. He gave me a bottle of champagne.'

'How can you be so certain?' asked Steadman.

'There's a gameshow I always watch on Wednesday. It helps improve my English and the presenter is cute.'

'Thank you, Stefan. There, are you satisfied now, Inspector?'

'Not quite. What time did they leave?'

'About eleven, I got their coats,' Stefan replied.

'Who was driving?'

'The old guy.'

'What colour was his car?'

'Blue.'

'What make?'

Stefan shrugged. 'A Ford, I think.'

'Well, that's that,' Pelham interjected. 'I'm sorry I can't be of more help.'

'One other thing – have you got a boat?' asked Munro.

'A boat? Good grief, no. If it's stormy outside, I have to draw the curtains – dreadful *mal de mer.* This room has a wonderful view of the waves. You'll have to take my word for it, Inspector Steadman, or ask your sergeant.'

It was a nasty remark, spiteful and laced with malicious glee. Munro came very close to giving Pelham a slap.

'Now, I believe lunch is ready. Isn't that so, Stefan? Goodbye gents, don't hurry back.'

The two men walked slowly back to the car. Munro was seething. Steadman was lost in thought. Had Shuster and Sidley only visited once? Had they drunk the champagne? There was no point in going back. Doubtless Pelham and his friend were already busy concocting a pack of lies.

Robbie stopped at one of the bushes trimmed into the shape of a heart and cocked his leg. 'My sentiments exactly,' muttered Munro.

CHAPTER 19

Robbie curled himself up into a ball in the footwell as Steadman buckled himself in.

'Good to go, sir?'

Steadman gave a little nod. Munro glanced at his colleague and put his foot hard down on the accelerator. The Audi shot down the drive, spraying gravel in every direction.

'Do you think Pelham's our man?' asked Munro.

'Impossible to tell, Alan. My gut instinct says no, but there again you saw how easily he flipped from niceness itself to uncalled-for spite. Maybe Shuster and Sidley pushed him too far.'

'What about the champagne, sir?

'I suspect that was simply to impress. They probably took the same to each of the people on our list, though I doubt if it would have been appreciated by the Drapers.

We had better do some background checks on Pelham's chum, Stefan Radu.'

'I'll get immigration to check him out. He's probably here illegally,' suggested Munro.

'Perhaps,' Steadman replied. 'However, if he's living with Pelham he may well have landed on his feet and he's unlikely to do anything to rock the boat.'

'Unless, sir, doing Pelham's dirty work is the price he has to pay.'

'I think we both know, Alan, what sort of payment Pelham demands.'

Munro sniffed. 'I can imagine only too well, sir.'

The Audi purred along the road. Steadman could hear the intermittent flick and squeak of the wipers. It had started drizzling again.

'Where to now, Alan?'

'I thought we should go and see Madam Chu next. It's lunchtime and I don't half fancy a sweet and sour chicken with maybe a couple of spring rolls on the side.'

Steadman tried not to appear alarmed. Eating out using normal cutlery was challenging enough; attempting to eat rice with chopsticks would be a disaster.

★ ★ ★

Madam Chu's Palace occupied one of the old customs houses down by the docks. It had been a rather grand, austere building in its day. Now, it was like an elderly widow wearing too much makeup and jewellery. The Victorian sandstone facade was festooned with red and gold Chinese Lanterns. Huge ceramic pots of bamboo had been placed at regular intervals along the pavement and two enormous stone lions stood guarding the gilded portico leading through to the main doors of the restaurant and casino. A large neon sign flickering in the gloomy afternoon light ensured that no one was left in any doubt that they had arrived at Madam Chu's.

There were other doors too, more discreet. And windows on the upper floors, several with their curtains still tightly drawn.

'I presume she has a lot of staff living on the premises,' Munro speculated after describing the scene to Steadman. 'It still seems a lot of rooms to me. What do you think goes on behind the closed curtains, sir?'

'Nothing good, I'll warrant, Alan.'

Munro held the door open for Steadman and Robbie. The restaurant was vast and sumptuously decorated, but only partially lit. Plants and screens broke up the spaces between the tables, giving a feeling of intimacy. In the centre was a large ornamental pool where koi carp swam lazily round, occasionally breaking the surface for gasps of air. The only other people in the restaurant were a group of about a dozen noisy businessmen enjoying a liquid lunch.

'Very impressive,' remarked Munro.

Steadman nodded. It was several years since he had been here, yet he could still recall it vividly in his mind's eye.

A small Chinese waiter approached them.

'Sorry pal, we're no doing lunches today.' He had the broadest Scots accent Steadman had ever heard; it made his colleague sound like a BBC presenter. Munro's mouth fell open in a mixture of surprise and disappointment.

'Gotta problem wi' that, big fella?'

'No – it's just that I expected...' Munro stammered.

'Aye, ye thought I'd offer ye "flied lice". Listen pal, I'm frae Glasgow an' proud o' it.'

The two men eyeballed each other. It did not pay to cross Munro when he was hungry. A phone tinkled and the waiter turned to answer it.

'Right... Right... What table?... okey-dokey...' He put the phone down. 'Your lucky day it would seem. The boss says you can have lunch if you like.'

Munro's face broke into a huge smile and he clapped the waiter's back.

'Good man – I'm starving.'

The waiter gave him a withering look. 'Dinna push yer luck. Follow me.'

He led them through the maze of tables to one neatly laid for two by the fishpond.

'Let me take your coat,' he said to Steadman. 'Will the doggie be all right?'

'Thank you, he'll be fine,' Steadman replied.

'Make yourselves comfortable and I'll bring you some menus.'

Steadman was wary. Who had phoned the waiter? How did they know they were there? And why had they made an exception?

'Alan, could you escort me to the toilet? I need to wash my hands.'

Munro took his arm and guided him to the back of the restaurant.

'Not a word about the case,' Steadman hissed.

Munro looked puzzled. 'Why, sir?'

'We're being watched, and I suspect listened to. I'll bet it wasn't by chance we were taken to that particular table.'

The waiter returned carrying two menus. He handed one to Munro and was on the point of offering the other to Steadman.

'Nae point, I suppose,' he mumbled.

'I think I'm going to have the lunchtime special. What about you, sir?'

'Do they do scampi and chips?'

Munro was slightly taken aback. He flicked through the menu. 'Yes, no problem. Are you sure you don't want anything Chinese?'

'I might risk noodles and sauce in the privacy of my own flat. I wouldn't dare attempt such a feat in public.'

'Aah! Sorry sir, I didn't think about that.'

The waiter came back and took their order.

'And may I have a fork and knife?' Steadman added.

Munro's food smelled delicious. Steadman regretted not risking being more adventurous.

Halfway through the meal an elderly lady dressed in a beautiful Chinese silk dress hobbled past flanked by two stocky, unsmiling men. She hesitated by their table, cast a sharp glance at Steadman and Munro, then gave a small bow before walking towards the door, pausing only to have a word with the waiter. Munro raised an eyebrow and continued eating.

'Do you want a dessert, sir? I'm having a banana fritter.'

'Not for me. I think it's about time we made a move.'

Munro called the waiter over and produced his ID.

'We are police officers,' he said.

'I would never have guessed,' the waiter replied with more than a hint of sarcasm.

'We would like to speak with Madam Chu.'

'You've missed her. She gave you a wee nod on the way out.'

Munro let out an oath. 'When will she be back?'

'She didna say – late I expect. She hopes you enjoyed your meal and says tae tell you it was on the house.'

'At least that's something,' grumbled Munro.

Steadman, however, insisted on paying. He took out his wallet and carefully produced two twenty-pound notes, each with a corner neatly folded over to distinguish them from the tens.

'That ought to cover it,' he said. 'Please keep the change.'

★ ★ ★

The two men and Robbie made their way back to the car. Despite his enormous meal, Munro was in a foul humour. He told Steadman about the entourage that had passed by their table and how Madam Chu had stopped, looked at them and even bowed in their direction.

'I've been played for a fool,' he moaned.

'You're not the first, Alan, nor will you be the last.'

'What do you mean, sir?'

'There is no Madam Chu. It's all an act, a charade. I should have told you earlier. Her real name is Elsie Entwistle. She's from Chorley in Lancashire originally. That's why you couldn't find any police records. I'm surprised Sergeant Grimble didn't tell you.'

'My ignorance probably made his day. No wonder he was grinning like the Cheshire Cat when I said we were going to interview an old Chinese lady.'

'That's not been her only alias. For years she played at being a French madame and ran a high-end strip joint and brothel. When she was younger, she posed as a film star and conned goodness knows how many deluded wealthy older men. She's had a string of fake companies both here and abroad – oh, the list goes on. She knows me of old.' Steadman scratched his forehead but didn't elaborate. 'I wonder if I would have better luck going back by myself. I'll need to clear it with DCI Long.'

Munro gazed back at the building, more intrigued than ever to know what was going on behind the curtained windows.

A white van pulled up at the door. Written on the side in big letters was 'Helmsmouth Office Solutions' and a phone number. Underneath this, for no obvious reason, it read 'Vancouver Brisbane Sydney Singapore'.

A familiar shape emerged from the driver's door, a huge man with no neck.

'Now what's he doing here?' said Munro.

'Who?' asked Steadman.

'Phil the Shed, of all people, or Philip Aintree to give him his Sunday name.'

The man was well-known to the police. He was a thug, a criminal and a wheeler-dealer in everything from drugs to stolen goods.

'What's he up to, Alan?' asked Steadman, frustrated that he couldn't see for himself.

'His van says Helmsmouth Office Solutions, and in fairness it looks like he's delivering a load of paper. Do you think he's gone straight, sir?'

'Is there anything unusual in the sky?' replied Steadman with a derisory sniff.

Munro squinted up at the low clouds. 'What had you in mind?'

'I was wondering if there were any flying pigs. The last

thing Phil the Shed did that was straight was drawing a line with a ruler when he was at primary school.'

'Why do you think he has Vancouver Brisbane Sydney and Singapore written on his van?'

'Possibly cities where he has a criminal record,' Steadman replied with a shrug. 'Who knows?'

★ ★ ★

The inside of the car had misted up. Munro switched on the engine and turned the fan on to full blast, and slowly the windows cleared. He had just pulled out when something caught his eye in the rear-view mirror.

'That's him again!' he exclaimed.

'Who?' asked Steadman.

'Seth Shuster's double. Hold tight.'

Munro jerked the steering wheel hard and pulled up the handbrake. Steadman felt himself being pressed up against the window and grabbed hold of the edge of his seat. The Audi's back end slid round on the greasy road surface. Munro pressed his foot to the floor and with a screech of the tyres shot off in pursuit. But the man, whoever he was, had disappeared into the myriad of lanes and alleyways that surrounded the docks. They crawled up and down the tiny roads for what seemed like an age.

Munro slowed down several times, peering into cul-de-sacs and doorways.

'He could be anywhere,' he said with a sigh.

'Are you absolutely sure it was the same person, Alan?'

'Oh yes, no doubt about it, sir.'

CHAPTER 20

The Audi crawled along the modest row of terraced houses. Munro was looking for number 102. They were small houses, crammed together, and originally built to provide cheap accommodation for railway workers. Those workers had long since gone and, for a time, the street had fallen into disrepair. Now, with property prices rising, the area was becoming desirable, even gentrified. "Bijou residences for executive first-time buyers", the estate agents proclaimed. And they were right, for at either end of the street the houses were having their windows and doors replaced and painted in muted Farrow and Ball colours. In between the clapped-out old bangers were impractical four-wheel drives, BMWs, a Porsche and even a bright red Ferrari.

Nothing was parked outside 102. The paint was peeling, and the windows covered in condensation. It would appear that the Draper's protection racket had fallen on hard times, thought Munro.

'Here we are, sir,' he said as he helped Steadman out of the car.

Robbie followed and gave himself a good shake before looking up at Steadman as if to say, 'Where to now?'

Steadman sensed that Munro was still in a bad mood, no doubt smarting from being hoodwinked by Madam Chu.

'Do you mind if we walk up and down for a bit to let Robbie stretch his legs?' he asked. 'And you can tell me what the street looks like. The last time I was here it was fairly dilapidated.'

They walked and talked for no more than ten minutes; long enough for Munro to regain at least some of his usual sunny disposition.

He hammered on the door of number 102. A dog barked loudly.

'Bugger off, whoever you are!' shouted a voice from inside.

Munro bent down and lifted the flap of the letter box. 'Police! Open up!' he shouted back.

The door was eventually opened by a pasty-faced giant of a man, taller and broader than Munro, but with a surprisingly small head. On a tight leash at his side something related to a bull terrier was slavering and growling.

'For Christ's sake, I've been out of the nick for five

minutes and you heartless bastards are hounding me already,' the man, said scanning Munro's ID. 'Who's your quiet chum?'

'This is DI Steadman?'

The man looked Steadman up and down and turning to Munro said, 'I heard he was blind.'

'Blind, yes – deaf, no,' Steadman replied. 'I assume you are Wally Draper. It's your father we want to speak to.'

Wally's dog suddenly caught sight of Robbie, who had remained motionless at Steadman's side. The dog bared his teeth and made a lunge at Robbie's throat. Fortunately, Wally was stronger than the brute and yanked him back before giving him a kick, much to Munro's dismay.

'Where did you get a dog like that?' he asked.

'Tyson's a rescue dog.'

'As in rescued from a dodgy dog breeder up the Old Kent Road?' queried Munro.

'Don't know what you mean,' Wally replied.

No, you probably don't, thought Steadman, *you're not one of our brighter brethren.*

'I think it would be better for us all if you could put Tyson somewhere out of the way for the time being,' suggested Munro.

Wally dragged the protesting animal into the house. There was a loud crash, and the two men could hear him shouting, 'Stay in there, Tyson, and shut up.'

He came back and blocked the door. 'What's the old man meant to have done, then?'

'Hopefully, nothing. It's information we're after, that's all – at least for the moment,' said Steadman.

Wally glared at the two men, and with a frown, stood aside.

'You had better come in. Keep your voices down. The old man's not well. They let me out early to look after him.'

The small house smelt of death, dog and take-away food. It was grubby and very untidy. Dirty plates and cups lay on every available surface. A large TV was playing in one corner, but the sound had been turned right down. Four whisky glasses and an open bottle of cheap Scotch stood on a coffee table. Why four, Munro wondered?

A frail old man sat on the only available armchair. He was emaciated and gasping for breath. Gary Draper bore little resemblance to the photo of the grim-faced man in his police record. Clear plastic tubing wound around his neck and over his ears, trickling oxygen to his nose from a machine that thrummed and hissed at his feet.

Steadman recognised the sound of an oxygen concentrator; it didn't bring back pleasant memories. There was another sound in the room he couldn't place, a repetitive tapping and jangling. He turned his head from side to side, furrowing his brow.

'There's a budgie in a cage in the corner,' Munro explained.

Gary Draper opened his eyes just a crack and glanced at the two detectives, flicking his gaze from one man to the other, finally resting on Steadman.

'Good grief,' he said at last, 'Detective Inspector John Steadman – how the mighty have fallen. I barely recognised you. And you wouldn't recognise me if you could see me now. Cancer.' He almost spat the last word out. 'So far gone, they don't even know where it started. Who's the gorilla with you?'

'DS Alan Munro,' Steadman replied.

'A detective sergeant now – well, well. You've left it a bit late to pay me back, don't you think?' Draper chuckled, then started coughing. Wally slapped the old man's back.

'Thanks son – not quite so hard next time. So, why are you two here?'

'We're investigating the murders of Seth Shuster and Rupert Sidley,' Munro explained.

Gary Draper almost choked. He looked up at the two detectives and ran a thumb nail over his stubbly chin.

'I shouldn't be surprised – a right pair of greedy back-stabbers. It's amazing that Shuster has lasted so long considering how many people he has pissed off big time over the years. I thought he was in America. I wouldn't waste my time on either of them if I were you. Here, Wally, clear some space for these two gentlemen.' Reluctantly, Wally moved the dirty crockery off the sofa. 'That's a nice dog you've got there. What's his name?'

'Robbie,' Steadman replied snapping his fingers. Robbie obliged by spread-eagling himself at his feet.

'Look at that, Wally. That's how a dog should behave, not chew lumps out of the furniture like that wild beast you brought home.'

'He's a guard dog,' Wally protested. 'Just needs a bit of training, that's all.'

Munro interrupted them. 'Getting back to Shuster and Sidley...'

'Like I said, drop it. No one will miss them,' Gary wheezed.

'You know that's not how it works,' said Steadman. 'We believe it may have been a professional job. We can't let them get away with it, otherwise there will be no end to their killings.'

'Maybe,' the old man conceded reluctantly.

'Has either Shuster or Sidley approached you recently?' Steadman asked.

'Why would they?'

'We think Shuster was trying to buy himself back into the market.'

'I have nothing left to sell.'

Wally was starting to get restless. He kept shooting furtive glances at the sideboard. Munro followed his gaze. There was a fruit bowl containing some grapes covered in mould. Propped up against it was a large brown manila envelope. The writing looked familiar.

'Still offering protection to the vulnerable?' Steadman

queried. 'I thought that would be worth something. Or maybe you were planning for Wally to take it over.'

'Leave him out of it. He's done his time and he has more sense than his father. Wally's going to get a proper job – aren't you son?'

Wally grinned. Munro noticed that his front teeth were missing and wondered just who on earth would employ him.

'Besides,' the old man continued, 'my other two lads are on the inside, as I'm sure you already know.'

'You met with Rupert Sidley recently,' Munro challenged him.

'Yeah – to write my will. His little bit of fluff, Miss Devine I think you call her, can vouch for me.'

'What about Phil the Shed? Does he still work for you?' Steadman persisted.

Gary Draper opened a weary eye. 'Not for some time. He has his own business.'

'Yes, we saw his van.' Munro referred to his notebook. 'Here we are – "Helmsmouth Office Solutions". Is it legitimate?' he asked.

The old man laughed until he almost choked. 'How long have you known Phil the Shed, Inspector Steadman?'

'Over twenty years.'

'And has he ever done anything legitimate in that time?'

'Not that I'm aware of,' Steadman admitted.

'I think you have your answer, DS Munro.' Gary Draper

bent down and switched off the oxygen concentrator. 'I need a fag.'

Wally produced a cigarette and lit it for him, as the old man's hands were shaking so badly. He inhaled deeply and started coughing again. This time it seemed he would never stop.

Munro turned to Wally. 'Go and get your father a glass of water.'

The old man was bent double with his head in his hands. Munro saw his chance, darted over to the sideboard, and grabbed the envelope. He was still reading the contents when Wally returned.

'What the hell do you think you're doing? That's private, that is. He pushed his face into Munro's.

'Keep your shirt on, Wally. Go and tend to your father.'

'What is it, Alan?' asked Steadman.

'Some sort of legal document between Seth Shuster and Mr Draper senior, signing over the rights to his so-called Security and Surveillance Services.'

Wally was muttering furiously. At least his father had stopped coughing, although he now seemed to be making a peculiar rasping noise. Steadman tilted his head – no, it wasn't coming from the old man. Of course not, Steadman suddenly realised, it was coming from the budgie, who was cheerfully scraping its beak on a cuttlefish bone. It was the only sound in the room as Munro finished reading the document.

'It's signed and dated last week. I thought you said you

hadn't seen Shuster recently?' said Munro angrily.

'I never said anything of the kind, sergeant. I chose not to answer the question.'

'You said...' Munro checked his notebook again. '"I have nothing left to sell".'

'And that's the truth. I had sold it already.'

'When were they here?' Steadman asked.

'Who said they were here?'

'That wouldn't be hard to prove,' Munro replied. 'There are four dirty whisky glasses and a half-empty bottle on the table. I'm sure their fingerprints are all over two of the glasses.'

Wally made to grab them, but Munro had his collar in a vice-like grasp.

'I'm waiting for an answer, Mr Draper,' Steadman said in a quiet voice.

'Tuesday and Friday of last week,' the old man replied.

Steadman noticed his voice was getting weaker.

'And had they paid you?'

'Alas, no,' he said with his eyes closed. 'Which means, Inspector Steadman, we had no reason to kill them.'

Steadman weighed this up and nodded.

'Thank you – you've been most helpful.'

The old man smiled. 'I never thought I'd live to hear a copper saying that. I can die a happy man.'

CHAPTER 21

Seth Shuster looked at his watch and noticed there was a tiny speck of dirt on the glass. He picked it off with his nail and polished it until it gleamed. The watch said it was six forty-five, and he knew that if his Patek Philippe said that, then that was exactly what it was.

A bus rolled up outside the hotel and lazily honked its horn. Out of the window Seth could see several bleary-eyed people stumble aboard, some clearly nursing dreadful hangovers. He was aware he should have been with them. The bus had been sent by the liner to pick up the crew. He would walk. It was part of the plan. He wanted to be the last to embark.

★ ★ ★

The liner was enormous. Seth looked up at the towering decks shimmering in the sunlight. They seemed to go on for ever. His initial awe was soon replaced by the thought of endless possibilities. He smiled to himself and walked slowly up the covered gangway.

'You're late. Missed the bus, did you?' The man asking the questions was red in the face and flustered.

'Sorry, sir,' Seth replied. 'It's my first contract. I thought I would have one last walk on dry land. It was further than I had imagined.'

The man riffled hastily through the paperwork, stopping only to check the dates. He barely looked at the photo in the passport. 'We keep this,' he said putting the document to one side. 'The first thing you'll have to learn as a new hire, Henshaw, is crew discipline. An order is an order. If you're told to get on a bus, you get on a bus. Understood?'

It was the first time anyone had called him by his newly acquired name. He would have to be careful.

'Yes, sir,' he replied. 'Got it.'

'Good – now, get out of my sight. This gentleman here will take you to your cabin and get you kitted out.'

An officer with a clipboard appeared from nowhere.

'Gregory Henshaw?'

'That's me,' Seth replied. He quite liked the name; it wouldn't be too hard to get used to.

He followed the man into the bowels of the ship. Seth was like a rat in a maze, sniffing at every turn and every corner, noting the numbers of the decks, the steps and the passageways. Never let yourself get trapped, he reminded himself.

The constant thrum of the engines was getting more noticeable, as was the whiff of diesel. The cabin was tiny, airless and windowless. There was a small desk, a wardrobe, a mirror and a doll-sized bathroom with a shower and toilet.

'You sleep on this,' said the officer, putting down his clipboard and unfolding a narrow bed from the wall. 'It's called a flip-flop. After a couple of nights you won't want to sleep on anything else.'

Seth was not convinced. He noticed there was another flip-flop clipped to the opposite wall. 'Am I sharing the cabin?' he asked.

'Oh, my apologies, Henshaw – were you booked into a suite with a sea view?' came the sarcastic reply. 'You were meant to be, but he hasn't turned up. Bloody casino staff – you can never trust them.'

Seth smiled. No, you never can, he mused.

'Right, you have to report to the Food and Beverage Manager in twenty minutes in the restaurant on deck three. That's your first test of initiative. There's the map.' He pointed to a plan of the liner pinned to the wall. 'Don't get lost.'

'I'll try not to,' Seth replied. He scanned the diagram and reckoned he could have found his way there blindfolded.

The Food and Beverage Manager was an older woman. She had seen it all, done it all and was now, frankly bored with it all. She gazed wearily around her assembled staff. There were old faces and new faces. She paused at Seth, her latest recruit, and took an instant dislike to him.

Seth was fitted with a uniform, given a perfunctory tour of the liner and had the law laid down to him. Certain areas were strictly off limits, especially the passenger cabins. Exceptions were rare and had to be authorised. No hanging around in the guest areas. Mix with the guests and be friendly, nothing more. Be warned there are security cameras everywhere. And so it went on – there were two crew bars, one for smokers, and a café, and a recreation area... Seth was getting restless.

A man in a tuxedo burst into the meeting.

'Sorry to interrupt,' he said. 'Staffing crisis.'

Seth's ears pricked up. One man's crisis was another man's opportunity.

'What is it this time? I don't think I've ever been on a trip with you when there hasn't been a crisis in the casino.'

'I know, I know, and I apologise. This time three have not turned up and I'm desperate. Could you spare two or one, even? I don't suppose any of you have any casino experience?' he said turning to the assembled staff.

Seth's was the only hand raised.

The Food and Beverage Manager gave Shuster a contemptuous look. If she could have chosen one member of her team to lose, it would have been him. There was something about him she didn't trust.

'OK, you can take him,' she said.

'You're an angel and a life-saver,' he replied blowing her a kiss. Turning to Seth, he continued, 'Follow me, young man.'

The casino manager was a short, tubby man with slicked back wavy hair and a pencil moustache. He was pale and twitchy, like a creature of the night caught in daylight.

'I'm Mr Bagshott – and you are?'

'Gregory Henshaw, sir.'

'Very good, very good,' he replied rubbing his hands. 'Got a bit of experience working in a casino, have you?'

'Yes, sir. I've worked in several of the big London casinos.'

'Why didn't you apply for a casino job? It pays better than bar staff.'

Seth had anticipated the question and flashed Mr Bagshott a smile. 'I only applied at the last minute – bar staff was all that was left.'

The carpet underfoot was thicker now, the walls illuminated with discrete uplighters and decorated with modern abstract paintings. Mr Bagshott rubbed his hands again. 'Almost there,' he said.

Seth could hear the tinkling and chiming of the slot machines. They turned a final bend. Even Seth was amazed at how many machines there were. Row upon row of flashing lights twisted and weaved in a vast glittering cavern. Interspersed with the slot machines were several card tables and, in the centre, two roulette wheels. It was a garish temple to greed and desperation. Mr Bagshott gleamed with pride, and Seth felt instantly at home.

'Strictly out of bounds for all the crew, Gregory, except the chosen few,' he enthused clapping Seth's back. 'Now tell me, what games are you familiar with?'

Seth reeled off a list. 'Blackjack, baccarat, the usual poker games – Texas Hold'em, Three Card, Let It Ride, Caribbean Stud... I've also worked as a croupier,' he added nodding at the two roulette tables.

'Impressive,' said Mr Bagshott. There was a note of uncertainty in his voice. 'Sit there.' He pointed to one of the dealer's seats. 'Talk me through a game.'

Seth was slick and smooth. He knew all the jargon. He shuffled, cut, and dealt with lightning dexterity.

'Slow down a bit,' said Mr Bagshott. He reached out a hand and grabbed Seth's wrist. 'Deal at that speed and they will think you're cheating them.' The watch caught his eye. 'Is that genuine?'

Seth gave him another enormous smile.

'If it is, they will definitely know you are cheating them. Don't wear it when you're working in the casino. Get yourself a cheap watch from duty-free – you'll even get staff discount. Let me see how you are on the roulette table.'

Seth spun the wheel and sent the ball rolling while Mr Bagshott placed ever more complicated bets. Seth never faltered.

'You start tonight. Be here at seven thirty. Here is a set

of house rules. I expect you to know them off by heart by this evening. Any questions?'

'Are there any high stakes tables?'

Mr Bagshott flicked a glance at a padded door behind one of the roulette tables.

'If there are enough clients who want to play a high stakes game, I may arrange it. Sometimes the guests in the luxury suites will ask me to sort something out for them in their cabins. They're not really the high rollers of Vegas or Monte Carlo, but certainly people who don't lose sleep over losing a few thousand. Have you worked with high rollers?'

'Yes, in London. Mainly Asians.'

'Did you make a lot in tips?

Seth grimaced. 'Hardly a bean. I guess that's why they're so rich,' he replied with a sardonic smile.

Seth spent the rest of the day exploring the liner. It was vast. Below deck it was extremely easy to get lost and disoriented. He poked his nose in all the nooks and crannies. There were a lot of security cameras. Their positions were, however, entirely predictable. It didn't take him long to work out how to move around without being observed. He was only stopped twice in his exploration, and both times his smile saved him.

'Sorry – first day on board and completely lost.'

By the afternoon, all the guests had embarked. They were noisy and excited. A full emergency drill was held.

The old hands dutifully made their way to their muster stations, picking up stray passengers on the way. A safety video played. The Captain's face beamed reassurance. It was the only time Seth saw him on the entire voyage. The exercise was completed, and with much clamour and celebration they set sail.

He did as he was told and bought a cheap watch in the duty-free shop. The Patek Philippe remained in his inside pocket.

The casino was busier than he had imagined. In the early evening, middle-aged and elderly ladies trooped in to play the slot machines. Usually they were in groups of twos or threes, occasionally accompanied by a husband who had seen better days. The ladies didn't appear to derive much pleasure from the activity, even on the rare occasions when they won. It was simply a way of passing an hour or two; spend some money, dress up and pretend to be glamorous. Seth passed among them, smiling, giving a word of encouragement, congratulating them on their wins and commiserating with their losses.

A little later in the evening, the clientele changed. There were young men out to impress their lady friends with their gambling prowess. Poor suckers, thought Seth. Two older croupiers guarded their roulette wheels. This suited Seth. He was much happier at the card tables. He dealt – they lost, they won, they lost again.

Mr Bagshott wandered among the guests, keeping a watchful eye on everything that was going on. He took particular notice of Seth. *He's a natural*, he said to himself, and once more rubbed his hands.

It was now late. The elderly ladies had almost all left, dragging their husbands from the bar. Only a few hardened veterans continued to feed the slot machines. The roulette wheels were still spinning. Seth noticed a few anxious faces as the piles of chips disappeared. They would be back tomorrow, he thought. Some people never learn.

Two men entered the casino and immediately caught Seth's eye. He reckoned they must be in their fifties, sixty at most. The taller of the two was heavily built with thinning hair and wore dark glasses. The shorter man was dressed immaculately. He took in the surroundings with an air of superiority. Raising an elegant hand to cover his mouth, he whispered something to his companion. Seth noticed the large diamond ring on his little finger. *My type of people*, he mused as he drifted towards them.

Somebody tugged at his sleeve. 'Be careful,' hissed Mr Bagshott.

Seth ignored him. 'A game, gentlemen?' he asked. 'My table is over here – a little quieter.'

The shorter man nodded, and Seth led the way.

A waitress materialised from out of the shadows. 'What can I get you?'

'Two bourbons.' The big man had a strong American accent. 'Wait – what's your name son?'

'Gregory, sir.'

'And something for our new friend, Gregory. What's it to be, son?'

'Just a mineral water.'

The big man waggled a finger and looked at his companion.

'When you're playing with us, you drink with us,' said the smaller man.

Mr Bagshott was hovering nervously in the background. He gave a curt nod.

'Very good,' said Seth, 'I'll have a bourbon as well.'

They chose a game. Seth shuffled and dealt. All the time he watched the two men closely. The bigger man was loud and quarrelsome. The smaller one, also American, was much quieter, interrupting the flow of cards with only the odd dry comment. It was clear he was in charge.

After a few hands, Seth noticed a change in play. They were signing to one another. It was subtle but unmistakable. Seth let them win. The big man was gloating. He made one barbed comment too many for Seth. Over the next hour, Seth cleaned him out. The smaller man's eyes twinkled. He had neither won nor lost.

'Son of a bitch!' the big man exclaimed. 'You are one lucky bastard, Gregory.'

'No, he's not,' said the smaller man in a soft voice. 'He just cheats better than you do. I don't quite know how, but he's good, aren't you, Gregory? If that's your real name.'

Seth gave the man a huge grin.

'Let my companion win a little of his money back, otherwise he gets indigestion and can't sleep,' he continued.

So Seth let him win back some of his losses. The smaller man's eyes were fixed on Seth's hands as he shuffled and dealt. He had known plenty of cardsharps in his time. This one was in a league of his own, he thought.

'What's the name of your pit boss?' he asked.

'Mr Bagshott,' Seth replied, 'although he prefers to be called casino manager.'

The small man signalled to Mr Bagshott, who was hovering nearby.

'I'm wanting to organise a private game tomorrow night in my suite. I would like to borrow young Gregory.'

There was no need for Mr Bagshott to ask which suite. As casino manager he had been given details of all the VIPs. In his pocket was a list of names and photographs which he had duly committed to memory. Theirs was the most expensive suite on the liner.

'Of course, Mr Kent. What time would you like Mr Henshaw?'

'Better make it a bit earlier if the old boy is going to play,' suggested the big man.

His companion agreed. 'Let's say nine o'clock.'

'I will arrange everything, gentlemen. Leave it with me.'

Mr Bagshott rubbed his hands together so vigorously Seth was surprised they didn't catch fire.

CHAPTER 22

It had been a long day for Steadman. By the time Munro dropped him back at his flat, he was completely exhausted. He trudged wearily up the stairs behind Robbie and let himself in.

'You look awful, dad. Let me take your coat. Tea? Coffee? Or Something stronger?' asked Ben.

'I'm fine, really. I just don't have the same stamina, that's all. A mug of tea would be splendid. How's your day been?'

Ben put the kettle on. 'I've been to see Linda and Dominic. They never change. Linda's very worried about you and made me promise to spoil you while I'm here.'

'I hope that doesn't mean trying to get me drunk every night,' Steadman replied.

The doorbell rang – TW in Morse code again.

'That will be Tim come to take Robbie out. Can you let him in, Ben?'

'What do you reckon – boy soprano or basso profundo? Fancy a small bet?'

Steadman raised an eyebrow. 'You've been in Australia too long. Go and answer the door.'

A gravelly-voiced Tim asked if Robbie was ready for his walk. Damn, thought Steadman, I could have made some money there, before realising he would only be winning his own cash back. Tim was not his usual chatty self.

'What's up?' Steadman asked.

'Dr Yorke has given me triple detention,' he growled.

'That's impressive. I don't think even Ben at his most rebellious ever managed more than a double. What on earth did you do to receive such a lengthy sentence?'

'First, I forgot my homework. Then I didn't understand it, so I got it all wrong. I tried to explain, but he kept interrupting me and I lost it. He may be a doctor of physics but he's a git and a crap teacher.'

'Did you say that to him?'

Tim nodded. 'Yeah – and a few other things.'

'Nice one, Tim – good on you!' said Ben.

'I dunno know about that. I wish DS Munro was my teacher.'

'After this case is over, I'll ask him to give you a few lessons,' suggested Steadman.

Tim brightened up. 'Would you? That would be cool. Come on Robbie – let's go.'

Ben shook his head as Tim headed out through the

door. 'Poor lad, I know how he feels. I never got on at school. I think I learnt more after I was kicked out. And to add to my cultural education, Dominic has asked me to an art exhibition tonight – Helmsmouth College of Art Winter Fair. Do you fancy joining us?'

Steadman was slightly bemused. 'Without stating the blindingly obvious, Ben, and I choose my words carefully, an art exhibition would be wasted on me.'

'Ah, that's where you're wrong, dad. There's free wine and cheese.'

'Not even remotely tempted. No, I'm going to stay at home and think. Are you hungry?'

'A stupid question that almost trumps me asking you to an art show. I'm always hungry. And as I have promised Linda that I'll try to fatten you up, I've brought in some provisions. Go and chill, while I rustle us up some grub.'

Touching the furniture lightly, Steadman made his way across the living room, found the radio, and switched it on just in time to catch the tail end of the local news.

"Police are continuing their investigations into the two bodies washed up on Helmsmouth's eastern beach. A spokesman stated that they are following new leads and hope to make an arrest very soon."

It was a stock response with no meaning, and annoyed Steadman intensely. He wondered who had authorised the statement – Crouchley maybe? Or perhaps the new Divisional Superintendent?

"And now an update on the weather. The dismal conditions

are set to continue for the next five days due to the persistent Atlantic low."

The voice was as miserable as the forecast.

"However, I hope to bring you a warmer, drier spell next week with even a little sunshine."

The announcer was suddenly upbeat and cheerful. It was as though the bad weather was no fault of his, but he was personally responsible for the improving conditions. Steadman got even more annoyed. 'What a git – just like Tim's teacher,' he said under his breath as he snapped the radio off. Only then did he appreciate that he, like Ben, was ravenous.

A delicious aroma drifted in from the kitchen. Steadman sniffed. It was unmistakable: bacon sizzling in a pan.

'What are you cooking, Ben?'

'A full English all-day breakfast. They do good breakfasts in Australia, but sadly not a decent full English. Do you have any brown sauce?'

It may not have been what Steadman would have chosen but it was tasty, and he enjoyed chatting with Ben. There were even a couple of sausages left over for Robbie and Tim when they returned from their walk.

'Any progress with the case, dad?'

Steadman drummed his fingers on the table.

'Dead ends and loose ends,' he said distractedly.

Ben recognised the signs. His father didn't want to talk.

'I'll tidy up, then I'd better be going. Dominic likes to arrive at exhibitions early, before anyone else snaps up the only talent.'

Great as it was to have Ben back, Steadman welcomed the silence. He made his way to the bedroom, Robbie padding by his side, and changed into more comfortable clothes.

'Well, Robbie, what is it going to be tonight? Let's start with some Bach. The French Suite number two, I think,' he said lifting the lid of the piano. Robbie stretched himself at his feet with his head just touching Steadman's left ankle, reassuringly close but not in the way.

The music was slow, the harmonies perfect, the twists and turns of the melody almost predictable. Steadman knew the piece so well he could play it and let his thoughts wander without hindrance.

Captain Perkin and his dog – did he really know anything, or was he simply playing with DS Fairfax? Henry Bridges-Treston – what would the Divisional Superintendent Olivia Campbell think if she found out he had been raking about in her past? An expensive boat and equally expensive hobbies – interesting, but was it of any relevance? The boat was called *The Poppy* – a girl's name perhaps, Steadman wondered, or the flower? *Papaver somniferum*, the opium poppy – the source of the drug and much human misery. Now there was a thought.

His fingers danced over the keyboard. The tempo had

changed, a little faster now. His thoughts chased the music. The irascible Miles Pelham and his enigmatic friend, Stefan; the dying Gary Draper and Wally, his violent son; the elusive Madam Chu, in reality Elsie Entwistle; a most dangerous chameleon, a criminal empress. She too had met Sidley recently, that was for sure, but had she also met Seth Shuster? 'I need to speak with her,' Steadman muttered to himself. 'But I'll have to be more careful this time.'

The Bach had ended. Without thinking, he was now playing some jazz – slow, bluesy, late night, and entirely improvised.

Philip Aintree, better known as Phil the Shed – a man with a van and a criminal record as long as his arm. Had he really gone straight, and if not, what was he up to?

And, of course, there was Sam Griffiths. He had hoped she might call by this evening. Feeling a little guilty, he admitted to himself that was probably the real reason he didn't want to go with Ben to the exhibition.

His watch told him it was nine thirty. With a sigh, he resigned himself to the fact that she wouldn't be calling this evening.

'An early night, I think, Robbie,' he said closing the lid of the piano.

They made their way downstairs and into the small garden at the back of the café. A fine drizzle was still falling.

No point in staying up, he thought. Doubtless Ben and Dominic would, by this time, be putting the world to rights over a couple of pints.

* * *

Linda had encouraged him to listen to audible books. It seemed like a good idea. Some of the books were excellent and well read, but he was not enjoying Linda's latest choice, a complicated tale of modern slavery. His eyelids felt heavy and his concentration was starting to slip. He switched off the machine, turned over and felt himself drifting off...

It was very dark, and he was shivering. The binoculars felt cold in his hands. Lifting his head above the barnacle-encrusted groyne, he scanned the shoreline. Sparkles of phosphorescence marked where the waves were lapping the shore. Was there another light a little way further out? Steadman couldn't be sure; it was very faint and bobbing. His eyes started to water. He let the binoculars drop and rubbed his eyes with the back of his hands. No, there was definitely a light and it was getting bigger. He could now hear a small outboard motor.

And there was another noise. Steadman turned his head and saw a van park on the edge of the shingle. It was pointing out to sea. The headlights flashed twice. He dropped down behind the groyne. The clouds parted and the whole scene was illuminated by cold, blue moonlight.

The van was white and there was writing on the side. With his binoculars, Steadman could make out the words, 'Vancouver Brisbane Sydney Singapore'. A large man with no neck heaved himself out of the van and crunched his way to the water's edge.

The small boat had beached on the shingle. A man, much slighter in build than the van driver, stood up, raised an acknowledging hand and beckoned the driver to join him. Between them they lifted another individual to their feet. Steadman could not be sure, but it was probably a woman with short hair. Whoever it was appeared to be either drugged or drunk. For a brief moment a flashlight lit up her face as her head lolled back. She was gagged and her hands were bound behind her back. Steadman didn't recognise either the woman or the man in the boat. There was, however, no mistaking the bulk of Phil the Shed. He hoisted the woman over his shoulder. A small package passed between the two men.

Steadman ducked down as Phil the Shed made his way up the shingle beach. He heard the van doors slam. When he looked up again there was no sign of either the van or the boat.

In an instant, the groyne with its barnacles and saltwater tang was replaced by a hedge. Steadman parted the branches. In the early morning light, he saw the van parked on an immaculate gravel drive outside a pink villa. The side of the van had opened like a market stall. Inside it was bright. Shelves were full of watches, handbags, jewellery, and perfume. Miles Pelham was nonchalantly picking through the goods.

'I've got something more interesting round the back,' said Phil.

The two men disappeared from Steadman's view. He could hear Miles exclaim, 'Not my scene! You should know I've no use for young women.'

Steadman shut his eyes. Raised voices brought him to his senses. He blinked and wound down the car window. He was parked in a terraced street just opposite number 102. He could see the van again. Phil the Shed and a younger Gary Draper were standing about an inch apart. Draper was gesticulating wildly.

'Wally doesn't need a plaything,' he shouted. 'God knows what sort of game you're playing. I employ you for your brawn not your brain. Now get lost.'

With a jolt the scene shifted again.

'Do you think I could use her, Inspector Steadman?' asked Madam Chu. 'She's a bit older, but pretty enough, don't you think?'

Steadman had difficulty in focusing. The room was small and crowded and smelt strongly of stale incense. A body-shaped bundle lay beside Madam Chu. Behind her, and lining the walls were at least two dozen Chinese waiters all jeering and laughing at him. He felt dreadfully sick.

'Let her speak,' he demanded.

Madam Chu propped up the limp body and undid

the gag. Steadman stared at the woman. Her hair was dishevelled, and she had been crying. He felt sure he knew her but couldn't place the face. She looked back at him with pleading eyes.

'I thought you were meant to be protecting me, John Steadman,' she said in a soft Welsh accent, her voice almost breaking.

'Sam Griffiths!' he shouted. 'What are you doing here?'

Steadman woke with a start. He sat bolt upright, his heart racing and sweat pouring down his face.

The laughter stopped. Ben knocked lightly on his bedroom door.

'Are you all right, dad? I heard you shouting. Are you alone? Can I come in?'

Ben didn't wait for an answer.

The nightmare was fading fast, like mist on a summer's morning. The sound of Sam's voice was still ringing in Steadman's ears.

'A bad dream, that's all,' said Steadman. 'I thought I heard laughter.'

'Tim came over to walk the dog. I was telling him about my exploits at school. We're just having a bite to eat. Do you fancy a *pain au chocolat* and some coffee?'

Steadman nodded. He was still trying to capture his dream. It was all jumbled – a boat, a van and Sam's voice were all he could recall.

'I need a shower first, then I'll join you.'

By the time he had finished, Marco had brought up fresh coffee and a further supply of pastries. Tim returned with Robbie.

'Do you really think Dr Yorke will fall for it, Ben?' he asked in a squeaky voice.

'No!' said Steadman firmly. 'Do not attempt anything my son has been suggesting under any circumstances. Ben, I am shocked at you.'

Ben put a finger to his lips and winked at Tim.

'You mustn't encourage the boy, Ben,' said Steadman after Tim had left.

'It's only a bit of fun,' Ben protested. 'What are your plans for the day, dad?'

The phone rang before Steadman could reply. Ben answered.

'Yes, I'll tell him... That was Sergeant Grimble. There's a pow-wow at ten in the Eyesore. Dr Rufus will pick you up in half an hour.'

'What about you, Ben? What are you going to do?'

'Dominic liked the work of one of the students at last night's exhibition. We're going to visit his studio later today.'

CHAPTER 23

The rain had stopped. Even so, there was still a dampness in the air. Steadman and Robbie huddled in the doorway. It was cold and, in his haste, Steadman had forgotten his scarf. He turned up the collar of his coat and listened intently for the familiar rattle of Frank's old Volvo.

'Good grief, John. What are you doing standing outside?' Dr Rufus chided him. 'If I remember rightly, you claimed you had a caught a chill after loitering on the beach last Sunday.'

Was it only last Sunday, thought Steadman? 'Ah – that got better,' he replied. 'It must have been those lozenges that you forgot to buy me.'

'Placebo by proxy, I call it,' said Dr Rufus as he ushered his friend into the car.

'How was Southampton and your corpse in the freezer?'

'Southampton, from the little I saw of it, was as dismal as Helmsmouth. The post-mortem proved a bit of a challenge. He wasn't fully thawed out when I arrived. A bit like a frozen supermarket turkey – the breast and thighs were soft, but the giblets were rock hard.'

Steadman winced at the analogy. 'You have such a way with words, Frank.'

'The cause of death was obvious,' Dr Rufus continued unabashed. 'He had been strangled from behind – classic fractures to the hyoid bone.'

'Isn't that the little horseshoe-shaped bone that sits a bit below the jaw?' asked Steadman.

'That's it,' Dr Rufus replied. 'You get a bonus point if you can tell me why it is unique.'

Steadman thought for a moment. 'I believe the hyoid is the only bone not attached to any other bone.'

'Correct. I'm pleased to note there is at least one worthwhile piece of information in amongst all the useless bits you collect.'

'Were there any signs of a struggle?'

'No – he was probably drugged to the eyeballs. I've sent samples for toxicology. I'm not holding my breath. After all this time, even in a freezer, we may find nothing.'

'Have you any idea how long ago he died, Frank?'

'Not directly from the post-mortem. The stomach contents, when they eventually defrosted, showed he had very recently consumed a large Turkish meal. According to the local police, there was only one Turkish restaurant in the vicinity. It opened eleven years ago and shut down three years later.'

'What about the warehouse?' Steadman asked.

'It was abandoned just over ten years ago.'

'So our corpse had been there for between eight and ten years,' Steadman concluded. 'Has the body been identified?'

'Not yet. We have plenty of DNA, but that takes some time to analyse. Because of the freezing and desiccation, the first lot of fingerprints weren't satisfactory. They've been repeated.'

Steadman was trying hard to visualise the scene. 'Was there anything else unusual in the post-mortem?'

'You mean apart from the fact that he was stark naked and stuffed in a freezer? Not really – he was fit, had been working out, his hair was dyed blonde, he had been on a sunbed... There was one little thing. His earlobe had been torn, probably just after he died. I presume he had been wearing an earring. Maybe it got caught when he was bundled into the freezer, only, the forensic team couldn't find any trace of an earring.'

'Suggesting that possibly our killer took it,' Steadman added. 'Did he have any other jewellery?'

'A flashy watch and a heavy gold chain,' Dr Rufus replied.

'But only an earring taken – now, that is interesting,' Steadman mused.

'Oh, the crime scene gets much better than that,' Dr

Rufus said with relish. 'Apart from traces of cocaine on the table, everywhere had been wiped clean of prints except for one. On the inside of the lid of the chest freezer there was a single clear handprint.'

'And this print didn't belong to the body in the freezer?' Steadman queried.

'No,' replied Dr Rufus. 'It belonged to Seth Shuster.'

★ ★ ★

There was nowhere to park in front of the Eyesore. Dr Rufus edged the Volvo into the last remaining space in the car park at the rear of the building.

'I'll get the door for you, John. There's not much room.'

Steadman and Robbie squeezed out of the car.

'Here, let me take your arm. There are loads of potholes and I don't want to have to pick you up if you trip. My back is not as good as it used to be.'

They reached the front of the building without mishap. Steadman was back on familiar territory. With Robbie leading the way, he climbed the short flight of steps and made his way in. Sergeant Grimble had a doggie biscuit ready in his hand.

'How is Robbie today, and are you going to stay with your Uncle Bertie?'

Steadman knew there was little point in arguing and undid the dog's harness.

'So, they found Seth Shuster's handprint on the inside of the freezer,' Grimble continued as he slipped Robbie the treat.

'How did you find that out?' exclaimed Dr Rufus.

'I heard it through the grapefruit.'

Dr Rufus frowned. 'I think you mean grapevine.'

'No – definitely grapefruit. Kim Ho was in the canteen having breakfast with a colleague and I overheard the conversation. I distinctly remember she was eating grapefruit.' Grimble glanced at the clock. 'I think you had better be going up. You are the last to arrive.'

The conference room was not as crowded as last time. DCI Long and Sam Griffiths were standing at the front chatting. Dr Rufus guided Steadman to a seat beside Fiona Fairfax and Alan Munro. Steadman could hear Cleo Osborne and Will Lofthouse, the two detective constables, sharing a joke. Behind them, and with a surly expression on his face, sat Inspector Crouchley.

'Let's make a start,' said DCI Long, 'we have a lot to get through. We'll begin with Dr Sam Griffiths, who has been doing a detailed analysis of Seth Shuster's case files.'

'More bleeding psychobabble,' muttered Inspector Crouchley in a voice just loud enough for everyone, including Sam, to hear.

'Thank you, DCI Long. In preparing my victim report, I have endeavoured to keep things simple. However, if there is anything you don't understand, Inspector

Crouchley, please feel free to ask.' A faint smile flicked over her face. Crouchley, on the other hand, turned puce.

Sam sped quickly over Shuster's early life. His mother, Claudine Turner, had been abusing drugs from an early age and walking the streets by the time she was sixteen, probably encouraged by Adelina Monke, her own mother. The aunt and uncle had given no support. Joshua Reynolds had a record of violent behaviour even as a juvenile, and Clara Drinsdale, from what Sam could glean, was of limited intellect. From the time of his birth, Adelina Monke had been Shuster's main carer. Sam had found nothing to support the mythical American airman, his alleged father.

'What I can't understand,' said Steadman, 'is why she didn't have a termination.'

'Claudine Turner believed she couldn't get pregnant. When she discovered that she was, she was already too far gone,' Sam replied.

'What did I tell you? Born bad,' Crouchley interrupted.

Sam turned on him. 'Perhaps, but that's not to say he didn't suffer dreadful childhood trauma. Adelina provided an extremely basic upbringing, and certainly no love. She taught him only what she knew – greed and cruelty.'

Crouchley harrumphed and folded his arms. Sam continued, recounting Shuster's first and subsequent brushes with the law. And as she spoke Steadman was transported back over the years. He could hear the interviews, recall details that had long been forgotten and could visualise the youth as he turned into a handsome, and at times, charming, young man.

Sam had uncovered an early psychological assessment which included an IQ score that put Shuster in the top five percent of the population.

'Which meant,' Sam continued, 'that he could outwit most people he encountered, an attribute that made him unpopular. Not that this appeared to bother him. There is no record of him ever having any friends. He only got close to others in order to manipulate or use them like pawns before ruthlessly discarding them, the one exception being his grandmother, Adelina Monke.'

Steadman nodded. He had come to much the same conclusions.

'In psychological terms, forgive me Inspector Crouchley, Shuster had typical features of an antisocial personality disorder, showing many of the traits of a psychopath.'

'Can we infer he was capable of murder?' asked DCI Long.

'Of murder, assault, robbery – you name it. All without a shred of remorse,' Sam responded.

Silence descended on the room like a pall.

'I don't know about anyone else – I need a coffee,' Dr Rufus announced.

There was general agreement followed by a scraping of chairs and the clinking of crockery. Sam lightly touched Steadman's arm.

'How are you today, John?'

'I'm fine thanks. Can I ask you something? Why do you think Seth came back to Helmsmouth?'

'Part of a well-constructed plan, I would say, to get back into criminal activity. Weren't you and Alan Munro interviewing some possible business links yesterday?'

'I think we're about to hear all about it,' Steadman replied as DCI Long called the meeting back to order.

First up was DS Fairfax. She briefly recounted her meeting with Captain Perkin.

'Was he sober?' asked Dr Rufus.

'To begin with, at least,' Fairfax replied.

Steadman bit his thumbnail and frowned.

'Have you anything to add, John?' DCI Long asked.

Steadman was thinking about Superintendent Campbell's ex-husband, Henry Bridges-Treston, and what he had uncovered in the newspaper's archives. Should he say something? No, now was neither the time nor place. He shook his head.

'Have your officers uncovered anything, Inspector Crouchley?' DCI Long continued.

'We're working on it,' came the terse reply.

Munro blushed as he always did before he spoke in public. He fumbled with his notes and cleared his throat.

'Inspector Steadman and I visited three persons of interest yesterday, or at least we tried to,' he began. 'These had been identified by DCI Long from Rupert Sidley's diary and discussions with his secretary. All had recently

met with Sidley and also, we believe, with Seth Shuster.'
Once he got into his stride Munro spoke eloquently, even
managing to temper his Scottish accent.

As a child Steadman had always been able to think of
two things at the same time. Not just random thoughts
but two separate streams of consciousness. It had
made playing the piano easy. And now, without visual
distraction, he could hold three or even four flows of
thought in his head, weaving them, platting them,
unravelling them until they made sense, or in some
instances, no sense at all.

Munro's voice was soothing and as he spoke
Steadman could recall every word Miles Pelham had said.
Simultaneously, he brought to mind his past encounters
with the man; the lengthy, tedious interviews, the weaselly
words loaded with innuendo. And his bizarre dream of
last night... Had Miles Pelham ever had dealings with
Phil the Shed?

'Then he summoned his friend, Stefan Radu, who
confirmed both Sidley and Shuster had visited,' Munro
continued.

Stefan Radu – was he involved? No, thought Steadman,
it was all too trivial. Pelham wouldn't kill two people,
even with Radu's help, over a couple of massage parlours,
no matter how lucrative.

Munro had moved on to Madam Chu. Steadman
recalled the disastrous meeting he'd had with her all
those years ago, and his cheeks flushed. Munro's face

was burning too as he recounted how he had been hoodwinked by the old lady.

'Who should show up to deliver office supplies to Madam Chu's Palace?' Munro was in full flight now. 'None other than our old chum Philip Aintree.'

Steadman saw Aintree as in his dream, delivering, not office supplies, but a dazed Sam Griffiths. Although he knew it was not real, he still found it very disturbing.

'And as we left, I noticed Seth Shuster's double in the rear-view mirror,' said Munro. 'I gave chase, but I lost him.'

He will come to us when the time is right, mused Steadman. Still, it would be good to know who he was, although he believed he already knew.

'Finally, the Drapers,' Munro announced.

In an instant, Steadman was back inside the house with its stale smells, the chirruping budgie, and the constant thrum of Gary Draper's oxygen concentrator. A far cry from the belligerent man Steadman had arrested and interviewed on numerous occasions, a man who was no stranger to extreme violence, something his son, Wally, had inherited. Could the Drapers' meeting with Sidley and Shuster have got out of hand, and Wally lost his temper? It was a possibility, Steadman concluded. They would still need to dispose of the bodies. Steadman recalled his dream and immediately thought of Phil the Shed and his van. What was it that Gary Draper had said about Phil? – 'And has he ever done anything legitimate...'

Dr Rufus gave Steadman a nudge.

'Are you still with us?'

'Yes,' Steadman replied. 'I was just considering the alternatives.' It was one of his favourite phrases.

DCI Long rose to his feet.

'Before I ask Dr Rufus to give an update, I would like to open the floor to suggestions as to where the investigation should go from here.'

Steadman had made a list in his head. He held back, only too aware of the unusual role he played in the investigation.

DS Fairfax was the first to speak.

'I think one of our priorities should be to find Seth Shuster's double, sir. It can't be a coincidence that he keeps reappearing. He knows something.'

'Ah yes, the young doppelganger,' DCI Long said in a soft deep voice. 'Any ideas how we can flush him out? Anyone?'

There was a long silence. Eventually Steadman raised a hand.

'I've been thinking about that, sir. I believe I know how we can increase our chances of finding him. Is there still the large map of Helmsmouth in the room?'

All eyes turned to the map.

'Go on, John,' DCI Long encouraged him.

'Firstly, we need to consider Seth Shuster's movement. We know he went to visit Adelina Monke in The Oaks Care Home. Can someone put a mark on the map?'

Will Lofthouse was nearest and placed a large red pin on the site of the care home.

'We also know he visited the cobbler in Sainsbury's.'

Another pin went on the map.

'And finally, we know he bought flowers from the florist in Humboldt Street.'

A third pin went in, neatly marking out a triangle.

'Thanks to the work of DC Osborne, we know that Seth did not hire a car.'

'And he's not been using taxis,' Inspector Crouchley interjected. 'My men have circulated photos to all the taxi firms and drawn a blank.'

'So it is likely that Seth walked to all of these places.'

'How does that help us find his double?' Dr Rufus asked.

'Bear with me, Frank. We also know from Inspector Crouchley that Seth Shuster wasn't staying in a hotel, guest house or bed and breakfast. Where was he staying, then? Not with a friend. Sam, our forensic psychologist, assures us he had no friends. That leaves only family. We know he wasn't staying with Josh Reynolds and Clara Drinsdale…'

'Sorry to interrupt,' said Munro, 'I've just remembered something. Didn't Clara start to say something about Seth's family before her brother shut her up?'

'Indeed she did. If I correctly recall, Clara's exact words were, "And it wasn't to see his family either, unless he wanted to see his…" I believe she was about to refer to Seth Shuster's son.'

'His son!' exclaimed Crouchley. 'That sounds far-fetched even by your standards, Steadman.'

'I would welcome a better explanation if you have one. No, I'm certain that the double is his son, and that Seth Shuster was staying with him. I am also certain that it's within walking distance of the triangle marked out on the map. What we need is someone who lives in the area.'

'My flat is close by, sir,' said DC Cleo Osborne.

'Is it, now?' DCI Long remarked. 'How long have you lived there?'

'Almost three years, sir.'

'I don't suppose you recall ever seeing him?'

'No sir, but there again I wasn't looking. I know all the cafés, bars, and clubs in the area, the places someone of his age is likely to frequent. I could easily check them out.'

'Excellent,' DCI Long concluded. 'I will arrange for you to have some photographs and you can start this afternoon.'

'And if that fails,' added Steadman, 'I'll join you.'

'No disrespect, John,' said Dr Rufus with a puzzled expression, 'but how do you think that will help?'

'Bait,' Steadman replied.

'Bait? What do you mean?'

'Other than DS Fairfax's initial encounter with Seth's double outside the Eyesore, I have been present on every occasion. Obviously I can't be sure, but I also believe the man that was standing in the mortuary car park was the same person. I think he wants to speak with me.'

CHAPTER 24

Inspector Crouchley was having none of it. 'Seth Shuster never had a son, Steadman. For one thing he was as gay as a maypole.'

Sam Griffiths leapt to Steadman's defence. 'The records clearly state he was bisexual.'

Crouchley made a derisory grunt. 'Listen little lady, bisexual is just a term that gays use when they don't want to admit the sordid truth.'

Sam held her nerve. 'Did you learn that at your latest Equality and Diversity Training, Inspector Crouchley? I think I must have been on a different course.'

DCI Long rapped loudly on the desk, ignoring Crouchley's protestations. 'DC Osborne, you will start this afternoon asking around the area. John, we won't take you up on your offer yet. DS Fairfax and DS Munro, you will go back and re-interview Josh Reynolds and his half-sister, Clara Drinsdale. I'm sure you can think of a way of separating the two of them. Clara may feel more comfortable speaking with someone of her own sex. Now, what other avenues do we need to explore?'

Steadman waited, biting his tongue.

Munro was the first to speak. 'I suggest we probe the activities of Phil the Shed, sir.'

Steadman breathed a sigh of relief; it was exactly what he was thinking.

'I agree,' said DCI Long. 'DC Lofthouse, find out all you can about his business, Helmsmouth Office Solutions. I want to know where he's based, who his clients are, his bank details – the lot.'

'I'm on to it, sir,' replied the dreamy detective constable.

'And, Eric,' DCI Long continued, turning to Inspector Crouchley and deliberately addressing him in a familiar tone as the Inspector was still seething, 'could you put some men on to tail Phil the Shed? It will need to be round the clock and not in uniform.'

Crouchley brightened up. 'I would love to nail that particular bastard. I've been wanting to for years.'

'Quite so,' DCI Long replied tactfully. 'Will your men continue their hunt for the boat that dumped the two bodies?'

Should I mention *The Poppy*, thought Steadman? Yes? No? Maybe later perhaps, outside of the meeting, he decided.

'Is there anything else, before I ask Dr Rufus to present his latest findings?' DCI Long asked.

No one spoke. Steadman raised a hand.

'Yes, John – you have something to add?'

'Thank you, sir. I would like to go to back to Madam Chu's Palace, and I think it would be better if I went on my own, or at least without another police officer.'

Steadman could hear DCI Long sigh.

'I have known Madam Chu, or Elsie Entwistle to give the lady her real name, for years, as you know,' Steadman continued. 'She's as slippery as an eel and will, I suspect, avoid any attempt to be interviewed formally. I may have better luck by myself.'

'How and when were you proposing to go?'

'I thought I would take my son, Ben, there for an evening meal either tonight or tomorrow night.'

DCI Long sighed again. He knew how headstrong Steadman could be, and even though he had been brought in to help with the investigation, he was not obliged to obey commands in the same way as other officers.

'Don't you think you may be taking an awful risk, John? God alone knows what goes on in that den of iniquity.'

Steadman shrugged and grinned broadly. Sam thought he suddenly looked ten years younger and very much like his son.

'What's life without a few risks, sir?'

DCI Long frowned. 'I'm not sure. What do you think, ma'am?'

The smile evaporated from Steadman's face.

'Is Superintendent Campbell in the room?' he whispered to Dr Rufus.

'Yes – has been from the start. Didn't you know?'

'How could I?' Steadman replied, only too grateful that he had kept quiet about her ex-husband and his boat.

Superintendent Campbell walked to the front of the room and gave DCI Long a curt nod.

'I doubt if we can officially stop you, Inspector Steadman. And having read your file, I doubt if you would pay the slightest attention to any recommendation. However, I would not wish you to compromise your own safety or the reputation of Helmsmouth Police Force. May I ask that you do nothing for twenty-four hours? I need time to reflect on your request.'

Reluctantly, Steadman agreed.

★ ★ ★

Dr Rufus took the floor. He had barely said two sentences when Inspector Crouchley interrupted him.

'What the hell has you swanning off to Southampton and a mouldy corpse in a freezer got to do with us?'

'O ye of little faith, Inspector Crouchley,' Dr Rufus replied. 'You must be the last person in the Eyesore not to know about Shuster's involvement. I am surprised. Even Sergeant Grimble is fully cognisant of the facts.'

It was like a red rag to a bull. Inspector Crouchley's loathing of the elderly desk sergeant was well known.

There was a roguish twinkle in Dr Rufus's eye. He was only too aware that others in the room probably didn't know either, but goading Eric Crouchley was irresistible.

'Let's just say, at this stage, that we recognise the hand of Seth Shuster. And by the way, the body wasn't mouldy. It was remarkably well-preserved.'

Dr Rufus continued in his inimitable fashion to give a graphic description of the body, the post-mortem and finally the crime scene.

'I don't understand,' said Inspector Crouchley. 'What was Seth Shuster's handprint doing on the inside of the freezer lid?'

'I think that's easily explained,' said Steadman. 'The lid fell down on his head as he was bundling the body into the freezer.'

'I'm trying to puzzle out why Shuster took his clothes,' said DS Fairfax.

'And only his earring – not his watch or gold chain,' added Munro.

All eyes turned towards Steadman.

'The only rational explanation I can come up with is that he was trying to steal this person's identity. We know that he was roughly the same age, size and build as Seth Shuster. If you want to pass yourself as someone else, the first thing you do is dress in their clothes. I bet the earring was quite distinctive. Dr Rufus said his hair was dyed blonde. I'm sure Shuster could have charmed a hairdresser into doing the necessary.'

'Why not take his watch and gold chain as well?' persisted Munro.

Steadman waved a hand. 'I can only speculate. Maybe he had a watch and a similar chain already. If we knew the corpse's identity, then we might get some clue as to Shuster's next movements. The most likely being that he somehow managed to secure a passage on a liner heading for America.'

* * *

There was a gentle knock at the door.

'Come in,' boomed DCI Long.

Kim Ho, nervous as ever, entered carrying a slim file.

'You have some news for us, Kim?' DCI Long asked.

'Yes, sir. We have a positive ID for the body in the freezer. He was a local Helmsmouth man by the name of Gregory Henshaw.'

'Good grief!' Steadman exclaimed, remembering his dream of several nights ago.

'Do you know him, John?' queried DCI Long.

'It must be ten years ago. I was still in uniform,' Steadman replied. 'I recall going to the house quite distinctly. It was very odd. The mother was distraught as she had lost touch with her only son, whereas the father seemed almost glad to be rid of him, virtually denying his existence. I discussed it with Sergeant Grimble at the time, and he advised me not to get involved in domestics. With hindsight I regret not taking it more seriously. If I remember correctly, Gregory Henshaw had a police record for minor criminal offences.'

'I have it here,' said Kim Ho. 'He was fingerprinted at the time.'

'Does his family know yet?' asked Steadman.

'I wouldn't have thought so,' said DCI Long. 'I'll get Rosie Jennings, the family liaison officer, to call this afternoon.'

Steadman knew Rosie well. She had been shot in a car chase while being pursued. Steadman had been in the passenger seat and always believed that he had been the intended victim. He felt an enormous burden of guilt, as Rosie's left shoulder and arm had never fully healed.

'I would very much like to go with Rosie Jennings, sir, if that's allowed?' asked Steadman. 'I feel I owe it to Gregory Henshaw's mother.'

'I'm sure Rosie would appreciate that,' DCI Long replied.

* * *

The meeting concluded. Amid the murmur of voices and shuffling of feet, Sam made her way over to Steadman, who was having a quiet word with DC Osborne.

'What are you doing for lunch, John?' Sam asked.

'I was proposing going to the canteen. Would you care to join me?'

'Do you need to ask?' said Sam. There was laughter in her voice, and it sent a shiver down Steadman's spine.

'What are you two up to?' asked Dr Rufus.

'We were thinking about having lunch in the canteen, that's all,' Steadman replied.

'Excellent idea – I was wondering about risking it too.'

'Frank, after what you said last time we were there, I wouldn't be surprised if they did try to poison you.'

'Oh, they do that to everybody,' Dr Rufus said with a loud guffaw. 'They will have forgotten about it by now.'

Judging by the expressions on the faces of the staff behind the counter, they had not entirely forgotten. They slapped the food noisily on to his plate. Dr Rufus was completely oblivious. He sniffed the food.

'Well, it smells all right,' he said.

Sam had found a free table and fetched sandwiches and drinks for Steadman and herself. Sergeant Grimble returned with Robbie.

'He's been a very good boy for his Uncle Bertie. We've been out and had a little walk, haven't we,' he said as Steadman slipped Robbie's harness back on.

'Funny that the body should turn out to be Gregory Henshaw, and you only asking about him a few days ago,' Grimble remarked.

Steadman's ears turned bright pink.

'I was just thinking about missing persons that I

had dealt with, nothing more. Pure coincidence,' he mumbled. He knew that if he mentioned his dream Dr Rufus would only mock him, and heaven knows what Sam would think.

'Have you found a way of cleaning the Superintendent's windows?' asked Steadman, hastily changing the subject.

'I'm working on a plan,' Grimble replied as he made his way back to his desk.

There was little need for conversation with Dr Rufus at the table. He was amusing and outrageous. At one point, when he did pause for breath, Steadman asked him what his plans were for the afternoon.

'Paperwork – always bloody paperwork. And an unnecessary post-mortem on a ninety-seven-year-old who died unexpectedly. I would have thought it more unexpected to find her alive, but we have a new Coroner, and I haven't whipped him into shape yet.' Rufus looked at his watch. 'Goodness me, is that the time? You two mustn't keep me chatting any longer.'

On his way out, Steadman heard him remark to the canteen staff, 'Thank you, that was passable. If I'm still alive tomorrow, I may chance it again.'

'I bet that went down well,' said Sam.

'Don't worry. They're used to him,' Steadman replied. 'What about you, Sam? What are your plans?'

'Like Dr Rufus, it will be paperwork. At least I'm spared having to do post-mortems. Here's Rosie Jennings, if I'm not mistaken.'

Steadman stood awkwardly and held out his hand. 'You've met Sam – Dr Griffiths – before?'

'Yes, we've met,' Rosie replied. 'May I join you?'

'Of course, do take a seat. Have you eaten?'

'I'm all good. You don't mind coming with me this afternoon?' Rosie asked.

Steadman shook his head. 'Not at all. I feel it only right. I was the officer that dealt with Henshaw's disappearance ten years ago.'

★ ★ ★

Rosie Jennings and Steadman walked slowly to the car.

'How is your shoulder?' he asked.

'A bit stiff but not sore,' she replied, and if to prove a point she slipped her arm in Steadman's. 'The holes in this car park are a disgrace,' she added. 'Sam Griffiths seems really nice, don't you think?'

She turned to look at her colleague.

'Why Inspector Steadman, I do believe you're blushing!'

It was a very small car. Rosie slid the passenger seat back as far as it would go.

'Mind your head,' she warned Steadman.

'Do they know we are coming?'

'No. If you tell them you're coming, they'll want to know why. It's much better face-to-face, I find. News like this shouldn't be broken over the phone.'

They arrived at the Henshaw's house. It wasn't far and Rosie was able to park almost directly outside. Ignoring the fact it was still drizzling, she removed her hat and rang the bell. The door was opened by a diminutive lady, aged beyond her years. Steadman would not have recognised her.

'Mrs Henshaw? I'm PC Rosie Jennings and this is Detective Inspector John Steadman. May we come in?'

She hesitated, grief already written over her face.

'It's about Gregory, isn't it?' she said.

Rosie nodded, and Mrs Henshaw stood aside to let them in.

'Do you remember me, Mrs Henshaw?' Steadman asked. 'I came here ten years ago when you first reported your son missing.'

She looked at Steadman, and then the dog. A flicker of recognition passed over her face.

'Yes, I remember you.' There was no bitterness or rancour in her voice, for which Steadman was grateful. 'A lot has changed since then.'

'It most certainly has,' Steadman replied as he encouraged Robbie to walk on. 'Is your husband here?'

She took them through to a tiny sitting room. Rosie led Steadman to a chair.

'No, he dropped down dead in the pub. It must be two years ago. They reckoned he had choked on some peanuts, but the doctor said it was his heart.'

'I'm sorry for your loss, Mrs Henshaw,' said Rosie.

The old lady shrugged.

'And even more sorry that I have to add to them,' she continued. 'I regret to inform you that Gregory's body has been found.'

She stifled a sob. Robbie made a move as though to comfort her. Steadman laid a calming hand on his head and listened while Rosie gently told the story.

Mrs Henshaw dried her eyes.

'At least I know now, though I've known in my heart for some time. Can you understand that?'

Both officers nodded.

'In a way, I'm glad his father went before him. He could not accept Gregory for what he was. The shame of all of this would surely have killed him.' She paused again, slowly letting the news sink in. 'Do you know who murdered my son?'

Steadman sat forward in his chair. 'We do, Mrs Henshaw.'

'I hope you find him, Inspector Steadman.'

'We have, but I'm afraid it is rather too late.'

Slowly and patiently Steadman recounted what he knew of Seth Shuster.

'I think they met entirely by chance,' he said. 'They were about the same age. Helmsmouth is not that big and my guess is that they may have known each other. I believe Shuster murdered your son in order to steal his identity and flee to America.'

'He did say something in one of his letters about

getting a job on a liner and going to America. Mr Henshaw found the letters and made me burn them all.' She moaned very softly. 'When can I have his – his body?'

'When the Coroner releases it, which shouldn't be too long,' replied Rosie. 'Is there anyone who can help you?'

Mrs Henshaw shook her head.

'Would you like me to come back? We could go through things together.'

'That would be most kind. And Inspector Steadman, I appreciate you making the effort to come and see me as well.'

Steadman swallowed hard. 'Given the circumstances, Mrs Henshaw, it was the least I could do.'

They walked the short distance back to the car in silence.

'Takes it out of you,' Steadman remarked.

'It does,' Rosie replied. She gave Steadman's arm a squeeze. 'Thank you for coming with me, sir.'

The mobile phone in his pocket rang.

'Where are you, dad?' asked Ben.

'I'm just on my way back to the flat, Ben.'

'Good. We think we've found the lad who took the photos on the beach.'

'Oh – who is he?'

'Dominic's latest discovery. One of his paintings was of a mutilated corpse being mobbed by seagulls. Dominic spun him a yarn about having a potential client who may be interested in his work. We've provisionally said we would call back this evening.'

'I would like to be there. Obviously, we'll need to bring Fiona Fairfax or Alan Munro with us.'

'Might be best to bring both, dad,' Ben replied. 'He's a bit twitchy.'

CHAPTER 25

Light drizzle was still falling. Munro gazed bleakly up at the sky.

'Let's take the Audi,' he said to DS Fairfax.

'Or we could take my motorbike. You would barely notice the rain once we got going.' She sized up her companion; he really was massive. 'Perhaps you're right – the Audi it is.'

Munro beamed. 'So, let's get this straight, Fiona, I'm going to question Josh Reynolds about a burglary in a property that he's supposed to have been decorating.'

'And when he gets angry at the accusation, which he will because we've made it all up, I will take Clara Drinsdale to the kitchen and see if she'll spill the beans about Seth's son.'

'I'll enjoy this,' said Munro. 'I like a bit of amateur dramatics.'

Josh Reynolds was none too keen to let the two officers in. Munro, however, was not an easy man to dissuade.

It didn't take long for the conversation to get heated.

'Where is this burglary meant to have taken place?' Reynolds demanded.

'I'm not at liberty to say,' replied Munro. 'The owners assured me you were working there recently.'

'Produce an invoice, did they?'

'When was the last time you wrote an invoice? It's always cash in hand, isn't it? You tell the punters you'll knock ten percent off for cash. I know how dishonest you are, Reynolds.'

Josh slammed his hands down on the arms of his chair. 'Oh, yes – and what exactly is it that I'm supposed to have nicked?' He jabbed a finger in Munro's face.

'Jewellery and money,' Munro replied. 'The same as you always do.'

Josh Reynolds stood up and shouted. 'That's a bleeding lie, and well you know it. Go on, prove it.'

Clara Drinsdale was fretting. She had screwed up her apron into a ball and would have stuffed it into her mouth had DS Fairfax not intervened. She touched Clara lightly on the shoulder and pointed to the kitchen.

'Let's leave the men to talk, come on.'

Clara didn't take two tellings. She trotted off to the kitchen, closely followed by Fairfax.

'What about a nice cuppa, Clara? I do like your lipstick. Where did you get it?'

It was a garish shade of red.

'Free with a magazine,' Clara replied. 'Josh says it makes me look like a tart. Me, a tart? At my age?' She shook her head at the very thought of it.

'I bet he's difficult to live with,' Fairfax continued.

'Tell me about it. He won't have anyone around to the house, not friends or even… It's not fair.'

'What? You mean not even your nephew, Seth?' Fairfax tried to appear shocked. Fairfax tried to appear shocked.

Clara glanced up sharply. 'Especially not him. Do you take milk in your tea?'

'No thanks – just as it comes. Didn't Seth and Josh get on, then?'

'You didn't know our Seth, did you? Charming, handsome, but…' she struggled to find the words. 'If he called, it was always because he wanted something – money, a bed for the night because someone was after him, a place to hide things.'

'What about his son? Does he ever call?'

'He used to – 'til Josh threw him out.'

'So, Seth does have a son!' Fairfax exclaimed.

Clara realised she had fallen into the trap. 'I never told you that,' she squealed. 'I never said anything about a son.'

Josh Reynolds burst through the door before Munro could stop him. Fairfax had never seen a man look so angry in her life. Clara dropped her teacup and cowered behind the kitchen table.

'What have you been saying, you stupid woman?' he demanded.

'Nothing, Josh. Honest,' Clara whimpered.

Munro placed a beefy restraining hand on Josh's shoulder.

'We were only having a little chat, that's all, Mr Reynolds. Nothing more,' Fairfax said in a soothing voice.

Clara looked terrified. Josh glared at the two officers.

'I don't trust either of you. I know my rights. Get out.'

'I was just about to use your bathroom, Mr Reynolds.' Fairfax brushed passed him into the bathroom and swiftly locked the door.

Clara was still whimpering. 'I didn't tell her anything, Josh.'

The toilet flushed and Fairfax reappeared.

'I think we should go now, DS Munro,' she said.

'I agree, DS Fairfax,' responded Munro.

'Thank you for the cup of tea, Clara. I enjoyed our natter. We must do it again.'

Josh slammed the door behind the two officers.

'Did you find out anything?' Munro asked.

'Yes. Seth Shuster definitely has a son, but that's as far as I got.'

'I'm worried about Clara's safety,' said Munro. 'He might be getting on a bit, but he's a bully with a nasty, violent streak.'

'I think Clara wants to talk. I went to the bathroom to find her makeup bag. I left a card with my contact details in it.'

Munro frowned. 'What if her brother finds it first?'

Fiona gave him a pitying look. 'Alan, have you ever even peeked inside your wife's makeup bag?'

'I wouldn't even know if she had one,' Munro confessed.

'Exactly. A women's makeup bag is strictly out of bounds to all men, trust me.'

★ ★ ★

DC Cleo Osborne spent a fruitless afternoon going around the shops, cafés, gyms, and leisure centres. She gave up counting. Maybe the old photo wasn't a good enough likeness. Some people thought they might have seen someone looking a bit like him. No one was certain. 'He looks vaguely familiar, love. No idea who is, though,' was the stock reply.

Methodically, Cleo Osborne ticked off the streets one by one, keeping a note of all the bars and clubs that she would have to visit later. Steadman had drawn her aside after the meeting and advised her to pay particular attention to the florist.

'It was odd,' he had said, 'that a florist should definitely recognise a young man. It suggests he was a regular customer.'

Unfortunately, the florist was closed. A note pinned to the door read, "At a Wedding – Back Tomorrow." Cleo Osborne sighed, and made another note.

★ ★ ★

Steadman was pale and weary by the time he arrived home.

'Is everything all right, dad? You're looking tired.'

'Thanks, Ben. You know exactly the right thing to say to make an old man feel good about himself.'

Ben smiled. 'Go and put your feet up. The kettle's on.'

Steadman almost fell into his chair. He laid his head back and closed his eyes. Within seconds, he had drifted into a deep, dreamless sleep. Ben tiptoed back to the kitchen with the cup of tea.

There were footsteps on the stairs. Ben managed to open the door before Tim Warrender had time to press the bell. He put a finger to his lips. 'Ssh! Dad's asleep.'

Tim poked his head round the sitting room door. Steadman was breathing heavily.

'Is he all right?' Tim asked in a quavering voice.

'Yeah, he's fine. He needs a lot of sleep, that's all. It's something to do with being shot in the head, I think.'

Tim nodded and took Robbie out for his walk. Steadman was still asleep when he returned.

The sound of laughter in the kitchen woke him. Very carefully, he made his way through to join them, counting the steps and trailing a guiding hand along the wall.

'Sorry, dad, did we wake you?'

Steadman pressed the button on his watch and was amazed to discover he had been asleep for over an hour.

'No problem, I need to waken. Any chance of a coffee?'

'I'd better be going,' said Tim. 'Robbie's had his walk and been fed.'

Steadman sipped his coffee. 'Tell me about the art student. We need to make a plan. What's his name?'

'He's called Stevie Deans,' said Ben. 'Dominic spotted his talent straight away at the exhibition.'

'Is his work any good?' asked Steadman.

'Head and shoulders above the rest – a different league entirely. By the time the exhibition officially opened, Dominic had already bought two of his paintings and arranged to visit his studio to look at some more.'

'You say 'studio' – that sounds a bit grand for an art student.'

'They are just fancy halls of residence for the final year students built on some waste ground behind Helmsmouth College of Art. The accommodation is a bit basic, but the light is good. I'm surprised he doesn't try growing cannabis plants.'

'I'll pretend I didn't hear that,' Steadman replied. 'Tell me about Stevie Deans. What is he like?'

'Quite short, scruffy, tousled dark curls streaked with paint. Seemed on edge the whole time we were there. He kept running his hands through his hair. He could do with a bath and getting out in the fresh air.'

In his mind's eye, Steadman conjured up a clear vision of the youth.

'Drug user, do you think?'

'Find me an art student that hasn't tried at some time.'

Steadman let that pass. 'Tell me about his paintings.'

'He uses a lot of paint – layer upon layer thickly applied. I guess he uses palette knives as well as brushes. The final effect is almost three-dimensional. Different surfaces catch the light depending on where you're standing. The colours are quite muted with just the odd splash of bright red or blue that catches your attention.'

Steadman tried to imagine what they might have looked like. It was virtually impossible. 'What sort of subjects does he paint?'

'He's dabbled a fair bit. Over the last year he's concentrated on seascapes, beaches and the coastline.'

'So, tell me about the painting.' There was no need for Steadman to explain which one he meant.

'It's a large picture, about six feet by four. At first, you think it's simply a flock of squabbling abstract seagulls. Then your eyes are drawn to a gash of red on the beach and you realise that half-hidden by the birds is the body of a man. You can just make out the torso, but the head is little more than three vermillion stripes. As you look back up the canvas you notice the gull in the centre of the canvas has an eyeball in his beak.'

A very vivid image sprang into Steadman's mind of the eyeball in the painting staring directly at him.

'Would you describe it as art, Ben?'

'Without a doubt. It is a deeply disturbing picture. Not what you would want to hang in your living room perhaps, but certainly something a large gallery would display.'

Steadman drummed his fingers. 'And this was recently painted?'

'The canvas was still wet,' Ben replied.

With Ben's help, Steadman phoned Fiona Fairfax, Alan Munro, and Dominic.

'You were right about Seth having a son, sir,' said Fiona. 'Clara blurted it out, much to Josh's dismay. Disappointingly, he interrupted us before I could get a name.'

Munro agreed to pick up Fiona and Steadman while Dominic offered to collect Ben. Steadman put his phone back in his pocket.

'Better not to mention you're related to me, Ben,' he cautioned.

'No worries, dad. As far as Stevie goes, I'm Dominic's business partner.'

The car was warm and snug. Fiona sat in the back; Steadman and Robbie took up their familiar places in the front.

'I wonder if Stevie Deans will recognise me?' Steadman pondered. 'He'll certainly not forget you, Alan.'

'I've not met him,' said Fiona.

'That's true. I think you should be the potential buyer and, if he asks, I can be your wealthy uncle. Ben said he was very twitchy. If he gets wind of what we're up to, he may try to do a runner. I've asked Ben to hover by the front door.'

'I know my place, sir,' said Munro with a grin. 'I'll stand out the back.'

★ ★ ★

The studio smelt strongly of turpentine and body odour. There was another smell that Steadman struggled initially to place. Cannabis, that was it, he said to himself at last.

Stevie Deans was indeed nervous. The hand that clasped Steadman's was decidedly clammy.

'This is a first – a blind guy coming to look at my pictures.' He sounded sceptical.

'My niece is the connoisseur. I am merely the banker,' Steadman responded.

Stevie showed her several of his paintings. Fiona played her part to perfection.

'What's the big picture hiding in the corner?' she asked pointing to the large easel facing the wall.

'It's not dry yet,' Stevie said. 'You can look at it if you like.'

He wheeled the picture around and Fairfax scanned the large canvas.

'It's definitely the body on the beach, sir. It's Seth Shuster all right.'

Stevie ran his hands through his hair. Alarm bells were

ringing. Who calls their uncle 'sir', he asked himself? He looked again at Steadman and Robbie.

'You were on the beach with the big guy. You're the police!'

Ben was standing casually by the door, his outstretched arm blocking the exit.

Stevie's eyes darted around the room. He sprinted to the back door, pulled it open, and ran straight into Munro's arms.

'Well, now you've met the big guy again,' said Munro who had been listening at the door. He marched Stevie back into the studio.

DS Fairfax produced her ID. 'And this is DS Munro and DI Steadman.'

Stevie stared at the floor and swore. Turning angrily to Dominic, he said, 'I thought you were genuinely interested in my work.'

'Oh, I am a bona fide art dealer, Mr Deans. It so happens that I am also Detective Inspector John Steadman's brother-in-law.'

'I suppose you're going to arrest me now,' Stevie sniffed.

'That all depends how the next bit goes,' said Fairfax. 'You don't deny being at the beach and I'm sure you won't be stupid enough to deny taking the photos and selling them to a newspaper. You could be charged with obstruction of a coroner and preventing identification of a corpse contrary to Common Law, and that's just a start.'

'What do you want?' asked Stevie. He sounded utterly defeated, and Steadman felt sorry for him.

'A full statement under caution. DS Munro will write it down, then you will read it and sign it.'

'We need your phone as well,' Munro continued.

Stevie nodded and handed over his mobile.

'What's the code to unlock it? You might as well tell me. I only want to see the photos. I promise I won't tell your mother about all the porn you've been watching.'

There wasn't much in Stevie's story. He had been out walking and stumbled on the body by chance. He thought it would make an interesting subject. Only as he ran away did it occur to him that he could make money from the photos.

'One final thing,' said Steadman. 'Seth Shuster was wearing a watch when he was dumped at sea. It was removed while he was lying on the beach. May we have the watch?'

Stevie hesitated. 'What watch?' he replied, glancing nervously at his bedroom.

Munro was scrolling through the photos. He paused at one and zoomed in. The watch was clearly visible. He held it up to Stevie.

'Inspector Steadman means the one you can see in this photo. Maybe I'll take a wee look through there, Stevie,' said Munro pointing at the bedroom door.

'Don't bother, I'll get it.'

The Patek Philippe was still ticking and had not missed a second. Stevie handed it over to Munro. 'Is it an expensive watch?' he asked. 'I thought I might get something for it.'

'Too expensive. You would never have been able to sell it without questions being asked,' Munro replied.

Stevie turned to Dominic. 'I don't suppose you'll be wanting any of my paintings now.'

'On the contrary, Mr Deans, I'm going to devote my entire gallery to your work and make the painting of the body on the beach the central exhibit. You have no idea how a story like this will attract the critics and the paying public – utterly brilliant!'

★ ★ ★

DC Cleo Osborne was having less luck. The pubs and clubs were now open, and she trudged around every one of them. Not a single person recognised or ever recalled seeing the man in the photo. She was bitterly disappointed.

Her route home took her past the flower shop. There was a van outside, and a middle-aged lady was carrying displays back into the shop. Cleo Osborne introduced herself.

'If I give you a hand emptying your van, would you have another look at the photos?'

'If you give me a hand to move this lot, I'll not only look at your photos, I'll make you a cup of tea as well. I'm knackered,' said the florist.

It didn't take long for the two of them to do the job. The florist lived above the shop and, true to her word, she made them both a cup of tea when they were finished.

'It looks so like him, but not quite, if you know what I mean,' the florist said.

'We think the person we're seeking might be Seth Shuster's son. This is actually a photo of Shuster taken about twenty years ago,' Cleo replied.

'I see, that makes sense. The man that comes to the shop is a peculiar chap.'

'Peculiar in what way?'

'Well, for one thing he always pays cash, so I have no idea of his name. And secondly, he only ever buys white flowers – usually lilies or chrysanthemums.'

CHAPTER 26

It was most unlike John Steadman to be frustrated and irritable. If there was one thing that becoming blind had taught him, it was infinite patience. Everything took that bit longer. Life's daily tasks seemed, at times, to run in slow motion. There was nothing to be gained in getting angry. If buttons were done up incorrectly, you simply had to undo them and start again. If you dropped loose change on the floor, you bent down and retrieved what was at your feet. There was no point in scrabbling for the coins that had rolled away.

It wasn't just the loss of sight; it was also the loss of independence that riled him. Robbie, his guide dog, had given him a new-found freedom. Unfortunately, Robbie could neither do up buttons nor pick up pennies that had rolled under the sideboard.

The day had not started well. Tim Warrender had

phoned in a panic. He had slept in. Ben fed the dog, then decided to go for a long jog before spending the day with Linda and Dominic. His bath had used all the hot water.

A pair of discarded running shoes had caused Steadman to stumble and drop his toast. Without being asked, Robbie had helped to clean that up. But these were minor distractions. There was an on-going investigation, and for the moment, he did not feel involved. However irrational, he felt excluded, and that was what was really bothering him.

'Sod this,' he said out loud. He pressed the intercom and Marco Lloyd answered. 'I would like a large coffee and eggs Benedict.'

'Eggs Benedict?' queried Marco. Steadman had never ordered this before. Marco knew that Steadman avoided any food that was runny or covered in sauce.

Steadman's mood was defiant. 'Yes, eggs Benedict,' he snapped and instantly regretted it. The Lloyd family had been exceedingly kind to him since he had lost his sight and moved into their apartment above the café.

The meal arrived and he apologised before Marco was through the door.

'It is quite all right, Inspector Steadman,' Marco replied. 'If I were in your shoes, I would throw all the china out the window, as my grandmother used to say.'

The eggs Benedict were delicious. Steadman didn't care if he dribbled. The dressing gown could go for a wash and, once the water was hot, he would have a long shower.

'What do you think, Robbie? Shall we invite ourselves to the Eyesore and find out if there have been any developments?'

The dog wagged his tail.

Steadman dressed carefully. The colour scanner confirmed it was a white shirt. He stroked through his ties. The one he wanted had a textured weave. It was silk and expensive, a Christmas present from his sister. As a final act of rebellion, he splashed on some aftershave.

It was foggy outside. Steadman didn't care; the weather matched his mood. He was familiar with the route and its various smells and sounds, the large clock ticking above Eldon's jewellery shop, the unpleasant sulphide odour of setting lotion from Upper Cuts hairdressing salon, the honey, herbs, and chatter from the Greek delicatessen.

It was still early, and he had the pavement to himself, or almost to himself. The dog's harness twitched.

'You've noticed as well, Robbie?' he sighed. 'Well, I've had quite enough of being stalked.'

He stopped suddenly and turned.

'Why don't you just talk to me? I may not be able to see you, but I know you're there, and I know who you are,' Steadman called out angrily.

It was the wrong thing to say. The man dived across the road. There was a squeal of brakes and a car horn blasted, but no bump.

'Come back,' Steadman yelled.

Two old ladies emerged from a shop.

'Is there anything the matter? We heard you shouting.'

'I'm being followed and whoever he is doesn't have the courage to speak,' Steadman replied.

'Well dearie, there's no one here now,' she said as though trying to soothe a recalcitrant child. 'Maybe you should go home. We could call a taxi, couldn't we?' she said turning to her companion.

'It's a disgrace,' her companion muttered. 'People like him shouldn't be allowed out by themselves if you ask me. It's not fair on the rest of us.'

Steadman was fuming. He was saved from further comment by the sound of someone running towards him, someone in high heels.

'Is everything OK, John?' asked Sam Griffiths.

Steadman shook his head. 'Someone was trailing me again. Foolishly, I confronted him...'

'And he ran off,' said Sam.

'Do you two know each other?' interrupted the old lady.

Sam nodded.

'You'd better take him home,' added her companion. 'Shouting like that in the street – it's not decent. We should call the police, you know.'

Sam looped an arm through Steadman's. 'Come on, John, before the cops arrive and arrest you,' she said trying hard not to giggle.

They walked in silence and Steadman calmed down.

'Obviously, I can't be certain if it was the same person,' he said at last, 'although I'm sure it was.'

Sam tried to reassure him. 'He'll speak in his own time. I think he's scared – or desperate.'

'You're right. The one thing I don't feel is threatened by him. I've been a policeman long enough to have developed a sixth sense for danger.'

'What do you think he wants?' Sam asked.

'If I'm right, and it is Seth Shuster's son, I know exactly what he wants.'

The fog gradually lifted, and a frugal sun made a timid attempt to brighten up the day. Steadman's spirits rose a fraction as its barely perceptible warmth touched his face.

'What have you got on today, Sam?' he asked.

'More paperwork, and I've been asked to see a youth that Inspector Crouchley has in the cells. I gather Crouchley wants him locked up for good and the key thrown away. I suspect the lad needs to go into care, but we'll see. What about you?'

'I don't really know what I'm doing,' he confessed. 'I thought I would find out if anything new has happened, and maybe if I stand around looking pathetic, they might find me something to do.'

'Oh, John, I don't know whether you need a hug or a kick in the pants – perhaps both!' said Sam with a smile.

'Is that your professional opinion? You're right, of

course. I need to lighten up. Self-pity only fans the flames of depression.'

'Talking of fanning the flames,' Sam replied, 'there's an enormous fire engine outside the Eyesore – not one with ladders, bigger than that. It's got a cage-like thing with firemen in it, on the end of long folding arms. There are people and water everywhere.'

'A hydraulic platform, I think they're called,' replied Steadman, wrinkling his nose. There was no smell of burning. 'Can you see any smoke, Sam?'

Sam paused. 'No, nothing. How curious.'

'How far up the building are they working?' asked Steadman.

Sam counted the storeys. 'I'm not sure – fifth or sixth floor, maybe.'

Steadman hummed a little tune to himself and pushed his dark glasses up on to his forehead. He covered one eye then the other. Was it his imagination or could he just make out a flashing blue pinpoint of light?

'I wondered how he was going to do it,' he said at last.

'You're not going to tell me what you're thinking, are you? You can be quite annoying at times, John Steadman!'

'Come on,' he replied. 'If I'm right, you'll find out soon enough.'

By the time they arrived at the Eyesore, the fire crew were tidying up. Sam steered Steadman around the puddles. Robbie led the way up the steps, eager to get a biscuit from Sergeant Grimble.

Divisional Superintendent Olivia Campbell was standing in front of his desk with her hands on her hips. She was soaking wet and furious. She ignored the new arrivals.

'I assume, Sergeant Grimble, this was one of your idiotic ideas,' she bellowed.

'I was only trying to...'

She interrupted him. 'Look at me. I'm drenched. My clothes are ruined. I expect you find this amusing.'

'No, ma'am.'

'Well, all your colleagues do. I can hear them laughing at me behind my back.'

'I'm terribly sorry, ma'am. I heard that you wanted your office windows cleaned and I've been racking my brains trying to think of a solution.'

'So you dialled 999 and told them my office was on fire.'

'No, ma'am. The Chief Fire Officer is an old friend of mine and some of the new recruits needed a bit of practice with the hydraulic platform, and...'

'You didn't think to warn me?'

'I didn't know you were in your office, ma'am. Besides, none of the windows have opened for years. All painted over, I believe.'

'As you can see, Sergeant Grimble, I managed to open one of them.'

'Ah! That would explain why...'

'I look like a drowned rat – precisely.' She wagged a

warning finger in his direction. 'This is not the last you'll hear of this, Sergeant, not by a long chalk.'

Superintendent Campbell turned on her heel and, mustering as much dignity as circumstances allowed, strode off slamming the door behind her.

'I hope you appreciate the nice clean windows and all the effort I've gone to,' muttered Sergeant Grimble at the retreating figure. 'And don't you look at me like that, Robbie. I've even run out of doggie treats.'

'No Brownie points for you then?' queried Steadman. 'I've got to hand it to you, a most ingenious solution, though.'

'Ruddy woman!' Grimble exclaimed. 'Pardon my French, Sam. Nobody has managed to open a window in that office for years. Mind, I would've loved to have seen her face when they turned the water on. I wonder what she meant by "this is not the last you'll hear of this"?'

'I wouldn't worry,' said Sam. 'She'll probably bill you for the dry cleaning, that's all. And I'll buy you a cake of chocolate to cheer you up. Now, I must go and do some work. See if you can find something for John to do. He's like a bear with a sore head.'

A deep voice boomed behind them. 'That won't be necessary. I was about to phone Inspector Steadman. Can you come up to my office, John?' said DCI Long.

'I hope you'll leave Robbie with me,' pleaded Sergeant Grimble. 'I could do with somebody that appreciates me, and I've found a broken doggie biscuit in my pocket.'

★ ★ ★

DCI Long's office was cool and spacious. The room was filled with a sweet, spicy fragrance that Steadman couldn't place. He knew the Chief Inspector was a keen gardener and usually had a vase of something he had grown on his desk.

'You'll have to put me out of my misery, sir. I can't work out what the lovely scent is. I presume it is something from your garden?'

'Yes, witch hazel. The blooms have been spectacular this year. The perfume is quite heady, and it certainly cheers up a winter's day.'

Steadman tried to recall the spidery flowers in shades of yellow, orange and red.

'Hang on a second, John. I think I hear DC Osborne.'

DCI Long stepped out of his office and returned with a worried-looking Detective Constable. Steadman stood up as she entered and held out his hand.

'Our newest recruit has been busy,' said DCI Long. He turned to Cleo Osborne. 'I'm sure Inspector Steadman would like to hear how you got on yesterday.'

DC Osborne shuffled in her seat. 'You were right, sir. The florist was the most helpful in the end. Several of the shopkeepers and two of the café owners thought the photograph appeared vaguely familiar, but that was as far as it went. The florist wasn't open during the day, apparently she was off to a wedding. I went back out in the evening to check out the pubs and clubs. I showed the picture to all the bar staff and doormen. Remarkably, no one claimed to recognise the person in the picture. I thought that was odd if he was a local man.'

Steadman agreed.

'As chance would have it,' Cleo Osborne continued, 'I passed the florist just as she was returning home. She is definite that somebody looking remarkably similar to the photo of Seth Shuster as a young man lives in the area. He is quite a regular customer, and well turned-out. He always pays in cash, so she doesn't know his name. Invariably he buys white flowers, usually chrysanthemums or lilies.'

Steadman stroked his chin, deep in thought. As so often happened on occasions like this a tune popped into his head. In this instance, not Bach or jazz but a simple song, 'Morning has Broken', and he recalled with sadness the last time he had heard it play.

'I think the white flowers are our best clue,' he said. 'They always bring to mind funerals or weddings. It's interesting that he doesn't frequent the bars or nightclubs. It suggests maybe that whatever he does, he has some standing in the community.'

'What have you in mind, John?' asked DCI Long.

'Maybe he works for a funeral director, or in the registrar's office. He could even be a man of the cloth.'

'You mean like a vicar or a priest!' exclaimed Cleo Osborne. 'Is that possible with a father like Seth Shuster?'

'Stranger things have happened,' Steadman replied.

CHAPTER 27

DC Cleo Osborne stood up. 'I'm on to it, sir.'

DCI Long gave her a quizzical look. 'Much as I admire your enthusiasm, you will do no such thing. You worked fifteen hours solidly yesterday tramping the streets of Helmsmouth. This morning, you will finish writing your report, then take the rest of the day off.'

Cleo Osborne made to say something. DCI Long raised a hand. 'No arguments, constable, 'that was an order,' he said genially. 'The identity of Seth Shuster's son can wait at least another day. What do you say, Inspector Steadman?'

'Most definitely. You've already done a sterling piece of work, Cleo.'

DC Osborne appeared pleased, relieved, and suddenly exhausted. 'Thank you. May I start tomorrow, sir? I'm keen to finish the job.'

'You may,' replied DCI Long. 'Good, that's settled.' He closed the door behind the DC and returned to his desk.

'What I would like you to do, John, requires a little finesse. As you are aware, I have asked DC Lofthouse to investigate Philip Aintree's business activities. I find DC Lofthouse a bit like a suspect box of fireworks. Sometimes he goes off with an enormous burst of brilliance, but sadly at other times, no matter how often the blue touch paper is lit, he fails to ignite. This is going to be a bit of a challenge for him. I would like you to keep a fatherly eye on him, without, of course, undermining the young man.'

Steadman was fully aware of DCI Long's methods. He too had been trained by him.

'I think I can manage that, sir,' Steadman replied.

'I have no doubt, otherwise I wouldn't have asked you. I have already been to the Crown Court and obtained the necessary warrant to search his bank accounts and phone records, as well as his office and home, if need be. There is the usual team at our disposal to do the legwork. I don't want DC Lofthouse going off at a tangent and getting lost. I have a feeling that Philip Aintree may be crucial to our investigation.'

Steadman recalled his dream and the van with its awful bundle. 'I agree, sir. I'll try and keep Will Lofthouse on a not-too-tight leash.'

There was a knock on the door. Without prompting, Sergeant Grimble, who had been shamelessly listening to their conversation, entered.

'Talking of not-too-tight leashes,' he said unabashed, 'can I hand Robbie back to you? I've been summoned to Superintendent Campbell's office to survey the damage. Maybe I should take a bucket and mop. I don't know why I bother sometimes.'

'The best laid schemes of mice and men' quoted DCI Long in a conciliatory tone.

'Talking of plans, sir, has the Divisional Superintendent reached a decision about my proposed visit to Madam Chu's?' asked Steadman.

'I'll ask once she has dried out,' replied DCI Long.

★ ★ ★

It was obvious that DC Will Lofthouse was a bit peeved at Steadman's presence.

'I suppose the old man doesn't trust me?' he said.

'You mean DCI Long,' Steadman corrected him. 'He does trust you or he wouldn't have given you the task.'

'But he sent you over to keep a beady eye on me,' Lofthouse interjected.

'My beady eyes are, alas, not much good for anything these days.'

Lofthouse started to apologise for his crass remark, but Steadman talked over him. 'No, it's a complex case and DCI Long thought you might appreciate bouncing ideas off me as you went along. It remains your investigation.'

Lofthouse ran a hand through his wavy black hair. 'To

tell the truth, sir, I wouldn't mind a hand. I'm not quite out of my depth but not far from it. Let me get you a chair and I'll tell you where I've got to.'

Steadman sat down and Robbie lay spread-eagled at his feet.

'I started with Phil's van. I reckoned it would be the easiest,' said Lofthouse. 'I checked with DVLA. The van has neither an MOT certificate, road tax nor insurance. Before we do anything else, we can open a charge sheet with that lot. What I don't understand, sir, is why he would risk something as stupid as that.'

'Because he's a criminal,' Steadman answered. 'If there is a right road and a wrong road, people like Phil the Shed will always choose the wrong path. What else have you got?'

'I asked the HMRC to look at his tax returns. He's still registered with them as a self-employed security operative.'

'No mention of office supplies?' queried Steadman.

'None flagged up to the tax man. Which got me thinking – maybe the business doesn't exist at all,' Lofthouse replied. 'I rang round the wholesale suppliers. He does have an account with one of them. I asked for details of what he had bought in the past six months. They were reluctant at first. Eventually I got chatting to the young lady in sales, who sounded rather attractive...' Lofthouse's voice trailed away and Steadman got the impression that the DC's thoughts were elsewhere.

'And this young lady told you what, exactly?' Steadman asked.

'What he had bought would barely keep a small independent retailer in business for a month.'

'What about his bank statements and phone records?'

'The team are working on them as we speak. I haven't heard anything from Inspector Crouchley yet, although I know his officers have got him under twenty-four-hour surveillance. He lives in a nice apartment which he rents privately, and he has a lock-up less than a hundred yards from his flat. Do you fancy a coffee?'

The drink was warm and wet, but otherwise tasteless. Steadman grimaced.

'How am I doing, sir?'

'Apart from the dreadful coffee, you're doing just fine.'

Lofthouse wasn't listening. A far-away look had come into his eyes. 'I have just had an idea, sir. I must make a call. Back in a moment.'

Steadman considered it likely he had gone to phone the young lady in the wholesalers to ask her for a date. He scratched the back of his head and sighed. After ten minutes Lofthouse returned.

'That was interesting, sir. I wondered what would happen if I phoned Phil the Shed's mobile and pretended to be a potential customer.'

It was one of Lofthouse's flashes of genius, and Steadman felt ashamed for doubting him.

'I didn't immediately tell him exactly what I was after.

Phil assured me he had some very special deals available. We fenced around for a bit without him specifying what he had on offer. When I made it clear I only wanted a few reams of paper and a gross of envelopes he got shirty with me and told me he wasn't taking on any new clients. I tried to press him on the special deals, but he hung up on me.'

'Did you dial from a headquarters phone?' asked Steadman.

'No, I've got an old pay-as-you-go mobile that I hardly ever use.'

Steadman could tell that his young colleague was pleased with himself, and he didn't want to dampen his spirits.

'Good work – only be careful. We don't want to be accused of entrapment,' he cautioned. 'I think, however, it confirms our suspicions that Helmsmouth Office Solutions is a sham.'

The bank statements arrived, showing a bewildering array of traffic in fleeting sums of money. Large payments in, large cash sums withdrawn, a few regular payments, but no overall pattern. It was going to take hours to tease out, and this was only one account. Three others had been tracked down.

Some of the payments had been highlighted. Lofthouse read these out aloud. Written in blue pencil next to three of the most recent transactions was "Possibly Madam Chu's Palace".

'Perhaps she uses a lot of paper clips,' said Steadman wryly.

Lofthouse was staggered by the sums involved. 'What do you think he does with all the money?'

'Although they're big amounts, I'm willing to bet his profit margins are not that great,' Steadman replied. 'What he does make will be stored under a different name in some off-shore account. Like most of us, even crooks like Phil the Shed dream of retiring one day.'

Sergeant Grimble arrived with sandwiches for their lunch.

'How did you get on with Superintendent Campbell?' Steadman asked.

Grimble shook his head. 'A damp patch on her carpet, about a cupful of water on her desk and a couple of soggy reports that no one will ever read any way. You would think it was the end of the world the way she was going on about it. Come on Robbie, I'll take you for a quick walk and get you a drink. Maybe I should take you up to the Superintendent's office and you could lap up the water left on her desk. Do you think she would like that?'

Robbie gave him a lopsided stare.

'No? You're probably right, she wouldn't.' He turned to Steadman. 'I swear that dog of yours understands every word I say.' Grimble strolled off with Robbie in tow.

'I'm sorry to interrupt your lunch,' boomed DCI

Long. 'I have spoken with Superintendent Campbell and you have the go-ahead, John. She is none too happy, and to be honest, I have misgivings. When are you planning on going to Madam Chu's? Are you still intending to take your son?'

'Tonight, if you have no objections. Ben will surely come with me if it means a free meal out.'

'I'll need to speak with him beforehand. How can I get hold of him?' asked DCI Long.

'He's with Linda and Dominic this afternoon.' Steadman rattled off the number.

'Thanks. Are you making any progress?'

'DC Lofthouse is doing an admirable job. To be honest, sir, I believe I'm more of a hindrance than a help.'

Will Lofthouse tried hard not to look smug.

'At the very least it is keeping me out of mischief,' said Steadman.

DCI Long raised an eyebrow. 'From past experience, it will take more than that,' he said as he headed back to his office.

'Would you like another coffee, sir?'

'If it's the same brew as last time, I'd rather have a glass of water. Before we start again, I ought to phone Madam Chu's Palace.'

DC Lofthouse dialled the number and handed Steadman the receiver. It was the Glaswegian waiter who answered.

'A table for two at seven-thirty, Inspector Steadman?

Nae problem. Will you be bringing the big fella with you again?'

'No, no – not even a police officer this time,' Steadman reassured him. 'I would like a private word with Madam Chu after the meal if that's possible.'

'The boss usually takes a wee nap in the evening, 'cos she likes tae poke a nose into the casino later on. I'll ask her, but I'm no promising anything.'

DC Lofthouse replaced the receiver.

'I've got Phil the Shed's most recent phone records,' he said. 'It's a fairly long list, but some numbers keep cropping up – The Red Chip Casino...'

Steadman knew the place, one of Helmsmouth's less salubrious haunts.

'Swingles Nightclub...' Lofthouse continued.

Another venue with a shady reputation, thought Steadman.

'Several bars in the red-light area. Possibly all places where Phil the Shed has worked as a bouncer,' suggested Lofthouse.

'A ruck of mobiles that haven't been traced as yet, and not surprisingly even more with caller ID withheld,' Lofthouse continued.

'Are any of the numbers more frequently called or received than others?' asked Steadman.

'Four or five, by the looks of things. We'll concentrate on those, sir.'

It was frustrating for Steadman not to be able to see the

list. He would have liked to check for patterns of activity. Was any number called at the same time every week, or month? Were some called at odd times, suggesting international calls? Which were the bars that were being called? Steadman knew most of them. There were a dozen other questions he wanted to ask. He frowned and clenched his fists.

Lofthouse glanced up from the sheets of paper and caught Steadman's expression. 'Are you cross, sir? Have I done something wrong?'

Steadman reassured him and told him how he would tackle a list like that. He could hear Lofthouse scribbling it all down.

'What about text messages? Are they to hand yet?'

'I've got a couple of months' worth, sir,' Lofthouse replied leafing through some more pages. 'Some of the numbers match the calls. Most of the messages are brief – some are no more than letters and numbers, a code I presume.'

'What about the others? What do they say?'

Lofthouse glanced up and down the columns. 'These are typical – "call tomorrow", "6pm", "confirmed", "plans changed", "same price", "bring cash", "deal's on", "deal's off", "usual place", "will be 30 minutes late", and so on.'

'Are any of them signed?'

'I can't see any names, sir.'

'What about places? Are any mentioned?'

'A favourite rendezvous is the multi-storey car park at Helmsmouth West Shopping Mall. I'll check if they've got CCTV.'

I bet they don't, mused Steadman.

'There's also a layby on the Upper Bridgetown Road, a couple of bars down by the docks and "casino" crops up more than once but not actually specified.'

There were hours and hours of work involved, thought Steadman. Everything would need to be cross-checked and cross-referenced. The team in the backroom would have their work cut out.

DC Lofthouse had come to much the same conclusion.

'Any suggestions, sir, or is it simply hard slog?'

A possibility struck Steadman. 'Just suppose for the moment that Phil the Shed was mixed up in the murders of Seth Shuster and Rupert Sidley,' he said. 'I don't mean the actual killing, although we can't rule it out...' he continued as though thinking aloud. 'What if he was asked to use his van to move the bodies?'

'So we are looking at calls and texts on the Friday evening going into the early hours of Saturday morning,' Lofthouse replied. He flicked through the sheets of paper. 'No calls but a text just before midnight. "Urgent drop off of envelopes required". Caller ID withheld, I'm afraid, sir.'

'Who requires an urgent supply of envelopes?' said Steadman. 'I'm sure it means something else. Does he respond?'

'Nothing has been recorded,' Lofthouse replied. 'But there's an interesting text at one in the morning – "Merton Cove in forty minutes H".'

Steadman tried hard to picture Merton Cove. He was fairly sure it had a shingle beach protected by wooden groynes leading down to the sea. Who or what "H" stood for, he was at a loss to explain.

CHAPTER 28

Seth slept soundly despite the narrowness of his bunk. After a hearty breakfast he explored what parts of the ship he could get to without being stopped. He took a turn around the area reserved for crew exercise. It was located under the helipad and decidedly scruffy. Smokers huddled together, sheltering from the stiff breeze, coughing and commiserating. Seth had never been a smoker. Even with the gusts of wind the air smelt of stale tobacco. He made his way to the railing and stared out at the sea for a few minutes. It was only water and he got bored very quickly. This could be an awfully long week.

He returned to his cabin, lay down and closed his eyes. The two Americans interested him. Both were crooked, that was obvious. Only time would tell exactly how crooked. Mr Kent, the smaller of the two, was, without a doubt, higher in the pecking order. He didn't even know the name of the other one. A big fellow, a bit old to be a bodyguard, Seth surmised, but big enough not to be meddled with. They had mentioned the 'old boy'. He must be Mr Kent's father, mused Seth, and probably a bigger rogue than the other two put together. My kind of people, he said to himself. What were they into? It had to be gambling of some sort, he concluded, and he was sure tonight was going to be more than just a card game. He was going to be tested – they might even have work for him.

There was one big problem. Gregory Henshaw had been remiss. His papers lacked the necessary visa to enable entry into the States. Seth had neither the time nor the resources to rectify the omission. Could the Americans help him get ashore? He was not sure how it would work out. Then he smiled to himself – things always have a way of working out.

Seth knew tonight was going to be a long session. He laid out clean clothes and determined to sleep for a few hours. There was no need for an alarm; he knew he would wake on time.

At six o'clock precisely Seth woke, showered, and dressed. He glanced at his bare wrist. What the hell, he said to himself, as he strapped on the Patek Philippe watch. He ate something in the crew mess. It was not that he was hungry, he just wanted to line his stomach. He guessed he would be plied with copious amounts of bourbon.

One final check in the mirror. He was pleased with what he saw. A final touch – Gregory's earring. He patted his pocket to make sure he had Mr Bagshott's note authorising him to stray into the exclusive realm of the luxury suites. He needn't have worried, for at twenty to nine precisely Mr Kent's personal steward knocked on his cabin door.

'Henshaw? Follow me,' he sneered as though it were below his dignity to speak to casino staff.

Seth nodded. What did he care? Tonight was not the night for impressing stewards; he had much bigger fish to fry.

* * *

True to his word, Mr Bagshott had laid out a table, and provided gambling chips and sealed packs of cards. The suite was enormous. There was no whiff of diesel here, or even a thrum from the engines. It felt more like being in a five-star hotel than on an ocean-going liner.

Mr Kent, as suave and debonair as on the previous night, was there to greet him. 'Glad you could make it, Gregory,' he said, knowing full well the man had no choice.

'A pleasure to be here, sir,' Seth replied, flashing a smile and trying to sound sincere.

'Felix, please. And I don't believe you were properly introduced to my associate last night,' Mr Kent continued. 'Gregory, this is Mr Clem McKinley, better known as Mount, because that's what everybody calls him on account of his size and his surname being McKinley. I mean, what else would you call him?' He gave a small laugh.

The reference to America's highest peak was not lost on Seth. Mount stood up and glowered in Seth's direction.

'Pleased to make your acquaintance again, Mr McKinley.'

Mount grunted. Mr Kent placed a friendly hand on Seth's shoulder.

'Don't take any notice of him. He's still smarting from you whipping his butt yesterday.'

'Maybe he will have better luck tonight,' Seth replied.

'Now, Gregory, you and I both know that luck has very little to do with it,' said Mr Kent.

A stooped old man had joined them. His hair was pure white and swept back to reveal a wrinkled face and a misshapen nose. A few too many scrapes in his youth, thought Seth. But his eyes were the most striking feature. They were gunmetal grey and quite terrifying. He looked at Seth Shuster as though reading his soul.

'Pops, I'm so glad you could join us. Gregory, this is my father, Mr Julius Kent.'

'Is this the card-shark you told me about, Felix?'

His son nodded.

'Good evening, Mr Kent,' said Seth with a slight bow of his head.

'Don't bother with the Mr Kent, it's too confusing. And I can't stand Julius either – never could abide the name. You can call me Pops like everybody else does.' His voice was sharp; each sentence was like the crack of a whip. He glanced at his son. 'What did you say his name was?'

'Gregory Henshaw, Pops,'

The old man again turned his piercing gaze on Seth Shuster.

'Like hell it is.'

Seth smiled by way of reply.

'No matter,' the old man continued, 'he's not a cop, and I'd wager what's left of my miserable life he has a criminal record as long as the Mississippi.' The old man neither waited nor expected a reply, instead he teetered over to the cocktail cabinet and opened a fresh bottle of bourbon. He poured Seth a large glass.

'You may need this, Gregory. I do believe Mount is out for revenge,' he cackled. 'Let's all sit down. I'm only going to watch to begin with.'

'What game would you like to play, gentlemen?' asked Seth. They chose a game. 'And would you like me to deal?'

'That's the idea, Gregory. Felix and Mount tell me you're pretty nifty with the cards. I want to see just how nifty,'

Seth opened a pack and discarded the Jokers.

'Go on, you shuffle them,' Pops continued.

Seth shuffled. The old man appeared unimpressed.

'Would you like me to shuffle a little faster, sir?'

'I said call me Pops. Let's see how fast you can go.'

The cards whirred in Seth's hands. Backwards and forwards, in and out, spiralling with dazzling speed until he finally laid them back in a neat stack on the green baize.

The old man lifted an appreciative eyebrow.

'What's the top card?' he asked.

'Four of Hearts,' Seth responded without a pause.

The old man turned over the top card. Sure enough, it was the Four of Hearts. He cut the pack several times and placed it back in front of Seth.

'Now deal,' he said shoving three equal piles of chips in front of each man.

They played in silence. To begin with there seemed to be no pattern to the game. Sometimes Mount won, sometimes Felix Kent and sometimes Seth. After twenty minutes of play, however, Seth had all their chips neatly lined up in front of him.

'Damn, but you're good, Gregory,' declared the old man. 'I've been watching you like a hawk and you only faltered once. I bet the boys didn't even notice.'

Felix gave a little shake of his head. Mount merely grunted again.

'I like your watch,' said Pops appreciatively. 'A family heirloom?'

Seth looked at his watch. 'No,' he replied, 'I won it playing poker.'

The old man cackled again. 'Mount, you better go put your Rolex in the safe before young Gregory has it on his other wrist. More bourbon,' he declared. 'And I'm going to play this time. Real money and a different game...'

Seth feigned ignorance of the game.

'Oh, you'll pick it up as we go along. Get a fresh deck.'

Seth unwrapped a new pack, shuffled and, following the old man's instructions, dealt the cards.

After quarter of an hour, Pops looked Seth in the eye. 'I want to win,' he said.

Seth duly obliged.

'Now him,' said the old man pointing to his son.

Felix Kent's pile of chips rapidly increased.

'Better not leave Mount out of it – his turn.'

Seth dealt, and folded. He knew precisely what cards the others had in their hands. All were good, but Mount's was the best.

'I reckon you've blown it this time, Gregory,' said the old man pushing more of his chips out to the centre of the table.

Felix grinned and did the same.

Mount was sweating. To stay in the game and call his opponents would have meant putting all his chips on the table. He was about to fold when Seth gently touched his arm. 'Call them,' he said softly with a hint of a smile.

'If you're wrong, Gregory, so help me, I'm going to rearrange that smile on your goddamned face,' he said.

They showed their cards. Mount let out a loud whoop and scooped in the chips with a fat greasy hand.

'Well, I'll be...' said Felix.

The old man found the whole thing highly entertaining. 'Where did you learn to play like that, son?'

'Here and there. I'm mainly self-taught.'

'You are a naughty boy, I'll swear. Mind you, so was I in my day. With talent like that, why are you stuck on this floating heap of junk? No, don't tell me – you're trying to get to the States because England's got too hot for you, too many people breathing down your neck.'

'You could say something like that,' Seth conceded.

'Maybe somebody wants their fancy watch back,' Pops suggested. 'What are you going to do for money?'

'Get a job, I guess,' Seth replied.

'Go take a comfort break, Gregory. I want to have a quiet word with the boys here.'

Seth spent some time in the bathroom. He admired himself in the mirror. The evening had gone well, he thought. He flushed the toilet and opened the door noisily.

'It's OK, you can come back in, son,' said Pops. 'Take a seat.'

Seth's glass had been refilled during his absence.

'We run some of the major casinos in New York, and a few other things,' explained the old man. 'You've probably figured that one out already.'

Seth nodded and picked up the abandoned pack of cards. He began to shuffle them slowly.

'I'm going to offer you a job. What I don't know is if I can trust you.'

Seth flipped over the top card. It was the Joker. 'Can you trust anybody these days? How much are you thinking of paying me? Or shall we cut for it?'

The old man laughed. 'I like your style, but I wasn't born yesterday, nor the day before that. I pay top dollar.'

Seth cut the pack and offered Pops a card. He turned it over – the Ten of Clubs, the card of fortune and financial success.

'However, if you cheat us...'

'We make you disappear,' chipped in Mount with evident satisfaction.

Seth flicked over the Ace of Spades. 'I get it,' he said, nonchalantly shuffling and cutting the cards again. 'With a surname like McKinley you must have some Scottish blood in your ancestry.' He tossed the top card in Mount's direction. The big American turned it over slowly – the Nine of Diamonds, the curse of Scotland.

'Don't get smart with me, Henshaw.' Mount rose to his feet.

'Sit down,' barked the old man. 'It's only a playing card.'

'One problem, sir,' said Seth.

'What's that?'

'I don't have the necessary visa.'

'You mean, Gregory Henshaw didn't have one when you stole his papers?'

Seth didn't answer.

'I guess it comes to the same thing,' the old man continued. 'I'm sure we can organise it. Are you in?'

Seth stopped in mid-shuffle and dealt four Kings followed by four Aces.

'Damn, but you're good,' said Pops.

'Maybe too damned good,' added Mount.

CHAPTER 29

Steadman came out of his bedroom. 'How do I look?' he asked.

Ben pulled a face. 'You're not going to wear a tie, are you?'

'Why not?'

'It's a Chinese restaurant. Nobody wears a tie to a Chinese restaurant unless they're having a business lunch with the boss.'

'May I remind you, Ben, that I'm going there on a semi-official basis. I'm hoping to have a chat, albeit informally, with a person of interest in a murder investigation.'

'How you can have an informal chat while wearing a tie beats me, dad.'

Before the debate could get even more heated, the doorbell rang. Steadman was perplexed. He pressed the button on the side of his watch. It was way too early for the taxi.

'That will be Sam,' said Ben.

Steadman was even more baffled. 'What do you mean, "that will be Sam"?' he asked.

'There's been a change of plan,' Ben explained. 'If you are going out on a dinner date, wouldn't you rather take Sam than me?'

Steadman was livid. 'No, Ben, no...' Images of the dream flashed through his mind. 'Madam Chu's Palace may well have a very nice restaurant, but all sorts of other things go on there. I'm sure of it. There is a risk to this enterprise tonight. I don't want to put Sam in any danger...'

'Oh, I see – it's OK to put your son in that position,' said Ben, but he was smiling.

'That's not what I meant. You've been in plenty of scrapes in your life. You can take care of yourself.'

The doorbell rang again.

'I'll get it,' said Ben.

Sam had heard the row and was clearly upset. 'It's all right, John, I'll just walk back to the hotel. I thought you knew, or I would never have come.'

Steadman's anger turned to confusion and embarrassment. 'Knew what? I'm lost.' He threw up his hands.

'I forgot to mention,' said Ben. 'DCI Long phoned.'

'Ben, why didn't you tell me?'

'I didn't want to spoil the surprise,' Ben replied giving Sam a conspiratorial glance.

Sam stared at her feet, not knowing whether to stay or leave.

Steadman broke the awkward silence. 'Let's all sit down and hear what DCI Long has suggested, and what my errant son has failed to tell me.'

They made their way to the sitting room. Perhaps because he sensed her distress, Robbie opted to lie on Sam's feet.

'It's quite simple really,' said Ben. He sounded contrite, realising that he had blundered. 'DCI Long didn't want the two of us to go by ourselves.'

'But...'

'Let me finish, dad. Don't worry I'll be there as well, only at a separate table with Cleo Osborne. Fiona Fairfax and Will Lofthouse will be joining us. I gather Fiona took a bit of persuasion as Will has been pestering her for a date for ages.'

Steadman would have been more comfortable if Alan Munro had been in the party. As though reading his thoughts, Ben continued, 'And Alan Munro and possibly a couple of others will be in a car not far away, just in case.'

A horn tooted outside the flat. Ben looked out of the window.

'There's your taxi.'

Steadman sighed. He turned towards where Sam was sitting, not really knowing what to say or do to make the situation better. Eventually he spoke.

'Sam, would you like to have dinner with me at Madam Chu's Palace tonight?'

Sam looked up. 'I'd like that very much, John.'

'Would you like me to take off my tie?'

'Whatever for? It suits you. It wouldn't be you without a tie.'

'You are outvoted, Ben,' said Steadman. It was a petty triumph, but a triumph, nonetheless.

★ ★ ★

In sharp contrast to the chill night air, the taxi was hot and stuffy. Steadman and Sam squeezed into the backseat followed by Robbie. Sam's perfume filled the cab and Steadman felt his heart race.

'I'm sorry if I appeared rude earlier,' said Steadman. 'I don't know what Ben was playing at by not telling me.'

'Do you really think there might be a risk?' asked Sam.

Steadman bit his thumbnail. Should he mention his dream?

'If you promise not to mock me,' he said after a pause, 'I'll tell you the reason I am so apprehensive about taking you to Madam Chu's.'

Sam listened attentively. Like all dreams, it lost its sparkle and realism in the telling.

'It was so vivid,' Steadman concluded almost apologetically.

Sam gave his hand a squeeze. It must have been very

distressing,' she said, although she was more intrigued to know how Steadman had visualised her in his dream. She didn't dare to ask.

★ ★ ★

The Chinese lanterns shone red and gold. Even the huge pots of bamboo were illuminated. The taxi pulled up by the two enormous stone lions guarding the portico.

'This all looks very grand, John,' said Sam.

'If I recall correctly, it is even more lavish inside,' Steadman replied.

They were met at the door by the same Glaswegian waiter.

'Good evening, Inspector Steadman,' he said as he held the door open for them. He cast an approving eye over Sam Griffiths. 'I've given you the same wee table as last time. Follow me, though I expect your clever doggie would remember the way.'

Sam linked her arm in Steadman's. The restaurant was spectacular with candles on every table, twinkling fairy lights, a profusion of greenery and oriental artefacts. There were even floating lanterns on the large fishpond. A small waterfall tinkled over some rocks and the ghostly shadows of the koi carp flitted between the lily pads. Music played softly in the background. Many of the tables were occupied and Steadman was vaguely aware of murmured conversations. But with the plants and furnishings the restaurant didn't feel at all crowded, as each table was nestled in its own intimate arbour.

'This is enchanting, John. Very romantic.'

'You're nae English, ma'am, are you?' asked the waiter.

Sam confirmed she was Welsh.

'Ah! – a fellow Celt,' he said warmly. 'Talking of things English, Inspector Steadman, I hope you are not going to have any of that muck you had last time. It's the top chef tonight and he's awfully easily offended.'

Steadman assured him he was going to sample the Chinese cuisine.

'Excellent. You won't be wanting these,' he said, discreetly removing the chopsticks. 'I'll bring you some cutlery and the menu.'

Sam pondered the lengthy menu. 'Do you know what you're going to have, John?'

'Yes – largely based, I'm afraid, on what is least likely to dribble down my tie,' he replied with a smile. 'I'm going to start with the prawn and sesame toasts followed by egg foo yung. What about you?'

'I can never resist spring rolls, especially if they are homemade, and then I think I'll have the Peking duck – it's the house speciality.'

Steadman ordered the food and a bottle of German Riesling. He opened his wallet and offered one of his cards to the waiter.

'Perhaps you would give this to Madam Chu and let her know I'm here?'

'There's no need. She kens fine you're here.'

'Will she see me?'

'That all depends,' he said enigmatically.

'He's not the easiest man to understand,' confessed Sam. 'His accent is very strong.'

'Oh, I don't know,' Steadman replied. 'After years of working with Munro...'

His explanation was cut short by a noisy party being led to an adjacent table. Ben's laugh was unmistakable.

'The cavalry has arrived,' he mumbled under his breath.

The food and wine were delicious, but there was no hint from the waiter as the meal went on that Madam Chu would see him.

'Damn,' he muttered as he finished and laid down his fork and knife. 'I thought she just might play ball. Still, the meal was superb and the company extremely pleasant.'

Sam agreed. 'It has been a memorable evening, John.'

The waiter brought them coffee and two fortune cookies. 'Compliments of the house,' he said.

'Oh, I love fortune cookies,' said Sam with girlish glee. 'Shall I read your one for you?'

Steadman cracked open the cookie and handed her the slip of paper. Sam scanned the note.

'Well, that's not what I expected. It's handwritten. It says, "Madam Chu will expect you at nine".'

Steadman pressed the button on his watch, it was eight forty-five.

'A quarter of an hour to enjoy our coffee. Aren't you going to read your one?'

Sam tapped the cookie on her side plate and unfolded the message. It too was handwritten, only this time it read, "Why don't you tell him how you really feel?"

Hastily, she crumpled up the piece of paper.

'Nice coffee,' she said.

'So, what was your message?'

Sam was saved from answering by the return of the waiter. He grinned at Sam and gave her a playful wink.

'If you're ready, Inspector Steadman, I'll take you up now.'

Steadman nodded and slipped Robbie's harness back on.

'Just a moment, John,' said Sam. She took her napkin and brushed some crumbs off his lapel.

'If the young lady would care to join your colleagues, I've laid an extra place at their table.'

Sam looked over at Ben. He shrugged and pointed to the empty seat.

'Was it that obvious?' Steadman asked.

'Do you think I came down the Clyde on a water biscuit, Inspector Steadman?' the waiter replied. 'Now, will your doggie follow me, or will I take your arm? The place is cluttered with ornaments.'

Their passage through the restaurant caused a bit of

a stir. Eyes turned in their direction and conversations stopped as they passed.

'They probably think you're leaving without paying and I'm leading you to the kitchen to do the dishes,' said the waiter.

They left through a narrow door at the rear of the restaurant. There was a sudden draught and for a moment Steadman thought that he had been led outside. He need not have worried.

'Madam Chu's apartment is on the top floor. Will you manage the stairs?'

Steadman reassured him that Robbie would guide him safely without the need for extra assistance. The waiter watched fascinated as Robbie's head twitched, and Steadman safely put his foot on the first step.

'Tell me about my colleagues on the other table,' Steadman asked.

'Are you testing me out, Inspector? Well, only three of them are police officers, as far as I can make out.'

'Go on,' said Steadman intrigued by the answer.

'The laddie with the ponytail and goatee beard is no from the police.'

'What do you think he does?'

'He's an artist of some sort, I reckon – probably a performer or a showman.' He stopped suddenly and turned to face Steadman. 'Can I be very presumptive, Inspector?'

'Try me,' Steadman replied.

'Would you slip off your dark glasses for a second and let me see you properly?'

Steadman smiled and obliged.

'Aye – I thought so. The laddie's your spit. He's your son, isn't he? Although he did nae get that suntan in Helmsmouth!'

They continued up the stairs.

'He's getting on real well with the good-looking black lassie. I can't say the same for the other fellow.'

'No?' queried Steadman.

'No, not at all,' the waiter replied. 'He keeps giving the blonde woman lecherous looks, but she's having none of it.'

'You are very observant. Don't you think you're wasted working in a restaurant?'

'You think so? Tell me, how much does a detective inspector get paid?'

Steadman quoted a figure, and the waiter shook his head. 'You couldn't afford me,' he said.

'May I ask your name?'

'Everybody calls me Jockie Chan on account of the accent. It's as good a name as any, I suppose. We're almost here. I must ask you to keep Robbie in his harness. Madam Chu's a bit fearful of dogs. And another thing, she's adamant that you've not to pay for your meal tonight. If you insist, she won't see you.'

Reluctantly, Steadman agreed. 'Would you prepare the bill for my son's table? At least let me pay for that.'

They arrived at last on the top floor. Jockie Chan knocked lightly on the door and a quavering voice from within said, 'Enter.'

My, thought Steadman, Elsie Entwistle, otherwise known as Madam Chu, has aged, either that or I'm going to be treated to an extraordinary performance.

CHAPTER 30

Jockie led Steadman to a large, comfortable armchair. He eased himself into the seat and snapped his fingers. Robbie immediately lay down spread-eagled at his feet.

The room was very warm. Incense was burning. Steadman felt ill at ease, as the cloying perfume brought back a host of unpleasant memories.

'Thank you, Jockie. I will call you when the Inspector is ready to leave,' said Madam Chu.

'Very good, Madam Chu.'

The door clicked shut behind him.

'It's been a long time, Inspector Steadman.' There was no trace of her native Lancashire accent. Her vowels were imperceptibly lengthened, and the consonants clipped a fraction. This was no ham actor pretending to be oriental. She lived and breathed the part.

'It has indeed, Elsie,' Steadman replied.

The old lady clicked her tongue. 'I no longer recognise

the name. I am Madam Ying Chu and have been for so long that the past is but a dusty memory.'

'Are we alone?' Steadman enquired.

'We are. I have, of course, taken certain precautions – just as you have. I see now that I need not have bothered. Life has been most unkind to you, Inspector Steadman. I gather you are completely blind.'

'Occasionally, I can discern a flash of bright light. That's all,' Steadman replied.

'Sadly then, the charming décor of my beautiful restaurant would be lost on you.'

'I'm afraid it was. My companion appreciated it and thought the place enchanting.'

'And you?'

'I could feel the warmth of the candles. The food was excellent.'

Steadman relaxed a little. There was no rush to the conversation. He knew Sam was safe.

'Your companion is very pretty.'

'So I've been told. I wouldn't know.'

'What does she do? She is not a police officer.'

'No, she is a forensic psychologist.'

'Be careful, Inspector. She may well know what you are thinking.'

Robbie stirred and sneezed. The stench from the incense was upsetting his sensitive nose.

Madam Chu glanced down to where Robbie lay. 'I thought they might have given you an Alsatian as a guide dog. It would have been more fitting perhaps. I do not trust Alsatians. Your dog appears remarkably docile.'

Robbie sat up and Steadman gently patted his head. 'He is highly intelligent, with a streak of stubborn persistence.'

'Ah, a lot like you then, Inspector. I believe I read somewhere that they match a guide dog's temperament to that of their prospective owner.'

Steadman's eyes had started to water.

'Forgive me, Inspector. I forget that my incense is not to everyone's taste.' She hobbled from her chair, licked her fingers, and snuffed out the joss stick. 'How well I remember your first visit to this very room,' she continued. It was as though the curling smoke had brought back the memory.

'My recollections are rather hazy.'

Madam Chu gave a small chuckle. 'I don't suppose you have ever forgiven me. You were so young and pompous then. You needed taking down a peg or two. You were even sporting a ghastly moustache.'

Steadman had not forgotten the moustache. Holly, his late wife, had not approved. It had lasted less than a month.

'And you were smoking a pipe.' Madam Chu smiled wistfully. 'Who did you think you were? Sherlock Holmes?'

'I believe I was modelling myself on Maigret.'

'The Belgian detective?'

'I think you'll find that was Hercule Poirot. Although

Georges Simenon, who wrote the Maigret novels, was born in Belgium.'

Madam Chu dismissed the correction with a wave of her hand. 'We were very mischievous to steal your pipe.'

'It wasn't the purloining of my pipe that was outrageous. It was the fact that you put a small pellet of opium in it without my knowledge, then encouraged me to smoke the damned thing. I distinctly recall you saying how you liked the smell of pipe tobacco. In fact, that was my last clear recollection of our first meeting.'

Madam Chu chortled. 'I almost had you, John Steadman. I'm sure you will admit it was one of the most pleasurable experiences of your life.'

And for a fleeting moment, it had been. Steadman's memories of the events of the day were fragmented. He could recall lighting his pipe and an enormous weight being lifted off his shoulders as he inhaled the sweet smoke. He had felt an overwhelming sense of calm, with no aches or pains, no cares or worries, an overwhelming sense of calm, not an ache or a pain, not a care or a worry. He was numb, yet everything seemed perfect. How long it lasted he could only hazard a guess. He had never felt like it before or since.

Holly had found him slumped in their car outside his house. Still in a stupor, he had begun to tell her how wonderful the world was, and how great he felt. But she had noted his pinpoint pupils and the sickly, musty smell that clung to his clothing, and instantly she had realised exactly what had happened. Bursting into tears, she had slapped her husband as hard as she dared. Steadman could picture the moment vividly; Holly crying, completely distraught, and her words still echoed round his head. 'You fool, John, you utter fool. Wake up and look at yourself. You have a choice – me, a baby son, a career – or you can spend the rest of your life chasing the dragon, knowing full well you will never, ever catch it again.'

With that, she had turned and stormed back indoors, but she had left the door open. Steadman knew he had to make a choice, possibly the most important choice of his life: walk through that door and back to the harsh realities of normality, or risk losing everything. He walked through the door, and it was true, he had never forgiven Madam Chu.

Steadman shook his head as if to rid himself of the memory.

'I assume you still have your regular clientele,' he said after a pause.

'What do you mean, Inspector? I have loyal customers who frequent my restaurant and casino.'

'You know that's not what I'm talking about, Elsie.'

'No one calls me that anymore,' she snapped waspishly. 'And if you mean opium. Well, who smokes opium these days?'

Steadman noted the vagueness of her reply. She was neither confirming nor denying that she still ran an opium den.

'Old habits die hard, as you well know,' Steadman replied. 'A niche market perhaps, but a market nonetheless and potentially very lucrative. I believe you still have friends in high places.'

'I have no idea what you are implying, Inspector Steadman. A lot of people come to my establishment. I'm sure some of them are important in their own way, politicians, judges, wealthy businessmen, peers of the realm even. I'm not so sure I would call them friends.'

'They offer you a degree of protection.'

'They give me a steady source of income, nothing more. In return, I give them a place to relax, eat, entertain, and escape their everyday lives. Is that so wrong?'

Steadman drummed his fingers on the arm of his chair. 'And the police never bother you?'

'Why should they?'

'Because, Elsie Entwistle, you have a criminal record dating back to when you first learnt to read and write – fraud, forgery, drug dealing, running brothels – need I go on? '

Madam Chu bridled. 'Is that why you have come to visit me, Inspector Steadman, to hurl insults at an old lady?'

Steadman let her anger linger in the air.

'No, that's not why I've come at all. You know perfectly well why I'm here. I'm investigating the murders of Seth

Shuster and Rupert Sidley.'

Madam Chu tutted again. 'Why are you wasting your time? I thought the police would be delighted to see the back of those two. Let me give you some advice, Inspector. You knew Shuster better than anyone else in the police force. You will agree, I'm sure, that he was a most dangerous criminal. In fact, the most dangerous man I have ever met, and yes, it's true, I was no stranger to that side of life. Are you really telling me that the world is not a better place without him? Go home with your pretty lady friend and forget the whole thing.'

'Not even tempted, Elsie. You know I won't do that.' Steadman gave her a wan smile. 'Tell me about Rupert Sidley. He doesn't have a police record, although I gather, he should have.'

Madam Chu sighed. 'Another crook. He knew his legal stuff, I'll grant you, and I have even made use of his services myself. He exploited his knowledge at every opportunity to feather his already comfortable nest. Another one whose loss will not be missed.'

Steadman leant forward in his chair and put his long bony fingers together. 'Here's my problem. I do not disagree with you that Shuster was an abomination, and that Rupert Sidley was an amoral villain. However, both their lives have been taken. As a police officer, I can't tolerate that. If the police allow killings to go unchallenged, they will never end. Society as we know it will crumble.'

'An interesting point of view, Inspector, and perhaps with some justification. It doesn't explain why you are bothering me.'

Steadman sat back in his chair and stretched out his legs. 'Ah, here's the thing, Elsie. You see, we know that Shuster and Sidley came to see you, possibly in this very room.'

'And just why would they do that?'

'I was hoping you would tell me.'

Madam Chu did not answer.

'My guess is that Shuster wanted to buy a piece of the action,' Steadman continued. 'He too has a lifetime's experience of drug dealing, gambling, and prostitution. As you yourself said, you are an old lady – who is going to take over once you're gone? I believe Shuster made you an offer and brought along the loathsome Sidley with some sort of contract, and a bottle of champagne.'

Madam Chu puffed herself up. 'I detest champagne! My business is not for sale,' she replied haughtily.

'I don't doubt that,' said Steadman. 'Do you deny they were here?'

'I see your mind is already made up on that one, Inspector Steadman. My denial would be pointless.'

'What I can't understand, Elsie, is why you had them killed.'

'Killed? Do you really think I have killed anyone in my life?'

'Not you personally perhaps, but someone on your staff. Mr Chan perhaps? He seems very devoted to you.'

'I don't hire killers, Inspector. Mr Chan is my eyes and ears. There is very little that gets past him, and I pay him handsomely.'

'What about the chap sitting behind the door? You are not going to deny his presence as well? I can hear his chair squeak every time he moves. I presume he's being paid for his muscle and not for lighting the candles in your restaurant.'

'As I said earlier, I take precautions just as you do. I'm getting tired of all of this. Have you any more preposterous suggestions to put to me?'

Steadman pressed the button on the side of his watch. He had already been in the room for the best part of half an hour.

'Humour me a bit longer, Elsie. Supposing that Shuster and Sidley came here as I suggested.' Madam Chu clicked her tongue again. Steadman ignored her. 'I assume that Shuster made you an offer and when you declined, he threatened you.'

Madam Chu did not answer.

'I wonder what Shuster and Sidley knew that could be so damaging?'

The old lady's silence was deafening. Steadman's brain was in overdrive. Past images and faces, snatches of conversation and scraps of dreams rose and fell and whirled around in his consciousness like wheat grains being tossed into the air. And with each throw some of the worthless chaff blew away. The grains fell again, now clean.

An idea started to form in his head. It took shape, became more solid. It was a possibility...

He turned towards Madam Chu and smiled. 'Perhaps Seth Shuster had been speaking with Phil the Shed,' he said. 'His van has been seen outside your premises, with Phil carrying in packages. I doubt if you use that many envelopes. Now, what would Phil the Shed, a man who is a known drug dealer amongst other things, be delivering? And come to think of it,' Steadman added, 'what could he possibly be taking away, or even disposing for you?'

Madam Chu seemed amused, but Steadman detected a hint of nervousness in her forced laughter.

'What a vivid imagination you have, Inspector. You are flying a kite, and you know it. Philip provides me with office supplies, nothing more. You have no proof of your unfounded allegations. Admit it.'

It was true. Steadman plucked at his trousers. A tune started playing in his head, not Bach but Chet Baker's 'Almost Blue', slightly dissonant yet harmonious. What had he to go on? Phil's past form, a coincidence, payments on a bank statement, a hunch, a disturbing dream?

'You are right, Elsie, I have no proof, not yet anyway. However, I'm sure we'll get it, and when we do, I'll confront Phil. He'll squeal like the proverbial pig trying to save his own bacon. Even your money won't guarantee his loyalty.'

'I have no need to buy his loyalty.' She spat out the words. The faux oriental lisp slipped a little; there was a definite Lancashire edge to her vowels.

He had touched a raw nerve, Steadman thought with some satisfaction.

'Do you deny that Shuster and Sidley have been here?' he asked determined to press home the advantage.

'I'm tired of this, Inspector Steadman. You are wasting my time and yours. The police should drop this case. No one will miss either of them, especially Seth Shuster.'

The music in Steadman's head stopped abruptly and was replaced by a vision of a solitary figure standing in the shadows. A man who was so like the young Seth Shuster, he could have been his double, sad, and desperately wanting to speak. But as he started to speak, the words froze on his lips and he turned and fled.

'That's where I know you are wrong,' Steadman said after a pause. 'At least one person in Helmsmouth cares.'

Madam Chu must have pressed a bell, for the door opened and Jockie Chan entered.

'It has been a pleasure meeting you again, Inspector Steadman. I fear your charming companion is missing you. I mustn't take up any more of your time. Mr Chan will escort you back.' Any trace of her native accent had once again disappeared.

Robbie stood up and gave himself a shake.

'Thank you for agreeing to see me, Madam Chu,' Steadman replied. 'You have been extremely helpful,' he added, with more than a hint of irony. He did not offer to shake her hand.

★ ★ ★

'Did you find out what you were after?' asked Jockie as they made their way downstairs.

'You know I didn't. Your boss keeps her cards very close to her chest,' Steadman replied. 'How much is the bill for my colleagues' table?'

'Ninety-six pounds in total.'

They stopped on a landing. Steadman opened his wallet and gave the waiter six twenty-pound notes, each with a corner neatly folded.

'You've given me twenty too much.'

'Not at all. That's for looking after my companion.'

'Are you sure that's all she is, Inspector Steadman? I dinna think so. I've seen the way she looks at you.'

Steadman felt his face burning and quickly changed the subject. 'What do you know about Phil the Shed and his involvement with Madam Chu?'

'Aye, your tip was generous, but no that good,' Jockie replied as he opened the door to the restaurant. Without saying another word, he led Steadman back to the table where Sam was sitting.

'Are you all right, John?' she asked anxiously.

'I'm fine, but I would like to go home,' Steadman replied.

'I'll fetch your coats,' said Jockie.

'Would you possibly order a taxi as well?' Steadman added.

'There will be no need for that. Yon big fella has been cruisin' up and doon all night in a big green Audi with a worried frown on his face. You would think his wife was in here giving birth. I'm sure he'll give you a lift.' He vanished behind the foliage and fairy lights.

'Did you find out anything useful, sir?' asked Fiona Fairfax.

Steadman's face twitched. 'Possibly – it was more what was left unsaid than said. I need to think it over. I'll give you a full briefing in the morning. By the way, I've taken care of your bill.'

'You're a star, dad,' Ben chipped in. 'I may be late home,' he added, casting a glance at Cleo Osborne.

Munro was waiting at the door for them. He got out of the Audi and opened the rear door. In the shadow of one of the enormous pots of bamboo, his collar turned up against the cold night air, a man was standing. Sam pressed Steadman's arm.

'He's there again, just beyond the stone lions,' she whispered.

Steadman did not seem in the least surprised.

'I'm too tired to talk to him tonight,' he said. 'Let's go.'

In truth, Steadman was not at all sure what he could

say to him.

CHAPTER 31

Sam's perfume again filled the car. It was like a breath of fresh air compared to the repellent odour of Madam Chu's incense.

'I'm so glad you're safe, sir,' said Munro as he eased the Audi through the narrow cobbled streets around the docks. 'I'm just going to pull over. I have to phone DCI Long.'

Steadman could only hear half the conversation.

'He's fine, sir…Yes, completely unscathed…Tomorrow morning at ten… I'll make sure he gets the message.'

Steadman sighed. 'It appears I've put everybody to a lot of unnecessary work and worry.'

'A bit like Daniel in the lion's den,' said Munro.

'I'm not so sure, Alan. If I recall correctly, Daniel was thrown in, betrayed by his colleagues. Whereas I went voluntarily, and my colleagues were sitting not so far away, and you were circling the block. The only time I felt remotely anxious was when the Glaswegian waiter led me from the restaurant. For a moment, I thought he had taken me out to the alley behind Madam Chu's Palace, not to the foot of a draughty stairwell leading up to her private apartment. Besides Jockie Chan...'

Munro chortled. 'Get on with you! That's not really his name, is it?'

'I have no idea,' confessed Steadman. 'It's what he answers to. As I was saying, Jockie Chan recognised Fiona Fairfax, Will Lofthouse and Cleo Osborne as police officers. He even worked out that Ben was my son. He also noticed you driving up and down with a concerned look on your face. He's bright. There's not much going on that he doesn't notice.'

I wonder what he thought of me, mused Sam. The time wasn't right to ask, maybe later...

'I did try to get some answers out of him,' Steadman continued. 'Sadly, Madam Chu pays him too much. I'll tell you all about it at tomorrow's meeting. Ten o'clock did you say?'

Munro confirmed the time. 'Will I pick you up, sir?'

'No thanks. I would like to walk and gather my thoughts,' Steadman replied.

Robbie squirmed at his feet then butted his muzzle gently against Steadman's thigh.

'Where are we, Alan?'

371

'Just coming up to the Greek delicatessen.'

'Robbie's getting restless. Would you mind dropping us off? We know the way from here. I think we could both do with stretching our legs.'

Munro pulled up at the kerb. 'There you go, sir, right outside the door to the deli.'

'May I join you?' asked Sam. 'The restaurant was beautiful, but the chairs were not that comfortable.'

'Oh, I almost forgot!' exclaimed Munro. 'And Maureen would have killed me if I hadn't remembered. We're having a Burns Supper at our house tomorrow night. Haggis, neeps and tatties – the works! You are both invited, and Ben of course. Dr Rufus has already agreed to come, and he is going to do the Address to the Lassies.'

'What's that?' asked Sam.

'You'll see. Nothing formal – it will be fun.'

'I've never had haggis.'

'Well, Sam, you are in for a real treat,' Munro replied. 'Kilts are optional, an empty stomach obligatory.'

They got out of the car and Sam linked her arm in Steadman's. By way of an excuse, she declared that the pavement was a bit slippery and that Robbie looked tired.

'He is,' Steadman agreed. 'Robbie is usually off duty by now and fast asleep. It's a good thing I've got you to guide me.'

Sam glanced at Steadman. Was he teasing or being serious? In the half-light and not being able to see his eyes, it was impossible to tell.

The street was empty, and a gentle rain had started to fall.

'You seem very pensive, John.'

'I was thinking about a much earlier encounter I had with Madam Chu... damn it, I can't keep calling her that. Her real name is Elsie Entwistle. She's a sham. In fact, the whole thing is a great big fraud, a lie,' said Steadman angrily. 'She very nearly ruined my life, and I have never forgiven her.'

Sam said nothing. She knew that if he wanted to tell her, he would.

'I was young and arrogant,' he continued. 'Heaven help me, I even smoked a pipe. Elsie conspired to steal my pipe and stick some opium in the bowl, and then she watched me smoke it.'

'What was it like?' asked Sam.

'That's the point – it was wonderful. I'll never forget it, but it was, like Madam Chu herself and her Palace, all an illusion. And I nearly fell for it.'

Sam was intrigued. 'Do you think she still supplies opium?'

'Her answer to that, and her answers to all the questions I put to her about Shuster and Sidley, were entirely evasive. Only one thing rattled her during our whole conversation and that was when I suggested Shuster may have known about Phil the Shed's nefarious goings-on, and what he actually delivered to her Palace. I even hinted at what Phil might have taken away in his van. It was a spur-of-the-moment stab in the dark, yet it struck home. I'm hoping we will find out more tomorrow. Will Lofthouse has been going through all Phil's business dealings.'

Subconsciously, Steadman had been counting the steps. Robbie slowed down and they came to a halt directly outside his door.

'That's impressive,' said Sam.

Steadman pretended not to hear her. 'I'm sorry if I went off on a rant. Would you care for a nightcap?'

'Are you trying to lead a girl astray?'

Steadman became flustered. 'No, no – I was...'

Sam Griffiths put a finger on his lips. 'The correct answer, John, should have been "yes".'

'And, Dr Samantha Griffiths,' Steadman retaliated, 'the correct answer to my perfectly innocent question should also have been a "yes" – not an excuse to torment me.'

'In that case, Detective Inspector John Steadman,' she replied with mock formality, 'I would love a nightcap.'

They let Robbie out in the garden behind the café before climbing the stairs to Steadman's flat. He opened the door and the dog staggered to his bed. He was snoring gently by the time Sam and Steadman had taken off their wet coats.

'What's it to be?' Steadman had opened the drinks cabinet and his fingers were lightly dancing over the tops of the single malt whisky bottles. He hesitated over a large stopper. His fingers slid down the side of the dumpy, square, dimpled bottle. 'Cardhu,' he said with some satisfaction, 'Warming, with a hint of sweetness. That will do nicely.'

He poured two generous measures. Sam took the glass from his outstretched hand.

'*Iechyd da!* – isn't that what you say in Wales?'

'Now you're just showing off,' Sam replied, then added, 'Good health!'

They sipped their whiskies. The soothing glow of the spirit dispelled the cold and damp of the night that had seeped into their bones on the short walk home.

'Tell me about Holly,' said Sam.

Steadman was completely taken aback. Of all the things he had supposed they might talk about, his late wife was the last thing on the list.

'May I ask why?' queried Steadman.

Sam gave a slight shrug of her shoulders. 'I would like to know... I need to know... She was, is, so much part of your life. If I don't ask you now, I may never ask you, and then there will always be something between us. I don't want that, but I also don't want to cause you distress. Maybe I shouldn't have mentioned it.'

Steadman pushed his dark glasses on to his forehead and smiled. 'No, Sam – you have every right to know. Let's start at the beginning.'

For the next half hour Steadman painted a picture of his wife, how they had met at school, been childhood sweethearts, drifted apart only to meet again as adults.

'It was a charity event,' Steadman explained. 'Holly was always championing some good cause or other. We both realised the old flame still flickered and... well, you can guess the rest.'

He described how Holly was impulsive, how they got married on a whim at a registry office. Dr Rufus was there along with his sister, Linda, and how, within a year, Ben was born.

'That was probably the happiest day of our lives,' said Steadman. 'Ben was largely brought up by his mother. I was too busy catching criminals. I think she encouraged his rebellious nature.'

Sam had an image of a woman with a free spirit. A person who may well have needed a man like John Steadman behind her just as much as he needed someone like Holly to bring out the best in him.

'Have you a photo of Holly? I would like to know what she looked like,' asked Sam.

Without saying a word, Steadman got to his feet and with an arm outstretched felt his way to the bedroom. Sam could hear a drawer opening. He returned carrying a photo in a silver frame and handed it to Sam. She was surprised how alike she and Holly were. Holly's hair was fairer and longer than hers had been at that age, but they had the same sparkle in their eyes.

'That was taken on our honeymoon.'

'She's very beautiful. Shall I put it back for you or

shall I leave it out on the table?'

'Why not leave it out, if it doesn't upset you? Sadly, my last image of Holly is of her dying with blood trickling down her face.'

Sam put her hand in his. 'Why don't you think about the day Ben was born, or your honeymoon – something happy?'

Steadman gripped her hand tightly. 'She would have liked you – you're similar in many ways.'

'The good ways, I hope. Although I'm warning you now, I have a fiery temper.'

'Tell me about you, Sam.'

'There's not a lot to tell. I'm an only child, born in the Valleys where my mam and dad run a garage. Dad mends the cars, while mam does the shop. I'm the first in the family to go to university. They are insanely proud of me but haven't a clue what I do.'

Steadman hesitated before asking, 'You've never been married?'

'No – I think I terrify most men.'

'I could believe that. You can certainly hold your own against misogynists like Inspector Crouchley.'

There was a loud crash at the door.

'It's only me,' shouted Ben. 'Am I disturbing anything and if not, why not?'

He staggered into the room.

'You're drunk!' exclaimed his father.

'Such powers of deduction – I can see why Helmsmouth

Police Force can't manage without your detective skills, dad. And I confess, I've had one or two. In my defence I would like to point out that I'm still jetlagged.'

Suddenly he noticed the photograph of Holly.

'What's this doing here, dad?' he asked. 'I really will have to give you some tips on chatting up the opposite sex. If you think that dragging out pictures of mum…'

'I asked to see a photo of Holly,' Sam interjected.

Ben picked up the photo, looked at Sam then back at the picture.

'Good grief,' he said with surprise. 'You two could have been sisters. Dad, you wouldn't believe how alike they are. Excuse me, I must attend to a call of nature.'

As soon as Ben was out of the room, Steadman turned towards Sam. 'Do you see a resemblance? Are you really alike?'

'I noticed it straight away,' Sam confessed. 'My colouring is darker, but we have the same eyes and cheek bones. Listen, I ought to go.'

Steadman looked downcast.

'Don't worry, we have plenty of time,' she added.

The toilet flushed and Ben returned. 'Who would like a coffee?'

'Not me,' Sam replied. 'I'm going back to my hotel. In fact, Ben, you can walk me home and sober up. First, do up your flies.'

'Sounds like a plan,' Ben replied as he sorted out his gaping jeans. 'I'll fetch your coat.'

Sam turned and kissed Steadman lightly on the cheek. 'I must warn you that it is not only Burn's Night that is celebrated on the twenty-fifth of January but also Saint Dwynwen's Day.'

'Saint who?'

'Dwynwen, the Welsh patron saint of lovers – a bit like Saint Valentine. Goodnight, John. See you tomorrow.'

With Sam's words still ringing in his ears, Steadman fell into a deep and dreamless sleep.

CHAPTER 32

Seth Shuster was bored and restless. The days on the liner dragged. He discovered, to his horror, that the clocks kept getting put back by an hour. Five of the miserable days had twenty-five hours. During the entire voyage Seth saw neither land nor any other ship. The few thousand people on board could have been the last on earth. And what a dreary lot they appeared to be, he thought. The bulk of the passengers seemed to live for nothing more than gluttony, alcohol, and an expectation of constantly being amused, while the crew, for the most part, spent their time running after them and attending to their every whim.

True, there were others on board – the senior officers, the engineers, the staff running the clinic – but Seth never mixed with them, nor with the guests in the rarefied atmosphere of the luxury suites barring his one sortie there on the second night. Other than when he was in the casino, he spent most of his days living in the dingy world of the crew quarters with the constant throb of the engines and the ever-present hint of diesel.

It was not the grimy existence he was used to. He liked the streets, the meaner the better with their pimps, prostitutes, and pushers. A place where there were chances, a place where the rules only applied if you got caught. He couldn't wait to find out what New York had to offer.

Seth was never invited back to Mr Kent's suite. Felix and Mount dropped into the casino occasionally. They blanked him and opted to play only roulette.

Mr Bagshott was convinced Seth had somehow upset them. Seth only smiled.

'I'm beginning not to trust you, Gregory.'

'Don't worry,' Seth replied. 'Everything will work out – it always does.'

On the last night there was a huge gala dinner followed by a firework display. The casino was virtually empty. Mr Bagshott wandered up and down, rubbing his hands and beaming ingratiatingly at the few remaining guests in the hope of getting some financial reward. He was sorely disappointed.

At half past midnight Felix and Mount entered. Mr Bagshott raced over to them.

'Mr Kent, Mr McKinley – how lovely to see you both again. A bourbon on the house to celebrate your last night.' He snapped his fingers at one of the waitresses. She gave him a withering look before departing to the bar.

'What's it to be tonight, gentlemen? Cards or roulette?'

'Roulette,' Mount growled.

'Excellent choice. Please follow me.' Mr Bagshott was at his most oily and obsequious.

Seth looked on. It was cringing to watch, and Mount was getting increasingly irritated. Mr Bagshott was entirely oblivious.

'Will these chairs be comfortable enough for you?' he said patting two chairs that were no different from the rest. Felix and Mount sat down. 'I do hope,' he added in a confidential whisper, 'that young Mr Henshaw has not caused any offence. I apologise sincerely on his behalf, and on behalf of the company if he has.' And to emphasise the point he placed his hand on Mount's shoulder and gave it an overly familiar stroke.

For a second Mount just stared at Mr Bagshott's hand with his mouth open.

'Mr Shitbag, or whatever the hell you call yourself, take your hand off my jacket.'

'Of course, sir, of course. I do...'

'We liked Gregory, very much. Didn't we, Felix?' said Mount ignoring the casino manager's grovelling attempts at an apology.

'Indeed, we did. In fact, Mr Bagshott, we'd like to see him before we go.'

'I'll send him over straight away, Mr Kent.'

Mr Bagshott scurried into the shadows to find Seth.

'They want to see you, Gregory, now.' He was red in the face and sweating 'You must apologise immediately.'

'For what exactly?'

'Anything – it doesn't matter. Rule number one – at all costs never upset the VIP guests.'

Mr Bagshott was not reassured by Seth's grin.

Nonchalantly Seth walked over to the roulette table.

'I gather you wanted to see me, gentlemen' he said.

Felix pulled an enveloped out of his tuxedo pocket. 'Pops asked me to give you this to thank you for the other night.'

'And don't let Shitbag see you open it,' added Mount. 'Hey – and Henshaw, any tips on how to get even at this table?'

Seth bent over the table and pushed Mount's chips on to nineteen. He gave the croupier the tiniest of winks before walking away.

Back in his cabin, Seth opened the envelope. There was a hundred-dollar bill inside and a letter that read, "Be in Immigration at five past two precisely. Note the exits and head to the last booth on your left." He read the letter twice, crumpled it up, and flushed it down the toilet.

★ ★ ★

Even Seth was swept up in the excitement of arriving in New York. Passengers were up on the observation deck before dawn. Seth, in his exploration of the ship, had found a better and more private spot, higher up and with uninterrupted views. On his right-hand side were the lights of Long Island, then on his left lay Staten Island. The liner glided gracefully under the Verrazano suspension bridge. So close were the funnels to the underside of the bridge that he ducked and closed his eyes. On opening them, he saw the Manhattan skyline spread out before him in the early morning light. It was all that he had imagined and more.

It was chilly, and he started to shiver. He was determined to wait until he caught sight of the Statue of Liberty. And there she was, beautifully lit, surrounded by wreaths of mist with her torch and crown glowing.

Still shivering, Seth went below decks, grabbed a scalding cup of coffee, and returned to his cabin. There was nothing for him to do now except wait. He stretched out on his bunk and dozed.

* * *

Nobody seemed to notice him leaving. All the passengers had already disembarked, and a sort of torpor hung over the ship. The party was over.

Seth only had the bag he was carrying, so he walked straight through the terminal hall. US Immigration was no worse and no better than any other he had been through. If it weren't for the American flags and the different accents, Seth felt he could have been arriving in any major port. He looked around him, made a mental note of all the exits, judged the time it was taking each person to pass through, and checked his watch. It was too early to join the queue. He opened his bag and made a pretence of retrieving his papers.

The queue meandered slowly. Seth resisted checking his watch again, and besides a large clock on the wall told him it was five to two. He really didn't know what to expect. His heart was racing as the minute hand crept closer to the hour and the queue got shorter. He now had a clear view of the immigration officer, a large man with a shaved head and a surly disposition. Probably armed too, thought Seth.

There was now only one person in front of him. The minute hand moved to five past the hour. Seth's eyes darted around the room. A trickle of black smoke appeared from the air conditioning vents. The trickle eddied and suddenly billowed out of the vents, rapidly filling the space with acrid smoke. Genius, said Seth to himself, pure genius.

Alarms sounded and confusion broke out. People were coughing, their eyes streaming. The public address system blared a warning: "Fire – evacuate the building by the nearest exit – evacuate the building." The message kept repeating. Seth put a handkerchief over his mouth and walked calmly out into the sunshine.

Despite the warning, he found himself going against the crowd. Rubberneckers were rushing forward to get a better view, and some had their cameras out recording every moment. What is it about a disaster, Seth wondered, that the masses find so alluring?

* * *

Seth had expected to see a line of cab drivers holding up name signs for prospective customers, but of course, all the paying passengers had long since gone. There was only one driver left, a short fat elderly man with thinning hair and a baby face. His eyes were red and his lower lip trembling. He looked as though he had just been crying. His sign was a grubby piece of cardboard on which was scrawled "HANDSAW". As there was no one else about, Seth approached him.

'You wouldn't by any chance be waiting for Gregory Henshaw, would you?'

The little man looked at his sign and shrugged. 'Are you going to work for Pops Kent?' he asked.

Seth nodded.

'I'm sure he said "handsaw". Never mind – get in the cab.' His voice was high and shrill with a strong New York drawl.

It was an ancient yellow taxi. The back seat was plump,

lumpy, and worn. A bit like the owner, thought Seth. He threw in his travelling bag.

'That all you've got?' asked the driver. 'Don't sit in the back, sit beside me. I've been told to show you the sights.'

The taxi pulled away from the docks and shot into the traffic. The contrast between his poky cabin and the claustrophobic casino could not have been starker. Seth blinked; the noise, the people, the sheer size of everything was breath-taking.

'Takes everyone by surprise first time,' said the driver with a chuckle. 'Here – this is me.' He handed Seth a dog-eared card from a small pile on the dashboard. It read "Tovey's Taxi 24/7", and there was a phone number printed below. 'Keep it. You never know when you might need me.'

'Are you Mr Tovey?' Seth asked as he slipped the card in his wallet.

'Some of the time. And it's just Tovey – you can drop the mister.'

'I'm...'

'I heard you first time, Gregory,' Tovey interjected. 'See that over there – that's Wall Street. The only building in New York to house more criminals is the Metropolitan Correctional Center.'

For the next few hours Tovey weaved his taxi in and out of the traffic, pointing out the landmarks – the Flatiron, the Empire State Building, Times Square, Central Park, the museums, the churches and cathedrals. Seth struggled to take it all in. They drove through the neighbourhoods – Chinatown, Little Italy, Greenwich Village, Harlem. At each, Tovey told stories, almost invariably about crooks and gangsters – the Mob, the Mafia, the Syndicate, the Tongs, and countless others that Seth had never heard of.

'Crime is big business in New York,' Tovey concluded. 'But I guess you knew that already, Gregory.'

Seth gave a non-committal shrug. 'Do you work for the Kents?' he asked.

'Me? No, I work for myself, and anyone who'll pay me.' He turned a red-rimmed eye towards Seth. 'I'll give you some free advice. Don't cross the Kents – if you do, and they find out, you won't do it again. Get my drift? And watch out for McKinley – he's one mean bastard.'

The light was starting to fade.

'You've seen enough for one day,' he declared, pulling the car over and stopping outside a large nondescript building. 'This is where we part company.'

It was all in darkness. Seth could just make out the word "Casino" in an unlit neon sign.

Seth offered him the hundred-dollar bill.

'Mr Kent has already paid me. And if that small bag is all your worldly possessions, then I reckon your need is greater than mine. You've got my card – give me a call, day or night, if you need anything. I never sleep.'

Seth closed the car door and Tovey sped off into the evening traffic.

★ ★ ★

Felix Kent himself opened the door.

'Glad you made it, Gregory. Come on in.' He too noted the lack of luggage and added, 'Is that all you've got?'

'It saves having to tip the porters,' Seth responded with a smile.

'I'll show you to your accommodation.' Felix led the way up the stairs and ushered Seth into a large bed-sitting room with an adjoining bathroom. 'This comes with the job. You can eat in the restaurant. If you use the bar you must settle your account at the end of each week. Mount and I will be dining at seven. Come and join us.'

Seth unpacked and had a shower, and as he had found an iron and board in the wardrobe, he pressed his trousers and took the creases out of his shirt.

Mount and Felix were wating for him in a corner of the restaurant.

'Sit down, Gregory, please. Mount, pour our new employee a glass of wine.'

Without being asked, a large steak was place in front was placed in front of him. He cut into it, and blood ran out.

'We like it rare,' commented Felix. 'Sometimes I think Mount could eat his raw.'

'It's delicious,' replied Seth between mouthfuls.

'Yeah – but don't expect it every night,' Mount

grunted. 'The staff get what they're given.'

'Let me run through what's required of you,' said Felix. 'To begin with, Mount is the casino pit boss. You take orders direct from him.'

'Got a problem with that?' queried Mount.

Seth shook his head.

'For the first two weeks, I want you to get a feel for the place,' continued Felix. Note the faces, note who wins and who loses. If you're asked to be dealer, don't try any nonsense, at least not to begin with.'

'But if you see somebody cheating,' Mount interjected, 'scratch the back of your head to get my attention.'

'You see,' said Felix, 'what we run here is a business, and like all businesses we need to make money. Over the past few months some of our customers have been on an unusual winning streak. We need to recoup our losses – that's where you come in.'

* * *

Seth was a quick learner. By the end of the two weeks, he had made a note of who was winning, and why. They're good, he thought, but not that good.

Mount had worked out a complicated series of signs that Seth was meant to follow. He largely ignored them, much to the annoyance of the big man. Felix, and presumably Pops, were pleased as the casino was now turning in a handsome profit.

Seth's pay was generous, but he was greedy. In his spare time, he played in other casinos. He even devised an ingenious way of scamming his employers. He made contacts, lots of them, people almost as crooked and devious as himself. They weren't friends. Seth paid for their trust in hard cash.

And cash was a problem, in as much as he had no safe place to store it. To get a legitimate bank account, he would need a stack of paperwork. He also wanted to spread the risk and get some of it back to England.

There was only one man in England he could rely on – Rupert H. Sidley. What Sidley suggested appealed to Seth Shuster. It was simple, foolproof even. Sidley dealt in rare stamps. He would scan the auction sites, contact dealers and collectors. He told Seth what to buy and how much to pay. All Seth had to do was post them over. Sidley would do the rest and take his cut.

* * *

Time passed quickly. He had been living in New York for several years, and things were starting to get too risky. Seth knew he had to move on. Now, he had need of another identity, and this time an American identity. It was proving more of a challenge. He was already banned from many of the gambling joints. Worse still, Mount McKinley was beginning to get very suspicious. He remembered what Tovey, the taxi driver, had said –

"Watch out for McKinley – he's one mean bastard."

It was late and the casino was shutting. McKinley had cornered Seth and again threatened him.

'I'm watching you, Henshaw, or whatever your goddamned name really is. You're up to something and when I find out...'

'Relax, Mount,' Seth had replied, before foolishly adding, 'you won't find out.'

Seth quickly retreated to the safety of his room and bolted the door. His wallet dropped on to the floor and out fell Tovey's card. What the hell, he thought, the man said he never slept.

The taxi pulled up opposite the Kents' casino. Seth emerged from the shadows. Clutching his bag tightly, he sidled up to the taxi and slipped into the front seat.

'Where to?' asked Tovey in his high-pitched voice.

'Anywhere,' Seth replied. 'Just drive.' Once he had calmed down, he outlined his problems and needs.

Tovey nodded. 'It can be arranged, but it will cost you.'

Seth opened his bag. Tovey glanced over and whistled. 'You're pretty desperate, aren't you?'

'I know to the last dollar exactly how much is in here,' he replied. 'Ten per cent is yours, if you can keep it safe and sort out the rest.'

'Ten per cent, huh?' queried Tovey.

'I have the same amount again back at the Kents' place.'

'You have been a busy boy – I'll say that for you. Same terms?'

Seth agreed.

'You've got yourself a deal. Let's go see some people I know.'

It didn't take long for Seth to become Adam Monke.

'Why that name?' asked Tovey.

'Monke was my grandmother's name.'

'And Adam?'

Seth just shrugged his shoulders.

The papers were perfect, slightly worn and a bit grubby. He put on his best American accent and thanked Tovey.

'My but you have got that off to a tee,' Tovey remarked.

* * *

All hell broke loose at the casino one November night. Somebody had won big and had ordered champagne, lots of it, which he consumed rapidly. At a most inopportune moment he shouted across the casino, 'Hey Henshaw, you know how I promised you half, but guess what – you can take a run and jump!'

Mount seized Seth by the scruff of the neck and pushed him through the fire exit into the back alley, where he pinned him up against the wall. Seth was not a big man, at least not compared with Mount McKinley, so it came as a big surprise when Seth slammed his head into Mount's face, followed swiftly by a vicious kick to the groin. Mount didn't have time to contemplate his problems as Seth grabbed his hair and hammered his skull repeatedly against the wall. Stepping over the unconscious body, Seth brushed down his jacket, stepped back into the casino and made a beeline for his room.

Fifteen minutes later he was sitting in Tovey's cab, out of breath, and with everything that he owned hastily stuffed into his bag.

'You were right about McKinley being a mean bastard,' he said with a grin. 'I need a car. I've got to get out of town before he wakes up.'

'He'll follow you,' Tovey warned.

'Better add a gun to the shopping list,' Seth replied.

It wasn't the most dignified of exits from New York. Seth gave the bulk of his money and his UK passport to Tovey for safe keeping. He checked the gun; it was fully loaded. In the grey light of dawn, he headed south.

New York was getting colder and Seth knew from bitter experience just how hard and cruel the winters could be. He wasn't sure exactly where he was going, Texas maybe. He had seen a lot of TV programmes and everybody there appeared to be rich. Time to share the wealth, he mused.

He drove until he was falling asleep. He snatched a few hours, but his sleep was disturbed by visions of Mount McKinley's bloodied face. Grabbing only the occasional coffee, and eating a bag of nauseatingly sweet doughnuts, he pressed on.

His eyes felt as though someone had rubbed grit in them. Again, he stopped and dozed. It was not only Mount that disturbed his slumbers, both Pops and Felix Kent were now hammering at his door. It was almost three days since he had left New York. At one service station, he caught a glimpse of himself in a mirror. He looked terrible.

A car pulled in behind him. A door slammed and Seth nearly jumped out of his skin. He needed to rest, sleep in freshly laundered sheets, get a wash, and get some proper food inside him. One more push, he said to himself, just one more push.

The heat was unbearable. The air conditioning in the car worked only intermittently. To add to his misery, he was now hopelessly lost.

His eyes were dazzled by the sun. He didn't see the highway patrol car behind him, only noticing it when the siren howled. It pulled in front of him. He stopped.

A patrolman got out of the car, a bulky man who looked vaguely familiar. As he wandered over, Seth wound down the window. Whether it was because of the heat, the hunger or the lack of sleep, Seth was convinced he was Mount McKinley. He pulled the gun out of the glovebox, pressed it to the patrolman's chest and squeezed the trigger.

CHAPTER 33

Tim Warrender was busy towelling Robbie's paws.

'Is it still raining?' Steadman asked.

'No, it's just cold and damp. Robbie got a bit wet in the park, that's all,' Tim replied in a husky voice. 'Shall I give him his breakfast?'

Steadman nodded. 'Have you time for a drink of squash and a biscuit?' It was a foolish question; Tim invariably had time for an extra snack.

'How tall are you now, Tim?'

'I'm past your shoulder. I reckon it won't be long before I'm as tall as DS Munro. How's the case going? Are you any nearer making an arrest?'

The question took Steadman by surprise. Discussing an on-going investigation was strictly off limits; surely Tim hadn't forgotten.

'Slow, but making progress,' he replied cautiously. 'Why do you ask?'

'I was wondering when DS Munro would be free to give me some more physics lessons...' His voice tailed off; he sounded despondent.

'Is Dr Yorke giving you a hard time again?'

'And how! I've a good mind to follow Ben's advice and...'

'You'll do no such thing,' said Steadman hastily. 'Ben ought to be ashamed of himself for even suggesting whatever it was he suggested. I'll bet it involved either an explosion or an awful smell.'

'Both actually,' Tim replied with a grin. 'Is that Ben snoring, I can hear? It sounds like a sawmill.'

Steadman sighed. 'That's Ben all right. He claims it's jetlag. The truth is he had too many beers last night.'

'I don't like beer,' said Tim.

Steadman was intrigued to know when and where Tim had tasted beer, but he didn't dare to ask. He wouldn't have been at all surprised to find out that Ben had something to do with it.

'Is that the time?' exclaimed Tim. 'I must dash.'

'I'll remind DS Munro about your lessons,' Steadman replied as Tim ran down the stairs.

* * *

The meeting in the Eyesore had been arranged for ten. Steadman knew he would be cutting it fine. There was still no sign of Ben waking.

'Oh, to be young and carefree,' he muttered to himself.

He put Robbie in his harness, crept along the corridor and pulled the door gently behind him.

Tim was right; it was cold and damp, what Alan Munro would call "dreich". He turned up the collar of his coat and paused, hoping to hear the tapping of Sam's high heels. He was met only by silence.

'Go forward, Robbie.'

Immediately a part of his brain started counting, ticking off the steps with the regularity of a metronome.

Outside Eldon's jewellery shop, Robbie stopped dead. Despite Steadman's encouragement, and even the offer of a treat, the dog refused to budge. It was a situation Steadman hated. Clearly something was amiss; it was the only reason Robbie ever disobeyed a command. Exactly what the reason was, Steadman hadn't a clue. He drummed the fingers of his free hand on his thigh. The choice was simple, either go back home or wait for assistance.

'Can I help you, Inspector Steadman?'

The hairs on the back of Steadman's neck bristled. 'Do I know you?' he asked.

'Not yet,' replied the man.

What an odd answer, thought Steadman. Before he could say anything further the man spoke again.

'There's scaffolding barring the way. It looks like they're repairing the large clock hanging outside Eldon's shop. They've closed the pavement. May I lead you around the obstruction?'

The voice was gentle and kind. Steadman felt no threat.

'That would be appreciated.' He wanted to say more, for he was almost sure that the man was the elusive double of Seth Shuster's younger self.

'Mind the kerb! There you are – back on track.'

'Thank you. How do you know who I am?' asked Steadman.

'I think everybody in Helmsmouth knows about DI John Steadman, the blind detective.'

'Who are you?'

'I would be very surprised and disappointed if you haven't worked that one out. Let's just say that today I'm the Good Samaritan.'

Steadman frowned. 'Assuming I'm correct, and you are who I think you are, I had the impression you might want to talk with me?'

'Not yet,' he replied.

Again, Steadman was puzzled by the answer. 'When, if not now?'

But the man was walking away.

'Good luck in your investigations, Inspector,' he said over his shoulder.

★ ★ ★

The brass handrail on the steps leading up to the Eyesore was painfully cold to the touch. Steadman pushed open the door and was greeted by a rush of warm air smelling vaguely of bleach and humanity. But there was something different in the air, something he couldn't define. It was as though the atmosphere was charged with electricity. Even Sergeant Grimble seemed to have more purpose about him. Unusually, he addressed Steadman first before speaking to Robbie.

'Good morning, sir. Your meeting is up in the conference room again.'

'Am I the last to arrive?'

'No, we're still waiting for DS Munro – ah, here he comes now.'

DS Munro came in with a gust of damp January air.

'Alan, would you take Inspector Steadman upstairs? Robbie, you will stay here with me,' said Sergeant Grimble with uncustomary directness.

Steadman's brows furrowed. 'What's up, Sergeant Grimble?'

'There's been developments. It's not my place to tell you. Go on, the two of you. You don't want to keep DCI Long waiting.'

DS Munro ushered Steadman into a seat. From the heady perfume he guessed he was sitting next to Sam Griffiths.

'Good morning, John,' she said in her soft Welsh accent.

'Morning, Sam. Can you tell me who's here?'

'Fiona Fairfax, Cleo Osborne, Will Lofthouse, and sitting at the back with a face like thunder is Inspector Crouchley.'

'No Dr Rufus?'

'He's tied up in the mortuary,' explained Munro. 'Not literally. An old tramp was found dead under a bridge last night.'

How sad, thought Steadman, here we are pulling out all the stops to solve a double murder while some poor old chap dies unnoticed and uncared for sheltering under a bridge.

A little after ten, DCI Long strode into the room.

'Apologies for keeping you all waiting,' he said. 'I've been on a long-distance call to America. I'll come back to that in a moment.'

Steadman's ears pricked up at the mention of America.

'First, let me update you on events closer to home,' Long continued. 'Ten years ago, Gregory Henshaw was listed as a crew member on a liner heading for America. As his murdered body was found in a freezer along with Seth Shuster's handprint, we can safely conclude that it was not Henshaw but Seth Shuster who boarded the vessel and that is how he made his way to America. We know that he worked in the ship's casino and seemed to form a relationship with two men known to be part of New York's underworld. Despite not having the necessary papers, he got through immigration during a suspected fire that proved to be an elaborate hoax.'

DCI Long paused and poured himself a glass of water.

'Shuster spent several years in New York. Where he lived and what he did remains a mystery, although it was almost certainly criminal. Any questions so far?'

The room remained silent, apart from Crouchley stifling a theatrical yawn.

'The next time Shuster emerged it was as Adam Monke. You may remember that Monke was his grandmother's surname. To cut a long story short, he was pulled over by a Highway Patrolman while heading south. For no obvious reason, Shuster shot him dead. He was caught soon after, held in prison for some time undergoing numerous psychological tests, and made several court appearances. He refused to have a lawyer and refused to enter a plea. We know that Adam Monke and Seth Shuster are the same person. I have just taken a call from America – their fingerprints are identical.'

Crouchley could contain himself no longer. 'In my opinion, it's a blooming shame they didn't send him to the electric chair and save us a lot of bother.'

DCI Long chose to ignore the outburst. 'Some of you may recall an audacious jail escape some months ago involving a helicopter. Well, that was Seth Shuster. As yet, we have no idea how he made it back to Britain. I've put all of this in a summary which you can read at your leisure. Inspector Steadman, I'm sure somebody will assist you.' He looked at Sam, who nodded.

Steadman raised a hand. 'Thank you, DCI Long. If I recall correctly, didn't the prisoner pretend to be choking on a fish bone?'

'He did, you have an excellent memory. Neither Seth Shuster nor the helicopter were ever found. DC Osborne, have you anything new to report on the identity of the man who is probably Seth's son?'

DC Osborne shook her head. 'No luck so far, sir. He doesn't work at the registrar's office, none of the funeral directors know of him, and he is not listed anywhere as a clergyman, although there are far more of them than I would have credited.'

Steadman pursed his lips and frowned. But it was always white lilies or chrysanthemums, he thought; that must be significant.

He raised a hand again and cleared his throat. 'I may have met him on my way here,' he said and described the morning's encounter. 'I still get the impression he cared about his father.'

'He's the only bloody one who does,' Crouchley muttered.

DC Fairfax intervened. 'I'm afraid I've nothing to add either, sir. I was hoping that Clara Drinsdale would have got in touch.'

'I don't think she can read or write,' said Steadman. 'It may be worth checking her records.'

'And I've had a fruitless chat with Captain Perkin,' Munro added. 'I leant on him quite heavily. Either he was still drunk or too good at lying, or possibly both, but I got nothing out of him.'

Steadman tried to imagine the Jack Russell with his bright orange life jacket and thought how he would have loved to see the little dog.

'On the subject of boats – Inspector Crouchley, have you got any further?' asked DCI Long.

Crouchley harumphed. 'My men have scoured the coastline and...'

Sam Griffiths turned around and shot him a withering look. 'Men? Don't you have any female officers working under you?'

'By men, I mean men and women, as I'm sure the little lady understands perfectly well.'

Steadman could sense the anger rising in Sam.

'It's not worth it,' he whispered.

'Perhaps, Inspector Crouchley, the term "officer" would be more correct,' DCI Long announced.

'All right then – my officers, most of whom are men...'

Sam shook her head in disgust. If it wasn't so pathetic it would almost be comical.

'...have scoured the coast, as I was saying. I've lost count of how many vessels they've searched or how many of their owners they've questioned. So far with no joy. Mind, the weather hasn't helped. The visibility has been atrocious. Some days you could barely see your hand stretched out in front of your face. Any boat that wanted to avoid detection would only have to sail a short way out to sea.'

'And plenty of the larger craft are more than capable of that, despite the weather,' Steadman added.

'Have you any particular boat in mind, John?' asked DCI Long.

He did, but it was idle speculation. He remained silent.

'Perhaps, you could tell us how you got on with Madam Chu last night?' DCI Long continued.

'Elsie Entwistle, to give the lady her real name. Elsie and I go a long way back.'

Concisely, and without mention of his first encounter, Steadman described the events of the previous evening, how all Elsie's answers had been evasive, how she had neither confirmed nor denied dealing in opium, nor any recent meeting with Seth Shuster or Rupert Sidley. He told the room she had admitted to knowing both the men and, like most of the other people that had been interviewed, did not mourn their loss.

Crouchley butted in. 'So your visit was a complete waste of time. I don't know – all those hours and all that effort for a couple of worthless scumbags and we're no further forward.' He sat back in his chair, folded his arms, and stared at the ceiling.

'Not exactly, Eric,' Steadman replied, deliberately choosing to address him by his first name. 'I suggested to Elsie that Shuster might have been speaking with Phil the Shed, and in so doing knew what was in Phil's deliveries. I even hinted that Phil may have been disposing of certain things for her in his van. She became decidedly rattled. I went on to say that when we had the evidence, we would be interviewing Phil, and there was no way she could stop him...' He paused mid-sentence; a worrying thought flitted into his head. 'I wonder whether it wouldn't be a sensible idea to bring Phil in.'

Inspector Crouchley grunted. 'My men have got him under twenty-four-hour surveillance. Nothing will get past them. I say leave him out there. I would like to have something more incriminating than Steadman's anxieties before we nail the bastard.'

Steadman wondered if Crouchley was being deliberately contrary. If he had suggested keeping Phil the Shed under observation, would Crouchley have argued the opposite? Sometimes the man was impossible to fathom.

'Let's hear what DC Lofthouse has to say first, before making any decision,' said DCI Long.

Poor DC Lofthouse! He may have had no problem chatting up the ladies, but he was decidedly uncomfortable addressing a room full of his fellow officers. He mumbled and stumbled his way through. There was little that Steadman didn't know already. Lofthouse had managed to get more bank particulars and phone call details. These only confirmed what was already suspected; Phil's latest business enterprise was no more than a cover. The text messages caught everyone's attention. Both DS

Fairfax and Alan Munro were particularly interested in the mention of Merton Cove. Crouchley, on the other hand, dismissed it.

'Nothing but a load of old shingle – shallow almost to the horizon. You won't find anything there. My men have been over it with a fine-toothed comb.'

Sam bit her tongue.

'What do we conclude then, ladies and gentlemen?' said DCI Long pointedly stressing the word "ladies".

'Well, I don't know about you lot, but I'm going to be keeping a close watch on our friend, Phil the Shed,' said Crouchley.

Steadman frowned. DCI Long noticed the expression on his face.

'Am I right in thinking that you are unhappy with this proposal, John?'

Steadman spread out his long bony fingers and pursed his lips. 'It's not my call, sir,' he said with a slight shake of his head.

CHAPTER 34

Steadman had the wardrobe doors open and was flicking through his tie collection. Each occupied its own place on the tie rack. It had been so long since he had worn the tartan tie that he could not recall which one it was. His hand-held colour scanner was only of help if the tie was a uniform colour. In the end, he gave up.

'Ben – have you got a moment?'

His son pulled a face when he saw what his father was up to. 'Not a tie again, dad?'

'Firstly, I like wearing ties, and secondly, we are going to a Burns Supper tonight. I want to wear something appropriate. I think my tartan tie is either this one or that one.'

'It's neither,' Ben replied. 'It's the one lying on the floor at your feet.' He picked up the tie and handed it to his father. 'As far as tartans go it's pleasant enough, not too garish. Has it got a name?'

'It's Lindsay tartan. I bought it on the occasion of your great-grandmother's ninetieth birthday. Her maiden name was Lindsay. I don't suppose you'll be wearing anything remotely Scottish tonight?'

'You'll have to wait and find out,' Ben replied with a grin.

Steadman grimaced. Whatever Ben had bought would no doubt be outrageous and liable to cause offence.

'You can do me another favour,' he replied. 'Go and look in the whisky cabinet. There should be an unopened bottle of Ardbeg in amongst the others. It's an Islay malt – not exactly from Burns' birthplace, but it's the closest I've got.'

Steadman hummed a little tune to himself. He was looking forward to the evening. It would make a nice change, he thought, not to be worrying about criminals and corpses.

A car horn gave a friendly toot.

'Have a look out of the window, Ben, and see if that's Dr Rufus.'

Ben pulled the curtains aside and peered out at the street below.

'It's the same make of car, but way too clean to be Frank's.'

The car door opened, and a large, kilted figure got out and gave Ben a cheery wave. It was Dr Rufus.

'Good grief!' exclaimed Ben. 'Either Rob Roy MacGregor has come to collect us, or Frank really has entered into the spirit of things.'

Steadman and his son made their way downstairs, with Robbie taking the lead.

'Sam is in the front seat,' said Ben. 'We will have to budge up in the back.'

'We'll be lucky – Frank's back seat is always full of rubbish,' Steadman remarked. But to their surprise, the car was immaculate both inside and out.

'What you said about dodgy carwashes got me thinking,' explained Dr Rufus. 'Although why you never mentioned it before is beyond me. They made a good job of it, only the cheeky blighters asked for an extra tenner because it was so filthy.'

Steadman smiled to himself, knowing full well that his friend, despite his protestations, had probably handed over an extra twenty.

The car smelled of Sam's fragrance, air freshener and something less pleasant that Steadman took a moment to place.

'Hello Sam. How are you?'

'Feeling underdressed next to Frank,' she replied. 'I've only managed to get a white heather buttonhole.'

'Ah yes, the perennial Rufus kilt. I thought I could smell old-fashioned mothballs. Aren't they outlawed now?'

'Probably,' replied Dr Rufus. 'Just don't tell the moths.'

Sam turned in her seat. 'I see you're wearing a nice tartan tie, John. What about you, Ben? Are you letting the side down?' she asked.

'I'm not so sure about that,' said Ben, whipping a ridiculous hat out of his inside pocket and clamping it on his head. Sam shrieked. Dr Rufus caught sight of him in the rear-view mirror and let out an enormous guffaw.

'Oh no!' sighed Steadman. 'Somebody tell me please?'

'It is a genuine Scottish "See you Jimmy" hat,' Ben explained.

'Not one of those in bright red tartan with a straggly ginger wig?' Steadman queried.

'The very same, complete with a red bauble,' replied Ben. 'I bet Alan Munro will love it.'

Steadman wasn't so sure. Some Scots took Burns Night very seriously. Thank goodness he had brought a decent bottle of malt whisky.

'I suspect Melanie and Annie will appreciate it if no one else does,' he said.

'Remind me, who is the older of the two?' asked Sam.

'Melanie, by about two years,' Steadman replied.

'I'll see a big difference in them,' said Ben.

Out of the corner of his eye he noticed his father tightening his lips. It was just a fleeting expression, but he knew exactly what was going through his father's mind. Like photos in an album, the images he had of Melanie and Annie would never change.

It was a slow drive in the drizzling rain. Dr Rufus kept up a constant chatter about the great values of the kilt, how it never went in or out of fashion, how you could wear it at every conceivable formal occasion, how you could always let out a pleat should you gain weight (not that this applied to him, of course), and if you looked after your kilt, you could pass it down the family. Only the Scots could devise so economical a garment, he concluded with a chuckle and pulled up at Munro's door.

'You go on ahead,' said Steadman. 'I'm going to let Robbie stretch his legs.'

'I'll come with you,' said Sam. She linked her arm with his and they walked up and down the street.

'You've gone very quiet, John,' she remarked.

'I was thinking of previous evenings here and the phone ringing, shattering the peace with bad news. And I can't help thinking of what I said to Madam Chu about Phil the Shed. I only hope...'

'Relax, John. Let it go, for Alan and Maureen's sake if not your own. Crouchley has got him under observation, and DCI Long made the call, not you.'

'You're right of course. *Que sera, sera,* as Doris Day would say.'

Before Sam could ask who Doris Day was, Alan Munro hailed them from the front door. He was resplendent in full Highland dress. Steadman handed him the bottle of Ardbeg.

'Good man,' said Munro admiring the bottle. 'Is it a before or after the meal malt? What do you reckon?'

'It has quite a smoky flavour, so definitely after the meal.'

Munro ushered them into the living room.

'Now, what about a wee dram to warm you all up? We'll start with a Macallan and see where we go from there.'

Sam and Steadman both agreed.

'Sadly, I'm the driver, so not for me,' said Dr Rufus.

'No problem. I've managed to track down some Barr's Irn Bru – no alcohol, sweet and fizzy, and reputedly made in Scotland from girders. What about you, Ben?'

'I would prefer a beer.'

'That too can be arranged. I've got some bottles of Innes and Gunn all the way from Edinburgh. They're in the fridge – go and help yourself.'

Melanie and Annie rushed, in both wearing kilts. They loved Ben's hat, especially when he twirled it above their heads and produced chocolates from it.

'I would like a hat like that,' said Melanie.

'Well, you can have this one,' replied Ben, placing it on her head.

'What about me?' asked Annie.

'You will have to share, girls,' their father warned them.

'Oh no you won't,' said Ben as he produced a second "See you Jimmy" hat apparently from thin air. Sam was impressed.

'It's how I earn my living in the circus,' Ben explained.

The phone rang and Steadman's heart sank. Maureen answered it, but it was only her mother. She put the girls on to speak, slipped off her apron and joined the adults. The conversation was lively, and the room filled with chatter, laughter and the clink of glasses.

Once she heard the phone being put down, Maureen shepherded everyone through to the dining room. Although he was with friends, Steadman still had misgivings. To his relief the starter was smoked salmon on small pancakes, no cutlery needed. Sam watched, fascinated as he navigated his fingers delicately round the plate.

'Would you like a squeeze of lemon on your salmon?' asked Sam discreetly.

Steadman nodded. 'Thanks. I wouldn't dare risk it myself.'

The plates were cleared away. Alan left the table and signalled to the girls to go with him. Maureen returned, her face flushed.

'We're ready. We all have to stand.'

'Hurry up, I'm starving!' shouted Dr Rufus.

Two recorders, almost in time with one another and almost in tune, started playing a rather squeaky version of *Scotland the Brave*. Melanie and Annie preceded their father, who held aloft a steaming platter bearing an enormous haggis. Alan gave a much-abbreviated Address to the Haggis, as it was clear after the first few lines, he was the only one who had a clue what he was talking about. It didn't really matter as everybody was enjoying themselves, and he got a round of applause when he plunged the knife into the haggis. It was served, as tradition dictated, with mashed neeps and tatties.

'Turnips and potatoes,' Maureen whispered in Sam's

ear, seeing the baffled expression on her face. And to John Steadman, she whispered, 'The great thing is you don't need a fork and knife. There's a spoon by your right hand.'

'What do you think of the haggis?' Alan asked Sam.

'It's very tasty – a bit like faggots.'

Munro was having none of it. 'Nothing,' he said emphatically, 'tastes like haggis.'

They finished with cranachan, which Maureen explained was a combination of toasted oatmeal, cream, honey, whisky, and raspberries.

Suddenly, and for no obvious reason, Steadman wondered what Phil the Shed would be eating tonight – something instant in the microwave, or a takeaway delivered to his door perhaps. He felt sorry for the officers with the mind-numbing job of keeping Phil under surveillance. The cold, the boredom, and nothing to look forward to other than a flask of coffee and a sandwich. He remembered how as a young PC he had been put on surveillance duties, how he and his companion would take turns to doze, and one awful moment when they had both fallen asleep.

Sam gave him a nudge.

'Sorry, I was miles away...'

'And now, I call on Dr Rufus to give the Address to the Lassies,' said Alan.

Frank stood up, produced some crumpled notes from his sporran, and cleared his throat. He started by praising

Maureen for the outstanding meal and the generous hospitality. Everyone banged the table in appreciation.

'But there are other lassies here that deserve a mention,' Dr Rufus continued. Sam closed her eyes, terrified what Dr Rufus would say next.

'I am thinking particularly of lassies that have wormed their way into the heart of my friend John Steadman.'

'I can't think who he means,' said Alan, and everybody cheered except for Sam, who was staring at the tablecloth.

'And I know that certain lassies, with their good looks and charm have succeeded,' Dr Rufus continued. 'And, this is the most important point, I know that the feelings are equal on both sides.'

Another cheer and a burst of laughter filled the room.

'Name the culprits, Frank!' shouted Ben.

'If you insist,' Dr Rufus responded. 'Of course, I am referring to Melanie and Annie who adore their "Uncle" John!'

The two little girls ran round the table to give Steadman a hug.

'Goodness knows who you lot thought I was referring to,' said Dr Rufus as he sat down.

'Look at the time!' exclaimed Maureen. 'You girls ought to have been in bed half an hour ago.'

Naturally, Melanie and Annie protested.

'If you're good,' said Sam, 'I'll come up and sing you a Welsh lullaby.'

'What's that?' they chorused.

'There's only one way you'll find out,' Maureen replied as she led the girls out of the room.

'Time to open the Ardbeg,' Alan declared.

It was sweet and smoky with the sharpness of peat. Definitely a whisky to sip slowly among friends, thought Steadman.

He didn't notice Sam slipping out of the room and Maureen coming back in. She left the door ajar and put her finger to her lips.

They listened from downstairs. Sam had a beautiful voice. The melody was soothing and gentle. Although Steadman could not understand the lyrics, he was sure it was about warmth, sleep, and a mother's love.

When the singing had stopped, Sam tiptoed back down the stairs. 'There you are,' she announced. 'Two girls fast asleep.'

'Unless I'm sadly mistaken,' added Steadman, 'one son also asleep.' He nodded in the direction of Ben, who was dozing on the sofa.

'I think it's time we all went home,' said Dr Rufus.

'Are you OK to drive? Would you like a coffee?' asked Maureen.

'I've been on Irn Bru all night, and despite John Steadman's worries, we got through without interruption,' Dr Rufus replied.

Sam suggested that Ben, because he had the longest legs, should sit in the front. She, Steadman and Robbie squeezed into the back. The fog was dense, and Dr Rufus needed all his concentration to crawl back to Steadman's flat.

Ben was first out. 'Got to dash – too much beer on board,' he declared.

Steadman and Robbie followed.

'Well… Thanks for a pleasant evening,' he said rather awkwardly.

Dr Rufus's old red Volvo had gone no more than twenty yards when Sam asked him to stop. She got out of the car and ran back to Steadman.

'I almost forgot to give you your Saint Dwynwen's present.' With that she put her arms around his neck and kissed him.

★ ★ ★

Steadman had great difficulty in getting off to sleep. Maybe it was the whisky or the heavy meal. More likely it was jumbled thoughts about Saint Dwynwen, or possibly anxieties about the case. Should he have been more assertive with DCI Long? He had tried, and as Sam remarked, it wasn't his call.

Eventually he dropped off, but his sleep was disturbed by nonsensical dreams in which DCI Long, Inspector Crouchley, Dr Rufus, and even Sam, were pointing fingers at him and shouting, 'It's all your fault!'

The phone rang at six twenty. He knew precisely where the handset should be, but in that awful gap between sleep and wakefulness he dislodged it and it fell to the floor.

'Hang on a minute,' he shouted.

'Take your time, John,' said the unmistakable voice of Dr Frank Rufus.

Steadman located the handset and picked it up.

'I'm here now, Frank. What's happened?'

'We've got another body.'

'Who?'

'Phil the Shed, otherwise known as Philip Aintree.'

Steadman felt his chest tighten. He sat down heavily on the edge of the bed.

'Go on.'

'Crouchley got it into his head to pay him an unexpected call at dawn. As Phil didn't answer, his boys smashed the door down, no doubt with great delight. It appears that Phil the Shed has blown his brains out.'

'Suicide?' queried Steadman running his fingers through his hair.

'It would seem so.'

'I doubt that very much,' said Steadman.

'I thought that might be what you would say,' Dr Rufus replied. 'I'll pick you up in fifteen minutes.'

CHAPTER 35

It was noisy and cramped inside the helicopter. Seth Shuster pressed the ear defenders tighter against his head; it made no difference. He barely noticed the unconscious forms of the two doctors sprawled at his feet. All the coughing and gagging had left him with a dry throat. He looked around for something to drink. Out of the corner of his eye he saw a familiar travelling bag. He stepped over the bodies to retrieve it. Evidently, someone at the jail had decided he wasn't coming back.

His money was, of course, all gone, but his old clothes were still there. They smelt stale. He was desperate to be out of his prison uniform. There was not enough room to change. He could wait. After interminable months of confinement, he could last out a few more hours.

At the bottom of the bag, and much to his delight, he found his old shoes. The prison-issue soft-toed sneakers pinched his feet. It was a relief to kick them off and put on his old pair. They fitted like well-loved gloves. He sat back and, with a sigh, closed his eyes.

A sudden blast of cold air woke him. The would-be paramedic had opened the door slightly. He gestured to Seth to make sure his seat belt was securely fastened. The ground below was parched and desolate with no signs of habitation.

Despite the sharp drop in temperature, Seth noticed that the "paramedic" was flushed and sweating. He dragged the two bodies over to the edge of the open door and gave each a final shove with his foot. Seth watched them plummet and disappear from view. He felt absolutely no emotion. Whether it was the turbulence or the realisation of what he had done, the "paramedic" turned and vomited copiously into a paper bag.

The door was still open. Never one to miss an opportunity, Seth bent down, picked up his sneakers and flung them out. His eyes followed them twisting and tumbling down like a pair of birds shot in flight as they too fell to the ground.

Having emptied his stomach, the "paramedic" stood as best he could and threw the sickbag out of the open door. He closed it with a bang and turned towards Seth. For a few seconds, their eyes met. The look he gave Seth was filled with menace and loathing. Seth was on the point of returning a smile, but the man turned his back on him, spat on the floor, and rejoined the pilot in the cockpit.

Seth never found out his name and never saw his face again. He only hoped that Tovey, the New York taxi driver who had masterminded his escape, was paying him well enough.

He had left all the fine details to Tovey. The choking on a fish bone had been Seth's idea. Frobisher, the guard, had let slip one night that if there was a medical emergency at the prison, they always called a helicopter. And from that little seed of information, the plan had grown and taken shape. All Tovey asked was how much Seth was willing to pay. It was a breath-taking sum.

'Leave it with me,' was all that he said.

* * *

Seth wasn't sure where they were heading. He looked at his watch, then the direction of the sun and figured it must be roughly south. At last, the helicopter started to descend. Seth peered out of the window. The light was starting to fade, but he could make out some scattered roofs below him and the lights of a town on the horizon.

The helicopter circled around one particular group of buildings. Seth thought they might be warehouses or a garage for there were lots of vehicles parked haphazardly. As they got lower a small fire ignited belching black smoke, then another, and another. A man was running with a flare, lighting four oil drums that marked out a flat area no bigger than a tennis court. The cars, vans and trucks were not just parked randomly, but lay stacked on top of one another. Seth realised that they were landing in the middle of a massive scrapyard. The nearside of the yard fell away into a small ravine filled with the rusting carcasses of scrapped vehicles. In the centre was a large, battered crane and beside it, a car crusher that turned the metal remains into large blocks.

They touched down with a small bump. The motor was cut, and the deafening noise abated. Seth heard Tovey's voice address the two men in the cockpit.

'There are two cars by the gate. You take the blue one, and you the silver. The paperwork is in the glovebox, along with the money. Check it, then scram. You go northeast, and you, northwest. You've never met me, you've never seen me, and I've never clapped eyes on either of you – understood? Good – now beat it!'

Seth saw the backs of the two men making their way to the parked cars. A full ten minutes later he could see their taillights leaving the yard, then the door opened. Tovey had a big smile on his face.

'I hope you enjoyed your flight, Mr Monke – or is it Gregory Henshaw?'

'You know damn well what my real name is,' Seth replied beaming. 'You've got style, Tovey, I've got to hand it to you. Where are we, by the way?'

'Not far from the Mexican border. Come on over to the house and I'll fill you in on the next leg of your journey.'

Seth picked up his bag.

'I see you're still travelling light,' Tovey remarked.

★ ★ ★

The house was only distinguishable from the surrounding sheds in as much as it had a smaller door and some windows. Seth hadn't seen Tovey for a long time. He seemed to have shrunk in height, in marked contrast to his waistline, which had expanded. It was as though somebody had put a large weight on his head. Tovey started to puff.

'I've been thinking,' he said. 'Maybe this taxi driving is not good for my health. I need a new job.'

'What about professional jailbreaker and travel agent?' suggested Seth.

'Way too risky. You can only pull a job like this off once. You pay me well. Most of the other suckers who are stuck in chokey would rob their grandmothers blind of a bus fare. Let's eat, and we'll talk about tomorrow.'

Seth heard a noise and looked behind him. Two young men had scrambled onto the top of the helicopter and were dismembering the rotor blades. Tovey gazed at them with admiration.

'Yep,' he said, 'Bryson and his two boys will have that stripped, sorted and crushed before the morning. Pity really, I've always fancied a ride in one of those things.'

For a moment, Seth thought that Tovey was about to

burst into tears, but he knew that behind the soft exterior there was a cold and calculating heart.

'Come on in, I've cooked you some food. And change out of that goddamned uniform. Nothing personal, but you stink. Go take a shower and leave me your laundry.'

'I presume Bryson is the man running this place. Doesn't he have a wife?'

'Did have,' Tovey replied. 'But no woman with any self-respect would live in a dump like this.'

'How did you get to know him?'

Tovey shot him a cautionary look.

'Sorry – I shouldn't have asked.'

Tovey burnt his prison clothes and laundered the contents of his bag while Seth showered. Feeling fresher and more relaxed, he sat down by the big fire in the kitchen. Tovey plonked a bowl of stew in front of him and flicked open two beer bottles. It wasn't exactly haute cuisine, but it was better than prison food, and he was starving.

He pushed the empty bowl away and took a long slow draught of his beer.

'So, where to next?' he asked.

'Tomorrow, you walk to Mexico,' Tovey replied.

'Is it far?'

'Nah – I'll drop you off in Laredo. From there it's only about a ten-minute stroll. I've got all the papers you'll need here.'

Tovey shoved a fat envelope in front of him.

'And from Mexico?' Seth queried.

'You got here by boat, so you're going home by boat – only this time not some swanky liner.'

Seth frowned. 'Go on.'

'You're going back as a cargo passenger on a freight ship. I've booked you a passage from Tampico on the Gulf Coast to Nantes in France.'

'Won't I need my passport and a ticket?'

'Sure, you do,' said Tovey. 'All the paperwork is in the envelope.'

'How did you manage all that?'

'I cheated and lied, of course.'

Seth pulled a face.

'Aw, don't worry,' Tovey said. 'I mean no disrespect Seth, but you can bullshit your way through anything.'

Seth grinned. 'You know me better than I know myself.'

'I guess so, now go to bed – beat it. I'll wake you at six.'

* * *

Seth opened his eyes to find Tovey standing over him with a mug of coffee.

'Sleep well?'

Seth nodded and blew on his coffee. 'And you?'

'I told you, I never sleep. Your laundry is all done, I've even pressed your suit. It's all packed in your bag. Get yourself sorted out and I'll rustle up some breakfast.'

Seth jumped into the shower again for the sheer pleasure of being able to do so freely. He dressed and checked his bag. Everything was neatly stacked, and on top was the fat envelope.

Tovey placed a large plate in front of him.

'Eat up – I'm not sure when you'll get your next meal.'

There was no sign of Bryson or his two sons.

'They worked until four in the morning stripping and crushing the helicopter,' Tovey explained. 'If we had time, I'd drive you past the blocks. I bet you couldn't tell which one used to be a chopper.'

The sun was already up by the time they got in Tovey's taxi.

'What happens when we get to Laredo?' asked Seth.

'Couldn't be simpler,' Tovey replied. 'I'll drop you at the Greyhound bus station, and unless you're unlucky enough to get stopped, you'll be in Mexico within ten minutes. Follow the arrows. You'll need to buy a Gateway Pass to get over the bridge – it's less than a dollar, and some pesos to get an immigration form.'

It was the cue for the one question Seth had desperately wanted to ask.

'I don't have any money, Tovey. You have access to it all.'

'Relax, Seth,' he said and pointed to the glove box.

Seth pulled out another envelope, this time containing a wad of notes of various denominations and some small change in cents and pesos.

'There's about three thousand dollars in there, give or take. I suggest you divide it up a bit. Cash is the one thing the customs guys are looking for. If you let them help themselves to some of it, they usually let you through.'

'And the rest of my money?'

'All safe and transferred to Rupert Sidley. I hope you can trust him – it's a small fortune.'

'Sidley will take his cut, just like you,' Seth replied.

Tovey smiled. 'He's organising someone with a boat to pick you up in France. A guy called Henry something or other – fancy name, possibly double-barrelled.'

The only person that Seth knew fitting that description was Henry Bridges-Treston. He nodded; it would make sense.

'I guess this Henry person will make sure you get back to Helmsmouth,' said Tovey.

'I assume everyone has been paid?' queried Seth.

'All done and dusted, and in budget.'

'Then keep the change.'

'Don't worry, I have,' Tovey replied with a satisfied grin.

He pulled his taxi into a space next to a large Greyhound bus.

'On the other side of the bridge, just keep walking. Ignore all the taxi drivers who'll hassle you, go straight past them until someone calls your name.'

'What does this someone look like?' asked Seth.

'Imagine somebody about my shape and size, but

younger with dark hair and a moustache. You won't miss him – he's my cousin Miguel. Don't worry, he knows who you are.' Tovey switched off the engine. 'Sadly, this is where we part company. It's been nice knowing you and a pleasure to do business with you. But if anyone asks –'

'I know,' said Seth. 'I've never met you, I've never seen you, and if anyone asks, you've never clapped eyes on me. Right?'

'Right, but you've forgotten the last line…'

'Now beat it?' queried Seth.

'You've got it,' Tovey replied.

Seth picked up his bag, slammed the door shut behind him, and without a backward glance followed the signs to Mexico.

He walked past rows of scruffy shops. Some were boarded up and covered with graffiti. Others, despite the hour, were open for business. They were mainly crammed with clothes or selling a bizarre range of electrical goods. In the window of one shop, he noticed a white shirt and tie for sale complete with a pair of cufflinks in the shape of roulette wheels. The novelty appealed to him, even more so when he found they came with two complimentary packs of playing cards.

Closer to the border, every second shop appeared to be offering to exchange dollars. Seth wondered how they could all make money. The pavement was now narrow and uneven. Seth had to step onto the road to pass the slower pedestrians, being careful to avoid the increasing early morning traffic.

He turned into a fairly new concourse, went along an underpass then through a covered walkway until at last he came to the Laredo Bridge. There was a group of people crowding round the ticket machine. They nearly all spoke Spanish. Seth bought his pass, manoeuvred his way through the turnstile and walked over the bridge into Mexico, pausing only briefly to gaze at the muddy waters of the Rio Grande flowing slowly beneath him.

He bought his immigration form and had it duly stamped. Nobody bothered with his passport. Seth only saw one customs official. He was engrossed in a magazine with lurid pictures of guns and stuffing his face with a tortilla wrap. Seth edged past him and stepped out into the Mexican sunshine.

He walked briskly, ignoring the panhandlers, the buskers, and the taxi drivers. Somehow Mexico, even so close to the border, seemed wildly different from America. Seth couldn't say why; maybe it was the people. They certainly appeared less affluent but perhaps happier. The smells too had changed, spicier and more pungent.

A woman pleaded with him to buy some of her food. Seth wasn't sure but they looked like roasted crickets. He shook his head and moved on. What he liked most was the liveliness of the place. He could live here, he thought, if he hadn't already planned to go back to England.

★ ★ ★

'Hey, Signor Shuster!'

A man on the other side of the road was waving to him.

'Miguel?' asked Seth.

'My cousin Tovey ask you call me Miguel? OK, sure, I am Miguel. Get in car.'

It wasn't a yellow taxi this time, but a rather dilapidated Mercedes.

'So, you travel back to England in a stinking cargo boat.' Miguel tapped his head. 'You must be mad. Here we have sunshine and lotsa pretty girls. In England, ees cold and it rains, and the girls...' He finished with a look of disgust.

Seth didn't feel like offering an explanation.

'How long will it take us to get to Tampico?'

'Depends on the traffic, my friend, and how often we stop. Nine or ten hours, maybe. You have plenty time. The boat she don't sail until two in the morning.' He looked at Seth's bag. 'I hoped you packed some books. Three weeks at sea with nothing to do could drive a man crazy.'

The journey took over ten hours. The traffic was horrendous; they stopped, they ate, they refuelled... Miguel's chatter was incessant and when Seth closed his eyes, he would put on the radio. The music blared. The presenter could not have spoken louder or faster if he tried.

Finally Seth could stand it no longer. He reached over and pointedly switched off the radio.

Miguel looked offended. 'You don't like radio, my friend? It's not a problem,' he said. He started to sing.

It was a very long ten hours.

Night had fallen by the time they reached Tampico. From what Seth could see as they shot through the traffic, it was a large, prosperous city with beautiful old buildings and wide, bustling streets. The port area was vast and busy even at this time of night. Miguel had to stop twice to ask for directions. Eventually, he located the boat. Like most of the vessels docked in the harbour, it was enormous and could have done with a lick of paint. Miguel shook his hand and wished him luck.

Seth's passport and ticket were checked. He handed over his immigration form and made his way up the gangway.

The cabin was an improvement on the one he had had going over, in as much as there was a proper bed and a window. Sadly, the window was spattered with paint and rust, which obscured any view. At least it would let in some light.

There were only eight passengers. They were made to watch a video on emergency drill and given a tour of their quarters, and where to board a lifeboat should the need arise. Apart from two elderly ladies, his travelling companions struck Seth as remarkably dull. Miguel was right, it was going to be a long three weeks.

For the first few days Seth kept himself pretty much to himself. His other fellow travellers included a honeymoon couple who rarely left their cabin, an elderly man who spoke to himself and drank from early morning until he staggered to bed, and lastly, two middle-aged men with enormous beards. They spoke no English and conversed in a tongue that was so outlandish as to be completely unintelligible. There was a library of well-thumbed books in a variety of languages and a collection of DVDs ranging from the banal to the risqué.

Very heavy seas confined everyone to their cabins for the best part of a week. When they emerged, they were all paler and thinner, but having lived through the ordeal together, they had now lost some of their reserve.

One evening, Seth produced a pack of cards and started to play a game of Patience. The old ladies nudged each other and approached his table.

'My sister and I love a game of cards, but we forgot to bring any,' said the shorter of the two.

'Why don't you join me?' Seth replied, and introduced himself.

'I'm Freda, and this is my little sister Madge,' she said, waving a hand in the direction of the taller of the two. Both burst out laughing.

'I'm sorry, Mr Shuster. It's our little joke. I have a big sister who is smaller than me,' explained Madge.

'And I have a little sister who is bigger than me,' added Freda, and both of them began laughing again.

Seth smiled and pointed to the two vacant chairs. He cast an appraising eye over his companions. Neither wore expensive clothes or jewellery, and he doubted if they had ever gambled for anything more than matches. Still, it will beat playing Patience, he thought.

'What's it to be, ladies?' he said as he shuffled the cards. The two ladies sat mesmerised as the cards moved in a blur from one hand to the other.

'Goodness Mr Shuster, certainly not poker or you would have us down to our singlets in no time,' said Madge.

They played gin rummy, and this became a regular evening habit until Seth got bored. He taught them other games: Skat, Sergeant Major and Crazy Nines. They particularly liked Go Fish.

On the final week of the trip, Seth thought he would have some fun and taught both of them how to cheat at cards – fake shuffles, dishonest deals, and the best ways to conceal cards. Madge and Freda loved it and were quick learners.

'Wait till whist night at the Women's Institute,' said Freda.

'We'll whip the pants off every last one of them,'

declared Madge, and true to form, they both started laughing.

* * *

They arrived in Saint-Nazaire, the port of Nantes, in the early hours of the morning. Seth presumed Sidley would have been following the boat's progress, and he was not mistaken.

As he disembarked, he saw the familiar shifty face of Henry Bridges-Treston waiting for him. A taxi drove them to the marina where his yacht, *The Poppy*, was moored. Three handsome young sailors were waiting for their arrival. One of them gave Seth a salacious look. Seth ignored him; he was not in the mood.

There was something about Bridges-Treston that even Seth found abhorrent. He avoided his company during the crossing as much as possible. Compared to the voyage from Mexico this journey was very short, but quite bumpy. Feigning seasickness, Seth stayed below decks the entire time.

Thirty-six hours later, in darkness, they arrived in Merton Cove. They dropped anchor and Bridges-Treston launched the dinghy. Seth was helped down to the little craft by the sailor who had given him the eye. He held onto Seth for a fraction of second longer than was necessary.

The small motor belched and sprang into life. In no time, they reached the pebble beach.

'This is where we say au revoir,' said Bridges-Treston as he offered him a damp handshake.

Seth felt like wiping his hand after the encounter. He turned and saw another familiar figure coming towards him.

'Good grief,' exclaimed Seth. 'Philip Aintree. Don't tell me you're running a taxi service as well.'

'You know me, Seth, always willing to help an old pal.'

Yes, thought Seth, *but only if there's something in it for you.*

'Where to?' asked Phil the Shed once they had got into his van.

'Helmsmouth Christian Shelter,' Seth replied.

'You don't mean the doss house where all the winos and vagrants hang out? God, you must be down on your luck.'

Seth ignored the rebuke. 'Tell me Phil, who's doing what in dear old Helmsmouth?' He knew Phil the Shed was not well educated, but he was astute when it came to local illicit endeavours. He knew all the hardened criminals, both young and old, along with every brothel, gambling joint and drug den. Seth made a mental note of them all, though he was surprised that some of them were still active.

'And your pal Sidley has got a legal finger in almost every pie,' Phil concluded.

Good, thought Seth, *I need to buy me a large slice.*

They pulled up in front of the Shelter.

'Are you sure?' asked Phil in one last ditch attempt. 'I have a spare sofa.'

'Quite sure,' Seth replied.

He pushed open the door and rapped gently on the glass by the reception desk. A young man looked up from his work. The resemblance between the two men was uncanny. Identical smiles spread across their faces.

'It's good to meet you at last, father,' said the younger man.

Seth stared intently at him. It was like looking into a magic mirror that reflected back a youthful version of himself.

He took in the surroundings, his eyes darting back and forth. The Shelter was spotlessly clean, but drab and desperately in need of renovation. All the paint was flaking. There was damp in the ceiling and the corners. Every piece of furniture was worn. The place reeked of poverty and despondency.

One of tonight's residents shuffled passed him, muttering to himself, staring at the floor.

'Are you all right, Arthur?' Seth's son called after him.

The man raised a hand in acknowledgement but said nothing.

Seth gazed at his son and noticed the young man was clutching a well-worn Bible. How similar yet how different we are, he mused.

As if reading his thoughts, the young man said, 'It's never too late to change.'

Seth shrugged. 'Maybe one day...'

'Your friend is waiting for you upstairs in my flat.'

'Friend?' Seth queried. He didn't know anyone he would call 'friend'.

'Well, colleague if you prefer – Rupert Sidley. He's been waiting for over an hour. Come on, I'll show you up. I have to man the desk for a bit longer, then we can talk properly.'

The flat was as poor as the rest of the Shelter, but homely in its own way. Sidley rose to meet Seth scattering his papers on the floor.

'I hope your trip went well. At least you're here safely.'

Sidley had aged considerably since Seth last knew him. Despite the passing of the years, he still retained the look of a starving ferret.

'I have done as you requested and drawn up a list of potential business opportunities.' He picked up the fallen papers and gave Seth a page. On it were three names and some background details next to each.

Seth ran a finger down the list. 'OK. Can you fix up some meetings?'

'Already done,' Sidley replied. 'I thought next week. We don't want to appear too eager. I thought we ought to take a small gift with us. Champagne perhaps?'

Seth looked at the list again. He pointed to one name.

'Not champagne for this one. Better make it whisky, but nothing too expensive.'

CHAPTER 36

Steadman hammered on Ben's door. He paused, heard a moan, and hammered again.

'Ben, are you awake? I could do with some help. There's been a development.'

As a small boy, Ben had come to hate the word "development". It usually meant not seeing his father for days on end. Even now his stomach churned when he heard it.

'Give us a minute. What time is it anyway?' Ben replied stifling a yawn.

'About six-thirty, I guess. I haven't got my talking watch on.'

Ben heaved himself out of bed and opened the door. His father looked pale and drawn.

'Is everything OK, dad?'

'No, not really. Frank Rufus is calling for me in quarter of an hour. Would you lay out my clothes? I can wear most of what I had on yesterday. I'll only need clean socks and pants. I'm going to grab a quick shower.'

'No problem. I'll put the kettle on and make some toast.'

Ben knew exactly how his father liked his clothes to be laid out. He checked his father's shoes weren't needing a polish and that his coat was not still damp from the previous evening.

Steadman showered and dressed as quickly as he was able. Ben poured the tea and passed over a plate of toast and marmalade.

'I don't suppose you can tell me what's happened?' Ben asked. 'Another body I suppose?'

'Yes – and someone who was supposed to be under twenty-four-hour police surveillance.'

Ben whistled softly.

'It gets worse,' his father continued. 'I may be responsible for his death.'

Before Ben could ask anything further, the doorbell rang.

'That will be Frank. I'll get it,' said Ben.

Steadman finished his makeshift breakfast. Robbie padded through just in time for the last crust.

'You will have to stay here this morning, old boy,' said Steadman as he patted the dog's large head. An image of Robbie in a room with blood and brains spattered everywhere formed in his mind's eye. It was no place for a dog. 'Ben will look after you, I'm sure.'

'No worries,' Ben replied.

'Tim will walk him and feed him. Remember not to leave Robbie alone. He'll think he should be working and will get very anxious. Even if you nip down to the café, take him with you. Marco and Roberto won't mind.'

'Are you ready to go?' asked Dr Rufus.

Ben helped his father into his coat.

'Better take your hat as well. It's still raining.'

★ ★ ★

Dr Rufus opened the car door.

'Hang on a second, I'll throw these papers on the back seat,' he said. 'Damned car didn't feel like mine when it was all clean and tidy.'

'Who called you this morning, Frank?' asked Steadman.

'Crouchley himself. He wasn't very happy. Heaven help the officers who were on duty last night.'

'I can't say I'm very happy either,' Steadman confessed. 'Unless it really is a suicide, which I find hard to believe. If it's murder, then I'm probably the one who set the wheels in motion. I should have insisted Philip Aintree was brought in yesterday.'

'So that he could have been murdered when he was let out of police custody?' Dr Rufus argued. 'You know we couldn't have detained him, and barring putting an officer inside his flat, there's nothing more that could have been done.'

'I still feel guilty,' Steadman replied.

'Well stop it,' Dr Rufus said firmly. 'You're no use to me or anyone else if you're moping about wearing a hairshirt. I heard you made your views known at yesterday's meeting. If anyone should feel guilty, it should be Crouchley, and I'll bet that thought has never crossed his mind.'

Steadman's spirits lifted a fraction. It was difficult not to be heartened by Dr Rufus's support.

'Do you know if DCI Long is going to be there?' he asked.

'I got the impression from Crouchley that DS Fairfax was being sent. He won't like that it's a woman. Even so he'll probably spend his time ogling her as he usually does.'

* * *

It was quite a small apartment block with only four storeys. There were three flats on each floor except the first, which had two. It was surrounded by police cars, some of which still had on their blue flashing lights.

The two officers recognised Dr Rufus's old red Volvo and waved him into a parking space right by the entrance.

'Which floor?' he asked.

'First floor, middle flat,' one of the PCs replied.

Arm in arm Steadman and Dr Rufus walked in. They could hear the other officer ask his colleague, 'Isn't that DI John Steadman, the blind detective?'

'Oh, to be so famous,' Dr Rufus remarked. 'Damn it, they've cordoned off the lift. Will you be all right on the stairs?'

Steadman nodded. 'Tell me when we reach the landings, and I'll be fine.'

They could hear Crouchley shouting and swearing before they reached the first floor. DS Fairfax was waiting for them by the door.

'Thank you for coming, Inspector Steadman.'

'I doubt if I will receive such a warm welcome from Inspector Crouchley. Where have you got to, Fiona?'

'The photographers have been. Kim Ho and her forensic team are having a look around. I've managed to stop anything being touched or moved. You'll need to wear some plastic shoe protectors. To be honest, it's a most unpleasant sight in there.'

Dr Rufus wanted to ask if she was referring to Inspector Crouchley but resisted the temptation.

Steadman was right, Crouchley was not pleased to see him.

'What the bloody hell took you so long, Rufus? And what's he doing here?' Crouchley asked pointing a finger in Steadman's direction.

'You mean my deaf colleague?' Dr Rufus replied as innocently as he could.

'Are you being sarcastic? He's blind not deaf,' Crouchley said in a loud voice.

'In that case he can answer for himself,' Dr Rufus replied. 'To save him the blushes, I'll tell you – DI Steadman is here with me.'

'Why?'

'Because I asked him,' retorted the Home Office pathologist. He turned to Steadman and whispered, 'Don't move if you can help it. There's bits of bone, blood, hair, and brains strewn over the floor and halfway up the far wall.'

Dr Rufus had already pulled on some gloves and was surveying the corpse. Tentatively he tried to move an arm. It was set rigid.

'What time did he die?' asked Inspector Crouchley.

'Judging by the degree of rigor mortis, and the temperature in the flat, I would say yesterday evening about nine, ten at the latest. I'll give you a more accurate time after I've done the post-mortem examination. How do you know it's Phil the Shed?'

'Bound to be,' snorted Crouchley. 'Who else do you think it is?'

'With his head blown apart and half his face missing, it could be anybody. We'll check his fingerprints in case you're wrong. I would hate to give you a red face.'

Dr Rufus stood up with a groan. He looked at the body from several different angles, and again at the spread of blood and brains.

'What do you make of the gun, Kim?' he asked. 'It looks quite a fancy pistol.'

Kim Ho pushed her silky black hair behind her ears. 'It's a modernised Makarov pistol. It's the same make of pistol that was used to murder Seth Shuster and Rupert Sidley. I had the full report back from ballistics yesterday.'

How very clever to leave Phil with a Makarov pistol, thought Steadman, and probably the same gun that killed Shuster and Sidley.

'You haven't, by any chance, located the bullet, Kim?' he dared to ask.

'It's lodged in the far wall, sir,' Kim explained. 'about two metres from the floor.'

'What's the angle of entry?'

Kim gave a nervous giggle. 'Almost horizontal, meaning...'

'...he was shot while standing up.' Steadman finished the sentence for her. 'Now that is very interesting,' he concluded.

Inspector Crouchley was having none of it. 'What do you mean by, "he was shot"? Phil the Shed killed himself with the same gun he used to murder Shuster and Sidley. It's obvious. He knew we were on to him and took the coward's way out. Nice and tidy – we've got rid of all the trash. Done deal – all wrapped up,' he said smugly.

'Odd then that he shot himself standing up, don't you think?' Steadman ventured.

'You've spent too much time with that forensic

psychologist. Don't give me any more of that psycho-tosh nonsense,' Crouchley retaliated.

Dr Rufus interjected. 'We'll check his hand for gunshot residue, though it might be unreliable if he held up his hands at the same time as he was shot.'

'I have a question,' said Steadman. 'Which hand is he holding the gun in?'

'His right.'

'In that case, Inspector Crouchley, you may have a problem. Philip Aintree, otherwise known as Phil the Shed, was left-handed.'

'So, this is murder, unless we find large amounts of gunshot residue on his hand,' said DS Fairfax as she stared at Inspector Crouchley.

'In that case, Detective Sergeant Fairfax, it's your problem, not mine. I'm out of here,' Crouchley replied sarcastically.

Fiona Fairfax was not fazed by men like Crouchley. 'Before you go, I'll need some of your officers to question all the neighbours, locate and secure Phil's van, and track down any CCTV footage. I believe the caretaker lives in one of the ground-floor flats. You can leave one to guard the entrance. Oh, and I'll need to interview the officers who were on duty yesterday evening.'

'You can have what's left, after I've finished with them,' Crouchley replied before stomping out of the room. He paused as he passed Steadman and gave him a filthy look.

'A gun like that would go off with an enormous

bang. I would be surprised if the neighbours didn't hear anything,' DS Fairfax observed.

'Unless it was fitted with a silencer,' said Steadman.

Kim Ho shook her head. 'A silenced version of the Makarov pistol does exist, but it has a screw thread in the barrel. This gun doesn't.'

Steadman rubbed his chin. 'Frank, is there any possibility it's not Phil the Shed?'

'Of course not. It's undeniably Phil the Shed!' Dr Rufus responded gruffly. 'I just like winding Crouchley up, it does him good.'

Kim Ho emptied what pockets she could reach, and with Dr Rufus's help turned the body over to search the others.

'Not a pretty sight,' observed DS Fairfax.

Steadman wondered if it was any worse than the image he had conjured up.

'Thank goodness Munro isn't here,' said Dr Rufus. 'It's messy enough in here without him throwing up last night's haggis.'

And just as well Robbie's not here to stick his nose in it or worse, thought Steadman. If Robbie has one fault it was a penchant for rolling in anything gross and pungent.

'The wallet is Phil's– it's got his bank cards and driving licence,' said Kim. 'And here are a set of keys.'

DS Fairfax turned to one of the young PCs who was standing by the door.

'Go and see if you can find where Phil's van is parked.

Secure the scene, then come back and I'll arrange for it to be removed.'

'How will I know which van is his?'

'Oh, that's easy,' Steadman replied. 'I gather it's white with Helmsmouth Office Solutions displayed on the side, a phone number, and for some strange reason, Vancouver, Brisbane, Sydney and Singapore written underneath.'

'You two,' said DS Fairfax to the remaining officers, 'knock up all the flats and ask the occupants if they saw anyone or heard anything last night. And get the caretaker to give you any footage from the security camera while you're at it.'

Kim Ho was fidgeting anxiously.

'What's up?' asked Dr Rufus.

'There are two pizza boxes on the table,' she replied.

'What's bothering you about them? Looking at the size of the man, he probably lived on pizzas.'

'But if you look at his chair, on the arm there's a plate with the congealed remains of a fry-up,' Kim explained.

'The post-mortem will confirm if that was his last meal,' Dr Rufus asserted.

'If it does, why are there two boxes with fresh, uneaten pizzas in them?' she queried.

'Any clues on the boxes to suggest where they've come from?' asked Steadman.

'No,' Kim replied. 'They're generic unbranded boxes.' She lifted one of the pizzas out of its box and gazed at the underside. 'But this is interesting. This one has landed on the floor – there's blood and brains stuck on the underside. It's been picked up and put back in its box.'

'And certainly not by Phil the Shed,' DS Fairfax added.

Steadman suddenly found the room getting hot and stuffy. The image of the double-sided pizza was the last straw. Dr Rufus noticed him just in time.

'You need a breath of fresh air, John,' he said leading his friend out of the flat.

A cold draught came up from the stairwell and Steadman felt his head clear. He was about to thank Frank, but stopped before the words left his lips.

'I think I know how he was murdered. And I'll bet none of the neighbours heard a thing,' Steadman declared.

'Would you care to enlighten me?' asked Dr Rufus.

A wicked smile spread over Steadman's face. 'If I'm right, you'll find fragments of fabric and insulating material that don't belong to anything in the flat in amongst the remains of Philip Aintree's head.'

Dr Rufus scratched his beard and frowned. And then, as though a light bulb had been switched on, he beamed at his friend.

'The crafty devil!' he exclaimed. 'I knew you might come in useful if I brought you along. Let's go back in and see what DS Fairfax makes of it.'

They were overtaken by the two young officers, who nipped in ahead of them.

'I've spoken to all the neighbours,' said the first breathlessly. 'Nobody heard a thing.'

'And I've had a look at the CCTV footage from last night,' said his colleague. 'Phil returned at five past seven. Some of the other residents drifted in and out. The only stranger was a guy on a bike who arrived at nine fifteen and left quarter an hour later. He had one of those large cube things on his back – you know, the sort they deliver hot takeaway food in.'

'I don't suppose it showed his face?' DS Fairfax enquired.

'No. He was wearing a cycle helmet, goggles and gloves and had a scarf pulled over his mouth and nose. I've got the recording here.'

DS Fairfax turned to the first officer. 'Go back to all the flats and ask if anyone had food delivered yesterday evening.' And turning to the second officer, 'Find out who does takeaway pizzas near here. I don't expect any of them to be open.'

'Inspector Steadman has an idea to run past you,' Dr Rufus announced.

'More than one actually, Fiona. If Phil ordered the pizzas, we might be able to retrieve the call from his mobile,' said Steadman.

Kim held up a polythene bag. 'I've got his phone here.'

'Good,' said Steadman, 'but I doubt if there is a record of him ordering pizzas. Why nobody has come forward saying they heard a shot struck me as odd, and now we know that it's because nobody heard it. I've come up with an explanation, although it is a bit farfetched.'

'Go on,' said DS Fairfax.

'Those delivery cubes are very well padded. Let's say someone arrives at the door with two pizzas inside the cube. Phil would no doubt deny all knowledge. I don't know how Phil was persuaded to accept the pizzas. I guess the courier might have said they were already paid for and his name was on the order. Phil's not going to miss the chance of a free meal.'

Steadman tilted his head to one side trying to picture the image.

'This is pure speculation, but imagine Phil takes the pizzas, one in each hand. The courier finds an excuse to follow him in – maybe he asks to use the toilet. The Makarov pistol is still inside the padded cube. He needn't take it out – instead, he fires the gun from inside the cube at close range. Phil drops the pizza boxes, and one falls out. All the courier then has to do is put the pizza back in the box and stage the scene to look like a suicide.'

The room fell silent.

Dr Rufus was the first to speak. 'It stacks up. Maybe the post-mortem will turn up something to support the theory.'

'I'll deal with the gun and bullet and get them sent over to ballistics,' said Kim. 'I'll also get the whole team over to bag everything before we get the cleaning squad out and someone to secure the door.'

'Are you happy for us to move the body, Dr Rufus?' Fairfax asked.

'Yes, I'm finished here,' he replied.

There was a knock on what was left of the door. 'I've found his van and lockup,' said the young PC.

'Good, I'll arrange for it to be collected. Would you wait by the vehicle and keep an eye out for the pick-up truck?' instructed Fairfax.

The young officer made an attempt at a salute and left.

'Is there anything else I need to do before I phone DCI Long?' Fairfax asked Steadman.

Steadman frowned. There were still some missing bits of the puzzle, he thought, but they would have to wait.

'No,' he said at last. 'For the moment at least, I think we are done.'

'Before you go, Inspector Steadman, have you any idea why someone would want to murder Phil the Shed?' asked DS Fairfax in a quiet voice.

'Sadly, Fiona, I believe I know why he was killed and also who was behind his death. We will have to be meticulous in gathering all the evidence. The case will need to be watertight if we are to bring the perpetrators to justice.'

CHAPTER 37

With some difficulty, Steadman peeled off his plastic overshoes. Dr Rufus took them, and along with his own and his gloves, deposited them in a yellow bin bag by the door.

'How are we going to get you down the stairs?' he asked.

'If I can put one hand on the banister and the other on your shoulder...'

Steadman felt naked without his dog. Dr Rufus's efforts appeared clumsy by comparison. However, they made it safely back to the old red Volvo.

'May I borrow your phone before we start?' asked Dr Rufus.

'You haven't lost yours again?' replied Steadman as he fumbled in his pockets.

'No, it's not lost. I know exactly where it is. It's by my front door where I leave my car keys.'

It was useless pursuing the conversation. Dr Rufus's disdain for modern technology was renowned.

'I need to phone Nigel, my mortuary assistant, to let him know there is a body on its way in.'

Steadman raised a questioning eyebrow.

'This I can't wait to hear,' he said handing his friend the phone.

'It's very simple,' Dr Rufus replied. 'He taps the mouthpiece – once for no, and twice for yes. You have to allow for the conversation. It could be, "no, I can't", or "yes, I understand", and so forth.'

He dialled the mortuary number.

'It's me, Nigel. Can you hear me?'

'Tap, tap.'

'There's been a shooting. One body – male by the name of Philip Aintree.'

'Tap, tap.'

'Can you start the paperwork and make the usual preparations?'

'Tap, tap.'

'I'll be along later this morning. Have you baked any more cakes?'

'Tap.'

'That's a pity. I was hoping to entice DI Steadman to join us.'

'Tap, tap, tap – tap, tap, tap.'

He switched the phone off and hand it back.

'What was with all the tapping at the end?' Steadman asked.

'Oh, that was him laughing,' Dr Rufus explained. 'Judging by your colour earlier, I guess you wouldn't be too keen on attending another post-mortem.'

'No, I'd rather go back and see if Robbie's all right. He gets very anxious if I leave the house without him.'

And vice versa, thought Dr Rufus.

'Excellent plan, I'm starving and could do justice to a decent breakfast.' Very little seemed to put Dr Rufus off his food.

They arrived back at the flat, but there was no sign of Ben or Robbie.

'I need to wash my hands,' said Dr Rufus.

Steadman hung his coat and hat behind the door. Trailing a guiding hand along the corridor wall, he reached the intercom.

'Yes, they're both here, tucking into breakfast,' Marco reassured him.

Like Dr Rufus, Steadman felt somehow contaminated by the visit to Philip Aintree's flat. Odd how Phil the Shed had lost his nickname, he thought as he washed his face and hands. Was it, he wondered, out of some deep-seated respect for the dead that he was now given his full title?

The two men went down to the café. Robbie was ecstatic to see Steadman. Even without his harness on, he glued himself to his side.

Ben moved up to make room. As they sat down, DS Munro entered. He looked ghastly.

'Good grief, Alan, you could be one breath away from

the mortuary,' remarked Dr Rufus. 'In fact, there are at least two bodies down there that look better than you do.'

'It's all Inspector Steadman's fault,' replied Munro in a whisper.

Steadman's heart sank. He had no idea what he could have done.

'I wasn't sure about the Ardbeg whisky at first. It's very smoky – almost medicinal. I thought I had better try another wee dram, then another... Before I knew it, the bottle was, shall we say, a lot lighter than when you brought it. God, it feels like my head's a pot and somebody's clattering it with a spoon.'

'What you need is a large black coffee with plenty of sugar,' Dr Rufus suggested.

'I don't imagine you feel like eating anything,' said Steadman.

'I wouldn't say that. Maybe that's the problem – I haven't eaten enough,' Munro replied, his voice suddenly sounding a lot stronger.

Steadman ordered two full breakfasts and a bacon croissant for himself.

'I suppose you have heard about the latest development, Alan.'

'Yes, Sergeant Grimble called me. Philip Aintree murdered in his own flat while he was meant to be under twenty-four-hour surveillance.'

Even Munro is giving him his full name, Steadman noted.

'I gather Crouchley is going berserk down at the Eyesore,' said Munro. 'Did you hear that forensics have found another gun in Philip's van along with a suit jacket that matches Shuster's trousers?'

Steadman took a sharp intake of breath. 'I hadn't heard.'

'No wallet and no phone in the jacket, of course,' Munro continued. 'The gun possibly matches the description Sidley's secretary gave to DCI Long. He's asked me to go and show it to her. Hopefully, we can get a positive ID. I was hoping, Inspector Steadman, that you would come with me. There's something about Mzz Devine that gives me the willies – the way she looks at me when I pronounce her name...'

'I would be happy to come along. When were you planning to go?'

'As soon as I've finished my breakfast.'

Steadman nodded. 'What about you, Ben? Have you any plans for the day?'

'I've offered to dig over some of Linda's garden. I'll nip upstairs first and fetch your hat and coat, and Robbie's harness.'

Dr Rufus glanced at his watch. 'I'd better make a move as well. How much am I due you for the breakfast, John?'

'Don't worry. It's all been taken care of,' said Steadman.

★ ★ ★

The Audi was parked a little way from the café. Munro and Steadman walked briskly with Robbie in the lead. The dog held his head high, glad to be working again.

'I hope you don't mind me asking, Alan, but are you fit enough to drive?'

Munro turned bright red. 'You're as bad as Maureen. She made me do a home breathalyser test before she let me out of the house. I'm fine, especially now that I've got some food in me.'

Steadman's fingers were cold, and he struggled more than usual with the seat belt. Munro waited patiently, not daring to offer any help. He knew that Steadman hated unnecessary assistance. Eventually the belt clicked into place.

He patted his coat and frowned.

'What's the matter?' asked Munro.

'There's something in the pocket.'

He pulled out a small, intricate carving of a rat.

'That's pretty. Is it one of your Japanese carvings?' asked Munro.

'Yes, it's from my netsuke collection,' Steadman replied, running a finger delicately over the precious object, his fingernail tracing out its dainty ears and paws. 'This is the first one Holly gave me, and my favourite. I can only assume that Ben put it there.'

'Why would he do that?'

'For luck, I guess,' Steadman replied with a shrug.

'I didn't think you believed in such things,' Munro responded.

'You're right, I don't,' said Steadman, but his features relaxed, and he smiled as his fingers folded tightly round the little rat. 'Let's go.'

It wasn't a long drive to the Eyesore.

'I think I'll wait in the car,' said Steadman. 'Robbie is still fretful and I'm not sure he could cope with Sergeant Grimble fussing over him.'

Munro strode off leaving Steadman alone in the car. Gently he stroked his dog's head.

'Well, old boy, do you think we're any nearer solving the case? I fear, Robbie, it's not going to end too well.'

A melody started playing in his head. He couldn't place the tune at first. It was tranquil and soothing. Of course, he said to himself, it was the Welsh lullaby Sam had sung to Melanie and Annie last night.

Robbie stirred.

'What is it? Do you hear Alan coming back already?'

A man paused by the car and stared in. Robbie growled softly. Steadman felt a shiver run down his spine. He was certain that Seth Shuster's son was no more than a few feet away. Should he open the window? His fingers found the button on the arm rest. Damn, Munro had turned off the ignition; the window wouldn't move no matter how often he pressed it.

After what seemed like an age, the driver's door opened, and Munro heaved himself in.

'Sorry to keep you waiting. You know what Grimble's like once he starts.'

'Did you see anyone by the car, Alan?'

'No, there's nobody about.'

'He was here again, I'm sure – Seth's double.'

'What do you think he wants?' queried Munro.

'Only one thing – I believe he wants to know who killed his father.'

* * *

Munro placed a plastic evidence bag on Steadman's lap. 'Look after that for me,' he said as he started the Audi.

The bag felt cold and surprisingly heavy for its small size. Steadman traced a finger over the outline of a gun.

'Is it a Beretta?' he asked.

Munro was impressed. 'Yes, a Beretta Bobcat. Small, but deadly at close range.'

'I don't suppose there were any prints on it?'

'No – all wiped clean.'

Steadman hummed a little tune to himself. In all the years he had been involved with Philip Aintree, he had never known him to carry anything more offensive than a cosh and some knuckledusters. So where had the gun...

Munro broke his train of thought.

'Grimble reckons DCI Long will call a meeting before the day is out. I hope I can stay awake. My eyes feel like they're made of sandpaper.'

'It was a good meal last night,' said Steadman.

'I noticed Sam was fair tucking into her haggis,' Munro replied, his accent getting stronger with the memory. 'The girls were as high as kites this morning. The only way I could get them to go to school was by letting them wear their awful "See you Jimmy" hats. Heaven knows what their teachers will make of them.'

'Sam informed me that January the twenty-fifth is also St Dwynwen's Day – the Welsh patron saint of lovers.'

'Oh yes!' said Munro with a smirk. 'Would you care to elaborate?'

'Definitely not,' Steadman replied firmly.

★ ★ ★

Munro pulled up outside a small Victorian terraced house that had been split into two flats. Rupert Sidley's secretary lived on the first floor.

'Remind me how you say her name. Is it *Mzz* Devine or *Mz* Devine?' pleaded Munro, applying the full force of his Scots burr to the first rendition.

'You'll get away with the second version, but only just,' Steadman conceded.

Ms Devine opened the door before Munro had a chance to knock. She was dressed all in brown and looked even more angular than Munro remembered. He would bet she wasn't eating properly.

'One of your sergeants warned me you were on your

way. You had better come in,' she said pulling the door open wide.

Although he couldn't see it, Steadman sensed the austerity and starkness of the flat. Their footsteps and voices echoed very slightly, as though they had entered a church or a cavern.

Munro took in the surroundings. All the walls were white. The floors were polished wood, and the furniture, what little there was of it, was simple and modern. The only relief was numerous unframed paintings. They were all by the same artist and very abstract, yet Munro found them enchanting and vaguely haunting.

'Can I get you a coffee?' asked Ms Devine.

Both men declined.

'Do you mind my dog being here?' Steadman asked.

Ms Devine shook her head, before very quickly adding, 'Not at all. Does he always look so sad?'

'I don't think it's sadness,' Steadman replied. 'I think it's a pitiful attempt at getting a biscuit. Occasionally it works.'

Ms Devine looked lovingly at the dog again. 'If I had a biscuit, he would certainly get one.' Turning to Munro, she said, 'What can I do for you?'

Munro held up the clear plastic evidence bag.

'We've found this gun, and we were wondering if it could have belonged to Mr Sidley?'

Ms Devine stared intently at the gun. 'It could well be. It's definitely the same make. Where did it come from?'

Munro opened his eyes wide and tipped his head to one side, but remained tight-lipped.

'You can't tell me, can you?' said Ms Devine seeing the look on Munro's face. 'If it's Mr Sidley's gun, there ought to be some damage to the handle.'

'How do you know that?' asked Munro.

'I was with him when it happened. Let me explain. It was not often I accompanied Mr Sidley on his visits. Last summer he was dealing with a dispute over access the owners of the Red Chip Casino were having with their neighbours. It was exactly the sort of case Mr Sidley liked. He went armed with masses of documents and confused all parties to the point where they all thought they had won, when in truth he was the only person to benefit. I was there as a distraction and to help carry the papers. On the way back to car the gun fell out of his pocket and bounced on the pavement. Without batting an eyelid, he asked me to pick it up. As I was bending down, he said to be careful and not to touch the trigger as it was loaded. I noticed the fall had cracked one side of the handle. It's the side facing you, DS Munro.'

Munro inspected the handle, and sure enough there was an oddly shaped crack.

'Can you describe the damage?' he asked.

'I can do better than that, I'll draw it for you.' She fetched a pad and a small piece of charcoal. 'I studied art before I became a legal secretary. I have a good memory for detail.'

She glanced at the gun and quickly sketched it, but as a mirror image of itself.

'The scratch started at the base and branched out. Ironically, it looked very similar to the peace sign used by the ban-the-bomb campaign. Maybe that's why I can remember it so clearly.'

'The semaphore signs for N and D – nuclear disarmament,' said Steadman.

'You've lost me, sir,' replied Munro.

Steadman stood up. 'Imagine I'm holding a flag in each hand. The sign for N is both flags pointing down at angle, like so. Whereas a D is one flag held vertically with the other pointing directly downwards.' He moved his arms to demonstrate. 'Merge the two signs, put them in a circle, and there you have it.'

'You should join our pub quiz team, Inspector Steadman.'

'I fear I wouldn't be much use, Ms Devine. I only know random facts. Ask me about TV soaps or boy bands and I wouldn't have a clue.'

She handed the finished drawing to Munro. He peered at the gun, then the sketch, then back to the gun again.

'And you, Mz Devine, are wasted as a legal secretary. Your drawing is amazing. It perfectly matches the cracks on the gun.'

Ms Devine beamed at the compliment.

'Tell me, are the paintings on the wall yours as well?'

'All mine. I'm thinking of a change in career. I was

toying with the idea of teaching art.'

'I don't usually get modern art,' confessed Munro. 'But there's something about your paintings that fascinates me. I could certainly live with a couple of them on my wall.'

'You realise, Ms Devine, this is a first,' Steadman interjected. 'I never thought I would hear DS Munro enthusing about art. Have you ever thought about a public display?'

'Dreamt about it, maybe. I'm not sure my paintings are good enough, and I wouldn't know where to start.'

'My brother-in-law, Dominic, has a gallery in town.'

'You don't mean, Dominic's at Number Nine, the swanky new gallery?'

'I believe that's the pretentious name he's given it. He is particularly interested in discovering new talent. I could arrange for him to give an opinion on your work, once the investigation is over.'

Ms Devine hesitated, lost for words for a moment. Then she said, 'That would be incredible. When do you think that will be?'

'Very soon, I hope,' Steadman replied.

CHAPTER 38

Munro dropped Steadman back at his flat. A distinct smell of cooking wafting from the kitchen met him as he opened the door.

'Perfect timing – lunch is almost ready,' Ben shouted. 'I've made some eggy bread, roast tomatoes and smashed avocado.'

Steadman hung up his coat and hat and removed Robbie's harness. The dog followed the scent and scampered through to where Ben was laying the table. Robbie gave him a pleading look and was rewarded with a crust.

'What are your plans for the rest of the day, Ben?'

'I'm meeting up with some mates. I'll probably stay over if that's all right.'

Steadman didn't appear to be listening.

'You're very quiet, dad, what's up?'

'Sorry Ben – I'm lost in my own thoughts, that's all. No, you go out and enjoy yourself. I'll be fine.'

He needed to think. Having finished his lunch, he took off his jacket and tie and pulled on his favourite old blue jumper, the one that Linda, his sister, had been trying to dispose of for years.

It had to be Bach. Robbie sat at his feet as he lifted the piano lid and ran his fingers up and down the keys. A melody began, and Steadman thought back to the beginning with the body of Seth Shuster on the beach. No, it didn't start there, he mused, it was much earlier. In truth, it felt like he had known Seth all his life. Another melody, intertwining with the first; chords progressing; a subtle change of key... His thoughts turned to the various meetings, the encounters, the interviews. Each memory had its own little tune. Old Adelina Monke, now frail and forgetful but still full of spite... Josh Reynolds and Clara Drinsdale, unwilling to say what they knew about Seth and his young double. Were they too frightened or too stupid or was there something else?... Olivia Campbell, the new Divisional Superintendent... Distrustful and possibly disappointed. Did she still keep in contact with her husband?

The music grew sombre. Gregory Henshaw, strangled by Seth and dumped in a freezer for being in the wrong place at the wrong time. Rupert Sidley, a lawyer and a crook, murdered at the same time as Seth, yet his death had thrown up three likely names: Miles Pelham, Gary

Draper and Madam Chu. No, he said to himself, not Madam Chu – Elsie Entwistle – the oriental charade only served to confuse.

Finally, Philip Aintree. He could no longer think of him as Phil the Shed, and his fingers faltered. Could he have prevented his death?

The music turned to something softer and more gentle as he weighed each of the characters in his mind. He had a fleeting memory of being a paperboy collecting the weekly money on his Sunday morning round, then returning to the shop with his pockets bulging. He would stack the coins in neat piles of the same denominations and value before reaching the final total. As he had done then, he tallied all the information in his head. But no matter how often he counted, he reached the same conclusion. He knew who was behind the murders of Seth Shuster, Rupert Sidley and Philip Aintree.

Abruptly, he stopped playing, closed the piano and picked up the phone. Working carefully from the blip on the number five, he dialled the Eyesore. Sergeant Grimble answered.

'Would you put me through to DCI Long?'

'Right away, Inspector Steadman,' Grimble replied.

DCI Long picked up the phone on the first ring.

'Hubert? John Steadman here. We need to talk.'

'I've only this second finished speaking with DS Fairfax and was about to call you. Shall I send a car?'

Steadman's thoughts were still racing.

'I would rather walk. I need to clear my head.'

While he changed back into his formal clothes, Robbie stood by the door, head erect, eager to be working. It was as though he sensed Steadman's changed mood.

As he struggled to get his arms into the sleeves of his damp coat, his hand brushed against the pocket containing the little carved rat. It was no longer a question of luck. He fished the netsuke figure from his pocket and put it back with the rest of his collection.

Their journey to the Eyesore was uneventful. The scaffolding outside Eldon's shop was gone and there were few other pedestrians. He half-expected Seth's son to show up, and half-hoped that he would meet Sam Griffiths; neither appeared.

He became so engrossed in his thoughts that he lost count of his steps, only realising where they were when Robbie turned and led him away from a road junction.

'Go forward.'

The dog sat patiently waiting until a car passed When there was no further traffic, Robbie guided him safely across.

Sergeant Grimble held the door open for them. Another man, tall and slightly stooped, was standing by the desk.

'You made good time, John,' said DCI Long.

'Fortunately Robbie knows the way, sir,' Steadman replied.

There was a faint rustling behind Grimble's desk.

'I think he deserves a treat,' the portly Sergeant remarked. 'And are you going to keep your Uncle Bertie company while these two gentlemen put the world to rights?'

There was no point in arguing. Steadman passed him Robbie's lead. DCI Long took his arm and they made their way upstairs to the Chief Inspector's Office.

'I gather you have formed an opinion, John,' said DCI Long in his rumbling voice. 'Here, let me take your coat. There is a chair immediately to your left.'

Steadman touched the back of the chair and settled himself down.

'I have, sir,' he replied. 'Let me put the case, as I read it, before you.'

He spoke succinctly, counting the points off on his fingers one by one. DCI Long only interrupted him twice to seek clarification. Steadman reached the end and spread out his upturned hands.

'And there you have it, sir,' he concluded.

'What further pieces of information do you need to support your theory?' asked the Chief Inspector.

'I need the results of the post-mortem on Philip Aintree, the forensic analysis from his van, and any more details that DC Lofthouse has gleaned from the phone records.'

He paused and drummed his fingers on the arm of the chair.

'What else is bothering you, John?'

The drumming stopped. He scratched the side of his face. Should he mention his anxieties regarding Henry Bridges-Treston, the Divisional Superintendent's ex-husband? Eventually, he broke the silence.

'There is something bothering me, sir, but I have no evidence at all to support my concern.'

'Can anyone help you?'

'Only one person – Seth Shuster's younger double, who can only be his son.'

'DC Osborne has failed to locate him.'

'I know, but he's not far away and I'm sure he will come forward very soon.'

There was a knock on the door and DC Will Lofthouse entered, carrying a tray with tea and some biscuits.

'Thank you, Will. Were your ears burning? DI Steadman has a question to put to you.'

DC Lofthouse placed Steadman's mug on the desk.

'It's directly in front of you, sir,' he said in a hushed voice.

Steadman put his hands gently on the desk and brought them slowly together until he could feel the warmth of the mug. He picked it up and took a sip.

'Have you managed to trace any more of the calls that Philip Aintree made or received?'

He had, and they were exactly as Steadman predicted.

'That settles it,' said DCI Long decisively. 'We need to arrange a meeting of all parties concerned for tomorrow morning at ten. DC Lofthouse, can you organise it?

I want the following people there.' He reeled off a list. 'Have I missed anyone, John?'

'I would also invite our new Divisional Superintendent, Olivia Campbell.' He knew it was a risk, but one that he had to take.

DCI Long nodded to Will Lofthouse.

'I'll get on it right away, sir.'

Once the door was safely closed behind him, DCI Long turned again to Steadman.

'May I make one request?'

Steadman frowned. 'Of course, sir.'

'I would very much like you to lead tomorrow's discussion. You have a better grasp of the case than I or indeed anyone else has.'

It was not what Steadman was expecting. However, he recognised an order when he heard one, even though it was couched as a request.

'Very good, sir,' he replied.

DCI Long accompanied Steadman back to Sergeant Grimble's desk and left him as he attached Robbie's harness.

'I gather you're having a big meeting tomorrow morning,' said Grimble.

Steadman was taken aback.

'I'm not even going to ask how you know that.'

'Better not to,' Grimble replied. 'I'll be here ready for dog sitting duties.'

Robbie wagged his tail.

'And if I'm not mistaken,' Grimble continued, 'here comes Sam Griffiths.'

Steadman had already guessed from the distinctive clicking of her heels on the stairs.

'What a day!' she exclaimed. 'I've been stuck in a stuffy office from early morning. I desperately need to get some fresh air and stretch my legs.'

'You would be welcome to walk home with me if you don't mind going at Robbie's pace,' Steadman offered.

Much to his annoyance, Sergeant Grimble started to whistle 'Hello Young Lovers' as they made their way out of the Eyesore.

It was dark and damp. Sam took Steadman's arm.

'What kept you indoors all day?' he asked.

'I had to type up my final report on Seth Shuster, among other things. I did want to finish it before tomorrow's meeting, but it will have to wait. Will Lofthouse told me about the meeting. Is an arrest imminent?'

'I put forward an argument to DCI Long. If pending evidence backs me up and there are no dissenting voices, then yes, I think we'll have grounds for possibly several arrests.'

Sam knew Steadman well enough by now not to press him for more information.

'What are you doing for a meal this evening?' she asked.

'I hadn't given it much thought. Ben's out with his friends. I've got some microwave meals that Linda has prepared for me – there's more than enough for two if you care to join me.'

Steadman had considered inviting her to the café but was not sure if he could cope with ribald comments from his colleagues.

'Why don't you join me at the Equinox Hotel? I know you hate eating in public, but the hotel is virtually empty at this time of year. There will be no more than six other people in the dining room.'

'All right then, but don't say you haven't been warned if I send food and crockery flying,' Steadman replied with a smile.

They stopped outside his flat.

'I'm going to get a shower and change,' he said. 'After Tim has taken Robbie for a walk, I'll get a taxi and join you.' He pressed the button on his watch. 'Let's say seven o'clock.'

It was only when he was ready and waiting for the cab that it occurred to him that he might actually be going on a date.

To his relief, when he arrived at the Equinox Hotel, he found Sam to be equally as apprehensive. Neither need have worried. The meal passed without incident, the conversation never flagged, and they felt relaxed in each other's company.

They didn't mention the case until the very end of the evening.

'I'm not surprised that DCI Long has asked you to lead the meeting,' said Sam.

'Inspector Crouchley will no doubt be horrified,' Steadman replied. 'I'm relying on you to count how many times he pulls a face and swears under his breath.'

They both laughed.

'It's getting late,' said Steadman. 'Tomorrow may be a long day. I ought to be going.'

Sadly, the spell was broken.

'There will be other nights, Sam.'

'I'll hold you to that, John Steadman,' she replied.

★ ★ ★

Ben made sure his father was looking his best.

'Can I walk with you to the Eyesore, dad? There's something important I need to tell you. Don't worry, it's not about my lack of funds.'

'I would be grateful for your company, Ben.'

Steadman already had an inkling of what Ben was going to say. He didn't have long to wait. They had barely gone a hundred yards before he decided to speak.

'I know this is a bit sudden, dad, but...'

'Let me guess. You've got a last-minute deal on a flight today. Am I right?'

'How did you work that one out?'

'Simple. I heard you packing this morning and unless I'm mistaken, you've got your bag with you. Don't worry. It's fine. I'm really grateful that you managed to come back, even if it was only for a few days.'

Steadman produced an envelope from his pocket and handed it to Ben.

'That should cover your fare and get you a new mobile phone. Take it, and no arguments.'

'Thanks, dad. Can I give you something in return? If you and Sam want to make a go of things, then you have my blessing.'

Steadman was not sure how to reply.

'You're being a bit presumptuous, aren't you? Thanks all the same,' he said after a pause.

They continued walking, making only small talk until they reached the Eyesore. They hugged awkwardly.

'Take care, Ben, and keep in touch.'

* * *

Sergeant Grimble was at his desk chatting with Alan Munro.

'I hear Ben is going back to Australia today,' Grimble remarked.

Steadman shook his head in disbelief. 'Next you'll be telling me where I had dinner last night.'

'Actually, you went...'

Steadman interrupted him. 'Am I the first to arrive, Alan?'

'I believe there are two or three already in the room. I came down to fetch you.'

Robbie, of course, stayed with Sergeant Grimble and Munro escorted his colleague to the conference room.

At ten o'clock, DCI Long stood up.

'We are all here except for our Divisional Superintendent. One moment, I think that's her now.'

The door opened and Olivia Campbell edged into the room.

'Excellent,' said DCI Long. 'You will remember at the start of the investigation I invited DI Steadman to address us in this very room. A lot has happened since then. DI Steadman and I had a long chat yesterday. I have asked him to lead today's meeting and present his conclusions before we decide our next plan of action.'

Steadman was already standing by DCI Long, leaning lightly on the large desk at the front.

'There are some pieces of the puzzle still missing,' he began. 'Hopefully, some will turn up today, but not all. Irrespective of this, I believe we have grounds for making several arrests.'

The room was deathly silent.

'Early yesterday morning we were called to Philip Aintree's flat. The scene was set to look like a suicide, only the gun was in his right hand and Phil was left-handed, which makes suicide unlikely. Dr Rufus, you were going to carry out a gunshot residue test?'

'I did, and it was negative,' Dr Rufus responded.

'The gun he was holding was a Makarov pistol. The same make of gun used to shoot Rupert Sidley and probably Seth Shuster. Kim Ho retrieved the bullet that blew Phil's brains out and sent it to ballistics.'

'They have confirmed the bullet was from the same gun as killed Sidley,' said Kim Ho.

'So the three murders are linked,' Steadman continued. 'Kim noticed something else odd. It appeared that Phil had ordered two pizzas, yet there were the remains of a fry-up in his flat. I suppose, they could have been from a previous night.'

'But they weren't,' Dr Rufus cut in. 'Phil had eaten sausages, beans and fried eggs less than half an hour before his death.'

'When we arrived both pizzas were in their boxes,' said Steadman. 'Interestingly, one of the pizzas had in fact fallen out of its box onto the floor. It had been picked up and replaced. And not by Philip Aintree, for the underside of the pizza was contaminated with what remained of his brains.'

'Gross!' said a voice, possibly DC Osborne's.

'Inspector Crouchley kindly offered the services of some of his team to DS Fairfax. Maybe, Fiona, you could take up the story.'

DS Fairfax gave a small cough.

'They called on all the neighbours. None had left the block of flats after nine o'clock and no one had visited either. CCTV footage showed only one person – the cyclist with the delivery pack on his back.'

'That was confirmed by the two dozy beggars who were meant to be doing constant surveillance,' added Inspector Crouchley.

Steadman resumed. 'A Makarov pistol goes off with a loud bang. There was no silencer fitted to this particular model, yet no one heard a thing. It occurred to me that one way of concealing and silencing a gun would be to fire it from inside the padded pack used to keep the pizzas warm.'

'And at post-mortem I found fragments of wadding and fibres in the remains of Phil's brain,' declared Dr Rufus.

'Moving on,' said Steadman, 'Philip Aintree's van also threw up a couple of surprises. Firstly, a suit jacket that matched Seth Shuster's trousers, and secondly, a Beretta pistol. DS Munro and I showed the pistol to Ms Devine, Rupert Sidley's secretary.'

'And she positively identified it as belonging to her former employer from the unusual pattern of damage on the handle,' stated Munro.

'What else did you find in Phil's van, Kim?' asked Steadman.

'Traces of blood that matched both Seth Shuster and Rupert Sidley,' Kim Ho replied, 'as well as traces of drugs.'

'Excellent – we will come to the drugs later,' said Steadman, trying very hard not to look too pleased with himself.

He was beginning to feel warm, and slackened off his tie.

'Look out, he's starting to strip!' Dr Rufus whispered to Sam, who was sitting at his side.

'So Philip Aintree helped dispose of the bodies, but as yet we don't know who dumped them at sea.'

'We do have the cryptic messages on his phone, sir,' said DC Lofthouse.

'Go on, Will,' Steadman replied.

'Just before midnight on the Friday, he received a text saying, "Urgent drop off of envelopes required". Eventually we traced that call to Madam Chu's Palace. At one in the morning, he got another text that read, "Merton Cove in forty minutes H". We have not managed to trace the sender, nor have we identified who "H" was.'

Steadman would have loved to see the look on Divisional Superintendent Campbell's face at this revelation. He sighed and pressed on.

'In the course of the investigation, DCI Long, with the help of Ms Devine, identified three potential suspects, people that Shuster and Sidley had visited – Miles Pelham, Gary Draper and Elsie Entwistle, better known as Madam Chu. DS Munro and I interviewed all three.'

Steadman paused for a brief moment. Images from his bizarre dream flitted through his mind.

'Apologies, that's not quite true. We interviewed the first two together – I alone interviewed Elsie Entwistle. Correct me if I'm wrong, Alan, but I don't believe we mentioned Philip Aintree to Miles Pelham?'

Munro referred to his notes and confirmed that was the case.

'We did discuss him with Gary Draper, didn't we?'

'We did, sir. Draper said he hadn't used Phil's services for some time. However, we did find a legal document signing over the rights of Gary Draper's security company to Seth Shuster. It was unsigned, so Shuster was worth more to Draper alive than dead.'

'And Gary Draper is dying,' added Steadman. 'Finally, we come to Elsie Entwistle. I refuse to call her Madam Chu – we go a long way back. Her answers were all evasive, so I pushed her, and I believe I went too far. I suggested to her that Seth Shuster had threatened her by exposing what was in Philip Aintree's deliveries. Kim, what traces of drugs were found in Phil's van?'

'The usual – cannabis, amphetamines, cocaine, but also traces of opium,' Kim answered.

'Inspector Crouchley, do you know of anyone else in Helmsmouth, other than Elsie Entwistle, who deals in opium?'

'She's the last we know of,' he grunted and DCI Long agreed

'If only I had left it at deliveries, and not hinted at what he might be taking away, Philip Aintree might still be alive.' Steadman said with a frown.

'You weren't to know,' said DCI Long.

Steadman waved away his reassurances. 'That's why he had to die. It also explains the pizza delivery man.'

'My men have questioned every fast-food outlet, and no one admits to delivering anything to Aintree,' said Crouchley.

'That doesn't surprise me. We do know, however, that Madam Chu's Palace also runs a small chain of takeaways.'

'Where does Seth Shuster's elusive double fit into all of this?' asked DC Osborne.

'I have no doubt he is Seth's son,' Steadman replied.

Crouchley snorted. 'If he is, he's probably another bleeding criminal.'

Sam wasn't letting that pass. 'You don't believe in any of that "sins of the father" nonsense, do you?'

Steadman interjected before Crouchley could reply.

'I believe Seth has been living with his son. To the best of my knowledge, he has crossed my path seven or possibly eight times since the start of this investigation.'

'Why would he do that?' snapped Crouchley.

'Three reasons – I knew his father better than anyone, he knows I have been asked to help with the investigation and lastly, it is remarkably easy to follow a blind person.'

Again, silence fell on the room.

'There you have it, ladies and gentlemen. I don't know who killed Shuster, Sidley or Philip Aintree, but by my reckoning all fingers point to Elsie Entwistle and her entourage at Madam Chu's Palace.'

DCI Long took his place by Steadman.

'Thank you, Inspector. I believe we need to bring Elsie

Entwistle and company in. Does anyone disagree? No. Good, we must act swiftly.'

'I propose a dawn raid on the viper's nest,' suggested Crouchley.

'Will you be able to get enough officers together by then?'

Inspector Crouchley turned towards Sergeant Beattie who was by his side.

'I can get enough officers, sir.'

'That's settled,' said DCI Long. 'A full raid on Madam Chu's Palace at six tomorrow morning. By the end of today I want everyone's completed reports on my desk. We must leave nothing to chance.'

There was a general murmur of agreement.

Divisional Superintendent Olivia Campbell slipped out of the room.

CHAPTER 39

Dr Rufus put a hand on Steadman's shoulder.

'That must have been hard for you,' he said.

Steadman nodded in agreement. 'The biggest problem is not seeing anybody's face, that and the silence. I have no idea if people are agreeing with me, bored or possibly even asleep.'

'Sorry to interrupt,' DCI Long's voice rumbled. 'I need to go over the details of the raid with Inspector Crouchley. May I leave you in Frank's capable hands?'

'Very risky, Hubert,' Dr Rufus replied his eyes sparkling. 'I'm more used to dealing with corpses.'

A lighter hand touched Steadman's elbow.

'Twelve, but I lost count of the obscenities,' said Sam. 'Must dash if I'm to finish my reports by this evening.'

'In case you're wondering, Frank, I asked Sam to count the number of times Crouchley pulled a face or when he swore,' explained Steadman.

'I'm surprised it was only twelve. What shall we do for lunch?' asked Dr Rufus.

'I don't think I should risk the Eyesore canteen for a little while. They didn't appreciate my last light-hearted comments – no sense of humour.'

'If you don't have any work this afternoon, Frank, you could walk back with me to Lloyds' café and eat there.'

'As long as it's not pizza. I think after Philip Aintree's flat it will be a long time before I can face another one.'

Steadman collected Robbie from Sergeant Grimble and the two men walked slowly back to the café. For once it had stopped raining. There was even a hint of warmth from the sun as it did its best to break through the thinning clouds.

'I hear Ben's going back today,' said Dr Rufus. 'I hope you don't mind but I paid for his flight. He is my godson after all.'

'So did I, and I expect my sister did likewise,' Steadman replied with a wry smile. 'It was nice to have him here, if only for a short while.'

'What did he make of Sam Griffiths?'

Steadman felt his ears burning.

'They got on very well,' he replied cautiously.

'I think you're in with a chance there, you know.' Dr Rufus's eyes were twinkling again.

'I'm not so sure, Frank.'

'You're probably right. After all you're as ugly as sin, you've got wonky eyes, and you've only got a miserable police pension to offer her.'

'You're just saying all those things to cheer me up,' said Steadman, but silently he thought Frank Rufus was the best friend a man could have.

They had a leisurely meal: a selection of antipasti, followed by tortellini and homemade hazel nut cake. Marco Lloyd insisted they had some Valpolicella as well as grappa with their coffee.

'Will you be able to drive after all the alcohol?' asked Steadman.

'I've been counting the glasses and watching the clock. A brisk walk back to the Eyesore and a cup of tea with Sergeant Grimble and I'll be as sober as a judge. Mind, I've known some judges in my time who were rarely if ever sober.'

The afternoon was wearing late by the time they had finished their lunch. Dr Rufus insisted on paying.

'You paid last time – besides if you and Sam ever...'

Steadman didn't let him finish.

'That's quite enough, Frank.'

'I'm only saying...' he replied. 'And I do a cracking best man's speech.'

*　*　*
.

Steadman and Robbie were barely in the flat when the doorbell rang; one long ring, one short ring and a further two long rings – Tim Warrender's special code.

'Good heavens, is that the time?' said Steadman as he let Tim in.

'It won't be a long walk tonight, Inspector Steadman. I've got an early football practice,' said Tim in a raspy voice.

'That's all right. Robbie has walked to the Eyesore and back already today. DS Munro will be able to help with your physics homework soon. I'm hoping we are very near the end of the investigation.'

'Cool,' Tim replied as he left with the dog.

The flat was remarkably quiet without Ben. Steadman switched on the radio. Every station seemed to annoy him. Maybe he was turning into a grumpy old man.

Tim arrived back breathless with Robbie panting at his side.

'I've not got time for a drink,' he said as he gave Robbie his food. 'Could I take a biscuit with me?'

'Of course,' said Steadman. 'But I have a feeling Ben may have eaten them all.'

★ ★ ★

The lunchtime wine had made him drowsy. Once Tim had left, he sat down in his favourite armchair and, with Robbie lying on his feet, closed his eyes.

He was still preoccupied with the few remaining bits of the puzzle. How did the bodies get dumped at sea? It was a big risk for Elsie Entwistle to take. Either she paid an extortionate amount that would ensure silence, or she had an extraordinary hold over the person already – a craving for opium perhaps? He had no proof and wished now he had shared his anxieties with Sam. He was sure she would have understood.

His breathing became more rhythmic, and slowly he drifted off to sleep. Whether or not it was the red wine he couldn't say, but his dreams were broken, disjointed, and disturbing. At one point, he was back in the conference room speaking at the front, but everyone was laughing at him. He looked down and found to his shame that he was naked from the waist down. At another, Dr Rufus was objecting to his marriage: 'Can't you see he's as ugly as sin and has wonky eyes,' he shouted at the registrar. In his dream he turned to where his bride should have been and found himself facing a younger version of Seth Shuster: 'You knew I would turn up,' he said. 'You've let me down. My father's killer has escaped, hasn't he?' And then, in the most distressing sequence, Inspector Crouchley was putting him in handcuffs: 'I've been wanting to do this, Steadman, for effing ages,' he whispered in his ear. 'Now get in the back of the van.' His breath was hot and wet on his face. The van door closed with a thud, followed by another, and another...

He woke with a start. Robbie was trying to lick his face. Someone was hammering on his front door. It had to be Alan Munro.

He made his way down the corridor as fast as he dared and opened the door.

'Good – you're dressed. Madam Chu's Palace is on fire. I've got Sam in the car with me. Come on, I'll help you on with your coat.'

'But...' Steadman started to say.

'DCI Long's orders. He wants you there,' explained Munro.

The Audi's engine was still purring. Sam was sitting in the front, so Steadman and Robbie got in the back.

'It's a total disaster,' said Munro as he put his foot down on the accelerator. The Audi screeched away. 'None of Crouchley's officers were anywhere near the place. We only found out from the Fire Service. It could be arson for the whole building is in flames by the sounds of things. It's quite a coincidence that it's gone up tonight considering it was due to be raided in the wee small hours of the morning.'

It was no coincidence, thought Steadman. He only hoped Elsie Entwistle had had the decency to evacuate the place first.

Munro flicked on the siren and the blue flashing lights. No one spoke. It didn't take many minutes to reach Madam Chu's Palace. The building was surrounded by fire engines and police cars. A sizeable crowd had formed. Munro pulled up beside a waiting ambulance.

As soon as they opened the doors they were assailed

by the acrid stench of the smoke and could feel the heat from the flames that had by now engulfed the top two storeys.

Steadman pushed his dark glasses onto his forehead and tried to stare at the fire with one eye then the other. For a fleeting moment he thought he could make out a faint yellow glow. Sam gazed at him, not daring to ask if his eyes registered anything.

'DS Fairfax is coming towards us,' Sam announced.

'I'm not sure there's much we can do at this stage, sir,' she said.

'Is there any sign of life?' Steadman asked.

'It looks very much like they have all scarpered, sir. The fire crews were here first, and they haven't seen anybody fleeing the building. They think that maybe the fire was deliberate as it has spread so quickly. Perhaps Madam Chu received a tipoff.'

Steadman had already come to that conclusion.

The blaze roared. Above the din they could hear Inspector Crouchley cursing. He was arguing with the Fire Chief, who was insisting that he move his officers back from the conflagration as it was rapidly getting out of control. The Fire Chief was a woman, and Crouchley was making it abundantly clear he was not taking orders from her, or indeed any woman.

'Is there anything I can do, Fiona?' asked Munro.

'No, I don't think...'

Her words were cut short by a furious pounding on the plate glass door of the restaurant.

'Dear God, there's somebody still in there!' exclaimed Munro.

There was no stopping him. He ran towards the door pushing the fire crews aside and ignoring their pleas for him to stop.

'I think it could be Jockie Chan, the waiter,' said Sam.

Steadman could only imagine the terror on the man's face.

Munro charged against the door, only to bounce off. He gave his aching shoulder a quick rub. The pounding had stopped. Jockie lay slumped on the floor trapped behind the door.

Munro seized one of the enormous pots containing bamboo. He lifted it and spun on the spot – once, twice three times...

'What's happening?' Steadman asked anxiously.

Sam quickly explained. 'It's like he's throwing the hammer in some ancient Highland Games. It doesn't seem possible.'

Munro could hold the pot no longer. He let it go and it flew in the direction of the glass door. There was a sound like a gunshot. A small crack appeared, then another. Within seconds a maze of smaller cracks appeared all over the glass.

'Watch out!' screamed one of the firemen.

Munro turned his back just in time as the door

billowed and then, with an enormous whoosh and crash, blew out, showering Munro with hot sharp fragments of broken glass.

Flames licked out of the door like serpents' tongues. Munro was not deterred. He crouched, darted under the flames, and picked up the limp body of Jockie Chan. Barely noticing that the sleeves of his jacket were alight, he threw the man over his shoulder and raced towards the ambulance.

Sam had kept up a running commentary.

'Take me over to the ambulance,' said Steadman in a voice racked with emotion.

Flanked by Sam Griffiths and Fiona Fairfax, and with Robbie in the lead, he hurried as best he could towards Munro, Jockie and the waiting ambulance.

'Sam, can you hold Robbie? Fiona, help me up, please.'

Munro beamed triumphantly at them, oblivious to the burns on his hands and face, his singed hair and the blood trickling from the back of his head.

'That was a close one!' he said.

Jockie was coughing and trying to pull the oxygen mask off. He could barely open his eyes.

'That bitch,' he groaned, 'that fucking bitch!'

'Take your time,' said Steadman calmly. 'Tell us what happened.'

DS Fairfax had taken out her notebook and pen.

The paramedic gave Jockie a drink of water and persuaded him to put his mask back on.

'We really should get both of them to hospital,' she said.

Steadman nodded. 'One more minute, that's all.'

'Lunch had just finished,' Jockie began. 'I was summoned upstairs tae Elsie's lair. She was acting queer. I knew something was up. She made me tak' a cup of coffee wi' her. That henchman o' hers was standing grinnin' like an eejit. As soon as I took a mouthful of coffee, I knew it was drugged. I staggered and the oaf caught me. I can remember the smell of petrol, then nothin' till the smoke woke me.'

He took another sip of water. The paramedic was anxious to move, but Steadman held up his hand.

'Go on,' he said.

'I was locked in ma room, but the doors are paper-thin. I kicked it open and crawled along the corridor and doon the stairs. The restaurant was fair blazin', so I jumped in the fishpond tae soak ma clothes and cool down. Naebody else was about – they'd all done a runner. I made my way to the door an' that was when I spied ma big friend,' he said pointing at Munro. 'I owe you one, pal, big time.'

'No problem, Jockie. We Scots have got to stick together.'

'We really must go now, I insist,' said the paramedic.

'One last question. Did Elsie Entwistle kill Shuster, Sidley and Philip Aintree?'

'Aye – she ordered it. That henchman o' hers has nae qualms.'

Steadman could visualise the scene vividly. Seth Shuster standing in the room, glass of champagne in his hand, smiling, his jacket over the back of a chair, trying to convince Madam Chu what a good deal he was offering. The realisation that she was not interested, the veiled threats, the mention of Phil and his packages, and then... a sign to her henchman, the raised gun, the look of sheer terror on Shuster's face. The two shots ringing round the room. Did Seth even hear the second shot? Sidley starting to run – too late.

'And if he hadnae left his gun at Aintree's flat he would have done for me as well,' Jockie Chan continued. 'Elsie reckoned I had given you the nod about Aintree removing the bodies. That's why she wanted to get rid of me.'

Munro stood up awkwardly.

'Where do you think you're going?' asked the paramedic.

He looked at his hands, which had started to blister. With a struggle he retrieved the keys to the Audi from his pocket and tossed them to Sam.

'Looks like you'll have to drive,' he shouted.

DS Fairfax helped Steadman out of the ambulance.

'Are they all right?' Sam asked.

'Munro has burns to his hands and face. They don't look too deep,' Fiona replied. 'Jockie Chan sounds as though he has smoke inhalation. They're both going going to casualty.'

The ambulance doors closed, and it set off, wailing and flashing its way to Helmsmouth General Hospital.

Steadman turned towards DS Fairfax.

'If Elsie Entwistle finds out that Jockie has survived, she may make another attempt on his life. We'll need to get Inspector Crouchley to put an armed round-the-clock watch on him,' Steadman paused. 'It might be better coming from DCI Long,' he said with a slight shrug.

'Don't worry about that, sir. I can deal with men like Inspector Crouchley,' Fairfax replied.

A tremendous crash tore through the night air as the roof caved in. All eyes turned towards the building. Sam looked on in disbelief. A fire officer urged them all to stand further back. As Sam turned, she glimpsed a familiar face. She nudged Steadman gently.

'Seth Shuster's double is standing no more than ten feet away,' she whispered.

'I know,' said Steadman. 'He's been there since before Alan's heroic rescue.'

DC Cleo Osborne joined them. She too had noticed Shuster's double.

'Point me in his direction, Sam,' said Steadman under his breath.

He turned to face the man and held out his hand.

'I think,' said Steadman, 'it is time we were properly introduced.'

The man shook the outstretched hand. Steadman could almost feel his sense of relief.

'This is Dr Sam Griffiths, forensic psychologist and this is DC Cleo Osborne, although I expect you knew that already.'

The man turned and nodded to each in turn.

'Yes,' he said, 'I did know. I'm Abel Spencer, Seth Shuster's son,'

'Abel? Well, that explains one thing,' said Steadman.

Abel Spencer looked confused.

'You must excuse him,' said Sam. 'Sometimes he speaks in riddles.'

'Your father's last assumed name was Adam Monke. I could understand the surname but wondered why he chose Adam as a forename.'

'I'm still lost,' said Cleo.

'It's from the Bible,' explained Steadman. 'Adam had two sons – Cain and Abel. He must have remembered the story and knew about your existence.'

'He did, but that's another story altogether,' Abel replied. 'I am sorry, I should have spoken sooner. It's just that...'

'No matter,' said Steadman. 'Let's go somewhere where we can have a nice long chat.'

'Before we go, Inspector, I need to know if my father's killers died in the blaze.'

Steadman chose his words carefully.

'I don't believe so, Abel, but now we definitely know

who they are. Eventually they'll be brought to justice.'

Abel Spencer sighed. '"Though the mills of God grind slowly; yet they grind exceedingly small."'

'I agree. I think the poet Longfellow summed it up rather neatly,' said Steadman. 'Might I suggest all four of us go back to my flat? We will need to take a statement from you Mr Spencer. DC Osborne will take notes, and then get it typed up for you to sign.'

CHAPTER 40

The driver's seat in the Audi was pushed as far back as it could go to accommodate Munro's legs. Sam could barely reach the pedals. She adjusted the seat and drove cautiously through the gloom. Fortunately, there was a parking space right outside Steadman's flat.

'Not too much noise,' he said. 'We don't want to wake the neighbours.'

His hands were cold, and it took several attempts to get the key into the lock.

'Sam, would you switch on the lights?'

She did, and they made their way upstairs. Cleo Osborne was disappointed to find that Ben had gone.

'There's only one house rule,' Steadman declared as he entered his flat. 'Don't move the furniture. I know where everything is or should be.'

Cleo and Abel noticed that their positions were marked with tape on the floor. Sam made them all coffee.

'I've been thinking Mr Spencer...'

'Please call me Abel.'

'Very well – why don't you start at the beginning, Abel? How long have you known that Seth Shuster was your father?'

'From as early as I can remember, Inspector Steadman. I didn't have a glorious start in life. You can guess my mother's background. She knew she was pregnant by Seth. The pregnancy was concealed – I think that's the correct term. She went into labour in Marks and Spencer. The store was about to close so she hid in the toilets, and that's where I was born. A night cleaner called William Abel Jordan found her. He was an older man with a grown-up daughter some years senior to my mother. The daughter, Lydia, had a problem with her spine and had never married. William and Lydia took us both in. I was named Abel after him, and Spencer in memory of my place of birth.'

He took a sip of his coffee before continuing.

'My mother was flighty. I'm told she stayed for six months after my birth before disappearing. She came back from time to time, mostly for a few days – the longest was two weeks. I haven't seen her since my fifteenth birthday.'

'Was it then that she told you about your father?' asked Steadman.

'No – as I said, she made no secret of it,' Abel replied. 'And it was never in any doubt. She knew who Seth's solicitor was, and he has been a regular correspondent.

Money was sent every month to William and Lydia, and when I moved out at age seventeen, I received a regular allowance.'

'What were William Jordan and his daughter like?' Sam asked.

'They were kindness itself. They're both devout Christians, and it rubbed off on me. When most fifteen-year-old boys discovered girls, I discovered Jesus.'

'What do you know about your father's past?' queried Steadman.

'Pretty much everything. I know he was a crook and a murderer and that he was in jail in America probably facing the death penalty. It was a shock when Mr Sidley contacted me to say he was coming back to Helmsmouth. He asked if I would put him up. I had never seen my father, but I was assured I would recognise him instantly.'

Cleo looked up from her writing.

'Can you put me out of my misery? Where do you live? I've been searching everywhere for you.'

Abel smiled. 'I'm the caretaker of Helmsmouth Christian Shelter. I live above the premises. I did speak with one of your colleagues, who called with a fragment of material from Seth's trousers. He asked if any of my residents had a jacket in that fabric. I was truthful, though not entirely honest in as much as none of the residents had a jacket matching the description, but I recognised the cloth instantly. That was how I knew for certain that my father had been killed.'

'I'm surprised you took your father in,' Cleo Osborne remarked.

'I'm a Christian, and I believe no one is beyond redemption.'

'Is your faith the reason Josh Reynolds has nothing to do with you?' Steadman asked.

'Yes. Josh wouldn't let me back in his flat. I think Clara would have liked to learn more but she was terrified of her brother. I even met Adelina Monke. She insisted on calling me Seth. It was most embarrassing.'

'I have another question,' said Steadman. 'Do you know how your father got from America back to England?'

'He took a cargo boat from Mexico to France. There, someone called Henry Bridges-Treston met him and sailed him back to the UK. He arrived one night in a white van. I can clearly remember it had Helmsmouth Office Solutions written on the side. I caught a glimpse of the driver. I know you shouldn't judge on appearance, but he looked quite disreputable. May I ask you something?'

'Sure, go ahead,' said Steadman.

'Why was my father killed?'

'He was trying to buy himself a slice of the criminal action in Helmsmouth. With his solicitor, he had visited at least three elderly crooks. I think he pushed his luck with Madam Chu, known more correctly as Elsie Entwistle. I imagine he threatened to expose her. She has a full-time bodyguard who, on her orders, shot your father and then, of course, Rupert Sidley, who had probably tried to get away. We know their bodies were moved in the Helmsmouth Office Solutions van owned by a Mr Philip Aintree. He's been murdered too.'

'Who dumped their bodies?'

'I have my suspicions,' said Steadman.

'Could it have been Henry Bridges-Treston?'

'We have no proof,' Steadman conceded.

'But you believe that this Elsie Entwistle woman was behind the murders?'

Steadman nodded.

'She must have been warned,' Abel said with a shrug.

The room was quiet apart Robbie snuffling in his sleep.

'Can I ask you something else?' ventured Cleo Osborne.

'Of course,' answered Abel.

'Occasionally you bought flowers – always white – why?'

'Our residents are mostly frail and sick. Few have any next-of-kin. Quite often they die in the Shelter. They are given a public health funeral. Most people still call it a pauper's funeral. I'm a lay preacher. I make sure no one who dies in the Shelter is buried without some flowers and a prayer.'

Sam wondered what Inspector Crouchley would have made of this remarkable young man.

Steadman pressed the button on his watch and the tinny voice told him it was almost one in the morning.

'It's late,' he said. 'DC Osborne will type up your statement.'

'I can call by tomorrow,' she offered, and Abel nodded.

'May I say one more thing?' asked Abel. 'It's really an apology to you, DI Steadman. I shouldn't have followed you like I did, and I should have spoken to you sooner. I was sure you knew who I was, and you, probably more than anyone else, knew my father and what sort of person he was. Despite this, you pursued his killer, and I thank you.'

Steadman was moved by Abel's apology.

'Your father's remains are still in the police mortuary,' he said. 'You could claim them and arrange his funeral if you like.'

'I would like that very much,' Abel replied.

'He was probably quite wealthy. I expect he had a will lodged with Rupert Sidley. There will be some wrangling over it, I would imagine...'

'I don't want his money. If there is any, I'll donate it to the Shelter.' Abel paused and bit his lip. 'Just wish I had something to remember him by.'

Immediately Steadman thought of the Patek Philippe watch, Seth's most treasured possession.

'I believe that can be arranged,' he said.

Sam drove Abel Spencer and DC Osborne home. Steadman took Robbie down to Lloyds' back garden. The grass was damp and there was an earthy smell of spring in the air. New life, rebirth, and new beginnings, he thought.

Together they went back upstairs. Robbie settled himself down for the night. Steadman made his way over to the drinks cabinet and, on a whim, broke one of his golden rules. He poured himself a large single malt whisky.

★ ★ ★

The following morning, Steadman spent over an hour on the phone to DCI Long. At the end of their conversation, Long had a last question for him.

'Yesterday, something was bothering you, John. Can you tell me what it was? I fear there is still some unfinished business.'

'Abel Spencer answered one of my queries. It is now certain that Henry Bridges-Treston brought Seth back from France in his boat. I can't prove it, but I believe he may have also dumped the bodies at sea later. He was, as you know, fond of opium and Madam Chu's Palace, to the best of our knowledge, was the last remaining source in Helmsmouth.'

DCI Long made a note.

'I'll get onto it straight away. John, I have known you for a lot of years and I can tell you're still not happy.'

'Elsie Entwistle was tipped off. We know she has been

a police informant in the past, and that friends in high places have offered her a degree of protection.'

'I'm with you so far,' said Long.

'She must have been warned shortly after our meeting. There was nobody left in the Palace except Jockie Chan.'

'Are you suggesting it was someone from inside Headquarters that informed Elsie?'

'Not directly, sir. But there is one person who has an indirect link with her.'

The silence on the other end of the phone was so lengthy that Steadman thought he had been cut off. At last DCI Long replied.

'Do you know if she is still on speaking terms with her ex-husband?'

'I believe she is, sir.'

'That may explain the note sitting in front of me.'

'Would you care to read it to me, sir?'

'I now appreciate the predicament you were in, John. It reads, "Urgent – mother seriously ill in Jamaica. Have a seat booked on the late evening flight. Signed Olivia Campbell, Divisional Superintendent".'

'Her flight will have got there by now. We need to get hold of Henry Bridges-Treston.'

'You may, of course, find some interesting passengers on board, because I'm sure Elsie Entwistle will have left the country by now. Oh – and one last thing, sir, his boat is called *The Poppy*.'

★ ★ ★

The doorbell rang. Robbie gave a friendly bark and padded off down the corridor. Steadman was aware of her perfume before he even opened the door.

'And how is my favourite blind detective today?' Sam asked in her soft Welsh lilt.

'All the better for you being here,' he replied.

She jangled a set of keys.

'I have just been to see Alan Munro. He's home but his hands are in bandages and he's not allowed to drive, so I've still got the Audi.'

'How is Jockie?' asked Steadman.

'The smoke inhalation is worse than first suspected. He should make a good recovery but he'll be in hospital for a few days. Would you like me to drive you to the Eyesore?'

Steadman felt like a schoolboy who had outsmarted his teacher.

'No. I've said all I have to say to DCI Long already this morning.'

'Then where would you like to go?'

'I would like to take a walk along the eastern beach and listen to the sea. I believe it's stopped raining and the tide is out.'

★ ★ ★

They parked by the boardwalk in exactly the same spot where he and Munro had stopped. It seemed like a lifetime ago. They walked arm-in-arm with Robbie getting ever more excited as they got nearer the beach.

'You thought right from the start of this investigation that it had all the hallmarks of a local score-settling and that we may never solve it,' said Sam.

'I did, though I wish I had been proven wrong.'

'What do you think will become of Elsie Entwistle?'

'She'll reinvent herself as she's done before. I don't know – proprietrix of a steak house and brothel in Argentina, running a seedy nightclub in Berlin or a gambling den in Moscow. Who knows? She's as wily as an old fox, but one day she will be caught.'

They had reached the hard wet sand. A sea breeze was blowing, and it felt invigorating and pure. They continued right down to the water's edge before pausing. Steadman slipped off his dark glasses, blinked and let the sunlight play on his eyelids. Sam stared for a long time into Steadman's sightless eyes and wished, more than anything, that he could stare back into hers.

Printed in Great Britain
by Amazon